THE SILK AND THE SWORD

THE SILK AND THE SWORD

BY

RON SINGERTON

www.penmorepress.com

THE SILK AND THE SWORD by Ron Singerton

Copyright © 2016 Ron Singerton

All rights reserved. No part of this book may be used or reproduced by any means without the written permission of the publisher except in the case of brief quotation embodied in critical articles and reviews.

ISBN-13: 978-1-942756-38-5(Paperback)
ISBN -978-1-942756-39-2 (e-book)

BISAC Subject Headings:
FIC014000FICTION / Historical
FIC032000FICTION / War & Military
FIC031020FICTION / Thrillers / Historical

Cover Illustration by Ron Singerton
Cover by Christine Horner

Address all correspondence to:
Penmore Press LLC
920 N Javelina Pl
Tucson AZ 85748

A Statement of Appreciation

This novel could not have been completed without the unstinting encouragement of my wife, Darla. Her suggestions, as well as her literary input added enormously to this creation.

I also wish to thank my editor, Susan Wenger and, of course, Michael James, publisher and friend, for placing The Silk and The Sword and Villa of Deceit on the bookshelf of Penmore Press along with its other fine works.

Reviews

"A tour de force of Roman military survival across a long and arduous trek through the Parthian empire, the silk road, and into the celestial kingdom. Singerton delivers an astounding look at what it takes to survive, and ultimately to find forbidden love, in a harshly foreign land. A gripping read backed by the kind of historical research that enlivens a story."

—Sean P. Curley, Award Winning Author of *Propositum.*

Prologue

The screams from the temple, like the shredding of steel, ripped open the silence of the night. Tacitus and his girlfriend Tullia, hunkered down in a copse of trees, shivered in sudden terror. It had been a terrible mistake and something had gone horribly wrong. The leader of their gang had said that the priests would be asleep, the offering plate easily in reach, and they would be away in no time.

"No, don't go in there!" Tullia said, in a vain attempt to stop him.

"They need help. I have to," said Tacitus as he scrambled up the steps. The swift blow from an acolyte's cudgel slammed him against a pillar and three more men were instantly pummeling him. Blood streamed down his face and a blurred glance told him that one of his friends was lifeless and the other three were already trussed and awaiting execution. He tried to rise but the downward swing of a thick staff struck again and all turned to darkness.

It was mid-day when he woke and the first voice he heard was that of his father. There was an ominous threat, a demand, and then the hysterical voice of someone shouting, "How dare you storm into my temple with that sword! You didn't want my benediction before, but I suspect you want something from me now. Am I right, Centurion?"

"Actually there is something you will give me priest, and it's not your pitiful invocations. You will release my son."

"My title is now Lysippus, Most Exalted High Priest, and the scum that violated my sanctuary will die an extremely brutal death."

Tacitus heard the unsheathing of a weapon and a squeal followed by a plea from the priest, and then the two men appeared.

"You see him. He is alive. Now come with me," said the quaking priest as he led the centurion to his chambers.

Tacitus put his hand to his jaw and felt the swelling delivered by his father's fist the previous day. He detested the man and wondered how and why he came to be here. "Why would my father even care, and why would he have known this priest?" Leaning back against a wall, Tacitus could only hear snatches of their conversation.

The priest's rage dissolved into a muted lament and he said, "All your threats are hollow. I would gladly perish for my goddess, and I do not have to remind you that this temple was your late wife's sanctuary. Whatever clemency I give is in memory of her. I remember her name, Aspacia. All those years ago you introduced her as a 'Lady of Rome'. Of course I knew that she was still a slave, but in all other respects she was a lady, and her piety moved me. Do you forget that I married the two of you, and on the day she died I went to your house to extend my sympathy and give my blessing for her journey into eternal life? And you excoriated and humiliated me, an abominable insult which I have never forgotten!"

"Yes," said the centurion, "she prayed here and I prayed and gave everything to save her, but your goddess failed."

"The goddess Diana never fails. She had other plans for Aspacia. Now sparing your wretched boy will cost you every sestercius you have. He will never enter this holy place again. He will be banished!"

Relief flooded through Tacitus when he saw Tullia waiting outside. She threw her arms around him and the centurion waited for the briefest of moments before saying, "That's enough. Say your goodbyes; it's time to go."

Neither Tullia nor Tacitus knew exactly what Gaius, his father, meant but they did as ordered. Tacitus kissed her and painfully turned away, leaving her whimpering at the temple steps.

His father remained stonily silent as they walked on a road leading away from the city. Tacitus tramped beside him, shaken by his near encounter with death, and now the sweat that rolled down his battered face was from apprehension as much as the torpid heat. The man was implacably cold and terrifyingly resolute.

"This is not the way to Aunt Junia's house," ventured Tacitus, wary of what fate his father planned for him. It had been five years since he had seen his father, a man he'd disliked from the age of six. Gaius was a remote and dour soldier who had been away in Gaul with Caesar and his Tenth Legion. Now he had come back for his son's sixteenth birthday to give him a toga representing manhood, but nothing had gone well.

"We're not going to Aunt Junia's house. We're going to Campus Martius."

A horrible dread shot through Tacitus. Momentarily he stopped, then hurried to catch up. "Isn't that where your legion is?"

"That's right, and it's also where they train recruits."

Again Tacitus stopped. He could feel his heart pounding. "Recruits?"

"That's exactly what I said. Recruits. You will be joining the army today."

"No!" Tacitus screamed. "I don't want to be a soldier!"

"But you will be a soldier. At least for the next 20 years, if you live that long."

"You can't do this to me," Tacitus said beseechingly. He could feel his knees weakening.

"Of course I can. As your father, and by Roman law, I have the power to do anything I want. I can sell you, and I have the right to strangle you right here. But I'm giving you a choice. The only choice I will ever give you. You can become a slave or join the army. Which is it? Hurry now. I have 4,800 men to command, and I never waste time."

Tacitus's head was spinning. "Why can't you just let me go? You'll never have to hear from me again," he pleaded, feeling very insignificant.

"Because I can't trust you or any criminals you might collect, and I will not attempt to save you again. You have embarrassed me and you defiled your mother's temple. What would she have said? Were you trying to insult her memory or scandalize me?"

Tacitus imagined that that same look of hatred on his father's face was the last thing an enemy of Rome would ever see. The centurion grabbed Tacitus by his shift and said, "Don't you understand? That was your mother's holy place. That was her goddess, and she died giving life to you. And now you will pay for your violation of her and of her goddess. You will pay for the rest of your miserable life!"

The leader of their delinquent band had not told him the name of the temple. "I didn't go there to steal anything!" Tacitus pleaded.

"Maybe not, but you didn't stop your accomplices from doing it, did you? Now I have saved your life. Those who are not yet dead will be torn apart by bears and hyenas. You may die in battle, but not as a criminal with the name Aquila."

Despite his determination not to let them, tears streaked down Tacitus's face.

"Yes, cry if you must. Cry like I did when I buried your mother. She was more sacred to me than anything in this world. Cry now, but never cry in my presence again. A legionnaire does not cry."

Tacitus wiped his tears and stared at his father, whose bronze medals adorned his plated armor. He wore the red transverse crest on his spotless helmet and appeared indomitable. This, Tacitus thought, was something he could never be. And he would die with a spear or arrow deep inside him and no one, not even Tullia, would ever know. His father was speaking again, eyes boring into him.

"Now you listen. I have never lied in the 17 years that I have served the legion. But I'm going to lie today. I'm going to praise you in front of the recruiting officer and you will show respect and enthusiasm. Embarrass me again and you will pray for death every day of your life. I have a letter of recommendation from that priest, a total lie in your case, but from this day on you will behave as if no greater truth was ever told. You will learn to fight and you will learn to kill and you will do it remorselessly. Do you understand?"

Tacitus nodded.

"Say it!"

"Yes. Yes, father, I understand," said Tacitus, choking on his words.

They will make me into a miserable copy of the man so arrogantly standing before me. My life is over. Nothing matters. I'm as good as dead—the sooner, the better, he thought.

"One more thing. Many in the army pay bribes to get out of onerous details. You will never give or take a bribe. You will do exactly what you are told and you will do it willingly. Expect no favors or special treatment from me. You will acknowledge my presence only by saluting, and you will never speak to me unless I invite you to do so. If I do require you to speak, you will address me as 'Primus Pila, First Spear.' Fail me and the punishment will be swift and brutal. Do not fail the legion, do not fail yourself. You may not think so right now, but I have done you a great favor. You will reciprocate by showing your devotion and your loyalty. I expect nothing less."

"Will I ever get to see Tullia again?"

"No, it would be useless. A legionnaire is not allowed to marry. When your service is over, who knows? But both of you will have lived different lives by then. Certainly she will have married or even died. She is still a child and will soon forget what you even look like. By the end of the day you will be married to the legion. Your allegiance is to Rome."

But I will think of her every day and every night until I am killed, Tacitus thought. Sick and weak, he again stared at his father knowing that his life was over before it would ever begin.

Chapter 1

Gaius and Appian Dio, the trumpeter, ascended the parapet surrounding the city of Carrhae. One sentry after another saluted the "First Spear" as he walked along the raised fortification. "I want two more men at that post," Gaius said to the commander of the guard, then he and Appian Dio returned to the main street and strode through the open gates.

"Let's take a walk. I want to think and I don't like cities, particularly not this one," said Gaius.

"You liked Rome when we were kids," said Appian.

"That was a lifetime ago. I like encampments and tents, and neatness."

"This is a nice city and I like it," countered Appian as he glanced back to the settlement Alexander had built three hundred years earlier.

"You like it because there are plenty of women."

"I love women, always have. Can't get enough of them Gaius, you know that."

"You love them better than fighting?"

"That's a damn serious question," said Appian. "At least when I'm done with a woman she's still alive and happy."

It was nearing dusk and the Syrian desert was still cool. A pair of vultures floated past and Gaius watched their flight toward the Euphrates, where Roman ships offloaded cargo for the legions.

"No corpses for them to feed on right now," said Appian.

"They'll be fat before this is over," replied Gaius.

The two men left the road and walked to a low promontory. Appian said, "You started to tell me how this venture began."

"Where did I leave off?"

"You were at Caesar's villa in Cisalpine Gaul when he was waiting for Gnaeus Pompey and Marcus Crassus."

"I am no tribune or senator, just a simple soldier. So I was surprised that Caesar wanted me to remain in the atrium."

"He has little use for anyone except soldiers and you're the best he has. Were you able to hear everything?" said Appian.

"Yes, I think that's why he wanted me there. He's asked for my opinion on a few occasions. Anyway, he seemed quite anxious about the meeting; made sure that his slaves laid out a sumptuous table for the other consuls."

"Not the hardtack and swill we get on the march?"

"Not exactly. Exotic stuff: cooked sea urchins, ostrich, marinated hare and boiled pig brains."

"Ghastly! No ordinary soldier would ever eat that," said Appian with a shiver.

"Pompey got there first and was in a dour mood. Caesar told him that Crassus would be along that morning. Pompey called Crassus what the rest of Rome does: 'Dives,' which means greedily rich. What really rankled Pompey was Crassus's inflated self-esteem. Crassus is envious of the

Triumphal marches of both Caesar and Pompey through Rome following their victories; Caesar's in Gaul and Pompey's against the pirates in the Mediterranean."

"What else did Pompey say? Everybody knows what he thinks of Crassus," asked Appian Dio.

"Pompey was just warming up. He went on about how great Caesar was in comparison, how he'd conquered Gaul and how the barbarian, Vercingetorix, surrendered after the battle of Alesia."

"Julius must have enjoyed that. He never minds applause."

"He's not especially humble, but he's won his laurels."

"Then Crassus sweeps in and says, 'Friends, fellow triumvirs, a splendid day and such an honor to be in your presence!'"

"Pompey looked over at me and just rolled his eyes. But Caesar put his arm around Crassus's shoulders and led him to the dinner table."

"That must have pleased Crassus. Did he brag about his money? He is the richest man in Rome."

"Crassus knows what Pompey thinks of him. But, he did say that despite his wealth and his enjoyment of fine food he prides himself on living a moderate life and being a 'man of the people'. Then Pompey quipped that it took the right skill with the right fire-fighters. But Caesar became impatient and wanted to get on with his own agenda. He said, 'Enough, we have serious business to attend to and it's essential that we cooperate.' But Crassus was practically jumping up and down and said, 'Yes, yes, the Triumvirate, but you must listen to my idea. It's positively stunning and will make Rome and us exceedingly wealthy.'"

"I can only imagine how that thought played with Pompey," said Appian.

"I was watching Caesar. He just wanted to get a deal worked out, so he gave in to Crassus."

"And it was about this, us being here in his Syrian province."

"Basically, yes. Crassus clapped his hands and one of his slaves brought in a bolt of purple silk. Caesar admired it saying, 'It must have cost a fortune.' Crassus had the opening he wanted. 'It costs us a fortune, and that's the problem.'"

"I don't understand. What does silk have to do with us?" said Appian.

"That's where it gets convoluted. Crassus said that silk is sold to us by the Parthians and we have to pay for it in gold, and that's bankrupting Rome."

"You and I don't wear silk so what's it to us?"

"According to Crassus, silk comes from the Seres people and how it's made is a mystery. He said that we don't know if it grows on trees or is made from entrails from an unknown animal. But regardless, we can't get it from the eastern people because the Parthians won't let us cross their land."

"What did Caesar say about that?"

"He said that there's nothing we can do about it. We have a non-aggression pact with Parthia and they have strictly observed every aspect of the treaty. But Crassus was adamant and said that we must get them to accept our coinage or we must do to them what we did to Carthage, Greece, Spain and Gaul. He said that they must allow us to pass."

"So we're here because Crassus wants to go to war over silk?" said Appian Dio. "How did Pompey react to that?"

"Pompey was livid. He actually jumped up, spilling his wine and argued, 'If you want war, that requires additional legions and money. Who's going to pay for that?'" Crassus was equally furious, 'I will of course!' Then Pompey retorted, 'Let me guess who is going to lead those legions.'"

"The picture is becoming clear," Appian said with a smirk.

"Oh, it gets better. Crassus stuck his chin out like the prow of a war galley and said he would personally lead the attack against the Parthian capital at Ctesiphon. Pompey refilled his cup, sank onto a couch and said it was utter madness."

"What did Caesar think of Crassus's plan?" asked Appian.

"He lay on a couch and listened as if it were a debate in the Senate. Eventually Caesar pulled Pompey aside and said there was no need for all three Consuls to be in Rome at the same time. In the past, Rome only had two. Pompey smiled and replied, 'You're suggesting we get him out of the city; send him on his way to oblivion?'"

"An idea Pompey must have liked," said Appian.

"I'm sure he did. Then Caesar whispered to him that it was a quid pro quo; Crassus might succeed in getting to Ctesiphon, but they still needed him to secure the Triumvirate first. Because Crassus is popular with the Senate they would need his support. Then turning to Crassus he said, 'Yes, I believe that a victory over Parthia is conceivable, and I will support your plan.'"

"So, Crassus got what he wanted," said Appian.

"He was overjoyed and declared, 'As you will both agree, we are already in an economic war with Parthia. Not only will I crush them, but I will do everything in my power to continue our governance of Rome. I will win over the Senate and we will prosper!'"

"And then he left?"

"Not before Caesar told him he would not only back his venture, but lend him some of his best legionnaires and centurions. After Crassus left, Pompey said that the whole thing about silk—how it's destroying our economy—is a ruse, a flamboyant excuse to barge into a land that is at peace with us, and there really is no profit from it. He said even if Crassus wins we'll make a powerful enemy. His plan is deeply flawed. In fact, it's suicide! He's never fought in desert lands and hasn't campaigned for 20 years. However, Pompey said he would support Crassus in the Senate as he agreed, but that this quest for glory will end in unmitigated disaster."

"What do you think, Gaius? Is this an act of desperation?"

"It's all about strategy and timing, Appian. I was watching Pompey when he said, 'Julius, it's you who will have to clean up the mess, and it will be a very bloody mess indeed.' I was still standing at the entryway when Caesar motioned for me to come forward. I saluted and waited while he collected his thoughts. He then said, 'Crassus will need experienced men, so I'm lending you to him. Remember, you're only on loan. You should be back before the year is out, and I'll need you for my operation in Britain.'"

"So how was I so lucky to get into this mess?"

"Simple. Caesar asked if I had any requests and I said that I wanted you to come along."

"What did he say?"

"He laughed and said, 'My favorite trumpeter? I'll have to learn to play the damn horn myself!' Then he surprised me by ordering that I take several newly trained cohorts along with me. I asked him when I should report to Crassus and he said that I should go as soon as possible."

"And that's how we got here."

"Yes, but as I left the villa I heard Pompey say, 'I hope Crassus's adventure is over before summer. It will be damn hot in Parthia after that.'"

Chapter 2

It is a travesty!" shouted tribune Fabius Ateius. "Another secret deal. Have the consuls no shame?"

The Senate, having learned of Crassus's forthcoming adventure, was packed with supporters and opponents. "How many have been bribed by 'Dives' to cast their vote for this imbecilic scheme?" asked Ateius. There would be no discussion today over mundane lawsuits, divorces, or property rights. On this day, thought the tribune, the very future of Rome was at stake.

Ateius stood before the august body, his white linen toga etched with the purple stripe denoting power, wealth and status. He, like all statesmen, was trained in oratory, the most revered skill a patrician could have.

The cries of treachery subsided as the tribune called for silence. His theatrical voice could easily be heard by senators on the furthest stone benches.

"I know that Consul Marcus Lucinius Crassus demands that Parthia pay dearly for its manner of trade and its expectation of gold for the silk Romans buy. But, who says we must buy it? Why not enforce the rule against the purchase. Or, we could tax it to the hilt until the Parthians accept our coinage as do all other nations."

The murmur of approval grew and Ateius raised his hand for silence. "If we banned or taxed Parthian silk, how long before they would crawl to us begging for our coinage, their income devastated by our temperance and resolve? Certainly, a restraint by Rome on this one commodity is cheaper than war. And, may I remind the Senate, this would be a war against a power with whom we are at peace. If we unilaterally violate the treaty, what becomes of our word, our honor? Would we not be justifiably enraged if Parthia broke a treaty with us and then declared war and invaded our soil? All of Rome would rally to the cause of war. Indeed, the very gods would lead us to victory over such a treacherous foe!"

The tribune raised his voice, "But it is we who will be the culprits and it is we who will suffer calamity if Crassus's perilous course is sanctioned. Parthia is not a power to simply dismiss. It is a powerful state, greater certainly than Carthage was in the first Punic War. This venture is an unholy cause. Mark my words; it will result in the needless deaths of thousands of our brave legionnaires."

Many senators were on their feet cheering Ateius on. Summing up his oration, he proclaimed, "it is for vanity, greed and hollow glory that Marcus Crassus seeks this war. Not only must we deny him the invasion of Parthia, but we must condemn his right to consulship itself, for this is a reflection of his judgment. Rome must not be subjected to this calamity. Great Jupiter himself will condemn it!"

Ateius, having fired his bolt, left the podium and Senator Trebonius took his place. He waited until the tumult subsided and said, "We have heard the dire warnings of Ateius, but does he have the knowledge to defy Julius Caesar and Consul Pompey, who wholeheartedly support Crassus? It appears that the senator impugns the fighting ability of our illustrious legions and predicts failure before the great venture has even begun. Is this the speech of a patriot?"

A dozen senators rose to condemn Ateius. Trebonius waited, and then said, "What greater influence must one have beyond the support of Pompey and Caesar? I maintain that Crassus's cause is a righteous one. And how long, my friends, will it be before we must go to war against Parthia anyway? It is only a matter of time, and then we will empty our treasury to pay for it. However, the magnanimous and renowned Crassus, the 'Man of the People,' volunteers to pay the army's entire expense. Rome has nothing to lose. And the gain? Immeasurable!"

***

The legions stood in silent ranks outside the ancient walls of Rome. Having marched from Campus Martius, the Field of Mars, the troops watched as the city gates swung open for Marcus Licinius Crassus, who added general to his title of consul. A tribune ordered the legions to attention and Gaius Septimus Aquilius repeated the command. The red crests atop centurion helmets stirred in the morning breeze as all eyes focused on the great iron gates. Except for the oldest veterans the army was viewing its general for the very first time. Still dressed in his toga, Crassus, though portly, looked resolute.

The general was a dozen steps from the gate when Ateius darted into his path, the man's white linen toga etched with the purple stripe. The general stopped and glared at his nemesis.

The tribune placed a dish of smoldering incense on the ground and drenched it with oil. Flames shot upward. Thrusting an arm toward Crassus, he bellowed, "I curse you in the name of Great Jupiter and all the gods! You and your men will perish and bring shame to Rome. You defy the Fates and will die in agony!"

A crowd had assembled around the tribune and images of horror caused faces to blanch and the assembly to recoil. To invoke the name of the gods to invite the defeat of a Roman army was a sacrilege second only to damning Great Jupiter, father of the gods. Crassus glared at the man and moved forward to brush him aside, but Ateius held his ground.

"Your name will be reviled and your infamous pride will bring tears and lamentations to the mothers of brave soldiers whose lives will be snuffed out in the deserts of shame!"

Crassus drew himself up. "Coward. You made your treasonous opinions known at the Senate meeting. Nobody listened to you then, and nobody is listening now, least of all the brave men whose abilities you impugn." With that, he gathered himself and lumbered through the gates, followed by his scowling aides, and marched boldly before the ranks of legionnaires.

Crassus mounted his horse and rode to the front of the legions. The general made an effort to appear unfazed, despite the horrific omens.

Recovering from Atieus's vituperation, he looked forward to the great opportunities ahead. By Jupiter, he thought, he would have his victory and his Triumph and his detractors would cower in shame. This would be an adventure of his own making and he would go forward as a great Roman general.

Surely, legionnaires who heard the dire warnings were appalled and dismayed. Crassus was determined to inspire his troops and dispel the prophesy of doom. With bravado he shouted, "We shall march to the port of Brundisium, board our ships, and sail for our province in Syria. There we shall gather more legions and wreak havoc upon the detested Parthians, those ravenous vultures that defile Rome. We shall burn their cities and recover the gold they have stolen. You, my brave legionnaires, will be awarded a fine share of that treasure and you will become wealthy men."

He had their attention now and detected a growing resolve. "You shall gain honor and glory for your exploits and shall march through the gates of Rome in a great triumph. Together we are indestructible; no power on earth can defeat us. So, in the tradition of Roman arms, I ask you: are you ready to march?"

"Yes," came the legionnaires' expected reply, but it lacked vigor. As was the custom, Crassus repeated the question twice more.

"Are you ready to march?"

"Yes!"

"Are you ready to march?"

"Yes!"

"Then prepare to march," Crassus commanded.

"Prepare to march," echoed the centurions.

Marcus Crassus drew his gladius and pointed it toward the distant coast. "March!"

With one motion the legions swung in behind one another and began their trek to the port and the waiting fleet.

***

"This wouldn't be so bad if it weren't for the omens," said Sempronius.

The army marched at a leisurely pace along the tree-lined bank of the Tigris River. Sempronius, a diminutive blond legionnaire, was flanked by Tacitus and the giant Lupus

Ibericus. The three, along with their tent mates, had been conscripted into III Galicia, one of the seven legions Marcus Crassus now led into Syria. All along the route they passed farmers and herds of cattle and goats. Except for marauding armies and a change of potentates, it seemed to Tacitus that nothing about the land had changed since the time of the Babylonians, or the Sumerians before them. It was a great treadwheel of life that slowly revolved from one generation to the next.

A line of ships belonging to the Roman fleet, Classis Alexandria, was being rowed upstream. It carried provisions for the legions as well as sailors, who could be conscripted for land combat if necessary.

Tacitus gave the ships a quick glance. "Those won't be with us if we have to go inland. It may not be so cushy once we leave the river."

He and seven other Hastati tented together and, having just finished their training, had never seen combat. As the most expendable, they'd be in the front rank of battle. It made Tacitus feel terribly vulnerable, even though the enemy force was still hundreds of miles away.

Crassus and his tribunes rode at the head of the legions. Behind them marched the aquilifer carrying a staff emblazoned with a bronze plaque and the initials SPQR, "the people and senate of Rome." That was topped by the legion's eagle, its most important emblem. Losing the eagle, the *aquila*, was a legion's worst catastrophe.

From his position in the line, Tacitus could see those at the front of the legion. Between the bearer of the *aquila* and the legionnaires marched the *vexillarius*, who held aloft the cohort's standard. The *vexillarius* wore no helmet. Instead, he was crowned with the head of a wolf. Beside him marched the trumpeter and the legion's chief centurion, the Primus Pila.

Even on the dirt road the tramp of forty-five thousand men wearing iron-studded shoes sounded ominous. It would, thought Tacitus, take an experienced and dedicated army to match the skill and numbers of the legions. But, like the rest, he had witnessed the horrific omens.

Despite the curses of the senator there were few concerns the first weeks. But worries escalated when Crassus tripped and fell at the temple of Venus. A shudder sped through the assembled ranks as the men witnessed the general's clumsiness, for it was perceived as still another warning from the gods.

As the march continued, even greater doubts set in as calamitous events became more numerous. A violent thunderstorm drenched the army as it crossed the Zeugma River. Lightning bolts sheared across the sky, a bridge was carried away by hurricane force winds, and thunderbolts struck precisely where the army was to camp. In addition, the groom attending the general's horse was dragged into the river and drowned. That horror was followed by a thoughtless meal containing lentils and salt, food prepared for funerals.

Tacitus and the other men were appalled. A sacrifice was made to the gods, but the intestines of the animal were foul, and the seers were sickened by the putrid, slimy mass. They placed them in the hands of Crassus, who let them splatter to the ground. There was fear in the ranks.

Tacitus's cohort consisted of eighty men. Cresting a rise, he could see the front units led by his father, the chief centurion who seemed to never tire. He carried a golden ceremonial arrow, having won it 17 years earlier in the defense of a fellow recruit. With it came a golden crown of oak leaves and the title "Hero of Rome."

His father had earned the arrow when, on the Campus Martius, he'd killed two gladiators in the employ of a vicious tribune. That, however, had been when Tacitus was just an infant, shortly after his own mother had died following his birth.

"Do you still hate the army?" asked Sempronius.

"Of course I do. It wasn't my decision, it was his." Tacitus stared at the straight back of the Primus Pila.

"But you had little choice after what happened, or so I heard," said Lupus Ibericus, who carried his sixty-pound kit as if it were a knapsack.

"I had a choice."

"Sure," said Ibericus. "The army or slavery. I've known more than one father who sold his son."

"And you still despise him?" asked Sempronius.

"What do you think?"

***

Although the army could march over 30 miles in 12 hours, Crassus was in no hurry to reach the fortified town of Carrhae in Rome's Syrian province. He was awaiting his son, Publius, and his Spanish cavalry, who were returning from Gaul. The legion's trek became leisurely, not the usual fast military step. A halt was called, and Tacitus along with three of his tentmates walked a short distance to some shaded palms beside the river Tigris.

"Look at that silly oaf Ibericus," Militus Agacias said. "He sticks to Sempronius like tar."

"You weren't with us during training, so you don't know. We could have had Ibericus beaten to death—thirty, forty lashes in front of the entire legion. He actually deserved it. He tried to kill Sempronius a number of times. He was a different person then," said Tacitus.

"And now he's bosom pals with him? That doesn't make sense," said Agacias.

Lepidus, another legionnaire, took a chew of *bucellatum*, a hardtack tough enough to patch a sandal, and said, "Sempronius was easy to pick on. He's small and he had a stutter. During sling training Ibericus slammed a stone right through Sempronius's shield. It knocked him out, but he could have been killed. That was just the first time."

"Nobody tried to stop him or report him to the training centurion?" asked Militus.

"For a while nobody wanted to take him on," said Lepidus. "He was mean and he's big."

"But Ibericus also hangs around Tacitus," said Agacias.

"I'll get to that," said Lepidus. "The second time was during the swimming exercise in the Tiber. Sempronius wasn't a very good swimmer but had made friends with Tacitus. It was kind of strange because Tacitus didn't make friends with anyone then. Anyway, about halfway across, Ibericus grabs Sempronius, pulls him down, and keeps him under."

"Was Ibericus trying to murder him?" asked Agacias.

"Exactly, and it could have been the perfect murder in that Sempronius's body would never have been found, considering how murky the Tiber is," said Lepidus.

"But someone did. I mean, somebody must have seen Sempronius go under."

"Tacitus did," said Latinus. "He turned back and found Ibericus down there with Sempronius. Tacitus was a better swimmer and could have drowned Ibericus. At least that's what Sempronius told us. Then Tacitus dragged Ibericus to the sand. He was gasping for air like a dying fish. After that Ibericus was out to get Tacitus and Sempronius both."

"Was there a fight?" asked Agacias.

"No, well, not exactly." Lepidus took a swig of water from his drinking gourd. "About a week after the swimming incident a recruit was whipped in front of all of us for sleeping on guard duty. The man never recovered and was given a dishonorable and banished from Rome. We were all stunned, but Ibericus was terrified."

"A few nights later it was time to change the guard," said Lepidus, "and Tacitus and Sempronius were to take over from Ibericus and another recruit. I assigned Sempronius a position and Tacitus, Latinus, and I went to find Ibericus. He wasn't where he was supposed to be and he was leaning on his shield. We got real close and realized that he was fast asleep. We had him. Tacitus kicked the shield out and when Ibericus fell he found Tacitus's *puglio*, nice and sharp, at his throat. We tied him up and asked him how he'd like to have those forty lashes."

"Ibericus cried like a baby, begged that we not tell the training centurion. 'I'll do anything. I'll pay you everything I have,' he said, but Tacitus will never take a bribe," said Latinus. "We left him tied like a stuffed pig and let him sweat. He would die if flogged and he knew it. He said that he would apologize to Sempronius, become his protector, his best friend. Tacitus told him that if he ever reneged he would wake up with his throat slit."

"Wasn't Sempronius surprised by Ibericus's sudden friendship?"

"Stunned is a better word," said Lepidus. "But he's no fool. I think he knew and, strange as it is, they've become real friends. Ibericus is a giant but he's very sentimental when not in a fight. And for the sake of the gods, never make him cry."

"Pareculus, the training officer, said that Ibericus was making a fool of himself tagging along with Sempronius like a slathering puppy, but Pareculus was never told why," said Lepidus.

"Strange how one incident can change a person's life," said Agacias.

"Ibericus had the choice of befriending Sempronius or dying. He knew that his time in the legion would be 20 years, but dying is longer. We thought that Ibericus might go back to his old ways but he hasn't. But if I were you, I wouldn't talk to him about it," said Lepidus.

"He becomes violent?" asked Agacias.

"No, he'll become morose. There's little worse than a morose giant. It takes all of us to cheer him up."

As Lepidus walked away, he heard a voice call, "Munifex, a word with you." Being of the lowest rank, Lepidus turned about and sighed. A veteran with a pasty, pock-marked face came up to him and said, "I'm Quintillus."

"I know who you are. We have all heard about you," said Lepidus.

"And just what have you heard?"

"That you're the self-appointed complainer for the entire legion."

"Not true, but when I see problems, I make them known. I don't pretend that they don't exist, like some people do."

"Sure, so what do you want?"

"I couldn't help but overhear what the real complainer, Tacitus, said about hating the army. In my opinion, any man who hates the army is untrustworthy in battle."

"And you think he is untrustworthy, even though he has risked his life to save a fellow legionnaire?"

Quintillus ignored the parry and said, "I heard from a friend who spoke to the scribe at Tacitus's evaluation when he was enlisting. The scribe said it was his father who forced Tacitus to join after he and his girlfriend desecrated his mother's temple. His father had to get him out of Rome and away from the scummy girl. That's not the kind of person we want in the legion. I thought you and a few others would inform the Primus Pila. Maybe get him transferred before he becomes a problem."

"I think you're the problem, Quntillus, and I wouldn't use the word 'scum' about Tacitus's girlfriend."

"Why not? It's true from what I heard."

"Then you didn't hear it right, and Tacitus would slit your throat."

Quintillus puffed up and said, "I thought you would be helpful since you and all your tent mates have to depend on someone who has contempt for the army."

"So now you're going to complain?"

"I will bring it to the attention of the Primus Pila and he will know what to do."

"You do that. I'm sure he would like to know what you think of his son."

There was a moment of stunned silence, then Quintillus said, "His father? I didn't know that. Maybe I will wait and see how Tacitus..." But Lepidus was already gone. A group of legionnaires smirked as Quintillus scurried away.

***

Apollodoros shuffled up the steps of Carrhae's crumbling Greek temple. Eddies of sand blew across its scuffed marble

19

floor and piled up like wavelets at the base of its chipped Doric pillars. Alexander the Great, the Macedonian, had had the sacred edifice built over two hundred and seventy years earlier while on his quest to conquer the world. Time, war and the abrasive sand had taken their toll, but even as a stark ruin it projected nobility.

It was May and already Apollodoros, the former Greek slave, could feel the rising heat. A scorpion scurried toward a spider, stopped a few feet from him, and watched what might become his morning meal.

How bizarre, Apollodoros mused, that he had ventured here again at the age of thirty-nine. Nothing had really changed at Carrhae since he had last come as a boy with his itinerant father.

Apollodoros had stood in this very spot and memorized the text carved into the temple walls. As a child he had been instructed in languages, elocution, medicine, and fighting tactics by his father. On their travels his father had taught him how to set broken bones and sew up the wounds of fellow travelers. The wanderings of Apollodoros's mind were interrupted by the sight of a distant haze. Absently he watched the wall of desert sand rise skyward. The scorpion, postponing his meal, scurried to a niche in the temple wall. The shaking increased as thousands of riders, their horses pounding across the desert sands, tore past the temple. They held aloft multicolored banners, and their steeds were covered in bronze plates. The horsemen, all warriors, were likewise sheathed in armor.

"Cataphracts," Apollodoros said aloud. He touched two fingers to his forehead and wondered why such a large force would appear at Carrhae.

A pair of legionnaires quickly ascended the temple steps. One raised a hand in greeting. "The consul requires your immediate attendance. Bring your writing instruments. The Armenians are here."

The cavalry force had already assembled when Apollodoros hurried through the city gates. He was shown into a large hall and commanded to sit beside Marcus Crassus and six of his tribunes. Crassus was seated on a guilded chair that elevated him slightly above the other parties. A selection of Armenian gifts had been carried into the building, but few had been opened. The Armenian king, Artavasdes, and his entourage sat across from Crassus.

Crassus said "I really don't see why I would need the support of your army. As the governor of Syria, I'm entirely capable of raising all the legions I need."

"Excellency, the legions will be infantry. Roman infantry tactics are second to none, but you will be facing Parthian cavalry, cataphracts, and that could be catastrophic."

Apollodoros quickly recorded the exchange on his wax tablet. Though the conversation was in Greek, he wrote in Latin.

Crassus tipped a wine glass to his lips. He eyed Artavasdes for a moment. "Roman armies have encountered cataphracts and annihilated them. As I recall, some of them were Armenian."

The king stared at Crassus. "Yes, but the Parthians have powerful allies. I'm speaking of the nomadic horsemen, the Saka, in the far east of their empire. Of course you've heard of their tactics and extraordinary bows. Quite deadly."

"We also have tactics and nearly fifty thousand men to employ them," said Crassus, rearranging his stout body in his guilded chair.

Artavasdes stiffened. "We Armenians ask nothing of you. We have suffered under threats from Orodes, the Parthian King. It's only a matter of time before he attacks us. If he conquers us, his empire will be even greater, and we Armenians will be forced to join his army. That will make a Roman war with Parthia even more dangerous."

Crassus's expression didn't change. The king looked him in the eye and said, "I offer fifty thousand men if you ally yourself with us. And, one more thing. I presume that you intend to capture their capitol at Ctesiphon. There are only two routes available. One is across the desert. Summer is almost upon us; you can already feel its heat. Crossing the desert is madness. But my country is to the north, away from the desert. Take the route through my country, through the foothills of the Zagros Mountains, and your legions will arrive safely. And they will be fed by appreciative farmers."

"I don't need your men, Artavasdes, or your advice. Now you should leave and take your gifts with you."

The king stood. "You have made a grievous mistake, Crassus. I know this land and I know the Parthians. Orodes has terrible resolve. He also has a treaty with Rome, and your abrogation of it will be damning for you—as well as for us. His spies know we're here for only one reason: to join forces with you. Now neither of us will live to see the end of summer."

***

"I guess you saw Publius and his vaunted cavalry come in today," said Appian. "Big spectacle."

Gaius snorted. "Who could miss it? The great commander, son of Marcus Licinius Crassus, victor over the barbarians! His entire cavalry is only a thousand."

Publius was in his glory and Crassus had greeted him as if he were Alexander himself.

"And we've waited all spring for him to get here from Gaul. I hope his little horses make a difference. What have you heard about him?"

"He's extremely aggressive," said Gaius. "And in itself that's a good thing. But he's also impatient and compulsive. Apollodoros told me he's demanding that his father move immediately against the entire Parthian empire."

"We might as well. Sitting around here just gives them more time to prepare. Regardless, it's going to be bloody."

Chapter 3

"We concluded treaties with them over thirty years ago," said King Orodes. "We have scrupulously adhered to every provision, even if it cost us. The established boundary between the Roman province and Parthia is the Euphrates and we've never violated that!" he said in Greek.

Like many wealthy Parthians, Greek was his native language since Alexander had stamped Hellenism on the land centuries earlier. Greek culture was still honored, and old Parthian coins were adorned with the words 'Philhellene'—'Friend of Greeks.'

But it was not the Greeks who concerned Orodes, it was the Romans.

"Is it because Rome wants more territory and Crassus, a doting old fool, wants glory?"

Spahbod Surena, the king's foremost general and son of the wealthiest family in the land, didn't answer immediately. The two men walked through the palace gardens of Ctesiphon, the royal winter residence on the banks of the Tigris.

"Personally, I don't understand it," Surena said. "Our spies in Rome report that this is not a popular war. But

Crassus was backed by Caesar and Pompey. It's said that Crassus hopes to get as far as the land of the Seres people beyond the Great Wall. He boasts of taking us out of the silk trade."

"They don't even know where the Great Wall is, nor do they have contacts with the Middle Kingdom. He must be mad or the most narcissistic man in Rome," said Orodes. "Anyway, I sent envoys to Crassus. I said that we could negotiate any demands. He was also told that if there's a fight, Roman legions would be terribly vulnerable. But I guess he's made up his mind."

"So it's war," Surena said. With delicate features and hair carefully parted in the middle, he appeared unthreatening to those who didn't know him. "Are their legions already on the march?"

"Not yet. They're still at the river, a comfortable place, but that will change." Seeing a quizzical look, Orodes said, "There's a snake I'm setting loose in their camp, and he's damn venomous."

"I know who you mean, but can you trust him?"

"I pay him enough and he wouldn't dare cross me. He's a miserable viper, but he's our viper. He'll be on his way tomorrow."

The king stopped and gazed at the great arch standing before his city. "I also heard that the Armenian king met with Crassus and offered him his army, provisions, and a safe route through his country. I won't tolerate that."

"But Crassus turned him down. He wants to take us on alone so he can claim a great victory."

"Stupid of him not accepting the Armenian's help, but Artavasdes will pay dearly anyway. Before I slit his throat I'll remind him how he carried on about loyalty, and how

Armenia and Parthia are blood brothers. Well, Surena, there will be blood, a lot of Armenian blood."

"Do you want me to attack him?" Surena asked, excitement in his voice.

"No, Artavasdes is mine. I'll take most of the cataphracts and the infantry. All I want you to do is hold the Romans until I return. You'll have ten thousand of our Saka allies and a few hundred cataphracts. Slow the legions down but, whatever you do, don't tangle with them. Their strength is in close, pitched battle. The fight must be on your terms, not those of Crassus."

Surena nodded and Orodes could see the anticipation of glory on the young man's face. Perhaps too much so. That would be dealt with later; he knew that Surena had his eyes on the throne. So it would not be too much later.

***

"I knew you'd want to see it right away," said Ophelia, a slender thirteen-year-old girl with spritely ribbons in her hair. "It was put in with my brother's letter. I don't know why he would do that."

"Tacitus doesn't want his father to know that he's writing to me. It would get him in trouble again," said Tullia. She took the papyrus from Ophelia's ringed fingers and read the letter.

"How would his father know about it?"

"He's the chief centurion of the legion, the one Tacitus and Sempronius are in. He's against me and Tacitus having any kind of relationship."

"Why?"

Tullia smoothed out the simple white stola that came to her ankles and laid the three-month-old letter in her lap. "It's a long story. Suffice it to say that Gaius despises me."

A puff of wind blew through the atrium, lifting the papyrus from Tullia's lap. It landed near the door from which Junia emerged. She picked it up and looked at it, a dark, petulant expression on her face.

"I suspect that this is from Tacitus. Is it?"

"It is, Aunt Junia,"

Junia was Aspacia's sister and wasn't related to Tullia. A childless widow, she had raised Tacitus after her sister's death. She accepted Tullia's desire for friendship and allowed Tullia to stay in her home after her own mother cast her out, but, adhering to Gaius's warning, had discouraged her from communicating with Tacitus.

Junia looked from the cramped writing to Tullia and let out a measured breath. "Well, he's still alive, or at least was when he wrote this. What does he say?"

"He's with his cohort in Carrhae, an old Greek city in Mesopotamia. They've taken a few small cities from the Parthians, but nothing big has happened yet. He sounds worried, but everyone thinks they'll be back soon."

"Anything about his father?"

"Not really. He just tries to stay away from him. But I think he gets along with his tent mates."

"Sempronius certainly likes him; Tacitus saved his life," said Ophelia, hoping to dispel Junia's foul mood. "He's in the same cohort as Tacitus."

"I thought your brother was over there with Cassius, the tribune," Junia said.

"Oh, that's Servius, my older brother. He's at Carrhae but in Cassius's legion."

"I see." Junia brushed away a hank of grey hair that had fallen across her face and turned to Tullia. "You know what Gaius told you."

"I'm sor—"

"We had an agreement, Tullia. You said you wouldn't bother Tacitus or his father with useless letters when I took you in. And now this. You did write to him, didn't you?"

Tullia glanced at Junia, then down at her feet. "Yes. But I only wanted to know if he was safe. We had all heard terrible things about the crossing, all the ships that were lost in that storm. Surely you hoped that he arrived safely, didn't you?"

"Of course I did. But writing to him, encouraging him, won't make things easier for either of you. I'm certain you know that, Tullia. You have to face facts. Every boy must submit to his father's will, even when the boy is fully grown. Gaius is Tacitus's commanding officer now. You must stop this if they are ever to have a better relationship."

Tullia nodded. "I disappointed you. I should leave here."

"And go where? You have no money. I don't want you to do what your mother does, hanging around the baths, waiting for the next man." She sighed. "You have been a nice help for an old lady like me. I know what it is to be in love, especially with someone you can't have."

Junia sat on the bench beside the girls. "Someday Tacitus may have a posting near a town or a city and you may move there," she said softly. "A lot of women become attached to legionnaires, and they become wives in all but name. Gaius may look away if Tacitus is a good soldier or assigned to another legion. Then things may be different."

"Should I tell him that?"

Junia shrugged. "I suggest that you not write at all. But if you do, tell him that you pray for him in the war and that you will not be writing again for a very long time."

***

The great road upon which the silk trade travelled crossed the Tigris in Mesopotamia and proceeded east 2,000 miles through Parthia to the land of the Sogdiani at their capital at Marikanda. From there it continued 3,000 more miles through Central Asia. It wound its way over the Pamir Mountains and the terrible Taklamakan Desert to the nomad villages that lay only a hundred miles west of China's rough, unfinished wall. Behind the wall stood the empire of the Han Dynasty, the world of the Celestial Kingdom, a place of culture, art, learning, and general stability.

The land to the west of the Wall was, in the eyes of the Chinese, a geographical and intellectual wasteland. It was a place for exiles, a desolate existence peopled by unwashed marauders, whose only skill was their ability to raid Chinese villages and exact tribute for the Emperor of the Han.

In that land of dun-colored, treeless hills, Hera sat in a circle of women sewing trousers and jackets for the men of the village. They called themselves the Chanyu and had over centuries migrated from the steppes of Central Asia. After so many years in their captivity she did not have to concentrate on her sewing; she knew exactly where the needle should be. During lulls in their conversation she gazed past the felt yurts, and the goats and horses in distant fields, as her mind wandered aimlessly through the pathways of her life.

It had been 17 years since she'd last seen her son. He'd been a clever and funny child and had been purchased from their owner by a wealthy man. The boy had been nine then and his new master had told her that he would be treated well. She wondered what he would look like now, presuming that he was still alive. That had been in Parthia, the second land in which she was a slave. The memories flowed together like the water of converging streams.

She had learned many languages since her enslavement 26 years earlier. Her native language was Greek, but she had picked up the *linguae* of many tribes as she was sold from one to the other, each time, as she grew older, at a slightly lesser price. Once she learned Chanyu, the women asked her many questions and tried to visualize her far-off lands. They wanted to know about marriage customs, clothing, and the lives of women. None had ever seen a body of water larger than a small lake and could not imagine what a sea such as the Aegean or the Mediterranean could possibly look like. They could only shake their heads when she told them that the power of a single wave could sink a large ship, and of course a ship was something they would never behold.

Hera, they thought, had once been a very pretty girl, and they wondered why she had never been married. She would smile and say, "Someday I will tell you. It's not a very happy story."

"Few women ever have a happy story," the headwoman replied. "We all know our own, and they're much the same. So someday you must tell us yours."

Then one day when the trivial talk ebbed into silence, Hera, without preamble, said, "My father found a man who wanted a wife for his son. I was thirteen and we set sail for another island where I was to marry."

The women in the sewing circle looked up, surprised that Hera had finally decided to tell her story.

"We knew that there were marauders on the sea but we hoped to avoid them. Unfortunately, our boat was captured. My father was killed, and my mother and I were taken to a

Berber camp, a place of wild horsemen where the sea meets the desert. My mother was a beautiful woman, so we expected the worst. The worst happened the first night."

The women put down their needles and with rapt attention gazed at Hera.

"There was a boy, a Greek who had also been captured some time before and for some reason was favored by the slavers. That night Mother and I were taken from our cage to a large tent where the men, all drunk, were shouting and laughing with great expectation. The boy was brought in and told to rape us. He didn't want to but the other men ripped off our clothes and the boy, perhaps seeing naked women for the first time, became quite excited, if you know what I mean. He still protested but some men took out their knives and threatened to cut him if he refused."

"Why did they want him to do it instead of themselves?" asked one woman. Another said, "Hush, let her tell the story."

"I don't know why," said Hera. "Maybe he was special or we were a reward. Anyway, we were thrown onto a bed of foul horse blankets. The men were gaping at us as if they were waiting their turn. The boy entered me. I cried just as my mother did and in our language he said, 'I'm sorry,' over and over again. I really don't know how sorry he was. They had him do many unspeakable things to me while they cheered him on."

"Did they tie you up afterward?" one woman asked.

"They didn't have to. We couldn't run; there were dozens of them coming in and out of the tent. When the boy was finished with me they had him do my mother. Between her sobs she whispered to him and I'm sure he heard her. Rough men eventually pushed him away and raped us for most of the night. Then they left us for dead and went back to their own tents in a drunken stupor."

"I'm surprised that they left you and your mother alone," said the headwoman.

"We lay on the floor like rags. They had no further use for us, at least not that night."

Hera stared toward the herds of horses. "Before dawn my mother tried to console me. She found a knife one of the pirates had dropped. My mother got to her feet, gave me a kiss, then picked up the knife and left. Later I learned that she stole into Berber tents and slit the throats of the men who raped us."

"Did she do the same to the boy?" asked another woman as she wrapped herself against the ever-blowing wind.

"No."

"Did you learn his name?"

Hera shook her head. "What difference would it have made? I would never see him again."

After a long pause Hera said, "After Mother killed the men, we snuck into a corral. There were usually many horses, but all except one had been taken to another corral some distance away. Mother insisted that I take the horse. I refused and told her that I would get a horse from the other corral. She finally relented and rode off into the desert. I desperately wanted to follow her but I was in too much pain. I made my way back to the tent. There was great commotion the next day when the rapists were found dead. I prayed that they would never find her.

"They threw me into a cage with the other women and we baked in the hot sun. They beat me and sent riders to find her. Three days passed and I was sure that she had escaped. Then on the fourth day one of the riders came back. On his saddle he had tied her long black hair. I cried for many weeks. Then a ship came and I was sold. Nine months later I gave birth to my son."

"And the boy that defiled you, what happened to him?" asked another.

Hera shrugged. "I don't know. I never saw him again."

"Do you think he was your son's father?" asked the headwoman.

"Who could possibly know? I was raped by many men that night. After a while I just closed my eyes. They all looked alike and had the same stink. But my son was tall, even at the age of nine, and he looked more Greek than Arab."

"Then his father might have been the Greek boy?" said a young woman.

Hera gave a little smile. "Perhaps. It would be better if that was true."

"So what happened to you next?" another asked.

"I'm a little tired and this is a hard thing to speak of. Let me leave it for another time."

"Yes, another time. That's all we have here. Just time," said the headwoman as the horses in the field turned their backs to a cold wind from the steppes of Central Asia.

Chapter 4

Carrhae was a crowded place, being situated so close to both the Tigris and Euphrates Rivers. In many ways it mirrored Rome. The brothels, the street mongers, the slaves, and the wealthy Romans were all here. Gaius wove his way through the streets, ignoring the *alipili*, the hair removers, the masseurs, the *unctores* who perfumed foppish men, narcissistic fools who would never last a day in his legion.

Though it had only been seven days since he'd last bathed, entry to the *balneum* was cheap; a dip in the *baptisterium*, the cold bath, was followed by the warmer *tepidarium*, and, finally, the sweat room.

Gaius toured the many rooms of the elaborate bath. For a moment he thought he would enter the steam rooms where men and women could consort and arrange their trysts. Certainly he would be approached by one of the many prostitutes who frequented the baths. But he would not find comfort in their company. No woman had ever pleased him like the one he had loved and lost, even though it had been so long ago. No, he wouldn't share his time with them. They would only disappoint.

"That's why you're so dour, so intractably miserable, Gaius. You have to get laid. At the baths I've seen some exquisite women from Egypt, Cyrenaica, even Parthia. Come with me, we'll get them for the night. It will be good for you," Appian had said.

"It would not be good for me, you ass. I remember too well the last time we did that. It was one of the worst nights of my life."

"That was nearly eighteen years ago! You were a naïve kid who had never screwed a woman before. Aspacia was the most fetching girl you or I had ever laid eyes upon, but she's been gone for..."

Seeing Gaius's cold look, Appian threw up his hands and said no more. Gaius was a stubborn man, rarely moved by opposition or argument. It was why Caesar relied on him. How many times in Gaul would cohorts have wavered had it not been for his implacable determination to hold the ground? The hard look that said "Don't fail me!" was enough to maintain the line against the most determined enemy.

Gaius finally settled into the soothing tepidarium. On this morning the warm pool was quiet. Absent were the boisterous shouting, boasting, and laughter of bathers. Roman baths were raucous places. Besides bathing there were gymnasiums, ball courts, and vendors, all contributing to a cacophony of sound. But here in the tepidarium he was alone. There would be no need to exchange words with anybody else, not that he would be inclined to do so anyway. Now there were other things to think about.

His reverie was broken when an urbane, silver-haired man entered the pool.

"Centurion, I was hoping to see you. I hope you don't mind my intrusion."

"Not at all, tribune," said Gaius, hoping that his tone hid the lie. "I intended to give you the report on the legion's readiness."

"It can wait."

Marcellus Emiles Gracchus, unlike most tribunes, was not a wealthy youth seeking adventure or attempting to accumulate laurels, legitimate or exaggerated, for future political gain. Prior to joining the legions, he had served in the Senate with surprising competence. Gaius gestured for him to continue.

"I spoke with our general a short while ago. He's expecting another visitor, or should I say 6,000 visitors tomorrow morning."

"Not the Armenians again?"

"No, no. He pissed them off good. An Arab and his mob will be here. One of their emissaries brought word."

"How does Crassus feel about that?"

"He's looking forward to the visit."

Gaius nodded. Arabs would have valuable intelligence about the Parthians. "But why come to us? What could they gain? I have my doubts about them. They're a shifty lot, from what I've seen."

"I agree," said Gracchus, stepping into the warm bath, "but perhaps they know where the water holes are."

"Water holes? Are you talking about the desert?"

"The route was not my decision, but it would be important to know where the water is."

Gaius shook his head and was about to get into the *frigidarium* when the tribune said, "Wait, Gaius. There's something that I've wanted to say to you personally, but the time was never right."

"And that would be?"

"It's about your son. I know that things between you and him are tense, and I don't want to complicate it further, but I must express my gratitude. I would be remiss if I didn't. What Tacitus did … that is his name, right? What he did was selfless and quite amazing. It would have gained him the *corona civica* if he had saved a fellow soldier that way. Indeed, it would be the same laurel wreath and golden arrow you earned when you were his age."

"That he rescued your son was just a matter of circumstance. As you may recall, he was standing in the rain without his crossed belts because he violated an order. Moreover, he had embarrassed me in front of the *praefectus castrorum—*"

"And for that you hate the boy?" Gracchus said. "I think I'm a damn good judge of character, Centurion, and I'd say your contempt for him involves something other than that. Of course I won't pry, but I'll tell you this: my wife and I are grateful beyond words."

"You came on the scene after it was all over, so maybe you didn't get the entire story. My wife and I were talking to another tribune in his tent during that terrible storm. My son Lucus, who was only six, got bored and climbed back into the wagon. I should have stopped him; the horses were skittish with the lightning and thunder. You recall the storm?"

"I do," said Gaius, wishing he were now somewhere else.

"There was a thunderclap right over us and the horses bolted. The wagon with no driver tore down the road. Of course, we all ran after it, but the terrified animals charged through the Praetorian Gate and down that winding, muddy road beside the cliff. My boy was hanging on for dear life. We all expected disaster. Nobody could see anything in the downpour. Then we heard the crash and saw the wagon—or what was left of it—and the horses, at the bottom of the chasm. We feared the worst. My wife was hysterical. Legionnaires rushed down there and couldn't find him. Are you listening, Centurion?"

Gaius drew in a deep breath and said, "Yes, Excellency, I'm listening."

"Good. We were all standing around in that cold downpour wringing our hands when beyond the tree line and out of the gloom came that charger, the horse Tacitus was told to hold for a cavalryman. And, behold, my boy is in the saddle with your son and he's in one piece! We couldn't believe it. Tacitus hands Lucus to my wife, dismounts, and apologizes for leaving the spot where he was to stand. Think of it. He's riding that frightened horse at full tilt to grab a child just before the wagon goes over the cliff. It's a feat worthy of a Greek drama.

"What horsemanship! So of course the *praefectus castrorum* gave him back his belts. You should be the proudest father in the legion. If I were the Primus Pila I would have had him promoted."

Gaius weighed his next words. "You are right in assuming our enmity stems from something far more profound, more serious than an infraction. I'm gratified that he saved your son's life, but an earlier travesty is not excusable. And for that I refuse to show favor."

"You are a great soldier and an honorable man, Centurion. You may have every right to your hatred, but someday you'll have to come to terms with it."

***

Although a number of ships transporting Crassus's men across the Mediterranean had been lost, he still had enough troops to gain early victories against isolated towns within the Parthian orbit. While additional units were being trained, the Roman general spent his time adding up the acquired wealth of slaves, gold, and silver. The rest of the army dawdled as the land became warmer each day.

Nearly a week had passed after the departure of the Armenian king when Gaius Septimus Aquilius was joined by his friend from childhood, Appian Dio.

"The men are restless and anxious, Primus Pila. They should be marching and engaging in mock battle like we'd do at Campus Martius."

"We would be if I were Crassus, but I'm not. There's not a damn thing I can do but stay vigilant and make sure that Parthian spies stay out of this city."

***

With bravado and banners flying, 6,000 Arabs raced their horses to the walls of Carrhae. Apollodoros looked on as scimitars flashed in the brilliance of the morning sun, and the riders made a great show of horsemanship, wheeling their agile mounts in complex formations. The entire assemblage finally drew up before the gates and their leader, a bronze-colored man with a prominent nose and piercing eyes, awaited his invitation.

Roman trumpets blared in welcome as thousands of legionnaires stood in tight ranks. The dust settled, and the gates were swung open. Marcus Crassus, his son Publius, and the tribune Cassius walked out to meet the Arab. The desert nomad and his retinue were ushered into the legate's quarters, where they sat on plush carpets and were offered wine and sweets.

Apollodoros had been summoned from his medical duties to act as scribe and offer his linguistic skills.

With obsequious flattery the Arab accepted the refreshments and presented Crassus with a fine blade of Damascus steel and a gilded scabbard. The Arab, a Nabataean, spoke passable Greek, a smattering of Latin, and Arabic, his native language. He introduced himself as Achmed bin Ariamnes. Tall and swarthy, he curled his hair over his forehead in the Roman fashion.

"I am honored to say that I once had the pleasure of meeting the Roman Consul Pompey," said Ariamnes, while delicately sampling a plump date from a golden tray.

"It's always a pleasure to meet a friend of Rome, especially in far-flung regions. And though I am the governor of Syria, I have not been here before and I appreciate the visit of one so familiar with the region. I'm sure that there is much we can learn from each other."

The Arab gave a knowing nod with half-closed eyes. "I am a son of the desert and know every wadi, oasis, and waterhole as with the eyes of a falcon." He extended his arms and, with a slow smile, made a winging motion. The bird he imitated could have just as easily have been a circling buzzard. Both were both birds of prey. "But who," Apollodoros mused, "would they be preying upon?"

Crassus smiled at Cassius, whose mouth was set in a hard line. "See, it's good to have a friend so familiar with the land." He turned back to Ariamnes. "I must also commend the skills of your cavalry and their magnificent steeds. The Arabians you ride are certainly well suited for the desert. Publius, perhaps we should consider purchasing some."

"The animal has great endurance, but it might not do well in Europe, Father," Publius said. "Though I'm certain that they would be fine for lightly armed scouts."

Ariamnes nodded agreeably. "We would be pleased to give you some as a gift, a show of comradeship. In fact, you may experience their endurance when you enter the desert."

"The desert?" Marcus Crassus said.

"Yes, certainly you intend to attack the Parthian capital at Ctesiphon, and that's across the desert. I'm very familiar with the terrain between here and their capitol and that is the only reasonable route.

"It's all desert except the foothills of Armenia, and I'm sure you've already decided against that, or so the rumor has it. Certainly Orodes isn't going to bring his army to Carrhae where you are entrenched."

"So you know about my meeting with Artavasdes," Cassius said, unsmiling.

"Nothing in this land is secret for long, Excellency. By now I'm sure even the Parthians know that the Armenian king left in a huff. If I were an Armenian I would be quite concerned about Orodes."

"You speak of attacking the Parthians by way of the desert. I'm not that familiar with the terrain. If I go that way, I'll need a guide," said Crassus.

The Arab picked up another date. "Exactly. That is one reason for my visit."

"And the other reason?" asked Cassius.

"We Arabs, just like the Armenians, have a long and bitter history with Parthia. They want our oasis at Edessa and we would rather not give it to them. Allying ourselves to your splendid legions makes perfect sense. My cavalry plus yours will overwhelm any Parthian force we encounter. The gods cannot but favor our venture."

Crassus nodded. "What do you know about the Parthian force?"

"It will be a small contingent. I know the mind of Orodes. He will take most of his men and persecute the Armenians. Of that I have no doubt. What they will send against us will be negligible, a mere show, a holding action at best. It could be swept away before the sun is high."

Crassus nodded again, evaluating the Arab. Apollodoros looked up from his wax stylus and caught Cassius's eye. The tribune imperceptibly shook his head.

"Yesterday we sent a unit into the desert to find water," said Publius. "They reported seeing the tracks of many horses, a significant force. Do you think they were Parthian?"

The Arab smiled. "Many people cross the desert in search of water. Tracks can last a long time if there's no wind. We water our horses at the wells and even here at the river. Only camels carry their own water." With piercing eyes, he turned to Crassus. "If you intend to attack the Parthian capital you must enter the desert before the heat becomes unbearable. You have a week, two at the most. Spring in the desert is like a passing cloud; it brings little rain and then, like yesterday's whore, it is a distant memory. General, there is no time to waste. I, a friend of Rome, implore you to march and march quickly, or all will be lost."

"What did you think of the Arab?" Gaius asked Apollodoros that evening.

"He sees everything. He's calculating, deviously charming, and, above all, persuasive. He knows how to manipulate like a scheming sibling going after the entire estate. The Ariamnes spoke of friendship with Pompey, but Cassius knows that they were merely acquaintances. Cassius is suspicious, but Crassus likes the Arab, wants his cavalry, and enjoys the man's flattery."

"So the legions will be at the mercy of the consul's vanity," said Gaius. "The Arabs are coming?"

"It seems so. Ariamnes knows the desert and the location of the wells."

Gaius shook his head. "Did you hear when we will march?"

"I think it will be very soon. But it's still a secret."

"It won't be for long."

***

"It's from my sister. I guess it will be the last letter I get before we march," said Sempronius, unfolding the papyrus.

"Did she enclose anything from Tullia?" asked Tacitus as he arranged his kit.

"No. Maybe she didn't have time. Or maybe she wasn't around when Ophelia had the scribe write the letter."

"I doubt that. They spend a lot of time together. She would know what your sister was doing."

"I'll write to Ophelia as soon as we get back to Carrhae. I'm sure there's an explanation."

"No doubt." Tacitus snatched the letter from Sempronius. He looked at it closely, ran his finger over a broken wax seal, and handed it back.

"What?"

"Nothing. I was just hoping that she would write. I haven't heard from her since we got here, and Ophelia has written you four times."

"As I said, I'll ask her. We'll find out what's going on."

A centurion stuck his head into the tent. "Formation! Formation!" he bawled.

The eight men of the *contubernium* hustled into line. It was the third hour and the sun was already climbing above the desert floor. Forty-five thousand legionnaires and 5,000 auxiliaries stood in closely packed ranks awaiting orders. On the flanks were the Arab horsemen; to the front was Publius with his cavalry. Tacitus glanced back at the bastion of Carrhae with its 500 legionnaires. They would remain to guard the city. He would have given anything to be with them. A stiff wind blew and sand stung his eyes.

***

A legionnaire approached Gaius and saluted. "Primus Pila, you asked me to watch for this."

Gaius took the piece of papyrus, thanked the soldier, and quickly scanned the note. For a brief moment he considered tearing it and letting the wind carry the papyrus away. For a reason he could not explain, he folded it and slipped it into his kit. He would say nothing about it to Tacitus.

***

"Are you ready to march?" came the question from Consul Marcus Licinius Crassus.

"Yes." As usual, the answer was not as robust as it should be. So, as customary, it was asked again: "Are you ready to march?" And a resounding "Yes!" shot across the desert sands.

"Then we shall march!" shouted Crassus, and seven legions followed the Arab cavalry into the trackless waste.

"This is the desert; you didn't expect the flowers and fields of Campania. Did you think there would be bath houses and pretty girls to play with?" Crassus cajoled the legionnaires as he and Ariamnes rode beside the legions with good-natured companionship.

"Their shields are heavy and the sand is deep—that's why all Arabs ride, Consul. The only place my men would walk to is the brothel. In my humble opinion, all warriors should be cavalry. And yes, I'll sell you as many Arabian ponies and camels as you wish," bantered Ariamnes.

"No Roman would ride a camel, my friend. Cavalry is just fine for scouting and finishing off a routed force, but nothing in the world stands up to our infantry. You shall see."

"I look forward to that. But your men should conserve their water. The closest oasis is a full day's march."

Crassus nodded. He liked the insouciance of the Arab in his flowing vestments. But there was a mocking look about him now that things were in motion.

Ariamnes looked back at the formidable force and considered how far the Parthians would let the Romans march before they struck. Of course they would let thirst take its toll. He was pleased that the saddlebags on his men's horses contained many gourds of water and that water would not be shared.

The seven legions and their auxiliaries had crossed the Euphrates. The soldiers' spiked sandals sank into the sand as the infantry tried to keep up with Publius's cavalry.

The desert stretched to the horizon and the shimmering sand created a mirage. There was no vegetation to cool the earth and the sun scalded the legionnaires' plates of overlapping armor.

Crassus had waved off Cassius's suggestion that the legions rest and continue when refreshed. Rebuffed and knowing the general's flash point, the tribune said nothing more.

At dawn the next morning Apollodoros found Gaius staring into the campfire. "Centurion, perhaps you should speak to your son. He and his tent mates are nervous. It will be their first battle."

"Tacitus has been trained like all the others," Gaius said. "It's the duty of his own centurion to reassure him and his mates. I won't interfere with that man's responsibilities and I certainly won't coddle my son or anyone else. He'll live or die just like all the others."

The sun was already high by the time Gaius marched at the front of the first legion. A total of ten cohorts plus auxiliaries brought his legion up to six thousand men. Many of the auxiliaries came from the provinces as freed men, but they were not Romans. Apollodoros, a freed slave, marched with the auxiliaries, as only Romans could enter the regular army. Any foreigner who joined and was apprehended would be put to death.

Rarely was a legion given replacements, so after battles many units had far fewer than their 4,800. But the army of Consul Marcus Crassus was at full strength. Behind the legions came hundreds of vendors and supply wagons accompanied by men, women, and children, civilians all.

Gaius was flanked by the bearer of the eagle standard, the *aquila*. That emblem was followed by the general and the five tribunes assigned to each legion.

He turned and looked back at the legions moving as blocks in massed formations. The front rank of his own legion, where his son and his tent mates marched, were the newest legionnaires, the Hastati, who would absorb the first assault. They were armed with a stabbing sword, the eighteen-inch Spanish gladius, a knife, and the pilum, a javelin with an iron shaft on a three-foot wooden grip.

Behind the Hastati came the Principes, more experienced men who would fight tenaciously. Gaius was pleased to see the strength of the third and final rank, the Triarii, whose spears and swords would be expected to hold the line if the final outcome was in the balance. They were the old guard who had seen 15 or 20 years in the army and were inured to the vicissitudes of battle. These hardened warriors boasted many wounds and they wielded the gladius with brutal effect.

***

Sweat ran down Tacitus's face. He felt his head baking inside the steel helmet. He could see the giant Ibericus on his right and Sempronius on his left, but the helmet with its metal ear protectors made hearing difficult.

There was a brief halt in the march and the men were given a moment to gulp down water and chew on dried meat.

"Are you worried?" Sempronius asked Tacitus.

"Aren't you? You've heard the same rumors I have. General Surena's supposedly so rich that he supplements his force with 10,000 mounted archers. The man's no one to fool with."

Ibericus grunted and grinned. "But I've also heard that he travels with wagons crammed with 200 concubines. If you ask me, we should capture the women, forget about the archers, and just go home. How many girls would that give us each?"

"Enough to leave you dead in the sand," said Tacitus.

"You're no fun," Sempronius said.

"This isn't fun either." Tacitus shook sand and pebbles from his sandals while staring toward his father, who was impatiently tapping a golden arrow against his greaves. *Yes,* he thought, *you can't wait to see the blood run, especially mine.*

By midafternoon the heat became oppressive and men began to fall out. The *segmentata* of overlapping steel armor and the full kit amounted to sixty pounds. Thirty-mile marches three times a month accustomed men to great exertion, but the training marches were not through a desert's deep sand. The iron studs on Tacitus's sandals, so effective for stomping on the enemy, now made marching more strenuous.

His hatred of his father grew with each mile. His throat constricted and demanded water, but the cohort's centurion ordered that they conserve what little remained.

When the march slowed, Tacitus saw Marcus Crassus again ride past with Publius and Ariamnes, encouraging the men to step up the pace. There would be no more stopping until evening unless they encountered the enemy.

In training they were told that there would always be food and water along the march, placed there by auxiliaries. Now, in their haste, there were no advance troops.

Sempronius staggered. Ibericus grabbed him by the arm before he collapsed and relieved him of his four-foot shield. Usually that would result in a reprimand, but the centurion looked the other way. Tacitus put one foot in front of the other with great effort and wondered when they would engage in battle. The thought left him drained and despairing.

A young tribune on horseback rode to the Primus Pila and pointed. Six thousand Arabs had suddenly raced past the legions. Their horses sent up a column of dust that descended upon the marchers. Despite the noise, Tacitus heard his father say, "Where are they going?"

"I think they're to scout ahead for us, find out where the Parthians are."

"That's ridiculous," spat Gaius. "A scouting party doesn't require six thousand men."

The Arabs disappeared in their own dust and the columns lumbered further into the desert. Men who fell out were laid in the sutler's wagons to the rear of the formations. But the wagons fell further and further behind as their wheels sank into the soft white sand. Too often overheated horses and mules had to be cut from their traces, leaving the wagons and their occupants stranded. The animals fell on the spot or wandered off to die of thirst.

From the corner of his eye Tacitus saw Crassus and a clutch of tribunes ride to the front of the cohorts and stare into the dust created by the speeding Arabs. The consul seemed quite perplexed by Ariamnes's unannounced departure. The absence of cavalry on the flanks would leave the legions exposed. Publius was ordered to split his small force to make up for the loss, but they would only be able to mount a holding action at best. He then ordered 20 of his men to follow the Arabs and report back.

Marcus Crassus galloped in front of his legions. The tribunes followed. From his forward postion in the line, it appeared to Tacitus that Crassus's horse had tired. The general stopped and observed the last of his Arab allies disappear into the desert. All seven legions came to a halt. Tacitus expected orders to repel an attack, but there was no sign of an enemy. The word "betrayal" came to many lips. Tribunes, centurions, and legionnaires stood mute. Leaning on his shield, Tacitus baked in the midday sun.

There was again the sound of hoofs, and a dozen mounted scouts tore past the first cohort. Many had arrows protruding from arms and legs; their faces were marked by terror. Some held swords, but there was no blood on them. It appeared that they had never had a chance to close with those who had impaled them.

Wearing a scarlet cloak, Crassus hurriedly rode to join his son and Cassius. The scouts reached them, and an agitated discussion ensued as horses nervously pawed the sand. A moment later Marcus Crassus ordered a trumpet blown, a signal for the legions to form a continuous front line. The sudden excitement of approaching battle shot through Tacitus, his fatigue quickly forgotten. Orders were given and lines of men moved like waves in a rolling sea.

The consul appeared panicky as he gestured toward the lines of legionnaires. He wheeled his mount and raced from one position to the next. Tacitus turned to Sempronius, who no longer looked as though he was about to fall over. "Something is wrong."

Another trumpet blast rent the stifling air. Now the legions were given a second order, requiring them to form a single square. All 45,000 men and auxiliaries hurried into a box position. Wagons assembled within, their unarmed drivers dismounting. A haze rose in the distance.

"There must be cavalry to our front," said Sempronius. Probably the Arabs setting up a defensive line."

"Perhaps. But if it's not them, it's best that we are in a square. Otherwise someone may turn our flanks." With sudden anxiety Tacitus hoped his supposition made sense.

Once the maneuver was completed the legions stood in silence. Tacitus could hear the pounding of his heart. There would be death and most likely it would be his. Battle was the last thing he wanted. Until now it had still seemed remote, something distant, impersonal.

He would never see Tullia again.

Tacitus remembered their forest hideaway, the rain spattering on their makeshift tent, the girl's sighs, tears of happiness, and the blissfulness of everything that followed. It was over all too quickly. What would she think when she learned of his death and who would tell her? Looking about him he wondered how long would it take for his bones to be plucked clean by vultures, already circling high above.

When he was a child, his aunt Junia had told him to honor Great Jupiter, the most supreme of of all the Roman gods. Just how much good would Great Jupiter do any of them now? Certainly he was awed by the elaborate ceremonies in the god's honor, but the few prayers he gave were perfunctory. He never really believed. Junia had told him that the Primus Pila felt the same way but never explained why. Now he wondered how his father would react when he heard of his son's death. Would he offer up a eulogy? It was doubtful. The man would go on about his life as though it had never happened.

He had been ripped away from Tullia, the only girl he truly cared about. It was his father's doing and Tacitus hated him more than any foreign enemy, indeed, more than anybody who would kill him this day.

Now orders were being given. Each man held two javelins ready to be hurled on command.

"More dust," said Sempronius. "The Arabs must have found the Parthians. I think they're coming back to join us."

Out of the pall Tacitus saw horsemen emerge through waves of heat that rose from the desert sands. Like specters, the riders spread from one horizon to the next; the hoofs of their mounts shook the desert floor and plumes of sand shot skyward. Tacitus stiffened. The legionnaires clutched their throwing spears more tightly and aligned one shield beside the next. There was no need for another order. A sort of paralysis drifted over Tacitus, as if everything were a dream. For a moment even the sound of the approaching horde was swollen by silence. He stared at the stark blue sky, empty but for the waiting birds of prey.

The sound came back with terrifying resonance. Finding his voice, Tacitus glanced at his friend and shouted, "They're not Arabs; they're Parthians!"

52

Chapter 5

Marcus Crassus rode from one legion to the next, attempting to reassure them, but he appeared nervous and uncertain. The only sound in the massed ranks was the ceaseless wind. In the hollow square the men stood shoulder to shoulder, their red shields emblazoned with lightning bolts and steel, bowl-shaped centers that reflected the midday sun.

The thousands of charging Parthians came to a halt 200 yards to the front of Tacitus's cohort. These were light cavalry, not the heavily armored cataphracts that had been expected, and they appeared far less threatening against massed infantry than Tacitus had expected. Every legion had practiced tactics effective against a cavalry charge. During the campaigns against Carthage hundreds of years earlier, Roman legionnaires had even taken down charging elephants.

Then quite suddenly the Parthian riders split into two wings, which sped to the right and the left of the Roman square, revealing a line of densely packed horsemen. These riders wore polished steel helmets and held aloft banners that floated like ribbons in the blinding light.

"Silk," whispered Tacitus.

Translucent and shimmering in the sun, the banners fluttered in the wind, bathing the horsemen in varying hues. The cavalry moved closer and Tacitus stared at their armor with the overlapping metal plates that entirely cloaked the body. Their horses, far larger and heavier than Roman mounts, were also encased in a blanket of metal covering heads, chests, and flanks. Nothing in the Roman arsenal except the darts from the scorpion artillery could penetrate the hinged pieces of bronze.

The word "cataphracts" rippled through the ranks. These were the monsters that so terrified Roman cavalry. A stone wall would be no less impervious to spears and swords. No, Tacitus thought, he would not want to be in the cavalry today.

The Parthians painted their faces, black hair falling over their foreheads. The entire formation remained still, allowing the Romans a good look at what they would encounter before the day was over.

Mounted and surrounded by his officers, the tallest of the Parthians issued a command. The air was rent with the sound of hundreds of kettledrums creating a hollow sound like the bellowing of bulls.

"Hold the line. Its only noise," Gaius said as he passed between ranks of legionnaires. But the commotion to their front caused skittish Roman horses to break ranks in terrified lunges. Only by holding their mounts close-reined could the riders keep them from bolting.

Parthian horse archers had moved close to the Roman square. Crassus ordered the highly mobile auxiliaries to charge the bowmen. It was usually these lightly armed foreign troops who, with devastating effect, were committed to the first assault.

Tacitus watched a wave of 500 Syrians tear across the sand. It was a gallant and inspiring sight, but within seconds the enemy unleashed a torrent of arrows, spearing men protected only by leather vests. Screams and pleas for help wailed through the air as hundreds spilled into the sand. From a distance the arrows appeared like needles. Those who survived the fusillade ran back to their own lines. With baleful eyes they looked toward Crassus and his tribunes, no doubt praying that another charge would not be ordered.

"Who are those horsemen?" Tacitus asked Sempronius.

"I heard that they call themselves 'Saka,' nomads from eastern Parthia." Ten thousand of them tore around the Roman square. Firing eight to ten arrows a minute, their missiles cast shadows upon the ground. Armed with a composite bow of layers of bone, yew wood, and sinew, the riders plucked shafts from their quivers and aimed high, indiscriminately sending the shafts into legionnaire ranks. To Tacitus the entire sky was filled with deadly shafts, seemingly meant for him. Terror froze him in place. The bolts pierced the metal helmets and plates of armor that would easily deflect the arrows of a normal bow.

Latinus was the first of Tacitus's tent mates to fall as a shaft punched through his shield and pierced his eye. Screaming, he dropped his javelins and clutched the three-foot arrow. The scream lasted only a second. His body dropped onto the blistering sand and his place was quickly filled by another legionnaire.

"Form *testudo!*" ordered the tribunes. Tacitus in the front line held his shield directly before him. Those behind would raise theirs aloft so that each slightly overlapped the one beside it. The maneuver, the "turtle," created a ceiling of rectangular coverings like tiles.

Crassus ordered the formations to close the distance between themselves and the horsemen. But the Saka simply moved further away.

Each legion was equipped with dozens of scorpions, bolt-throwing catapults operated by a two-man team. Upon the command "Fire," hundreds of steel shafts tore Saka troops out of their saddles, bringing down their mounts as well. But the men operating the scorpions had no protection except their personal armor, and Saka arrows rapidly slaughtered the crews.

A tribune sent by Crassus galloped to his son Publius and pointed to the enemy horsemen. Publius nodded, raised his arm, and ordered a thousand cavalry, 500 archers, and eight cohorts forward. It was a sizable force. A great shout erupted from the horsemen. Their long swords were drawn, and infantry backed by archers sprang forward, lusting for a chance to close with the nomads.

A buoyant expectation rose within Tacitus. Finally the army was on the offensive, and Roman forces rarely failed in the assault. Thousands of arrows sped toward the Saka, tumbling the closest from their saddles. The remaining scorpions, firing high, brought down scores more. As the Romans charged across the sands, their foe turned away and Publius's cavalry pressed forward to close the distance. The Saka fanned out. In their pursuit, groups of Roman horsemen broke ranks and sped forward, leaving the infantry and archers behind.

Then, as in a much-practiced motion, the Saka halted and faced the Romans whose formations had become disorganized in the charge. The nomads drew their bows and unleashed a withering fire. Still over 200 yards from the enemy, the impaled Spaniards were ripped from their horses. An awed silence enveloped the ranks of the massed legions who moments before had expected a victorious day.

The cavalry that survived the counterattack turned in terror and drove their mounts through the infantrymen and archers, who tried desperately to get out of the way. On a signal from the tall Parthian officer, the Saka charged the foot soldiers and annihilated those left standing.

Again surrounding the legions, the nomadic horsemen stirred up so much sand that Tacitus couldn't see 20 yards in front of him. Blinded by dust, he hunkered beneath his shield. A roiling pall blew over him. There were impassioned calls for water, but water had long since run out. Tacitus was forced to hold his shield above his head to protect himself from the broiling sun; everyone around him did the same. One by one they began to kneel under the weight and Tacitus, seeing the others, did the same. As shields splintered, arrows found holes and dove into feet and legs, pinning men to the ground.

Hour after hour the horsemen circled the legions while men fell from thirst, fatigue and impaling missiles. Now very few scorpions were being serviced as legionnaires lay beside their machines. Men in the cohorts began to bunch up and attempt to overlap shields. Gaius, one of the few centurions still standing, pulled legionnaires to their feet. "Stand!" he shouted over the din. "We are not beaten!"

"They have to run out of arrows," said Ibericus, the onetime bully of the *contubernium*.

A gust of wind tore away the dust and Tacitus peered through it. "That's not going to happen." He turned in time to escape an arrow, only to see it pierce another man's knee. The legionnaire screamed and fell. Tacitus knelt beside his tent mate and broke off the shaft.

"Let me help," a voice said. Looking up, Tacitus saw Apollodoros holding an arrow-extracting instrument. It looked like two spoons facing each other, hinged and bound to a slender metal stick. The spoons fitted over the arrowhead and allowed the practitioner to extract the point.

"Tacitus is right," Apollodoros said, brushing sweat from his eyes. Blood spurted from the man's knee as the iron tip was pulled free.

"Can you see the camels out there?" Apollodoros said. "The Saka ride back to them and refill their empty quivers. There are hundreds of camels. They'll never run out of arrows."

***

Exhaustion settled over Tacitus. He wiped sweat from his face and peered into the hazy distance. He was surprised to see that almost 400 of the Roman cavalry still survived. Publius, in desperation, pointed to cataphracts assembled near a corner of the Roman square. He trotted his mount down the line of horsemen and gave them their instructions. A gap was made in the line of infantry and the cavalry charged headlong into the Parthians. With hopeless rage, the outmatched Romans ran their horses into the lances of the enemy knights. They spilled from their screaming horses, slid beneath the unprotected bellies of the huge Parthian mounts, and split open their stomachs. The animals fell, throwing riders encased in a hundred pounds of armor. Lunging and slashing between flailing hoofs, the Romans slit the throats of every downed enemy they could.

It was only a handful of legionnaires that escaped the carnage, and again Publius survived. He and a dozen others fled on foot to a low hill. The Parthians saw him and charged but Publius, his arm pierced by an arrow, refused to give them the honor of killing him. He turned to his aide, removed his armor, and said, "Better to die by a Roman gladius than a Parthian spear!"

With that the legionnaire thrust his sword through the tribune's heart. Only seconds later, the Parthian cataphracts descended upon the unhorsed band, slaughtering all. One Parthian found Publius's body, drew his knife, and decapitated the soldier. Moments later the knight spurred his horse along the tattered Roman line and displayed the sightless head on his spear.

Centurions and tribunes rushed to the front of the line to stare at the spectacle. The Parthians again hammered on their drums and one of their number appeared before the cohort. "From what family is this brave man and where is that coward Marcus Crassus?"

Tacitus looked with dismay upon the grisly head, and then toward their general. Crassus, mounted on his charger, sat dumbstruck, his hands covering his face. He spun his horse and shouted, "Countrymen, the loss of my son is mine alone, no one else's. We will fight on as Publius would have had us do. Take away their joy, do not dismay, for whoever tries for great things must suffer something."

It was the first resolute statement from Crassus in hours. The consul spurred his gelding and galloped to the knots of legionnaires, exhorting them to withstand the continuing onslaught.

"Stand for the general!" Gaius Septimus shouted to the cohorts. Tacitus staggered to his feet, as did many of the others. Crassus reached out to individual men as he rode the shrinking lines and exclaimed, "Lucullus did not overthrow Tigranes without bloodshed. Our ancestors lost 1,000 ships off Sicily. The Republic of Rome did not arrive at her height by fortune, but by perseverance through danger!"

Crassus ordered them to shout a war cry. There was only a weak response as more arrows rained down on the huddled men. Nightfall was their only hope. With their losses the legions shortened their lines and compressed the square. Many of the civilians who had accompanied the army had taken shelter beneath their wagons; hundreds more lay dead.

The day was drawing late when Tacitus saw his father hurry toward Crassus with the surviving tribunes. A heated discussion ensued, with officers pointing toward the camel trains that continuously re-supplied the enemy. Moments later Gaius was back and Apollodoros joined him.

"What was that all about?" the *medicus* asked, his tunic caked with blood.

"The army is beaten," said Gaius. "The tribunes are demanding that Crassus negotiate with Surena."

"What if Crassus refuses?" asked the Greek.

"There's talk of mutiny. I doubt that the Parthians will negotiate."

"Why should they?" said Apollodoros. "They can have the glory of annihilating seven Roman legions."

"I think you're right. Surena's status will only increase with total victory."

Gaius watched as another dozen men were cut down. "I rarely worry about seeing a Roman army defeated. I certainly didn't in Gaul when we were outnumbered and fighting for our lives. But then we were able to engage man-to-man and we prevailed. Here it's like fighting ghosts and shadows."

"Look," Apollodoros said pointing to a group of horsemen who galloped to a sand dune. "There go Crassus and his tribunes."

"Wait here." Gaius hurried toward the group of legionnaires closest to the knoll. Others who had been kneeling from fatigue rose to watch the heated debate.

A moment later a group of heavily armored horsemen galloped toward the general and his tribunes.

Sempronius turned to Tacitus. "Who are those Parthians with Crassus?"

"I think the big one is their general, maybe Surena, and there are Arabs, too."

Minutes went by. Suddenly there was shouting and a scream from the assemblage. Gaius rushed back to Apollodoros and Appian. "He's dead. Marcus Crassus was just killed. They cut off his head like they did his son."

"How did that happen?" asked Apollodoros. "From here it looked like Surena was giving Crassus one of his horses."

"He was," said Gaius, "but the Parthians forced him into the saddle and struck the horse to hurry it back to their camp. The tribune Octavius grabbed the bridal and there was a pushing match. Another tribune drew his sword and slew a Parthian, and then he and Crassus were killed."

Word of the general's murder spread rapidly through the Roman ranks. Despite the defeat and death he had inflicted on the legions, Tacitus let out a despairing moan when Crassus' head was displayed on a pole.

The brief respite from cascading arrows ended. Again, thousands of barbed shafts descended upon the legionnaires until the sun dipped below the horizon and the Saka horsemen withdrew. Survivors of the fusillade sank to their knees or lay prostrate on the ground. Tacitus, like others, had found sanctuary by burrowing under the dead.

With night, a sliver of moon glinted off the shields and armor of the living, the dead, and the dying. Exhausted and sickened, Tacitus peered out from beneath the body of a dead comrade and saw his father pacing the line as if the day had just begun. Dust coated his armor plates. The round bas-relief insignia of valor attached to his armor no longer glistened, but the centurion showed no fatigue. Watching his stoic father inspired awe, but also a terrible sense of rage. The man trod along the decimated line, looking from one live legionnaire to the next.

"Why is he doing that?" Tacitus asked Sempronius.

"Maybe he wants to see how many will be able to fight in the morning."

"We haven't been able to fight all day, how can we fight in the morning? Come sunrise they'll just finish us off." Then under his breath Tacitus said, "Why is he still alive? He should be dead like the rest of the centurions."

Gaius peered into a huddle of men. His eyes fell upon Tacitus with a piercing, contemptuous look. "Get out from under that man," came the brusque order. "Soldiers in my legion do not cower beneath the bodies of brave, dead men."

Shamed, Tacitus got to his hands and knees. Apollodoros, who had been walking with the centurion, reached down and pulled the youth to his feet as his father abruptly walked away.

"Don't despair, you're not alone" the Greek doctor offered in a quiet voice. "Don't hate him so much, Tacitus."

"Why not? He despises me."

"Almost 20,000 of your countrymen died today. They were all his men and they were never allowed to fight. He's bitter."

With darkness the Parthians camped a mile from the fallen legions. Tacitus could see the sparks of their fires. Shouts and peals of laughter were distinctly heard as Surena, surrounded by his lieutenants and Saka chiefs, reveled in their victory. The severed heads of Marcus Crassus and his son were put on view as trophies of war and would soon be on their way to the Parthian king.

The misery that would come with the dawn bore down on Tacitus. "I've never been so tired. I just want to sleep," he said. "Might as well," said Sempronius. "We will probably be annihilated in the morning, and then we can sleep forever."

Even more disconcerting, it was learned that the tribune Cassius had broken out with 6,000 survivors and was heading for the city of Carrhae.

Four thousand wounded men lay beside the dead. The fate of the wounded was certain. Injured men began to weep as word spread of the escape; with fewer numbers there would be even less resistance. Many prayed aloud to Mithra and Great Jupiter. Tacitus wasn't one of them.

A muffled sound from down the line and a hurried movement stirred Tacitus. A few legionnaires rose and stared at shapes barely visible in the moonlight.

"Be silent. No talking," Gaius said in a hushed voice inches from Tacitus and the six survivors of his *contubernium*. "Gather your *pila* and *gladius* and be ready to move. We're leaving here."

"We're going?" Tacitus said. The words croaked from his constricted throat.

"Are you wounded? Can you walk?"

"Walk? Yes, I—"

"Then move!" Tacitus's father pointed to a group and whispered, "Fall in with them and don't make a sound if you want to live."

Moving down the line of 400 legionnaires, the Primus Pila repeated the warning: "No talking, not even a whisper or we're all dead. Now follow me."

There was just enough light to see the silhouette of distant hills. The Parthians had posted sentries, but the legionnaires managed to hug depressions in the sand. When a horse neighed, the entire group froze. Gaius led the survivors on a circuitous route to avoid the cavalry.

The air had turned cold and the march toward the desert's edge seemed endless. On occasion a man would fall from exhaustion, but his comrades would pull him to his feet and support him across the sands.

With the half-light of dawn the men finally began to climb a series of hills. There were many hard, crusty ridges that over eons had been eroded by wind and rasping sand. They crawled up a promontory of rough boulders split by a gorge. The hoofprints of many horses had pummeled the sand in the narrow passage. In the dim light the centurion had the men lie on the rocks overlooking the depression.

Tacitus fell into a nightmare-filled slumber. After tossing and turning on the rock-strewn ground until he could no longer sleep, he sat up. In the silver of moonlight he saw his father leaning against a boulder, watching the horizon for movement. Always the soldier, always hard, unrelenting, brutal. Was he even human?

"Are you wounded?" Gaius had brusquely asked. "No," Tacitus had answered, because he'd hid under the corpse of a friend, praying the indiscriminate arrows would only enter his dead compatriot. Contempt marked his father's face. His live son seemed an embarrassment to him, an impediment.

Thoughts of the dead and the screaming haunted Tacitus. The shafts plunged again and again into Latinus, then Vinicias, whose body he had squirmed beneath. He had stared into the man's sightless eyes. When too many arrows pierced Vinicias, Tacitus had added Latinus to his human barrier, their combined weight nearly crushing him. For a time he wondered what the others might think. After a while he no longer cared. He'd believed it was only a matter of hours before his corpse would be carrion for vultures.

Then another thought crept into his mind. If he had been seriously wounded, would his father have left him there to be slaughtered or enslaved? He imagined his fate at the hands of the Saka or the Parthians.

"How many of our *contubernium* are left?" Sempronius asked in a hoarse whisper.

"Four, or five, if Gallius lives. There's me, you, Lepidus, Fortunius, and Ibericus. And also Quintillus, the complainer from the second cohort."

Sempronius nodded toward the battlefield beyond the hills. "There will be no funerals for them."

"Nor for us," Tacitus said. "This isn't over. It's just a lull, a matter of time."

***

Gaius Septimus walked the line of sleeping legionnaires. Four hundred and seven, he counted. Most were from two cohorts of the Tenth Legion lent by Caesar, but there were at least 30 from those legions raised in Syria. Though few of the men had serviceable shields, all had kept their javelins and swords. Many had minor wounds, and they all suffered from dehydration. For the moment he decided not to wake them; they would need every fragment of energy for what lay ahead.

Gaius had spent a sleepless night observing the distant Parthian fires and any sign of more survivors. There were none. He ascended the highest point on the crest and settled into a rocky crevice. Craving sleep, he began to doze, then shook off the temptation. Sunrise cast long shadows. From his vantage point he could see the glint of armor on the silent dead. Surely many were still alive but awaited certain death. On the perimeter of the annihilation were the bodies of Saka horsemen, casualties of the bolt-firing scorpions. Several hundred men and horses lay in a great circle. He perceived another knot of men and horses; these were Publius's cavalry and the Parthian cataphracts, all in their heavy armor with slit throats.

***

Beside the Parthian camp were almost 6,000 imprisoned legionnaires who had been herded into a holding area at daybreak. There was no sign of those who had escaped with Cassius during the night. Perhaps with only 10,000 horsemen, Surena didn't want to detach a sizeable troop to chase the Romans on uncertain ground. Only on a flat, spacious field with plenty of room to maneuver was cavalry truly effective against well-disciplined infantry. And perhaps Surena thought it doubtful that Cassius would make the same mistakes that Crassus had.

Gaius removed his helmet and lay motionless beside sand-effaced boulders and withering shrubs. His eyes followed a narrow trail leading from the split promontory to the desert beyond. There was movement in the distance. A whiff of dust ascended the cloudless sky.

"Horsemen," the centurion said to his slumbering trumpeter. Appian raised himself on an elbow and opened his bleary eyes.

"How far? Who are they?"

"They're not ours, that's for sure. Maybe twenty, thirty, coming fast."

Appian struggled to his feet. "I'll rouse the men."

"Have them stay low, no noise."

Crouching from rock to rock, Gaius placed his men in defiles on both sides of the crevice that divided the mount.

"No prisoners," he instructed the legionnaires. "Save the horses." To a few men with bows he said, "Stay at the end of the ravine. Kill any that try to escape. None must get away."

"Arabs and Sakas," Appian said to Gaius as the horsemen drew closer. The last of the riders entered the narrow passage between fifteen-foot walls. "Now!" shouted Gaius. With utter vengeance 300 legionnaires, gladii in hand, leaped from both sides of the precipice while others launched their javelins from front and back. As the unhorsed men were impaled, legionnaires grabbed the reins of panicked horses. Within minutes the slaughter was over.

"Strip the dead but save the clothing," Gaius ordered. "Arab garments here, Saka over there, bodies in that ravine." He turned to Appian. "Cover them with rock and sand. I want no vultures to give away our position. We'll remain here until dusk. Let the men have all the food and water the riders had and keep the horses out of sight. And no loud voices."

***

Only an hour had passed since the sun had risen. Long shadows spilled from the hills onto the desert floor. Tacitus, Sempronius, and Ibericus had been with those assigned to capture horses. With the animals tethered in the gorge, Tacitus peered toward the sight of yesterday's slaughter. A small number of wounded struggled beyond the bounds of the decimated square.

"Look," Sempronius said.

The Saka had mounted and they were heading for the wounded. Several dozen horsemen shot forward and rode down those attempting to escape, while others dismounted and slashed men's throats. It was too far for Tacitus to hear the screams, but the murders were quite evident.

"Maybe 4,000 wounded," said Ibericus, his eyes wide. "They're killing them all."

Bitterness rose in Tacitus's throat. "You didn't think they'd treat their wounds, did you? They were dead men last night."

"Do you think the Saka or Parthians will come here?" asked Ibericus, his huge body squirming into a slightly deeper hollow.

Tacitus laid his head in the crook of his arm and turned away. "I don't know. I don't really know anything except that I don't want to be here."

Thoughts of Tullia flittered through his mind. A vision of rain dropping onto the makeshift tent. The girl lay beside him, her warmth permeating his body, his soul. He held her close, felt her nakedness and his growing erection. She had kissed him and placed her hand around his organ but then somnambulant pleasure had turned to instant terror.

Daylight, grey and dismal, filtered through the cracks in their tent. He should have been back at Campus Martius hours before. He was late and he could only imagine the punishment to be inflicted upon him. He'd jumped up, kissed her, and was about to rush out when she tore a chain and amulet from her neck.

She said to wear it as a symbol of her love. She slipped the four-inch gold piece over his head.

"This is too valuable; it's worth a small fortune."

"Now you will have it. Come back to me, Tacitus."

"Wake up. Put these on."

It was his father's voice. Tacitus opened his eyes, his hand reflexively feeling for the talisman beneath his tunic. It was there, it was always there. He had shown it to only a handful of people. A foot nudged him and he stared at a clump of Saka clothing and weapons that had been dumped at his feet.

"Get down to the horses when you are dressed."

Saddlebags hung over the horses' flanks. Gaius assembled the ten men who were now wearing the foreign clothing. "Apollodoros will lead you. He can speak Greek the way they do, but avoid any contact with Arabs, Parthians, or Saka. None of the rest of you will say a word."

Tacitus stiffened at the mention of the Saka but no one said anything. He and the others mounted and took the reins of the extra horses. The sun was beginning to dip over the sands.

"How do we find our way back when it's dark?" asked Sempronius.

"I'll find you," replied Gaius. "Now go and act as if you own the place. Indecision or hesitation will get you killed."

Chapter 6

"Why did he choose me?" Tacitus asked Sempronius as they rode across the desert floor.

"Because you're the best horseman he has," his friend replied. "We were all trained to ride, but you're a natural. If someone's horse panics, he knows that you can run it down. He saw you do it before, remember?"

"My guess is that he thinks me expendable."

"My guess is that you're wrong."

Regardless, it felt good to be on a horse again. Perhaps he could become a scout. Of course, he would never ask his father, but he might suggest the idea to Appian. He knew little about the trumpeter except that he had been his father's childhood friend and even had something to do with preparing his father for entry into the army.

According to his Aunt Junia, it was an occupation the centurion would never have considered until his wife died. Junia said that Gaius had sat motionless beside the *impluvium*. He remained there for days after Aspacia's death, the world no longer part of him.

His aunt told him that prior to Aspacia's death his father had considered law, Apollodoros having taught him enough

Greek and oratory. It was a must for a Roman boy hoping to enter the political or legal arena. But Junia said that after his wife's death law was the furthest thing from his mind. She tried to console him, but it did no good.

Then one day he snapped out of his morose state and announced that he would join the army. But he did not want to enter like all the others, unskilled and weak like a civilian. No, he wanted Appian, already a veteran, to teach him everything that recruits were taught during six months of relentless marches and fighting drills. Finally, seeing Gaius's determination, Appian relented and the exhausting ordeal began. Day after day, he would practice hacking against a post as the recruits would do at Campus Martius, the Field of Mars. He was taught how to throw the pilum and fight with a knife, a shield, and a sling. Virtually every morning he loaded up with the required sixty pounds of gear a legionnaire totes and marched 20 to 30 miles.

Gaius's outlook had become dour, impenetrable, and horribly determined. He was brutal on himself and with others. Even in practice engagements against Appian, his only friend, he was unrelenting and vicious. Finally, on the last day of his training, Gaius challenged the veteran to combat, and had his aunt not rushed between the antagonists, Appian would have been killed. According to Junia, Appian had said that he would never fight Gaius again, nor would any man if he wished to live.

Now, all those years later, the same man was sending his son into the midst of an enemy that had slain 20,000 Romans. It was nothing but madness.

The billowing Saka shirt, the tight trousers, and the curved sword and quiver of arrows over his shoulder seemed surreal. Wearing the clothing of the enemy was the taste of ashes. The barbarian vestments felt unholy, accursed, an abomination.

Most of the Roman dead had been stripped of their armor earlier in the day, but a few hundred Parthians and Saka were still scavenging. Bands of them interrupted vultures that angrily flapped their black wings and scattered, only to pluck the eyes and entrails from another Roman a few yards away. Here and there wounded Romans still lived, and on them the Arabs employed their curved knives. Occasional screams and pleas rippled across the battlefield.

The bodies had bloated like pigs rotting in the sun. A fetid stench lay over the mass. Tacitus and the others kept their distance from the Parthians as they rode toward the battle site. He watched the carrion eaters gorge themselves until they could no longer fly. The odor made him gag.

The legions' implements of war lay upon the field, reflecting the rays of the fading sun. Tacitus and his fellows walked their horses amongst the bodies. The animals shied. Most of the dead lay in the square, though cavalry and many auxiliaries had fallen beyond the tightly packed cohorts when they'd been decimated in futile charges. Thousands of arrows still pinned bodies to the ground, dead hands vainly clutching the shafts.

The Primus Pila had given an assignment to each man before they'd left the promontory. Some were to retrieve Saka bows and quivers, while the rest gathered javelins, cloaks, waterskins, and any medicine not already stripped from the dead. Tacitus was charged with the task of collecting whatever coins he could find.

"We better dismount," Sempronius said, "We'll be less conspicuous. Even in this clothing we don't look like them."

Tacitus was leaning over a body when Sempronius whispered, "Quick, lie down and appear dead. Pull that man over you."

A hurried glance told him why. An Arab had strayed from his companions and was walking his horse toward them. Sporting a flowing moustache and wind-tossed beard, he watched Sempronius roughly pushing dead Romans aside as he stuffed coins into a leather pouch. Sempronius turned toward the Arab and nodded. The Arab gestured toward the coins and Sempronius tossed him a few. The desert dweller nodded, then fired off a question in rapid Arabic. Sempronius shook his head and pointed to his ears, pantomiming deafness. Instead of withdrawing to ransack more dead, the Arab stared at Sempronius's features and pointed to a blond lock of hair that had slipped from his headdress. Sempronius tucked the hair back in and bent to retrieve a ring.

With a sudden motion the Arab drew his sword and lunged. Sempronius stepped back and stumbled as he drew his knife. Tacitus reached up, grabbed the Arab's flowing robe, and flung the man to the ground. Before the Arab could react to the sudden rising of a corpse, Tacitus's knife ripped across his throat. He opened his mouth, but the only sound was a gurgling rush of air.

Sempronius regained his footing and stared. "You killed him. You actually killed him."

"We'd better cover him up before his friends start coming around." Tacitus grabbed a Roman body and dragged it toward the Arab.

"Sure, but, Tacitus, do you realize what you did?"

"Yeah, I killed him."

"Not just that. You're the only one in our cohort, perhaps the only one in our legion, that killed an enemy. No one else killed an Arab, a Saka, or even a Parthian."

Sempronius was no longer whispering. Tacitus saw a few Parthians glance in their direction. "Be quiet, they can hear you!"

Tacitus gazed down at the Arab, whose blood still ran out, and at his own clothing, covered in that same blood. His hands shook. It was nothing he hadn't seen before, but this killing done by his own hands unnerved him.

"We have to get out of here. I mean right now. We'll take everything we can." His hand still trembling, he returned his *puglio* to its scabbard and started to lead his horse away.

"Wait, Tacitus, I found this!" Sempronius pulled a horn from a dead Roman trumpeter.

He said it the same way a child would upon finding a push toy on chariot wheels.

"I don't know why you would want it, but don't blow it now."

Tacitus was about to mount when his foot caught on something—a half-buried pole held in the iron grip of a dead legionnaire. He pried it from the man's hand.

"I will take this standard now, if you don't mind," he said quietly to the corpse, the cohort's signifer. Signifers were men of exceptional courage who carried the emblem rather than a weapon into combat. Though the emblem was not the vaunted *aquila*—the Parthians would have been quick to snatch it—the bronze castings bolted to the standard were venerated objects signifying great battles in which legionnaires had fought and died.

Tacitus doubted that a Saka, Arab, or Parthian would have any reason to venture into the desert night, but he and

Sempronius were silent as they rode toward the hills that sheltered the survivors of Carrhae. Gradually the energy that had pumped through Tacitus's body began to ebb. Fatigue set in and Sempronius's words came back to him.

He, amongst hundreds, perhaps thousands, had been one of the few Roman foot soldiers to slay an enemy during the entire battle. Certainly those manning the scorpions had impaled the Saka, but that was from hundreds of yards away. They could not taste the blood or, amid the dust, see the damage their blots inflicted. Tacitus became aware of how quickly and unflinchingly he had killed. It was done without a moment's hesitation, without the slightest thought about terminating a man's existence.

All the grueling hours of striking the hated training post with the gladius, the forced marches and humiliation from vindictive centurions, had suddenly paid off. He had killed instinctively, just as he'd been trained. And now, like it or not, he was a killer. That was what it meant to be a soldier. He was just as violent in his execution as a hungry shark in the deep blue sea.

His father, he had heard, had slain hundreds of men. A hideous thought came to him. He had become a shadow of his father: a man revered and honored for impaling bodies and spilling entrails.

Tacitus felt no elation, no bravado. He had acted to protect himself and his friend and not for any other reason. For the briefest moment he wondered what Tullia would think if she could see what her lover had done. Would she be proud of him? He had no idea. He thought about whether he should tell her, then remembered that he would probably never see her again.

Tacitus held the standard low beside the horse's saddle, as if it were nothing more than a pole with metal pieces attached. It would have felt wrong to hold it aloft, as if he were leading a victorious squadron. Men rode up to him and looked at it. They said nothing, but stared at him and nodded.

Tacitus wondered what his father would do with the standard from an utterly defeated Roman legion. Would it be carried proudly before the ragged survivors? Perhaps he would just plant it in the ground, a simple memorial to thousands of men who'd stood and died like targets placed in the sand.

The air had begun to chill and the thin Saka and Arab clothing would not keep him warm.

"You needn't say anything about this," Tacitus finally said.

"You mean the standard?"

"Not just the standard. The whole thing."

"As you wish, but I suspect that others saw what happened. It won't remain a secret for long. Your father might even reward you."

"I don't want anything from him. I just want to get home, and I don't care how I get there."

"I hope you don't do anything stupid. But whatever you do, I'll be with you."

"I'm not asking you to come with me."

"Of course I will, but where will we go?"

"I don't know yet. Just don't say anything to anyone. I have to think about it."

A gust came up and blew sand in his mouth. He spit it out as if it were the embodiment of his entire life.

"It was an eerie feeling, being amongst all those dead men," said Sempronius.

"We were with dead men yesterday," Tacitus replied. "Did you think that was less eerie?"

"There was too much happening and no time to think. But today, with the dead, it was quiet. I felt like we were trespassing. It was as though they were watching us. I wonder what they were thinking."

"I doubt the dead think anything at all. But I'm sure we'll find out in a day or two."

"Maybe your father has a plan."

"Don't be stupid. We'll be just as dead as the ones back there."

"Maybe. It's just so strange. We joked and ate with them for months. Now they'll be nothing but bones in a few days. Like it or not, Tacitus, a lot of us are gratified that at least another Arab won't be waking up in the morning. Your father will be pleased, even if he doesn't say so."

"Nothing I do will please him. I just try to stay out of his way."

Out of the gloom 30 men appeared. Tacitus and the others stopped and waited.

"Saka?" said Sempronius, his hand reaching for his gladius.

"No, we would have arrows in us by now."

Without a word he rode up to his father and handed him the standard. Gaius took it, looked at Tacitus, but said nothing. In the pale moonlight it was too dark to see his expression. Tacitus turned his mount and fell in at the rear of the column.

Just as Sempronius had surmised, word of the Arab's death raced through the camp. To Tacitus's surprise his father placed the standard where the survivors could see it. No fires were allowed and talking was in whispers.

Exhausted legionnaires, upon seeing the standard, rose to touch it as if it were a spectral ensign of an army that had once existed.

***

After posting sentries, Gaius propped himself against the hollow of an ancient stump. Except for snores, there was silence in the camp. The weapons, valuables, and clothing his scavenging party had recovered would, he surmised, be useful in the coming days.

Exactly where they would go and how they would get back to Carrhae was something he would ponder in the morning. The beaten men in his small force were still soldiers. Even a few cohorts, well led, could be of significance. But that would also wait until dawn.

The Parthians, Saka, and Arabs slept. Many were undoubtedly drunk. If he had his legion he would launch a devastating attack upon their camp, but that had been taken from him. At least there would be no further danger to his legionnaires this night.

Tacitus, his one and only son, had retrieved the cohort's standard. It was a valuable thing, a badge of identity, a symbol of strength that the men would need. He had said nothing to the youth about its retrieval. It wasn't as if Tacitus had fought to bring it back. But he had fought. And he had killed. Apollodoros had witnessed the battle between Tacitus and the Arab, though he'd been too far away to lend assistance without raising an alarm. Perhaps he should praise his son, but, no. To do so would be a crossing of the Rubicon, and praise was not yet deserved. The boy's violation had been too great.

Forgiveness. He had forgiven his own father only because Aspacia had asked him to.

Gaius closed his eyes; it was alright to do so now. Sleep never came easy. She was the sacred image he saw each night. She never changed, never aged, always the enigmatic, taunting girl with bouncing curls. He imagined her teasing him, amused by his stories. He yearned for her love as she'd wrapped herself around him so long ago in the dark of the night.

She had been purchased, along with her plump sister, by his father, Toronius. The rape of Caladria, Aspacia's sister, happened as a matter of course. When he'd tired of the ponderous, plum-shaped girl he'd turned his attention to Aspacia, and what had merely been a bickering family became a violent one.

Like papyrus sheets, one over the other, Gaius picked through the memories, returning to the one dream he never tired of. The lithe, enchanting girl did not see him sitting on a bench beside the villa's garden. With an expression of disgust, she held a squirming door mouse by the tail, a delicacy for the evening dinner, and looked up and saw him grinning.

"Why are you staring at me?"

"I'm not staring, I'm just watching. I think you're funny. Why do you stare at me?"

"I don't stare at you," she said, one hand poised saucily on her hip. She shook her head imperiously. "At least not any more. Your father won't allow me to even look at you. But I have no reason to anyway. I care nothing for Romans."

"But you've been asking my mother about me. Pestering her when you do her hair in the morning. Questions like if I have a lover and what sports I enjoy."

She tossed her head and looked away. "Don't be silly. Why would that interest me? Besides, she told me that your father has found a girl for you, the daughter of a tribune."

She wrinkled her nose at the sight of squirming mouse, and he could detect the hint of a smile.

He remembered how his father had taken her from the slave market, Gaius and his mother tramping behind. The girl had glanced back to look at him and he'd loved her from that very moment. Now he resigned himself to simply staring at her. She belonged to his father and there was nothing that he could do to alter that.

She loved him, he knew it, or at least he thought she did. He felt quite proud standing before her when he turned sixteen and wore his new *toga virilis*, hoping that she would admire it. It acknowledged him as a man and an adult citizen of the Republic. Certainly she had to see how proud and grand he looked, no longer wearing a youth's knee-length tunic and the bulla charm around his neck.

Was she impressed, he wondered. He hoped that she was, but there was no reason for her to care for any man in Rome. She had been torn from her family and, except for her sister's, all their lives had been expunged by Roman hands.

Aspacia had been born free in Hispania and was enslaved along with her entire village, following a revolt. Her parents had drowned in the passage to Rome, and her grief was too deep for tears. Rome was a foreign and hostile place to her, a Republic priding itself on its civilized nature while so many were in bondage.

Of course, young Gaius had thought, why should she admire his gleaming white toga balanced just so over his left arm. He must have appeared haughty and presumptuous to her, the product of a bestial state. His smile vanished and he walked away, leaving her alone in the garden.

In his narrow *cubiculum* he lay on his bed and stared at the ceiling. She was a slave, but under his father's thumb he was no less in bondage. What could ever come of his love?

He knew so little about women, and this girl was spellbinding. She could have anything she wanted from him. But she wasn't his, not that he would ever have her as a slave. He did not want a slave, and though he would not say so, he found the institution despicable. Slavery was making Rome indolent. Did she know what he thought? How could he tell her that and, indeed, what good would it do?

The next day he had waited for her in the atrium. Before he could say anything she shook her head. "We can't play this game, master Gaius."

"I told you not to call me master."

"Oh, I forgot. As a slave I assume that every Roman is my master." There was no malice in her voice. "I belong to your father and I've been warned. I cannot be seen looking at you. You saw how angry he looked last night when I was serving dinner. You will get me in trouble and he will beat me."

Yes, he had seen the warning look and finger pointed at her, and he dreaded the idea of his father, bloated, crazed, and arrogant, pulling her into his *cubiculum* in the dead of night. His father, he knew, had been savoring her as a treat, a tasty morsel held aside. Then she would be a plaything like the other slave girls. And when he tired of her she would be sold. It had happened so many times before.

Gaius remembered his vow that he would not let his father rip in to her. He wanted to protect her, to make her his own. At that moment he could not imagine the terrible night still to come.

Now, 20 years later, half asleep in the crook of the tree, he dreamt of her green eyes, the bewitching smile, and her sensibility. He tried to hold the dream steady, keep it from sliding away into darkness. Anger and dismay would come with the dawn and he would no longer be that hopeful, anxious youth. Within moments he would morph into the intractable centurion, intolerant of ineptness and brutal to those who could not measure up.

There were nights when he spoke to her above the wind and the rain, and he listened for her whispered reply. He imagined that she heard him, smiled, and spoke tender and consoling words. Twenty years in the army had steeled him, but the vision of her made him bury his head in his arms and weep. Gaius believed in no gods or goddesses except one. That one was Aspacia, and she was dead.

***

In the morning, Gaius assembled the men in military order with the standard at the front. They had destroyed a small detachment of Saka and Arabs, but the once proud legionnaires lacked any spirit or determination. All appeared battered and beaten, having barely escaped death, and they now stood uncertain a few miles from thousands of the enemy.

Gaius knew that it was not a time for inspirational speeches. He had considered their predicament in the hours before dawn. Not hopeless, but his plan would require resolve that was in very short supply. Though he had seen defeated units before, rarely had he observed so much despair. Many had puncture wounds in hands, arms, and feet; they would likely heal. It was their spirit that had been so badly wounded.

They had to understand that he had not been bowed, that he was still the chief centurion who was unflinchingly in command. He stood before them, his eyes evaluating each man. He assumed a relaxed pose, almost nonchalant. He rarely allowed the legionnaires to see him like that, not even in the quiet hour following the day's endeavors.

The men looked at him quizzically. Gaius smiled, again a rare thing.

"You look like shit. Even you, Appian."

There was tittering, and then the men began to laugh. They looked about, pointed to one another, and repeated the accusation. A few stood straighter and dusted themselves off. Gaius removed his helmet, scratched his head, and blew dust from the red transverse crest.

Turning to his trumpeter, he pointed to himself. "Me too?"

Then his smile faded. "We have a choice to make, and I emphasize 'we' because, once made, we must adhere to it. All of us. And our decision may involve many years of effort and resolve."

At the mention of "many years" the men stiffened.

"Those people out there want to annihilate or enslave us," said Gaius. "Unfortunately, they stand between us and safety in Roman Syria. The bulk of their army might move on, but enough will remain along the route to make our escape extremely dangerous. So to stay alive and get home, what must we do?"

Turning to Appian, Gaius said, "What do you suggest, trumpeter?"

"I don't have a horn, Centurion, but if I did, I wouldn't blow it to begin a march. At least not now."

Half-amused laughter flitted through the lines. "Yes, you do!" Sempronius said. He broke ranks and handed the instrument to Appian. "You are a trumpeter again."

Appian took the dented instrument, smiled, and held the circular horn aloft. Sempronius returned to the ranks.

"Since you ask me, Primus Pila, I'm not so sure that we should return to Rome as a beaten fragment of an army.

How would we be received? How would even Cassius and his thousands be received? Remember, Marcus Crassus ordered a decimation for men who lost."

"Very true," Gaius replied. "But the general is dead, and we did not run from battle. In time the public will forget about Carrhae. Rome, I think, is where we belong."

There was a murmur of consent. Gaius pondered the matter for a moment. "Very well, you want to go back to Rome?"

The unanimous response was what he'd expected.

"Obviously," he said, as he walked before the formation, "we cannot march west because the Parthian forces are between us and Syria. We can go northeast into the Armenian foothills, but the Armenians are probably under the heel of the Parthians. They may be occupied by Surena's troops. And I don't have to remind you, we are a very small force against any army."

He gave the legionnaires a moment to think, then turned to Apollodoros. "Greek, what do you know of the lands to the east? You told me that you once took that route. Come here and speak."

Apollodoros emerged from behind the cohort and stood beside the centurion. The men peered at the tall, stooped *medicus* who had tended to their wounds.

"I traveled with my father, a trader, before I came to the house of the centurion's father. I have been to Parthia as well as Armenia. There is a road at the foothills of Armenia that extends many leagues east. Some call this the Silk Road because goods from the Seres people come from a distant kingdom to Parthia, then to Rome. No Roman or Greek has ever been to the land of the Seres. But I've heard that the road extends past great mountains and deserts, and even a wall, and eventually reaches a river that leads to the sea."

"A river that will take us home?" asked Appian.

"Possibly. The land of the Seres is a mystery, but a Parthian once told me he met a man from Sogdiana—which I believe is a kingdom east of Parthia—who had been there. The Sogdian told him that the land of the silk makers is a fabulous place with an emperor and a magnificent civilization. Their population far exceeds that of Rome, and their citizens are cultured and civilized. A march to that land will be difficult. Along the way there may be strange people, even barbarians, whom we have never seen or even heard of."

"How much time will the march take?" asked Gaius.

"Perhaps years. Remember that my countryman Alexander marched past the Oxus River to the Indus. It took years to get there and back, but many of his men returned to Greece."

"So," said Gaius, "it's a question of pushing through Parthia and likely facing another slaughter or marching east to the land of the Seres and the rivers beyond. Which is it? I will give you an hour to discuss it amongst yourselves. But this much is absolute: What you decide will be done by all of us. I will not allow this cohort to fragment. No groups or individuals will venture out on their own. Those who violate that order will be executed, for it will jeopardize the lives of all. Your decision must be unanimous, and then we will move as one. Dismissed."

***

"I don't like this," said Quintillus.

Tacitus brushed a strand of hair out of his eyes. "You don't think we should go east?"

"I don't think we should march east," said the burly veteran. "The Primus Pila still thinks of us as part of his

85

legion. That's ridiculous. We're no longer an army, we're a bunch of survivors stuck in the middle of a desert. Who is he to suggest we march for years in the wrong direction? Do you really think that will get us to Rome?"

"But *you* know how to get us back safely, I'm sure," said Latinus, still the leader of Tacitus's *contubernium*.

"Well, I sure wouldn't go east in order to go west! Oh no, I'll tell you what I'd do." Quintillus spread his arms as if he were arguing policy in the Senate. "I'd have us split up into tight units, say eight or ten men, and march at night. And I don't mean a formal march either. All groups would scatter so that any patrols would never see the bulk of us. They might find a few and take them prisoner, but most of us would get back to Carrhae."

"They wouldn't need to take more than one or two prisoners," said Sempronius. "After ripping off an arm or a leg, they'd know where every survivor is heading. Then Surena would put a cordon of cavalry outside Carrhae and annihilate every group trying to get through. We'd all be dead by the end of the week."

"But who says we'd go back to Carrhae? I'd head for someplace along the Euphrates. Surena would have to patrol a lot of ground and many of us would escape, that's for damn sure," said Quintillus. "And what does the *medicus* really know? The centurion will have us march on a rumor, the word of a slave who traveled when he was a boy. You all know that he walks around and talks to himself. Will you put your trust in that man? Personally, I think he's a lunatic."

"He pulled an arrow out of me," said Vincinius. "I don't think that was lunacy. I put my trust in the *medicus* and in the Primus Pila. He got us here in one piece. I don't like the centurion, no one does, but that doesn't matter. There's no better man in a fight, and we're going to see a lot of fighting.

If the Primus Pila wants to march to the end of the earth, I'll follow along."

"And Great Jupiter, he will march us to the end of the earth! His plan is nonsense. We'll never see Rome again!"

Quintillus, seemingly exaperated by his inability to sway opinion, stomped off. His old comrade, Julius Fortunius, ran after him. Tacitus watched as the two of them huddled together, speaking in hushed voices while staring at him.

***

Gaius watched the desert floor from his lookout. Puffs of sand rose in the distance as the Parthians and their Saka allies assembled their prisoners and marched them out of sight. The dead were left for the vultures, whose numbers grew with each passing hour.

"What's the consensus?"

"Most of the men are with you, but it's not unanimous. There are a few, perhaps four or five, who are siding with Quintillus. They may try to break away at night and get back to Carrhae or the Euphrates," said Appian Dio

"They won't make it," said Gaius.

"Because of the Parthians?"

"No, because I'll kill them first. Now have the men assemble so we can play democracy before we begin our march."

Gaius turned his attention once again to the desert below. He watched the sad procession of once-free legionnaires until his men repositioned themselves into tightly aligned ranks.

"Eyes front!" ordered Gaius. "You've had time to discuss the matter. I don't want it said that you never had a chance to consider alternatives. Of course, we soldiers never get to vote on what campaign we care to support. The opportunity I gave you is unusual, if not unprecedented. But now argument is past and it's time for a decision and unanimous agreement. And I repeat, no one, on pain of death, will violate it."

The mood in the ranks was deathly somber. Not a single head turned, though a few eyes strayed to the men on their right or left.

"I have been informed that there are a few who think that small bands can scurry across this desert without being hunted down by Saka and Parthians. Raise your hands if that suicidal idea sounds good to you."

Not a single hand went up. "Very well," said Gaius, making a show of checking closely. His eyes riveted on Quintillus, who only stared back.

"Now, say 'aye' if you wish to remain a determined and cohesive fighting unit. A force of combat-ready legionnaires who will follow me to the great river in the Seres lands, then on to Rome."

There was a chorus of ayes, but not all of them sounded enthusiastic.

"So it's agreed that we will march to the foothills of Armenia and take the route to the east?"

"Yes." The voices sounded more certain now.

"Are you ready to march?"

"Yes."

"Again, cohorts. Are you ready to march?"

"*Yes!*"

"Very well. Then we will begin tonight."

Chapter 7

A bizarre, hurried procession on little Mongolian horses surprised ten-year-old Princess Li Mae Tang. She stopped and turned to her soul sister, Princess Ming Zhaojun. "Who's that lady in the carriage behind them?"

"That's Lord Tao's favorite concubine, Lady Ti," said Ming. "I saw her during the Catching Cool Breezes festival last year. She taught the three perfections."

"To leave Chang'an forever and go with the barbarians. How terrible. And Lord Tao had to be very sad to lose such a beautiful woman."

"I wonder why the Emperor would allow the barbarians to take her."

"My father said that we have to give tribute to the Chanyu or they'll keep raiding the villages. They like princesses even more than our silk and money. It's a pity. The ladies never come back and their sons are born outside the Middle Kingdom."

"We must pray for her. She's so fragile. I just hope she doesn't die in their horrible desert."

"She may want to. My mother said that many of our women commit suicide because it's so desolate and lonely out there."

In silence they watched the treasure caravan leave Chang'an. The foreign warlord was accompanied by a boy, perhaps fifteen or sixteen, in motley garb. He leaned toward the warlord and pointed to Li Mae.

"Who is that strange boy?"

"Xion Wen Chanyu, the chieftain's son."

"He looks hideous," said Li Mae. "Can you imagine, they call their leader the Son of Heavenly Wisdom."

Ming giggled. "As if the barbarians ruled over anything but snakes and scorpions."

The young man pointed to Li Mae again and said something more to his father. The warlord shook his head. Xion Wen Chanyu made a face and turned his attention to his father's new concubine.

"I hope we never see that boy again," said Ming.

"We have nothing to fear," replied Li Mae. "Your father is the Minister of Histories and mine is the Emperor's favorite general. The Son of Heaven will never sacrifice us to the barbarians."

***

Built with the labor of 140,000 men, the city of Chang'an was the capital of China. A land of forty million, the "Middle Kingdom" had been ruled by the Han Dynasty for over 150 years. So important were the Han Emperors that the entire people called themselves Han.

Of the five palaces in the walled city, the Weiyang Palace was the most imposing. Covering five square kilometers, it was the meeting place of the Emperor and his court, and boasted 40 halls and pavilions. The largest had a foundation 350 meters long and 200 meters wide, and was situated on a rise known as Dragon Head Hill.

"I love the way you play the zither. I will never master that," said Ming as she and Li Mae waited for General Chen Tang.

"But your calligraphy is so elegant," replied Li Mae. "My mother says that you will be a perfect wife for a gentleman scholar or even a lord."

They stood anxiously beside the imposing stone dragons outside Li Mae's home and watched the high, two-wheeled carts being pulled by peasants down the wide boulevard.

"I am surprised that your father is letting us visit the court. I have only been there once and it was when my father became Minister of Histories," said Ming.

"My father expects all girls to learn the ways of Xiao so they will respect elders and have proper etiquette, but he also has his own ideas. That's why he is taking us to the palace."

"What kind of ideas?"

"He thinks wives should be able to give knowledgeable opinions if asked by their husbands, especially if it concerns matters of the court."

"But aren't there secrets we should not know?"

"I don't think we will be hearing any secrets today," said Li Mae.

The girls bowed when General Chen Tang appeared.

"Are you ready?" he asked his daughter and Ming as they climbed into a high, wheeled chariot. "I will be meeting with various ministers, and a few might not think it proper for young ladies to be present. They know you will be courteous, especially in front of me. Just remain silent. I think you will enjoy the day and see something girls usually never get to see —the ways of power.”

“The sight of the barbarians was too depressing,” said Li Mae. “Let’s think of other things.”

“Yes, Lady Ti’s fate is too sad to think about.” Then Ming brightened. “Tomorrow is the start of the Double Seventh Day festival.”

“That should be fun,” said Li Mae. The Double Seventh, also known as Girls’ Day, was her favorite festival. She liked it even better than the Dragon Boat Festival and the Spring Festival.

“It’s so romantic. Mother told me that it’s about a weaving maid, the granddaughter of the King of Heaven, who fell in love with a cow herder who played the flute.”

“I remember hearing about that,” said Li Mae. In the story the girl dropped her weaving and came down to the world to marry the cow herder. The King and Queen of Heaven were furious because she left without permission and they ordered her back for trial. The Queen Mother of the Western Heaven took a golden pin from her hair and drew a line in the air. A heavenly river appeared, with the maid on one side and the cow herder on the other so that they could only look at one another. But on the seventh day of the seventh month, the kindhearted phoenix intervened and formed a bridge across the Milky Way, so the lovers could meet once a year.

“Do you think it’s true?” asked Li Mae. “I mean, it’s such an old tale.”

“What does it matter, really? We get to put on our finest dresses and pray for nimble hands just like those of the weaving maid. It will be a wonderful day to go on a carriage ride in the city.”

"Maybe my father will take us to the Shanglin Garden in the Jianzhang Palace."

"Yes, please! We could see the acrobats and puppet shows."

Li Mae grinned. "I'll ask him tonight. Just promise you won't get lost again." Ming's father had taken her to the palace once. She'd wandered off and gotten lost, and he hadn't been able to find her for hours.

"It's easy to get lost there; the palace has a thousand gates and 10,000 rooms," said Ming. "It's even bigger than the Weiyang Palace."

***

Li Mae wandered amongst the elm trees in the Shanglin Gardens with her father, mother, and Ming. They admired the Taiye Pool, an expansive lake that surrounded numerous islands. LeiZhouu Island, like the others, offered pavilions strewn beneath leafy trees, lending a fairyland appearance to the landscape. A boat ferried the party across. Li Mae heard cymbals and horns.

"It's the Baixe event, the one hundred shows," said Li Mae excitedly. Her parents nodded and ushered her ahead. A dozen female dancers twirled and swayed to mystical notes. Each dancer wore a scarf made of a translucent cloth.

A little further ahead were face diviners who told a person's future by examining the muscle and bone structure of the face. Not far away were gentlemen scholars of the highest rank, the "Erudites" who had set up tables where they created custom poetry for their clients. The learned men grew their fingernails five inches long to show how removed they were from manual labor.

Soon they came to a pavilion where a pungent herb sullied the air. Ming peered in and instantly recoiled.

"What's in there?" asked Li Mae.

"I think they're torturing a man; everybody is holding him. I don't want to see it."

Li Mae's father poked his head inside the smoke-filled tent. "They're not torturing him. It's a medical practice called moxibustion. It's a cure for many ailments."

Li Mae peeked in and her father said, "Do you see those little cones? They're filled with an herb called mugwort. The cones are held close to the skin. It causes blistering and it's very painful. That's why they have to hold the man. Hopefully it will do him some good, but I think there are less painful cures."

A breeze ruffled the general's robe, and the girls rushed ahead to decorated tables surrounded by an excited crowd. Men were thrusting coins into the hands of one who held the rapt attention of his audience. Li Mae and her friend wriggled through and gazed at dozens of tiny, lidded boxes with slippery panels. Each box was decorated with intricate carvings of dragons, a symbol of good luck.

"Fighting crickets," said Ming. People were betting on which would win the next battle.

The crowd around Li Mae and Ming parted as General Tang approached. "Do you want me to buy you one?"

"Not one of those. I don't want to see them killed," said Li Mae. "I think it's very cruel."

General Tang laughed. "Perhaps, but I've seen a lot worse."

"We have other crickets, singing crickets," a man said, pointing to a table a few yards away. "It's not so noisy there."

Li Mae approached the table. The salesman motioned for her to come closer. "Can you hear this one?"

A mellifluous sound came from the two-inch-long insect. Its voice was at once deep and throaty, then higher.

The man held up four fingers. General Tang gave him round coins, each pierced with a square hole. The salesman smiled and handed one box to Li Mae and the other to Ming. Li Mae turned to see a fourteen-year-old boy cheering and holding aloft a cricket box where the crowd had assembled.

"Oh, he must have won the betting."

"Who?" asked Ming.

"That brat, Prince Shang Gao."

"You don't like him? I think he's quite handsome."

"He's loud and pushy, and thinks too much of himself."

"I've seen him looking at you," whispered Ming. "I also saw your father speaking to his father in the Nine Markets three days ago. Shang's father is quite important, you know. My father said he's become minister of security and censorship. He can speak directly to the Emperor, just like your father does."

"I don't care. I do not want Shang Gao's attention, and I don't care if his father is important," Li Mae said with disgust.

Li Mae's attention was on a lady playing the qin, the seven-string zither loved by Confucius, but she didn't want to be rude. "So what does he do that's so important?"

"It's a little scary, really. Sima Gao investigates treason and the corruption of people anywhere in the Celestial Kingdom. On his command, many people can be punished or even killed."

Li Mae shivered and vowed that she would never have anything to do with the son of the minister of security and censorship.

The following day, General Chen Tang was preparing for a meeting at the palace with the ministers of trade and the ambassador of Sogdiana, an empire on the Silk Road west of the Middle Kingdom. Still excited about her singing cricket, Li Mae asked her father if she and Ming might accompany him that morning.

"You may come to the palace but not to this meeting," replied the general. "There will be matters just for my ears." Then her father looked intently at her. "Oh, I know. How silly of me. You want to show your cricket to Tai Donc Quin, the Sogdian ambassador's son."

All Li Mae could do was blush and gaze down at her silk slippers. The general sighed. "Is he still teaching you their strange language? The one from the west?"

"Yes, but I'm sure he wants to see my cricket. He has one, too."

"My meeting won't take long, so don't wander away. I'll ask Wei Yao Quin if it's alright."

Tai joined the girls a few minutes later and listened. Li Mae's cricket made sounds, to which Ming's replied.

"I wonder how they would sing if I put my cricket in with yours," Shang Gao said as he approached the group.

A tremor seeped through Le Mae as she turned and saw Shang Gao. Before Li Mae could stop him, he tossed his cricket into the box containing Li Mae's.

"What are you doing?" she said, aghast. "My cricket is a performer, not a fighter!"

"All crickets can fight."

"Yours will kill it!" said the amassador's son.

"Hers might kill mine," replied Shang. "And besides, this is not a matter for barbarians like you." With that he pushed the Sogdian boy, who spilled onto the marble floor.

With horror Li Mae watched the inevitable; Prince Gao's cricket bit the head off hers and consumed it. She put her hands to her mouth to stifle a scream.

"Go away!" shouted Ming.

He ignored her. "Oh, I guess my cricket killed yours, little girl. I might buy you another one. Sorry."

"I don't want another one from you. Don't ever talk to me again!"

"I'll talk to you if I wish. No girl can tell me not to. Don't forget, I'm a prince." The boy grinned. "I think I'll visit my father. He's doing really important things for the Emperor. There's going to be an execution tomorrow and I'm going to see it. My father gets to cut off heads."

Tai got to his feet. "I'll tell my father about this. That boy is in trouble."

***

The high-wheeled carriage came to a halt along with all other conveyances and pedestrians when drums and bells were heard. All the streets of Chang'an had three lanes, but only the Emperor was entitled to ride in the center. Everyone bowed low, as the Emperor, wearing a purple robe, rode past in his carriage. Li Mae beamed when she saw that the Son of Heaven, the most important person in the land, recognized her father, General Chen Tang, and nodded ever so slightly as he passed.

Her father was a tall, slender man who did not have to wear elevated shoes like so many of shorter stature. His robe was crimson, the second most important color in the kingdom, and he sported a goatee and a long black moustache. Like all men, he wore a soft cap with black pieces of cloth extending from each side. However, the "feet" of his cap extended straight out instead of hanging down. Not even

Ming's father, Anshi Zhaojun, could wear the feet of his hat that way—it was an honor reserved for only the highest-ranking officials. But then, Anshi Zhaojun had never defeated a barbarian army, as had General Tang.

General Chen Tang's family lived in the affluent section of the capital, not far from the Weiyang Palace. It was known as the North Gate Mansions and was separate from the other one 160 precisely laid out communities. Unlike most houses, however, their residence was a two-story structure with a blue tile roof, the ends of which slanted upwards. Phoenixes topped the highest points of the sloping roof and looked down on an immaculately cultivated garden. A high wall surrounded the house and great stone lions guarded its gates. Over two dozen servants labored to maintain the estate and keep it prepared for visiting family and court officials.

Ming had been given permission to stay the night with Li Mae. The girls were up late after the servants had gone to bed. The women's rooms were on the second floor, and in the quiet of the evening, Li Mae could overhear her father in conversation with Jia Zhou Tang.

"As a woman I hesitate to ask," said Jia Zhou, "but I wonder what you and Count Sima Gao were discussing this afternoon over all your cups of wine."

The general put down his calligraphy brush of wolf hair and inlaid mother of pearl, a gift from lords who were grateful for his victories, and gave her an amused look. "All our cups of wine? You know what the Taoists say, don't you?"

"Oh yes, you've told me a dozen times, mostly after you drink too much. 'Only those who know the joy of wine remain immortalized in this world when they die.'"

"It's true. But more importantly, wine brings out one's real character. A little too much and a man reveals more than he might care to. Lord Gao might well be the head of security and censorship, but his talk is loose. There are things he's told that I'm not privy to. Court can be a form of warfare. Surely you remember what General Sun Tzu said."

"Yes, yes, husband, 'All war is deception'"

"Absolutely. Fortunately I'm not in the faction that opposes him."

"Who would be so foolish to oppose him?"

"No one who values his head, but you've heard the court gossip. The palace is like a den of snakes, some more venomous than others."

Jia Zhou made a minute adjustment to the jade butterfly in her perfect coiffure. "Count Gao's wife told me that Lady Wen, the Emperor's favorite concubine, hates Lord Gao and wants him replaced by a eunuch. Remember how she conspired with them to get into the Emperor's bed. She was one of the 'beautiful people' who fleeced rich men before she assumed the airs of a court favorite."

"Sima Gao's not worried about her. He and the Emperor listen to Grand Chancellor Hangyong. The chancellor is concerned about the intentions of the Chanyu and so am I. After all, I'm the one who will lead armies against the barbarians. At least I hope I will."

"You defeated them once," said Jia Zhou. "I'm sure the Emperor will entrust you with the army again."

"There are other generals who want to control the army, those who take bribes and have the ear of important lords." Li Mae's father sighed. "I may have defeated the bulk of the barbarian forces, but there are factions we did not destroy. That includes those of Zhizhi Chanyu, who just acquired Lady Ti. They're a miserable bunch. Their young men lust for power, and that means raids. Their leader retains control by distributing gifts, our gifts, to their young men, and that's supposed to buy peace. That's why the Emperor insisted on giving them silk and treasure and another princess."

"So I have heard. You don't sanction that?"

"The problem is, according to Sima Gao and his spies, Zhizhi Chanyu is becoming feeble and his son's angling for control. Of course, it may not happen for a number of years— the boy is only sixteen—but in time we'll have to deal with him."

Lady Tang looked out the window and watched the "pouring men" with their torches, as they collected the night's excrement. "Do you know that your daughter is very sad? That's why I invited Ming to stay with her tonight."

"Sad? We took her to the Shanglin Gardens yesterday. I even bought her a singing cricket."

"Well Count Gao's son had a fighting cricket, and it killed hers."

"Was it an accident? Did her cricket get out of its box?"

"I don't think so. Sima Gao's wife spoke to me while you were at the palace and apologized for her son. She said that what he did was bestial. Sima Gao whipped him for it. Worse yet, the Sogdian ambassador complained that his son was assaulted by Shang Gao. The count had to apologize. That was a great disgrace for the head of security, losing face to a barbarian."

"There are barbarians and then there are barbarians," said General Tang. "The Sogdians don't have hostile intentions toward the Middle Kingdom; they're worthy middlemen who just want to keep trade flowing. But still, I feel bad for Sima Gao, having been shamed by his son. It's a violation of *Xiao* and the boy will have to atone for it."

"But what about Li?" said Jia Zhou.

"You didn't answer my question, wife. Was it an accident?"

"Lady Gao would not have apologized if it were. The boy intentionally tossed his fighting cricket into the box. It was a malicious act. Shang Gao has a mean streak in him, and that worries me. I know that his father has been talking to you about a union of his son and our daughter."

"It was only an idle comment. He thinks that a binding of our two families would be quite formidable. Of course, Li Mae and Shang Gao are still quite young. But you do like Lady Gao, don't you?"

"Lady Gao, yes, but not her husband. Personally, I think he's dangerous. I wish you hadn't spoken to him about Li Mae. Now if we refuse the Six Etiquettes and the pledge of our daughter, we may find ourselves in front of his tribunal."

"That's not going to happen. Still, having him as an ally isn't a bad thing."

"But what about Li Mae? She detests the boy. Surely you won't bind her to such an unhappy marriage."

"The boy is acting like a rejected adolescent. That will change with manhood. My guess is that Shang wanted to gain her attention and was jealous of the ambassador's son. I'm sorry that his cricket killed Li's, but I think he already regrets his conduct."

"In my opinion, husband, it's a character flaw. Time doesn't change that."

The general waved his hand. "Shang is still quite immature and doesn't know proper etiquette. I'll speak to his father. And if I know Sima Gao, he will insist that his son apologize and buy another singing cricket for our daughter."

The next morning, Li Mae crept out of bed while Ming was still sleeping. She ran downstairs, hurried to the garden, and knelt beside her mother who had just completed a sorrowful poem.

"Father can't be serious; tell me he's not!"

Jia Zhou looked into her daughter's eyes. "Were you were listening to our conversation last night?"

Li Mae nodded, tears welling up in her eyes. "I don't want a singing cricket from Shang Gao. Please, Mother, don't let Father marry me to that horrible boy. I detest him, I really do!"

Lady Tang sighed and coaxed her daughter to her feet. Putting her hand on Li's head she said, "We'll do what your father thinks best for the family, but, as you heard, this is all years away. Besides, the astrologers and the face diviners must be consulted, and if things appear inauspicious, there will be no wedding with Shang. You know that the sorceress must consult the future and the first lords of the past. That takes time. So you see, my dear, there are fates over which neither Lord Gao nor your father have any control."

"But you'll talk to Father, won't you?" Li Mae pleaded. "If he decides against it I won't have to cry myself to sleep every night."

"I'll talk to him, but you must understand. Your future marriage is not just about you. Neither was mine. The point of marriage isn't love, it's producing and raising a son. We have to carry on your father's line. You must give him a male child, whether it's with Shang Gao or not."

Lady Tang's tone became stern. "You have been living a fantasy, with your father taking you to the palace to learn about politics and such. It's as if you were the son he doesn't have. But you're not his son. You are his daughter, and you must think and act like one."

Li Mae's mother had never spoken to her like that before and she suddenly felt silly, having strolled through the palace as if she were a visiting official. Men only tolerated her presence, she realized, because her exalted father allowed it. Her ridiculous questions about policy and matters of state would have to cease. From now on she would decline her father's invitations to visit the palace. She would never enter it again unless required by the Grand Chancellor or the Emperor himself.

Jia Zhou's expression softened and she held Li Mae's hands. "I know all this sounds terribly harsh, but you must learn how things are for a woman. It's been this way from the beginning, since the gods determined the way of yin and yang. The most important duty for a woman is to produce sons. It is to them you will give your love, and they will bring honor to the household. All wives shed tears for lovers they never held. I have, too, but I do what I must for husband and Emperor."

Still worried, Li Mae nodded and wiped tears from her cheeks. She looked into her mother's saddened eyes.

"What I've said is the way to heaven and eternal happiness. It's all in the hands of the diviners and the Fates. Don't worry. There's no need to rush into the future. It'll come for you soon enough."

Then she smiled and touched Li Mae's face. "I will have Lady Xie come this afternoon to help your study of the three perfections. And a gentleman artist will be here soon to paint a new mural. That should be enjoyable to watch."

***

In the morning the general attended a meeting at the Weiyang Palace. The Grand Chancellor was concerned about the dilatory construction of the Wall in the northwestern territories. The unfinished barrier was a weak point through which the Chanyu raided Han villages.

"Then we should conscript the peasants to build the wall," said the general. "After all, it would be to their benefit."

"I agree," said the Grand Chancellor. "But that will be expensive, and eunuchs don't want money diverted from their coffers. They think the wall will never be a barrier."

"So they want to continue buying off the Chanyu with princesses," said General Tang.

"It is an easy trade for a eunuch. They have little use for a princess," sighed the Grand Chancellor.

General Chen Tang, Sima Gao, and the Grand Chancellor, Bi Hangyong, were sipping tea and discussing the Wall when an aide entered, kowtowed, and said, "My lords, distressing news from the barbarian lands."

The Grand Chancellor lowered his cup and motioned for the messenger to continue.

"It's about Lady Ti."

Bi Hangyong looked puzzled until Sima Gao said, "Our tribute to the Chanyu, my Lord Chancellor. If you recall, she was the number one concubine to Lord Tao, director of the Bureau of Merit. She was quite accomplished on the zither and the three perfections, amongst other talents. The lady got his attention, her beauty not being insignificant, and became his favorite concubine."

"The Chanyu headman, Zhizhi Chanyu, claims that the woman was lost in a sandstorm when she and other local women were herding goats. But our man, a Chanyu who is well paid, thinks that she committed suicide. Or something worse," said the messenger.

"Worse?"

"Murdered, my lord. Our informant found her body. There was a knife wound in her chest."

"Since when does a princess herd goats? And murdered?" exclaimed the Chancellor.

"The barbarians do not accord privilege to a Chinese princess once she's beyond the Gate of Exiles. They live in yurts, worship war and horse skulls, and raise goats," said General Tang.

"I've lost count of how many of our ladies have perished in that desert. Suicide, mostly. But some have been murdered out of jealousy," said Sima Gao.

"Excellency," said the aide, "our spy also said that there's bad blood between Zhizhi Chanyu and his son, Xion Wen Chanyu. He thinks it's possible that the son wanted to steal the princess from his father."

"Lord Tao will demand an investigation, if it's murder," said Sima Gao. "The lady may have been tribute but she does, or did, represent the Emperor. Her death is a matter of state."

Chancellor Hangyong raised one hand to halt any further comment by the director of censorship.

"One more thing, Excellency," said the aide. "Our spy says that Zhizhi Chanyu will demand a replacement princess. That is, if Lady Ti took her own life and deprived him of the gift from the Son of Heaven."

"Really? What gall!" said Chancellor Hangyong.

The aide bowed again and hurried from the chamber. The Grand Chancellor turned back to his guests and said, "I can't believe that the barbarian expects us to give him another woman just to be murdered or commit suicide." He waved a jeweled finger. "None of this conversation will breach these walls. Obviously we cannot expect the Chanyu to carry out an investigation when they have done the killing. They won't accuse one of their own."

"Then it's up to us to find the truth," said General Tang.

"And how do you propose to do that?"

"I'll take 30,000 men, hold their people hostage, and interrogate anyone I choose."

"But that will precipitate another war," said Chancellor Hangyong. "And it will also give the Confucian academics, those idiotic idealists, ammunition to petition the Son of Heaven for our dismissal. They don't venture beyond the Shanglin Gardens and have never seen heads lopped off by a horde of insane barbarians. But they have influence with the Emperor's wife. She revels in their lustful poetry. No, general, we won't send you and your army into the wilderness. We have other ways to deal with them."

"As director of the Censorate I have connections that don't directly involve the military. Lord Chancellor, we might involve our Sogdian friends in this matter."

The chancellor raised his eyebrows. "How insightful, Lord Gao. But again, none of this will be mentioned to anyone except the Emperor. The last thing we need right now is another war."

"But we'll have to deal with the Chanyu sooner or later," said General Tang.

"We shall annihilate them when we can commit an army of 40,000 with the full backing of Emperor Wudi. It will take a greater atrocity than the death of a single princess, no matter how important she may have been," said the chancellor.

Chapter 8

There was no moon and the men, roped to one another, stumbled over the broken ground. Gaius leading the silent column carried a shielded oil lamp. If any Parthian had noticed the tiny glow he might have thought it a shepherd's lamp, nothing to warrant closer inspection.

The mouths of the horses had been bound and every piece of equipment tied tight. It was the fifth night since the escape from the catastrophe at Carrhae. The 400 legionnaires sought the relative sanctuary of the rugged Armenian hills where cavalry was not effective.

Now, on the forced march, there was no talking, no joking or exchange of comradely insults as the men had shared when along the banks of the Euphrates. Like a voyeur escaping an alarmed couple, the soldiers scurried through the night.

They finally reached a line of trees beside a swift river. Its water, chilled by the melt ice of the Zagros Mountains, replenished skeins and cleansed the legionnaires for the first time since the battle.

Gaius allowed the men a respite after they ascended a wooded promontory affording a view of the desert below. He posted sentries, as he did each night. At daybreak Gaius assembled all but the guards. The mood could not have been more somber; the uncertain road before them seemed to stretch for eternity.

They stood in groups. Shields and weapons lay about them, trappings that had been virtually useless only days before. The centurion looked over his men. He had not spoken on the route except to issue curt orders. The fear of whistling arrows was motivation enough to keep the legionnaires moving.

Ignominy. The humiliation showed on every face. This was not a military force.

They had survived the flight across the desert, Gaius would give them that. But it was one thing to hasten in the face of terror, another to stand and fight with determination as they had been trained to do. A deep contempt, a bile, rose in his throat as he eyed the despondency before him. He would not countenance rabble. That was contrary to everything that had defined him for 20 years. He fingered his *vitis* stick. Seething, he paced before them, saw their unmilitary postures, their expressions of defeat. From the corner of his eye he glimpsed a chiding, reproachful sneer that said, "We are beaten, what are you going to do about it?"

It didn't matter who gave him the look. Discipline mattered. With stunning speed the Primus Pila turned and slammed the stout vine branch into the stomach of one man, then another. They grasped their bellies, groaned, and fell to the ground.

"Stand!" he bellowed. "I said, 'Stand!'"

Sempronius, the first legionnaire struck, writhed with pain.

"Form ranks!" he said, slapping the stick against his bronze greaves. "I will not have soldiers of Rome looking like terrified sewer rats. Pick that man up."

Tacitus reached down and helped Sempronius to his feet. The desultory lines began to form; men edged in between others, held shields before them, and made an effort to appear soldierly.

"Straighten up!" commanded Gaius, striking shields as he paced the lines. Two junior centurions stood before their cohorts, but the third cohort had no centurion. The Primus Pila looked about, then spied the man he wanted.

"Cornicularius to the front."

Appian stepped forward, trumpet at the ready.

"I appoint you centurion of the first cohort. Take your post."

Gaius stood back and trained his eyes upon the ranks. Good enough for now. It was time to speak to them again.

"We did not fail in battle," he began. "We did not disgrace ourselves, because we were not allowed to fight. Certainly the cavalry and the auxiliaries did their best, but the rest of us were targets for superior bows. That thousands of our comrades died was the fault of strategy, not inferiority or cowardice. But I am not pleased by what I see before me. I will not abide defeat or shame or slovenliness."

There was grim silence in the ranks.

"You are legionnaires; you can fight and march 30 miles a day in full armor. We are four cohorts with many veterans, but four cohorts are not enough to challenge the horse archers of Parthia. Not if any of us is to ever see Rome again."

"A few days' march from here is the way of the caravans. It is the Seres Road that brings silk and jade to Rome from a land to the east. Our medicus, Apollodoros, has told us that the road goes many leagues through treacherous places but eventually leads to the silk people. Beyond that stands a wall and then a river leading to the sea. That water will take us home. We have already made the decision to march and we will do so in a military manner."

It was time to set the rules.

"To deter local raiders," he continued, "we must appear as the advance unit of a large army, not unlike that of Alexander. We will appear indomitable and undefeatable. We will be strangers to any who have not been to the Roman provinces, and that will be to our advantage since all hostiles will have to consider our fighting skills. A disciplined, cohesive unit will make them very cautious. To give the impression of strength we must show strength— overwhelming strength. That is imperative, and that is what I expect."

For many, thought Gaius, the march would be interminable and unrelenting, overseen by a man they despised. They would not crave adventure, there had been too much of that already. The monotonous march would likely be as bleak as the River Styx. But the decision had been made and there would be no dissension.

"No fires tonight," Gaius said. "We will post sentries as usual and march tomorrow with scouts to the front and a guard to the rear. The road is widening and we shall proceed in the standard line of four abreast. We will begin at first light. Be ready to march."

Gaius dismissed the men, summoned Appian, and found a place removed from the despondent troops.

"Why did you choose me?" the trumpeter asked.

"Why not? You've been in the legion even longer than me. You know how to lead and how to fight. That's what I need. I also need another pair of eyes and ears, and not just for the Parthians or Saka."

"You're thinking about deserters?"

"That and agitators. The men agreed to this march because I presented no viable alternatives. But they are a disgruntled and resentful lot. I would inflict severe punishment were we at Campus Martius, but I can't afford to lose so many. Keep an eye on them. I'll execute any who attempt to run or mutiny."

They watched as the men found shelter beneath the scrawny trees.

"The men are exhausted, more mentally than physically," said Appian.

"They can use a good rest. But there will be little of that after sunrise. I'm not worried about cavalry surprising us on this road."

"What about Parthian infantry?"

"They probably engaged the Armenians. That's why we weren't facing their infantry at Carrhae, and why I doubt that we'll encounter more than a patrol on this road. But we'll be vigilant."

"This isn't the only place they might be," said Apollodoros, joining them. "Years ago my father took me to a city called Merv, to our east. It belongs to the Parthians, and in a few months we'll have to pass it. There may be patrols all along the way."

"A good reason for haste and stealth," Gaius said. "Have your men attend to their weapons, Appian. They'll be needing them."

The Primus Pila slept for a few hours, checked on the sentries, and spent most of the night planning for the journey ahead. Then he dozed off until the first glimmer of dawn and, after inspecting the cohorts, led them silently through the forests toward the fabled Silk Road.

***

"Why did he hit me?" Sempronius asked.

Tacitus stepped carefully over a jagged rock as he and the others moved through the boulder-strewn hills. "Because that's the way he is, a pain in the ass."

"Do you think he has it in for me? He never hit me before."

"Not more than anybody else. He's a spiteful man with a lot of hate. Just stay out of his way."

They came to a fast-moving river. Gaius gave the cohorts a few minutes to rest and fill their water gourds. Sempronius looked about, then motioned to Tacitus. The two walked beyond the rear of the column. "Do you really think we can get back by going to that river? How many years did Apollodoros say we would have to march?"

"He doesn't know how many years," said Tacitus. "He doesn't really know if the river exists."

"I gave in. I voted for this march because everybody else did."

"You would have voted against it?"

"Yes, but now it's too late."

"Maybe not."

Sempronius looked at Tacitus. "If enough men petitioned your father ..."

An order was given and the men moved into position. Tacitus's reply was lost in the jostling movement of troops.

"Say nothing," said Tacitus when the ranks had assembled. "We'll talk about it later."

Tactically, there was little worse than marching along a narrow road with steep hills on one side and a river on the other. An enemy could tear down a slope, crash into a narrow column of troops, and push them right into the water. The cohorts ascended the rugged hills, keeping below the summit, with scouts observing from the crests.

The last thing Tacitus wanted was to be on that road. Every step east would take him further from Rome. But how could he slip away unnoticed? How could he possibly get to the Euphrates and then home to Tullia? If only it were possible. Once home, he would flee with her to a distant port where nobody would question him. It would have to be someplace where the Tenth Legion and survivors of Carrhae would never go. Indeed, it might be years before any of the cohorts returned to Rome. Others might decide to desert, but he would not go with them. He would go alone.

A dozen men were designated as pioneers and cut a swath through the brush. The progress was slow but afforded cover. It also gave them a vantage point from which they could see the road below and anybody on it. When a caravan or Armenian patrol was spotted, the men were ordered to lie prone and remain silent.

During the last night in the hill country, Tacitus, Sempronius, and the giant Ibericus stood guard beside a rocky outcrop. Appian had joined them. From their position they could observe the flat plain illuminated by a full moon.

"There's no cover down there. We'll be totally exposed if we have to march during the day," said Sempronius.

"We'll only march in the early hours," said Appian. "Anybody following us will have the sun in their eyes. Then we'll continue after the sun has set."

"But we'll still be in the open like before."

"Not exactly. The *medicus* said it's not a desert like at Carrhae. There's water, brush, and trees. Just not as much as up here."

Tacitus said nothing, his eyes searching for signs of life below.

"Still raging at your father, Tacitus?" said the trumpeter.

Tacitus only shrugged.

"You don't know anything about him, do you?"

"There's not much I care to know. He's mean and brutish, and if he wants me to hate him, well, he's succeeded quite nicely."

Appian grunted. "There's an old adage in the army: if you fear your officers more than the enemy, there is little to fear from your enemy."

"That's little comfort. You know I only saw him five times in my life before he dragged me into the army. The man is a total stranger to me. Even now I know almost every soldier better than I know him."

When Appian failed to reply, Sempronius said, "Centurion, how long have you known him?"

"Since we were kids in Rome. I never expected him to join the legion and he wouldn't have if ..." He stopped and looked at Tacitus. "The Primus Pila was once a very different person, kind, pleasant. But unforeseen circumstances can change us and we're never the same again."

Tacitus looked away.

"There are things you should know about your father," said Appian. "I mean as a soldier, a leader, because he's the man you must depend on. You must have faith in your leader."

"And you do?"

"Sit down, you can still see the road," said Appian. "Gaius is a stern and hardened man; war does that. It takes joy and humor out of life. Considering what you've been through, you should understand. Your father is devoted to the legion and all the men in it. It became his family long ago, and it's the only one he has. You're part of that, Tacitus, though you don't believe it. True, he's tough, but he knows that the enemies we'll encounter are also tough. The difference between him and almost every other centurion, tribune, or legate is that he's honest. That's what he's required of you—honesty. In many ways, like it or not, you two are much alike. You are, after all, his son."

"He enjoys killing people. I don't," said Tacitus.

"You'll kill people who want to kill you or your friends. Give it time."

The centurion paused. Tacitus met his gaze this time, unmoved.

"I was still a *munifex*, a common soldier like you, when he told me of his decision to join the army. That was shortly after his wife died, when he became a different person and rejected the gods. He asked me to train him, to teach him all the fighting tricks. He was ruthless, savage, unforgiving of himself. From the beginning he was different than other legionnaires. Most men try to avoid hardship and bribe their way out of onerous work. He never did. He wouldn't accept a bribe and he wouldn't give one. And he didn't talk glibly or say mindless things. He didn't brag about the women he laid or how many men he slew. Nor did he call for help from the gods."

"Because he doesn't believe in them,"said Tacitus.

"None of them, not even Great Jupiter?" asked Sempronius.

"None of them. He has his reasons," said Appian. "And they're not yours to question."

"What else do you know about him?" Sempronius asked.

"As I said, he's tough, brutal, but not for the sake of meanness. He became an expert with his weapons; even veteran legionnaires were wary of him. Because of a heroic act he received the golden arrow and the *corona civica*."

At that, Tacitus's eyes widened. The *corona civica* was Rome's highest award.

"Yes, Tacitus, the golden arrow wasn't a gift from Great Jupiter. Maybe I'll tell you about it sometime. The man has strength and cunning, but beyond that is the determination to win at all costs. Even when the goal appears hopeless. Some thought it strange, considering his father's influence, that he didn't join the army as an equestrian. He could have had a dashing and relatively safe life as a knight. But that's not him. He never chose anything easy and despises those who want the safe, redolent life."

"And that's why he joined the Tenth?" Ibericus asked.

Appian nodded. "He had to petition to get in; Caesar's personal legion was mostly made up of Spaniards and southern Gauls. It was newer and less experienced than the Seventh Claudia or the Third Galicia, but it was tough, and men who joined knew that they were going to war, not some sunny resort along the Nile. In time Caesar began to rely on the Tenth. The Primus Pila's first action was in a rebellious part of Spain. The Tenth was becoming a war machine. Julius Caesar was making his mark, and so was your father."

"You saw all this?"

"I was there beside him. You question me?"

Tacitus shook his head.

"Caesar's legions had already conquered most of Gaul," Appian continued. "We were in winter quarters, nice and warm, thinking that there would be no more fighting until spring. Then we heard that a tough bunch called the Belgic Confederacy had decided that it would be a good time to boot us out, that we wouldn't fight in such nasty weather. They assumed that we would scurry back to Spain and the warm beds of women."

"I like the warm beds of women idea," said Ibericus.

"Caesar had other ideas; he's not one to run away. We tore down the camp and marched through blizzards for 20 days. There were the Eighth, Ninth, and Tenth legions, as well as anyone else he could scrape up. We ripped into Belgae near the Scheldt River and completely destroyed two of the three Celtic tribes."

"Germans?" asked Ibericus.

"Yes, the Bellovaci and the Aedui, big, mean fighters who wouldn't surrender to anybody, especially not Romans. They were angry men protecting their families; they gave no quarter and expected none."

The trumpeter studied the moonlit plain below then. "By this time, Gaius was a middle-ranking centurion, stationed on the right of his cohort. As you know, it's a very exposed position, but it's from there that the fight can be directed. He reveled in the danger, though it was not a place to be envied."

"There was a third group, the Nervii, the largest of the barbarian tribes, and we engaged them at the Sambre River. As I said, the snow was deep. There were thick trees and we couldn't see into the hills. We of the Tenth were on the far left of the line. There were the river and the forest to our front, and suddenly 60,000 Nervii came screaming out of the forest and hit the legions. Our cavalry fled in total panic."

"Did the line break?" asked Sempronius.

"In places it did. The fighting was chaotic; scattered elements were banding together, trying to survive. I could see our Numidian slingers, Greek auxiliaries, camp followers, all running in one direction or another. The legions were spread too far apart and we were completely outflanked. All of us thought the day was lost; there would be total annihilation. Caesar was all over the field, rallying the men. He called the centurions by name; he knew the name of every one of them. At one point, seeing our men fall back, he grabbed a shield from a legionnaire and charged straight into the hulking, towering Nervii. Then I saw a tribune dash up to him and say that the chief centurion of the legion had been killed."

"Appian, enough of that, I need you now." Like a specter, Gaius had emerged from the shadows. "There's something I want you to see on the other side of this hill."

***

The two veterans ascended a rise and looked down at a river that meandered in the moonlight like a glistening snake. Beside its banks were pinpricks of campfires stretching to the horizon.

"Thousands," exclaimed Appian. "How is it we didn't see them before?"

"The guard just spotted them. Whoever is down there arrived a short while ago," said Gaius.

"A whole army. Why would they come this way? We're the only force out here and the Parthians wouldn't need that many men. And how would they even know we're here?"

Gaius shook his head, puzzled by the enormous numbers beside the river. "I don't think they're after us."

"But are they Parthians?"

"Maybe."

"If not Parthians, then Armenians? Survivors from the battle against Orodes?"

"That many would not have survived. It might not be a military force, Appian. They're too spread out, and they haven't set up any defense."

"Civilians, then? Refugees from the Armenian capital? It doesn't make sense, them being way out here."

"Maybe they're neither," Gaius said. "Have the men strike camp. I want to be far away by first light. Pick a few men and find out who they are and where they're going. Wear Parthian clothing and take Apollodoros."

"I'll also take Tacitus and Lepidus."

"It's your choice. Saddle horses and meet us at the base of the mountain when you find out more about them."

***

Appian and his small party found a narrow passage that led down to the river. Halting beside a tangle of trees, they tied their mounts a distance from the closest fire. The eerie quiet of the great encampment made Tacitus nervous.

"Stay here, Lepidus," instructed Appian. "Take the horses and ride, if we're not back by first light."

Tacitus walked silently beside the river with Appian and Apollodoros. When they came upon a thatch of reeds, they lay in it and listened to approaching hoofbeats. A dozen riders appeared just beyond the campfires. Peering through the brush, Tacitus saw that they appeared to be small, slender men with sheaths of arrows and recurved bows across their backs. They spoke in loud, boisterous voices while carrying out a quick sortie. Joking amongst themselves, they trotted their horses toward a distant picket line.

"They're the same Saka cavalry that murdered us at Carrhae," Tacitus whispered.

"The same," agreed Appian Dio. "Let's see if the others are also Saka."

They slipped from their cover and moved toward a fire surrounded by a dozen men. In the shadows they again crouched and listened to the quiet, despondent voices. Men spoke conspiratorially in hushed tones. The only other sound was of metal chains clinking against one another.

"Roman prisoners from Carrhae. Can we free any of them?" Tacitus asked.

Appian shook his head. "Not now. It would cause a disturbance. Even if we could cut their chains they have no weapons. We'd all be killed."

A tall horseman spotted them and Apollodoros stood. His Parthian clothing fluttered in the night breeze.

"Is everything okay?" a voice said in Parthian-accented Greek.

"All is fine, sir," replied Apollodoros. "They won't make any trouble for us."

Tacitus looked straight ahead, hoping the Parthian wouldn't say anything to him. He could speak Greek well enough thanks to Apollodoros's instruction, but his accent would give them all away.

"Be careful around them," said the horseman. "Even chained they can be dangerous, and we have a long way to go."

"How far is it, sir?"

"Merv? A thousand miles. With this many prisoners, maybe three or four months."

"We'll stay alert."

The officer looked at the three would-be Parthians, nodded, and guided his horse toward a group of chained men.

"That's it then," Appian said once the officer rode off. "Merv. I don't know how many will make it."

"Where's Merv?" Tacitus asked.

"At the eastern edge of Parthia," said Apollodoros. "It's a grassland beside the Oxus. Perhaps they want to sell the prisoners to their neighbors, the Sogdiani."

"Then they're not after us," said Tacitus.

"No, not unless they see us," said Appian. "Then we'll be like them." He nodded toward those who would be slaves for the rest of their lives.

***

At the end of the next day's march, Tacitus sat before the fire with Sempronius and Ibericus.

"I hope Appian Dio will join us," Sempronius said.

"Why's that?" replied Tacitus.

"Because he hasn't finished the story," Ibericus said, his bulk looming beside them.

Tacitus shrugged. "He'll finish it. He thinks it's something I should know about. But it's not going to change what I think. My father's never done anything for me."

"You have a short memory," a voice said behind them. "He saved your life. You would have been the excrement of hyenas in a Roman circus."

"You can't be sure of that, Centurion," said Tacitus.

"Cow piss. The guards had been summoned. The priests were furious; their temple had been defiled by you and your gang of delinquents. Be thankful you're alive, *munifex*."

Tacitus had never seen Appian truly angry. He had always thought of him as a mild-mannered, aging legionnaire. But now, as he met Appian's long, ugly gaze, he suspected that he had been wrong.

"A few nights ago you were telling us about the war against the Nervii at the Sambre River," said Sempronius. "How did it end?"

Appian turned away. "Forget it."

"Alright," Tacitus blurted. "He saved my life. I admit it. But I don't have to like him."

"He doesn't want you to like him. No centurion needs a legionnaire's affection. But he must be obeyed so he can again save your thankless life, Tacitus."

Appian returned to the fire and stared into the flames. Ibericus was about to put another log on the blaze when the trumpeter said, "No more wood. Sparks in this wind can be seen for miles."

Fortunius came to the fire, its coals glowing like tiny lanterns.

"As I said before," continued Appian. "Caesar's legions were nearly overrun by 60,000 Nervii. I was in the rear rank, the Triarii, the old guard. Being veterans, we were supposed to hold the line, keeping the younger men from folding. But we were all being pushed together. It's a dangerous thing when men can't maneuver. We lost the battle of Cannae against the Carthaginians because of that."

Gaius was to the right of the line directing the less experienced legionnaires. The *aquilifer* carrying the sacred eagle staff had moved too far forward and was cut off. A dozen barbarians surrounded him; their blood was up. Taking the eagle would make them invincible."

"Did they get it?" Ibericus asked anxiously.

"Be quiet," Sempronius said.

Appian, ignoring the interruption, took a sip from his wineskin. "Caesar was on a nearby hill, still trying to rally his men, and turned to see what was happening with our cohort. A tribune pointed to the *aquilifer* and the general stopped to watch. Gaius, in the thick of it, saw the eagle bearer go down. The man was mortally wounded. The Germans already had their hands on the standard."

Once more Appian went for his wine, but the bag was empty. Fortunius handed him a full one and the centurion took a long slow pull. Pointing directly at Tacitus he said, "Alone, your father charged the Nervii, grabbed the eagle, and slashed the throats of three so fast that they were dead before they touched the ground. Then he sliced off the arm of one and impaled another. Hundreds of men saw it happen, including Caesar. Amazingly, your father hacked his way back to our lines and handed the eagle to a tribune. The entire legion thought it an omen. We charged the Nervii and the slaughter began."

"And the battle was over?" asked Tacitus.

"Far from it. As I said, Caesar saw it all, dismounted from his charger, and ran down the hill with his tribunes. In the middle of the fight he grabbed you father's hand, raised it high, and shouted, 'This centurion saved our eagle! I elevate him to Primus Pila for his bravery on this day!'"

"Then I heard the general say, 'Stay alive if you can and report to me when this is all over.' The Tenth held. Even the cavalry came back, ashamed of their rout. The Nervii broke and ran. Only 500 survived out of the original 60,000."

"Now maybe you'll think differently of your father, Tacitus. After all, another man does, and his name is Julius Caesar."

Chapter 9

"We'll do it at dawn," said Quintillus to Julius Fortunius as he looked down the steep hill to the distant road below.

"Who else is coming with us?" asked Fortunius.

"Just Arelius," Quintillus said in a hushed voice.

"Did you get what we need?" asked Quintillus.

"I will when everyone is asleep."

***

"Clumsy idiot! Where are you going?"

Sempronius's voice woke Tacitus from a half-dozen yards away. Eyes half shut, he heard quick, fading footfalls. "Why are you yelling? It's too damn early."

"That fool fell on me."

"What fool? There are hundreds of them here."

"Fortunius. He just ran off, didn't even apologize."

"Did you expect him to?" groaned Ibericus. He rolled over and his melon-sized head poked out from his cloak. "Tacitus, I'm out of water. Give me some of yours, won't you?"

"You're always out of everything." Tacitus reached for the bag containing his water gourd. He patted around the ground and raised himself on his elbow.

"Just toss it, I'm real thirsty."

"It's not here, the bag's not here. Sempronius, did you see where I put it?" Tacitus peered about in the half light. The only things nearby were his armor and weapons.

Sempronius sat up and looked around. "When Fortunius tripped over me he had a heavy pouch. Do you think it was yours?"

"Maybe. I left it right here."

Why would he take it?"

"Because of what was in it. The gold medallion, the one that Tullia gave me. I put it in there and he saw me do it." Tacitus snatched up his gladius. "Which way did he go?"

Sempronius pointed. Tacitus, now fully awake, sprinted past snoring soldiers.

"Wait!" said Ibericus. "We're coming, too."

Wearing only their tunics, the three sprinted uphill, leaving the encampment behind.

"Are you sure he went this way?" Tacitus asked.

"Pretty sure."

Ibericus halted below the crest. "If it was Fortunius, he wouldn't have been alone. See the sandal tracks?"

Tacitus knelt and studied them. The soil on the hill was powdery. "There were others on guard last night. It might not be theirs."

"These were made by somebody running," said Sempronius. See the distance between the footprints and the depth of the tracks? Men leaving guard duty would walk."

"But why would they go this way? The road we took from Carrhae is behind us, not to our front."

"If they went down this track they'd get to the road." Ibericus pointed. "See it out there? They wouldn't have to take the zigzag mountain trail. They'd have at least an hour lead on anybody going after them."

"We can get down there too," said Sempronius. "We can catch them if we hurry."

Loose shale and tumbled rock caused by snow melt and earthquakes was strewn along the pathway. Sempronius and his friends grabbed branches and, following scuff marks, began their descent.

A gnarled branch gave way, and Sempronius pitched forward and careened full tilt into a boulder. A moment later Tacitus and Ibericus were at his side. Sempronius's head was a bloody mess. He collapsed when he tried to stand.

"Don't stop for me, go after them," he said, lying back against the rock.

"No, they'll slow down once they see that no one's after them. We'll get them later," said Tacitus.

"We'll take you to the *medicus*," said Ibericus. "You're all beat up."

They neared the summit after an arduous climb and heard a shout from the top. Tacitus looked up to see his father, along with Apollodoros and two dozen legionnaires, staring down at them.

"Get them!" The Primus Pila held a coiled rope. Ten soldiers scrambled down the hill, grabbing Tacitus and Ibericus, who were forced to drop Sempronius.

"What are you doing?" said Tacitus. "Sempronius is hurt!"

"No talking, just get them up here and bind that man's hands," said Gaius, pointing to Ibericus. The giant looked at Tacitus, a baffled expression on his face.

"I will not tolerate deserters. I made that perfectly clear before we started." Turning to the dozens of men now congregating at the hilltop, the centurion said, "You agreed to my proposal and you all know the consequences of desertion. These men, including the one lying down there, will receive forty-five lashes each. Tie them to the trees."

"That will kill them, Gaius," said Appian as he hurried up the hill.

The Primus Pila ignored the trumpeter and handed the knotted rope to a burly legionnaire and repeated, "Forty-five lashes and not one less. That big one first."

"No, by the gods, don't," said Ibericus.

"We weren't deserting," shouted Tacitus. "Fortunius stole my kit and ran down that hill. He and Quintillus are the ones deserting. We were going after him."

"It's true. We would have come back," said Ibericus.

"Traitors! Deserters! I've been watching you, Tacitus. You are a coward and a disgrace. The lash!" Gaius roared.

The legionnaire shook out the rope. Tacitus drew his gladius, sprang forward, and sliced it from the man's hand. Startled, the legionnaire jumped back.

"You will not whip Ibericus!" shouted Tacitus as he saw Gaius draw his own sword.

"You defy me? You defy my orders?" said the Primus Pila. He rushed Tacitus, swinging his weapon with a downward slash. Tacitus parried the blow but tripped and fell backwards. Seeing his father's advance and the killing sword, he grabbed a handful of dirt and tossed it into Gaius's face. Blinded by grains of sand, Gaius swung wild, and Tacitus leapt to his feet, gladius pointed toward his father's throat. The centurion brushed the dirt from his face and raised his sword again when Apollodoros rushed forward and grabbed his arm.

"No! Don't kill him!" he shouted. "Don't kill Aspacia's son."

The enraged centurion threw Apollodoros back. "Slave, get away from me!"

"Slave?" said Apollodoros. The two stared at each other. "You manumitted me in a Roman court. You made me a *libertus* after I helped you kill the men who murdered your parents. I heal your men. And you call me a slave? You may go to the river and that wall but you go without me. I am a free man and I owe you nothing!"

"Centurion!" shouted Appian, rushing between the two. "Tacitus is correct. It's Quintillus and two others. They're gone. They ran out with extra packs. They're the ones you want."

Gaius stared at the trumpeter. "When did they leave?"

"At dawn, Primus Pila," said a centurion, stepping to the front.

"I must speak to you alone, Primus Pila," said Appian. "Come with me, please."

Tacitus watched, his heart still pounding, as his father allowed himself to be led away.

***

"Tacitus and his friends were after Quintillus," said Appian.

"Why didn't they tell me they were going?"

"They had no time."

Gaius remained bitterly silent and stared into the distance.

"Look, I know you have it in for him. You're a stubborn and vindictive man. You've been that way ever since Aspacia died. But your son wasn't deserting, though he has every reason to. Your threats won't keep him here; he's too much like you. And believe it or not, he's a damn good soldier."

Gaius sheathed his sword but said nothing.

"Ask yourself, why would Tacitus and the other two run off carrying only their weapons? They took no water, no food, no clothing against the cold. This was not premeditated. I recommend, Centurion, that you have Ibericus untied and have Apollodoros tend to Sempronius. After this morning we'll be fortunate if an entire cohort doesn't just pack up and leave.

"Apollodoros is bluffing; he can't be serious," said Gaius. "He took an oath. He'll stay."

"Really? He's a *libertus*, an auxiliary, not a Roman soldier. What are you going to do, make an example by beating your only *medicus*? If I know Apollodoros, he's already leaving." Appian glared at Gaius. "Maybe you should say something to him if you're capable of doing that."

***

Despondency settled once again upon the cohorts. They had planned to march out of the mountains that morning, but no orders were given. Sempronius was taken to a tent. Tacitus and Ibericus stood in a corner and watched while Apollodoros, still in camp, gave him a quick examination.

"You'll mend. Nothing is broken, just abrasions and a bad sprain." Then the *medicus* proceeded to pack his few belongings.

"Are you coming with me?" Apollodoros asked. "I don't think your father will try to stop you now."

"I might if Sempronius could walk, but he can't, and I won't leave him. Are you going alone?"

Apollodoros shrugged. "Why not? What do I have to fear? People always need a trained *medicus* and I speak many languages. I can talk my way out of anything."

"When are you going?"

"As soon as I fill my water gourd."

"Get him to stay," Ibericus mouthed when the Greek wasn't looking.

"I never knew that you helped my father when my grandparents were murdered," said Tacitus with a brief nod in Ibericus's direction. "Tell me what happened. My aunt Junia never said much about it."

Again Apollodoros shrugged. "It was a long time ago and I really don't care to talk about it. All I'll say is that I was your grandfather's slave. I was with them on a road outside Rome when we were attacked by a gang of thieves. They killed your grandfather, then raped and killed your grandmother."

"I vaguely remember my grandparents. They treated me well."

"Yes, well they changed a lot over the years," said the *medicus*. His kit was nearly packed. "Anyway, Gaius was on leave from the army; I told him what happened."

Tacitus nodded. He had only been six at the time, but he remembered Apollodoros running across the field to meet his father. He had looked so tired. He found out later that Apollodoros had barely survived the attack.

"And the murderers?"

"Tacitus, you're holding me up," said Apollodoros ruefully. "You can ask your father about it if you ever talk to him again. I just want to get out of here."

"He won't tell me. If you don't, I'll never know. It's important to me; I know practically nothing about my grandparents."

Apollodoros sighed and touched his forehead with two fingers. "Only because you ask, but then I must go."

"I promise not to delay you a moment longer."

"Fine. I spied the murderers' camp up a wooded hill. That night your father and I went there. He had me stay at the bottom to report if any escaped. He killed them one after another. One tried to escape by running down the hill. I found a heavy branch and cracked open his head. We burned all the bodies after that."

"But you were still a slave, even though my grandfather was dead. So who did you belong to?"

"Your father inherited me. I didn't sleep that night because I didn't know what to expect. He could have sold me. The next day he took me to the Capitoline Hill along with Aspacia's sister, Caladria. In a legal ceremony he gave us our freedom."

"And then he forced you to join the army, like he did me."

"Of course not. I had nowhere else to go. I was under his command, but he depended on me. I was once his teacher, after all. When he was young we travelled with his father to Alexandria to buy antiques. His father sold them to wealthy Romans."

"I never knew about that."

"I imagine not. Your grandfather was enterprising, but he was also a crook and an accomplice to murder."

"An interesting story."

"Something else you might ask your father about."

"Was my father involved in it? He's good at killing."

"Your father was not an accomplice to anything. He used to seek my advice, but he certainly doesn't need that anymore."

Appian ducked his head into the tent. "Medicus, a word? The Primus Pila says that you are free to go as long as you don't divulge our position, and that it would be best if you appear as a Greek trader. But he would prefer that you stay. He wishes that you speak with him."

"Tell him that this *libertus* doesn't care to speak with his Excellency. I'm going back to Athens."

"You're as stubborn as he is. You have no money, no weapons, and you'll be under constant surveillance. You won't make it."

"You won't need to, Greek," said the Primus Pila, stepping into the tent. "I apologize. What I said to you was vile. Stay and I will never insult you again."

Tacitus watched as Gaius abruptly turned and walked away. His father had not even glanced at him or at Sempronius.

Apollodoros stepped to the tent's open flap and stared into the distance.

"What could have possibly made your father apologize?" asked Sempronius.

"Sometimes even a hard man can have one or two human qualities," said Apollodoros, almost to himself. "But he can be such an ass!" He turned to Tacitus. "I've known him since he was a boy. He treated me with respect even though I was a slave. We did dangerous things together, things I've never spoken of."

"Like what?" asked Sempronius.

Apollodoros stared at the young man for a moment. "Together, we killed a man to save his father. That's what we did."

"How did you do that?" asked Tacitus, wondering how many more secrets Apollodoros had.

The *medicus* found a seat in the tent and sighed deeply. He gave it some thought and then said, "We killed a slave your grandfather owned."

"You actually killed someone? Why? When?"

"Your grandfather had beaten a slave named Aztecas and the man wanted revenge. We saw him coming through the atrium with a weapon in his hand. It was your father who put the knife into the man. He had no choice if I was to live.

Tacitus nodded. If a slave killed his master, every slave had to die. "What did my grandfather say after Aztecas was killed?"

"Nothing. We never told him what happened. We buried the man in a field."

"I never knew about any of that."

"Your family has many secrets," said Apollodoros. "Your grandfather was cunning and brutal, even treacherous, in his attempts to make a sestertius. He got into a scheme to smuggle slaves into Rome without paying duties on them. One of his associates, a client of his, was murdered when the slaves slipped out of their chains. Then they went on a killing spree. Your grandfather barely escaped with his life and feared that he would be implicated in the plot. Most of his endeavors failed. But sometimes people can change if they're scared or realize their limitations. Your grandfather did, later in life. Your grandmother did, too, after the accident."

"Accident?"

"Livia was a beautiful, shrill, and willful woman. She conspired and copulated with gladiators and wealthy men, tribunes and the like. Did you know that she detested her husband? Yes, she hated him, though they had much in common. She was, like her husband, calculating and devious. The *domina* was an inveterate social climber, but her ladder had missing rungs." Apollodoros rubbed his temples. "But I'm not sure I should be telling you all this. Your father might not—"

"My father tried to kill me today. I don't give a damn what he thinks, so you might as well."

"You really want to know?"

"Why not? We have time on our hands since it seems that you're staying and my father is figuring out what mistakes to make next," Tacitus said from a well of bitterness.

The Greek stared at his hands and shrugged his thin, hunched shoulders. "I'll tell you, but I'd rather you didn't mention it to him."

"Sure, if it makes you feel better."

The *medicus* sighed again and said, "Traumatic things can change people. As I said, your grandmother hated her husband, and they rarely spoke except to excoriate one another. One day she was shopping for a new slave. Wagons were supposed to be off the streets before dawn, but one was left on a hill because of a broken axle. Somebody jarred the wagon and it toppled. It was filled with heavy jars filled with wine. They rolled off and crashed into people. One jar hit her, slashing her face. She was never the same—wore a veil and begged your grandfather to keep her. Strangely enough, he did. It was very touching, considering how much they had conspired against one another. After the accident he quoted her the classics I'd taught him."

"Was his change sincere?"

"I believe so," said Apollodoros. "He knew that he had failed in nearly everything. He was a tormented, frightened man. He knew that people wanted to kill him, and in a way I precipitated it."

"How could you, being his slave?"

"It's really quite involved—intrigue, murder, adultery, and even a plot to assassinate a Roman consul. I witnessed it all. A slave must know everything in a household if he hopes to survive."

"So why was he so scared? What was he into?"

"One nefarious scheme after another, and for years he looked over his shoulder, expecting to be murdered. Your grandfather had failed in the silk business, and I suggested that he purchase and sell Egyptian antiques to wealthy Romans, Old Kingdom stuff. Your grandfather, Gaius and I traveled to Alexandria and canvased the souks. Of course I speak much better Greek than your grandfather since it's my native language. I helped him purchase several fine pieces— Thoth, Seth, and other god statues, from an old Jewish trader. We took the antiques to an inn where we were staying. All the inns were bars as well as brothels. That night while your father and I guarded the treasures, Toronius led a prostitute, a relative of the innkeeper, to an adjoining room where he nearly beat her to death. In fact he left her for dead."

"Did she die?" asked Sempronius.

"No, the girl lived. During the beating the girl ripped a valuable Egyptian necklace off his neck. When he realized it was gone, he ordered your father to go back to the room and retrieve it."

"Did he?" asked Tacitus.

"No, he left it with the whore out of sympathy. We escaped that night, but the Egyptians found our villa in

Rome; they had many contacts with ship captains and traders.

"For years your grandfather claimed to see the Egyptians everywhere, and he was terrified. Eventually they found him and tried to incinerate him in an old barn but, like the prostitute, he lived. And he changed. So your grandfather became a different man, Tacitus. I guess that sooner or later most of us do. I did and so will you."

"I don't see myself changing at all," said Tacitus.

Apollodoros gazed at the young man but said nothing.

***

"I've been here before," Apollodoros said as he scrutinized the drowsy village from the foothills of the Elburz Mountains. "I was a boy, maybe twelve, when I came this way with my father. I remember that mud brick wall down there and the broken stone tower. We traded for rhubarb here. It's worth its weight in gold; did you know that?"

"My aunt Junia used it as a diuretic," said Tacitus. "She said that it came from the east, but we didn't know where."

Although they had been slowed by the tedious trek through the mountains, the cohorts had journeyed 900 miles since leaving the Euphrates River. It was a tedious march as they passed the Caspian Sea and skirted the towns of Shahrud and Sabzevar where Parthian units were stationed. Dust raised by thousands of Romans, prisoners of the Parthians, still rose miles behind the legionnaires.

Appian found Tacitus sitting with Apollodoros and said, "The Primus Pila wants us to gather foodstuffs from the village fields. We'll do it tonight, when the farmers are asleep. It will be a fast in and out. The Parthians may be sending out advance patrols to search for supplies, so we won't loiter."

"If the villagers wake up they'll tell the Parthians about us. Then they'll be looking for us, not food," said Tacitus.

"So we must be silent. No armor and only a dozen men. Once done, we're back on the road," said Appian.

High above the village the cohorts found shelter from the slanting rays of the sun. They were still 200 miles from the city of Merv, the destination of the Parthian prisoners.

"Have you been to Merv?" Sempronius asked Apollodoros as they observed the farmers tilling their fields.

"Once. It was the furthest east we ever went."

"What's the road like once we leave here?"

"It's serviceable until we come to mountains called the Pamirs," said Apollodoros.

"How do we get past them?" asked Tacitus, overhearing the conversation.

"There's a pass through it called the Torugart. It's at 9,000 feet and can only be crossed in good weather. Winter snows make it a treacherous place. Once beyond the mountains, we will pass a town named Balkh. It's still in Parthian territory. Traders there sell blood-colored rugs. But it's a fertile place and has a decent climate. Not a bad place to live," said Apollodoros.

"Unless you happen to be a Parthian slave," Appian said.

A sense of unease had settled over the columns as they'd ventured further into unknown lands. How unlike the march to Carrhae, thought Tacitus. This hot, tiresome march was devoid of enthusiasm.

Gaius had studiously ignored Tacitus and his mates. He largely kept to himself except to exchange concerns with Appian or the Greek. Small advance parties were sent out to hunt or forage so the cohorts would not have to divulge their presence by making purchases from villagers along the way. But wild animals had become scarce. Despite the dangers, Gaius saw little alternative to raiding.

It was nearly dark when Tacitus and others dressed themselves in Parthian clothing. They watched the villagers finish the day's harvesting and retire to their mud brick homes. One by one the oil lamps were extinguished. The Romans waited two more hours before Gaius said, "Appian, it's time to go. No noise. Carry your knife, gladius, and a sack. Be back within the hour."

Silently they clambered over the undefended wall to the fields and sheds of the slumbering town. In the glint of a shadowed moon the legionnaires tore fruit off trees and broke into sheds, ransacking foodstuffs as they went. Suddenly Tacitus, Appian, and two other legionnaires came to a halt. Tacitus pointed and whispered, "There, maybe four of them, sleeping in the field."

"We'll go the other way," the trumpeter said.

They turned toward an outbuilding, its door ajar. Inside, a candle flickered, issuing a weak light. Slowly Apollodoros edged to the door and made way for Tacitus and Appian. Their shadows merged with that of a beef carcass and a pile of vegetables on a two-wheeled cart. Tacitus was about to fill his bag when a youth leapt from behind a bale of hay. A girl screamed and with knife in hand, the boy threw himself at Appian.

The attack was swift but the assailant tripped, and the knife only grazed the trumpeter's arm. Quickly Tacitus drew his *puglio* and sliced the youth's throat. The girl wailed. Tacitus turned toward her.

"No, it's too late for that," Apollodoros said over the shouts of wakened villagers. Some had armed themselves and rushed the shed only to be cut down. Oil lamps began to flicker in nearby houses as the Romans scurried back toward the surrounding wall.

The townspeople, who had no unified defense, didn't follow. Instead they raged at the inconceivable and senseless murder of their family member.

"They will send for help. We march immediately," said Gaius as soon as the raiders returned.

Weary but hoping to outdistance heavy cavalry, the cohorts hastened to get past Merv before the horsemen found them. Gaius allowed a brief halt 60 miles from the Oxus River. To some it was known as the Amu Darya, near the border of Parthia.

"We can't outrun them," Appian said to Gaius as they studied the dust plume that had risen since mid-morning.

"Parthian cavalry or Saka. They must have met with the townspeople. You're right; we won't get to the river quickly enough. We'll have to make a stand."

"But it must be someplace of our choosing."

"Precisely," said the Primus Pila.

***

Gaius Septimus knew the look of worried men. Seeing the approach of the horsemen imbued the legionnaires with a sense of dread. He desperately needed a victory.

"We must reach the hills and make our defense there," he said to Appian. The men, sweating in their armor, began a labored jog.

"There," Gaius said as the cohorts crested a slight rise. Before them was a flat plain flanked by high cliffs that formed a funnel, wide at the entrance and narrow toward the rear. Flash floods had sent water rushing over the promontories to cut narrow channels into the cliff's walls.

Centurions assigned the cohorts their positions. "How many horsemen are coming?" Appian asked Gaius.

"Two or three hundred, maybe more. Their main force is still guarding prisoners. I think we're facing a punitive expedition for what happened in the village."

Gaius quickly assembled his centurions and directed 100 men to both sides of the funnel at the bottom of the cliffs. "You will lie flat and stay hidden until you see my signal arrow," he told the men. Then he had Appian form up another hundred and place them in a visible double line across the entrance of the plain.

"We're going to do to them what the Carthaginians did to us at Cannae in the first Punic War. Remember the tactic?" said Gaius.

Appian and the other two centurions nodded as men hurried to their positions. The grim defeat and annihilation of over 200,000 legionnaires had been seared into the mind of every Roman. The final destruction of Hannibal's army and the transfer to Rome of Carthaginian Spain had only come about after two more wars against the North African empire. Carthage lay in ruins, but no one ever forgot the price. If the tactic could be repeated here, even on a very small scale, the Parthians and the Saka would be entering a very dangerous field.

"We will take very few prisoners, but allow no one to escape," Gaius instructed.

Bowstrings drawn, the jubilant Saka rode over a low hill in a dead charge. In the late afternoon sun the horsemen's baggy, brightly colored vestments fairly glowed as they launched their arrows at the thin lines of legionnaires. Using the turtle formation employed at Carrhae, the front rank held their shields before them while the second rank raised them above their heads. There was anxious silence as the horsemen fired their bolts, brought their horses to a halt, and pulled back to the top of the rise. Arrows plunged into shields and several men were struck, but the line held.

"Retreat!" ordered Gaius, and the men hurried to the narrow neck of the field. The Primus Pila attached a burning cloth to an arrow and waited.

***

The Saka commander surveyed the legionnaires. They were a pitiful number, as he had expected, but wore their full armor and carried heavy shields, hardly suitable for a harried and desperate escape through enemy country. It was a mystery as to why they would so encumber themselves. Still, with few bows and no scorpions with their deadly iron bolts, the Romans were virtually defenseless against a sustained attack.

Just as at Carrhae, the shields would disintegrate from volleys of arrows. Three, perhaps four charges and the Romans would break, and then his men would eviscerate them. Even now, obviously frightened by his agile riders, they were giving ground. The commander had no camels carrying great quantities of arrows, but he was not worried. Before him was only a band of dispirited survivors. Still, he had a nagging feeling that he should have planned for an early morning attack, when the sun would have been in the defender's eyes.

He observed his massed cavalry, impatient for the next charge. He wished that he had arrived earlier and caught the legionnaires in the open, not between the narrowing cliffs. It would be impossible to surround them now; a frontal attack was the only option. But it would be over within the hour. He didn't expect to lose a single man.

The king needed a quick and decisive victory. Orodes would expect nothing less.

There would be no bravado, nothing like Surena's self-congratulatory proclamations and parades in which he displayed the captured enemy standards and eagles. This miniscule operation was nothing but a skirmish. For the Saka, bored with guarding a shuffling line of prisoners, it was pure sport. No, the skirmish wouldn't be worthy of mention unless he were asked by the king himself. Then he would refer to it as a very minor force that had littered the Silk Road.

The commander squinted into the sun and tried to pick out the weakest point of the line. That legionnaire bones would be picked by scavengers was hardly fitting for the remnants of a once gallant army. But that wasn't his concern.

The field had no impediments, none of the five-pointed iron "lilies" to pierce hoofs and feet. Nor had the legionnaires had time to prepare deep but narrow pits to break the delicate legs of horses. The commander raised his arm and pointed toward the line of shields. Again the composite bows were armed and a surge of arrows streamed skyward. A second charge was on its way. From the Roman line a single flaming arrow arched upward.

As the Saka closed the range, two cohorts, one on each side of the cliffs, remained in concealment. Another cohort, unseen by the passing cavalry, streamed from their positions with captured bows and lay in the sand, waiting for the riders' return.

The horsemen fired their arrows while turned in the saddle and began their ride back to the low promontory at a more leisurely pace, their horses now winded. Again they had not lost a single man; the whole activity had become a game. Laughing, jostling one another, they cantered their mounts toward their starting positions, arrows still in their quivers. Suddenly, 20 yards to their front, the legionnaire bowmen rose and fired. A second and third volley tore into the unsuspecting riders. Men and horses fell, and pandemonium ensued as those still mounted careened into kicking and dying animals. A final volley was fired. Drawing the gladii, the legionnaires charged into the frenzied mass.

***

On Gaius's command the second and third cohorts rushed onto the field from the sides of the cliffs. Hundreds slammed into the Saka flanks, swords slashing at fallen riders, while other horsemen were torn from their mounts. With a shout, the cohort that had formed the *testudo*, with shields over their heads, bounded forward, completing the envelopment. Quickly enfilading the frantic Saka, the legionnaires bolted between the terrified animals. A massacre ensued; the legionnaire's frustration and hatred had found an outlet. Pleas for mercy were ignored; the butchering lasted only minutes.

Gaius spied the Parthian captain in the midst of his dying men, vainly attempting to organize a defense. "Take him alive," he shouted as the captain was about to be impaled. "Bind him, kill all the others."

The last of the enemy were quickly dispatched. "Examine the horses," Gaius commanded. His men confiscated bows and quivers and slashed the throats of the wounded mounts. They led over 100 unscathed horses away, leaving the field a tangle of corpses.

"Take all rings, pendants, and gold jewelry," he ordered. "We'll need it later on."

"What about the bodies?" asked Appian.

"Leave them just as they left us at Carrhae. We can't get rid of them, and their army will spot the vultures anyway. It might give them pause. Form up the cohorts; I want to get across the Oxus."

"And him?" Appian said, pointing to the tall Parthian captain.

"He'll learn to march. Put him with the lead cohort. We'll have a chat with him soon enough."

***

Standing tall, with dark, piercing eyes, and wearing bright colors, Diomedes put two fingers to his forehead and looked down on Merv from a distant hill.

"Is that where they're taking them?" asked Gaius.

"Yes, there beside the Murgab River."

"Why does Orodes want them there?"

"To build fortifications, buildings, and maybe a water system—the things you Romans are good at," said the Parthian drily.

"We're also good at killing Parthians and Saka."

"So I noticed. Your men fought well; the tactic was brilliant. I'm angry at my own overconfidence. I rarely make such mistakes."

"Marcus Crassus, the consul, had a similar problem, and we lost thousands."

"But he was taken in by a very unscrupulous Arab. Without the Arab's intervention it might have been a very different battle."

Apollodoros and Appian joined the two, taking a good look at the prisoner for the first time. The captain studied them as well. "My name is Diomedes. I was in the service of General Surena who is, or was, the leader of the most important Parthian clan."

"Was?" Appian said.

"The general was accused by the king of arrogance and beheaded shortly after the battle. The head was put on display as a warning to others. Orodes doesn't tolerate competition."

"So, if you had escaped our recent battle, your disaster might have caused some embarrassment," Gaius observed.

"Centurion, I can never go back to Ctesiphon," the man said with a wan smile. "I would be scheduling my own execution. Besides, I'm not really a Parthian. I'm Greek, raised by Parthians since I was a young child."

"I was curious about your pronunciation. It's the way Greek is spoken in Athens, like mine," said Apollodoros, looking into the man's dark, unwavering eyes.

"But you became a captain of Parthian horse?" Appian said.

The man shrugged. "A long story. But I can make it longer if you have the time," he said, a telltale smile on his face.

"We don't," said Gaius. Then to Appian, "We leave at the first hour tomorrow."

"Don't you want to see the captives enter Merv?" Apollodoros asked.

"No, we can't do anything for them. They're guarded by, what? Two thousand?"

"Three," countered Diomedes. "And they won't make the same mistake I did."

"Then we march out of Parthia," said Gaius. "We'll cut your bindings once we're away from here. Don't think of escape. You won't make it, and this isn't a nice place to die."

"I have no place to run. Besides, I'm as good as dead already. I'll never see my wife or daughter again."

"War has its price, and we all pay in the end," said Gaius. He took a last glance at Merv, where thousands of legionnaires would spend the remainder of their lives.

Chapter 10

Lieutenant Shang Gao hastened through the palace to the door of General Chen Tang. He nervously arranged his long silk coat and officer's sword, then entered the opulent office and kowtowed low before the exalted victor over the barbarians.

"Sit," said the general in a quiet voice. He pointed to a chair. Shang Gao sat, replaying his strategy in his mind.

"My Lord General, I came as quickly as I could. I knew that you would want a full explanation." From the sleeve of his coat he removed a paper scroll and placed it on the general's desk. "My report, which I trust gives a full account of my, that is, the army's actions."

General Tang glanced at the scroll, a slight smile playing on his lips, and leaned back in his dragon-foot chair. "I appreciate your promptness and I'm pleased to see that you survived. I only heard sketchy information about your deployment after I assigned you this mission. You are not injured, I presume?"

Shang's eyes took in the pastoral scenes decorating the walls; they seemed out of place in a military office. For a moment he was lost for words, even though he had practiced his verbal report ten times the night before.

"And Prince Wen Dao, is he well? I'm surprised that he didn't come with you."

Shang gazed at the floor. "My Lord General, it grieves me to report that the esteemed captain was slain in battle with the barbarians. It happened not far from the Great Wall."

"My nephew is dead? Exactly how is that? I must assume that they attacked and broke the truce since your small force was not to engage."

"My lord ..." Shang's voice broke and he struggled to control it. "Prince Dao and I proceeded through the Gate of Exiles to the fort at the end of the Wall. And, I must say, it's in need of great repair. It can be flanked quite easily."

The general only nodded. After a moment of hesitation Shang began again. "As you instructed, my superior, Prince Dao, I met with the local sub-officer of the fort, a lieutenant Pang Kwan, who was assigned to accompany us as we surveyed the Wall.

"We had proceeded thirty miles when we spotted a Chanyu village. Lieutenant Kwan became quite excited, saying that the barbarians had kidnapped and imprisoned three of our peasant women. Prince Dao said that we should free them. He was quite adamant, despite the fact that we were only a reconnaissance unit."

"What did you say about that?"

"Although I was a junior officer and respected my captain, I reminded him of our orders. As a student and military officer I studied the lessons of the great Sun Tzu and I knew that Prince Dao was making a mistake. I argued quite strenuously, and was reprimanded for my impertinence. He said that since it was my first sortie I should just watch, listen, and obey. But I sensed disaster and told him that we had too few men for an attack against the hilltop position."

General Chen Tang studied Shang. "My nephew was a cautious man. He was only twenty-three—just eight years older than you—but he'd served me well in numerous battles. He must have been easily swayed by this commoner from the fort."

"Absolutely, Lord General," Shang Gao said nervously. "For him the thought of rescuing the women and delivering a punishing blow to the barbarians became an unwavering challenge. Try as I might, I could not dissuade him."

"What happened next?" asked the general, twisting his long black moustache.

"Prince Dao announced that we should have a diversionary move. He ordered me to take 30 infantry and attack the village from one flank while he, Lieutenant Kwan, and the rest of the men proceeded up a pathway beside a steep hill."

"And the barbarians? Where were they?"

"Captain Dao was certain that the Chanyu hadn't seen us and said that they were in the village, since it was dinnertime. This assumption worried me, but I continued toward the village as ordered. Quite suddenly the Chanyu cavalry swept down the steep hill and pushed Captain Dao and his soldiers toward a ravine. Those not instantly killed fell to their deaths. I saw Captain Dao fight bravely, but he had no chance against the onslaught."

"What became of Lieutenant Kwan?"

"I'm certain he also perished. And though we were some distance from the massacre, I saw it all."

General Tang rolled his calligraphy pen slowly between his fingers. "And what did you do while this was happening?"

"There were still four dozen Chanyu riders in the village. They mounted up and tore into my men. I knew that my small force would be outnumbered and outfought. Certainly we couldn't enter the village. My thoughts turned to assisting any survivors of my unit or that of Prince Dao. I must say that my contingent fought well; we impaled many horsemen with the *jian*."

"But you and some of your men escaped after this remarkable defense against at least 50 mounted?"

Shang stopped for a moment, not knowing whether he was being praised or mocked. "Sir, it was late in the day and the barbarians went back to their village, taking their dead and wounded with them. I'm only guessing that there were 50. There might have been more. I, and the few who survived, retreated. Unfortunately, all who survived were grievously wounded."

"So you escaped and returned to the fort. How many of your men did you save with this resolute action?"

"None, sir," Shang mumbled. "None of them survived their wounds."

General Chen Tang gave the youth a dark look and raised a palm, suggesting that he required further explanation.

"It was almost dark, my Lord General. I was on my horse when the Chanyu attacked us. It happened very quickly."

"But you lived," said Chen Tang. It was not exactly an accusation, but Shang swallowed hard and nodded.

"Perhaps I should have stayed and died with them. I fought the best I could. Many of the barbarians tried to pull me off my horse. I repelled them as I had been trained. But had I stayed, no one would have known of Prince Dao's heroic action against the Chanyu."

"Or his ineptness, Lieutenant?" The general's eyebrows rose again. "And what became of his body? I hope it has been recovered to be returned to his grieving parents."

"I pray it has. I couldn't wait for that to be done. I didn't expect any reinforcements. I hastened back to give you this report and my recommendation."

"Recommendation?"

"Yes, Lord General. You required my assessment. I recommend that the Wall be completed and fortified so that there can be no more barbarian raids."

"Fortified against further raids," General Tang repeated. A moment passed and he said, "You should tender your condolences to the family of Prince Dao and speak of his bravery. Say nothing of his indiscretion. We will not sully the family name."

The general studied Shang for what seemed an eternity. "Tragic things happen in war. Sometimes cautious men do imprudent things. So it apparently was with my nephew. But you arrived here safely.

"I know that this, your first battle, has been difficult for you. And it is equally difficult when a friend dies, regardless of the circumstances. You will become stronger as you continue your military career, and you were right to counsel restraint, even toward a superior officer."

Shang barely had time to feel relieved when the general said, in a more conversational tone, "Your father has suggested that our families might profit from a union between you and my daughter. It would be a few years from now, but I'm wondering how you would respond to that."

"I would be honored, Lord General. I do like her, but I don't think she particularly cares for me."

"She's an obedient girl and will do as required. I'm sure in time she will come to like you if you treat her well. Your father, I, and the soothsayers will determine the course of events. But this will be considered at a later time. For now you'll return to your barracks. I'll pass on your assessment of the Wall. It just so happens that I agree with you."

Shang's hands were shaking. Hopefully, the general would think it was due to anxiety and nothing else.

***

Sima Gao rubbed his temples. Compared to the wars between the Han Dynasty and the barbarian hordes, the brief conflict between Prince Dao and the Chanyu was trifling. And it would have been considered unimportant except that it violated a truce that cost the Emperor a distressing amount of treasure. The cessation of hostilities may have been violated by the kidnapping of three Chinese women, but Sima, the minister of security and censorship, felt that the dispute could have been solved through negotiation. He'd had a bevy of questions, since the attack on the village by Han forces resulted in many dead and the endangerment of his own son. And though all would mourn the death of Prince Dao, the entire debacle had to be truthfully recorded in detail.

Thus it was necessary that an officer from the fort be summoned to Chang'an to answer pointed questions. A lone lieutenant arrived two weeks after the incident and was escorted to Sima's office.

The young man seemed flustered, and kowtowed before the minister, his forehead touching the floor. He remained in that position until Sima ordered him to stand. The lieutenant favored one leg, perhaps due to a recent wound. The minister glanced over a scroll and said, "I have a battlefield report indicating that the officer from the garrison at the Wall was killed. His name was Lieutenant Pang Kwan of the Twenty-

Ninth Frontier Guards. So there are some matters to be resolved."

"My Lord Minister, I am Lieutenant Pang Kwan of the Frontier Guards."

"How could that possibly be? The report states that you were killed."

"I barely survived. I was wounded, as you can see."

"Yes, well, you may be seated."

"Thank you, Lord Minister. The journey here was long and my leg has not healed as quickly as I had hoped."

"We are pleased that you survived the battle. We also hope your wound won't hamper your service to the Emperor. From this report I read that you and your men were assaulted by the barbarians after Prince Dao initiated a reckless attack against a Chanyu village. The engagement, I understand, was initiated because three Han women had been taken by the raiders—a piece of information you gave to Prince Dao."

"I did indeed tell the Prince that three of our women were held in the village, but I also told him that they were to be freed the next day. Their release had been negotiated for the cost of five horses."

The Minister of Censorship and Security knitted his brow and scanned the paper.

"Strange that something so important is not mentioned in the report," said Sima, adjusting his exquisite silk robe. "What I find vexing is how insistent Prince Dao was in attacking the village and how stubborn he remained in the face of sensible counsel."

"Sir, I'm not sure I understand."

"It's all right here, young man." Sima waved the scroll. "Prince Shang Gao strenuously attempted to dissuade Captain Dao from attacking the village."

Seeing that the minister was quite agitated, the young man lowered his head. He was ready to comply with anything the exalted man required. He looked up again when Anshi Zhaojun arrived. Anshi, holding the office of Minister of Histories, would be responsible for keeping a record of the incident.

Sima nodded to his old friend, handed him the battle report, and turned his attention to the lieutenant. "You must realize the significance of the action beyond the Wall, and I want you to know that everything said here will be presented to the Emperor. But, unless instructed otherwise, you will say nothing about this interrogation. Is that understood?"

"Yes, absolutely. I will say nothing."

"According to that report the senior lieutenant was killed, but it fails to mention that the release of the female hostages was already negotiated. So why was the attack even necessary, except for hotheaded revenge or glory?" Sima Gao stared, mystified, at the lieutenant.

"Perhaps the officer should relate the entire misadventure in detail," said Anshi Zhaojun, handing the paper back to Sima.

"I think that's advisable. Now, Lieutenant, we want the truth and you are honor bound to give it. We will not judge your actions at this time." Sima spoke softly, hoping to put the young officer at ease. "If you have done nothing wrong you have nothing to fear. One's rank or court position is of no consequence in this matter."

Lieutenant Pang Kwan sighed.

"I was beside Prince Shang Gao and Prince Dao until the unit was split into two parts. We inspected the condition of the Wall and progressed 90 li when we saw the barbarian village. We had parlayed with the headmen for the release of the women. That was before the arrival of Prince Shang Gao. We had met the Chanyu in the desert where the transfer would take place, but they warned us not to come near their village. They were afraid we would bring bad spirits and said that they would fight to keep us out.

"When Prince Shang Gao heard that Han women were being held, he immediately demanded that we launch an attack against the village. I tried to explain about their scheduled release, but he ignored me and taunted Prince Dao in front of the infantry."

"What was Prince Dao's response?" asked Zhaojun.

"He said that the attack was unwarranted, that destroying Chanyu villages was not his mission. He also cited Sun Tzu and said that the Great Sage would be opposed to such an attack."

"But Prince Dao did attack," said Sima.

"Yes, because he began to look weak and cowardly in front of the men. This reflected badly upon him because he was known as an overly cautious man. He became angry. In the face of insults he said, 'Okay, if you want war, there will be war! But if it turns to disaster, Shang Gao, it will be on your head!' It was very uncharacteristic of him. He told Lieutenant Gao to take 30 men and, as a diversionary tactic, attack the village from the south while he led the bulk of our force up the hill from the north."

"The report says that the barbarians rode down a hill into your column," said the Minister of Histories.

"That's correct, my lord, we were in columns of two and had to climb a steep uphill path toward the village. The barbarians' massed cavalry plowed into us. We were nearly annihilated. I and several of my men rolled down a steep cliff and landed on a ledge. Others were not so fortunate, including Prince Dao."

"Where was my son during this time?" said Sima.

The lieutenant's eyes grew wide, and a tiny squeak escaped his throat. Gao was a common name; apparently the lieutenant had not realized the connection until that moment.

"Prince Gao was already in full retreat from the village when we were swept away. Instantly we saw the folly of our action; our assault was senseless," the lieutenant said, bitterness in his voice.

"What happened to Prince Shang Gao's force?" asked Anshi Zhaojun.

"They were surrounded and cut down."

"But Prince Gao stayed and fought alongside his men, did he not?" pried Sima Gao.

"He did for a brief moment, until he saw that all would be killed. Then he spurred his horse. I waved from the ledge, hoping to get his attention. I don't know if he saw me or not, but he didn't stop. He was in full flight. I and four others waited until darkness so that we could escape."

There was a lengthy stillness. The Minister of Censorship and Security looked at the lieutenant, stone-faced. "I say again, none of this will be repeated to anyone in this palace or anywhere else. Is there anything more?"

"Only this, my lord. We took the five horses to the barbarians two days later and brought the women back. The Chanyu then allowed us to retrieve our dead."

"So, Minister," said Anshi Zhaojun, "there is no need for any reprisal against the Chanyu."

"Apparently not."

Anshi Zhaojun rose from his gilded chair. He approached Sima, leaned over, and whispered, "Don't be concerned; nothing about your son's action will enter the record. The case is dead." With that the Minister of Histories quickly left the chamber.

Sima turned back to the lieutenant. "You are dismissed. I suggest that you return to your post at daybreak tomorrow."

The young man kowtowed. He began to back out when Shang, hurrying through the door, bumped into him.

"So sorry." Shang Gao stopped short and stared at the officer. He looked to his father, then Lieutenant Pang Kwan. "Thank the Fates that you survived," he said in a thin voice. "I feared that you were dead."

"Did you not see me on the ledge that day?"

"No," stammered Shang. "I assumed that everybody in the ravine was dead. How were you able to run from there?"

"We who survived did not run. You did."

The lieutenant looked hard at Shang and stormed out of the room.

"Father, I had no idea that—"

"Silence! I'll tell you when to talk. Come here."

Shang glanced once at the door, then stood before his father.

"You reported that he was killed; apparently you were wrong. I just interrogated him and he contradicted virtually everything that you reported to General Tang. According to Pang Kwan, it was you who instigated the attack, after insulting Captain Dao. Then you fled the field, leaving your men to die at the hands of the barbarians. I could have you executed. Indeed, if the Emperor learns of this, he'll order it. What have you to say?"

Shang Gao dropped to his knees, his forehead banging on the floor. "No, I beg you, Father, don't tell him. Please don't. It was foolish of me and I must, I will, make amends."

"You most certainly will! You were thinking of your own glory. Did you believe that you would be rewarded by the Emperor for attacking people with whom we have a truce?"

"It was about the Han women, rescuing them from the barbarians, Father. I thought it would be noble. I had no idea that we would be ambushed and destroyed."

"Nonsense! Lieutenant Kwan told you that the women were to be released. But you decided to vilify your commanding officer in front of his men and go to war over three peasants!"

There was dead silence until Lord Sima Gao finally said, "Get off your knees. You are fortunate that I and the Minister of Histories are the only persons in court who know exactly what happened. I don't know what General Chen Tang will do if he ever learns the truth."

Shang stood, visibly shaken. "Will you tell him or the Emperor?"

"No," Sima said in a barely audible voice. "But not for your sake. For our family's and my own reputation. The Emperor's anger may not stop with your head alone."

"What of Lieutenant Pang Kwan? He knows everything. What if he or his commander goes directly to the Emperor?"

"He was ordered to say nothing, but his commander might write his own account of the battle and inform General Tang. Of course I would try to intercept it, but there could be a further inquiry with repercussions."

"What if Lieutenant Kwan's commander is immediately reassigned to a distant station? Perhaps even promoted and given a command of his own? He might forget about the entire incident."

"A cunning idea," admitted Sima. "But the orders would be initiated by General Chen Tang. There would have to be adequate reason, lest he become suspicious."

"Father, it could be said that the lieutenant fought bravely, saved some of his men, and deserves special consideration. Pang Kwan can be detained here to avoid communication and a fast courier could be sent to his captain at the Wall."

"I'll suggest the idea to General Tang, but you will say nothing about any of this."

"Yes, Father." Shang hesitated for a minute. "I reported right away to General Chen Tang as I was required to do. He didn't question my report. But, quite strangely, he asked me how I would feel about marrying his daughter."

Strange indeed. Why would Chen Tang discuss the subject with the boy instead of with his father? "What was your reply?"

"I said that I would be pleased, indeed honored."

"That's the most intelligent thing you have done for a very long time. I, too, would like to see such a union; our status would rise greatly. The idea should be encouraged, but it must be done subtly."

"But surely, Father, it is he who should be indebted. You, after all, are Minister of Censorship and Security. That's an honored position."

"It would behoove you to learn more about court politics," said Sima. "I am the Minister of Censorship and Security, but I serve at the whim of the Emperor, who is influenced by the Empress, his concubines, and the eunuchs. I am hardly invulnerable and, having sent many dignitaries to the executioner, I have many enemies. You of all people should know that the court is a snake pit. Ministers come and go at the Emperor's whim. They're in an audience with him one day and a slave the next. But General Tang is formidable. He won a war against the barbarians. The Emperor favors his counsel. None of those Court vipers will dare sully his name—he's beyond reproach. You must give General Chen Tang the greatest respect, and it's imperative that you cultivate the trust of his wife and daughter."

"Thankfully, Father, it's not up to Li Mae Tang to decide upon the marriage. She quite detests me."

"Make her not detest you!" Sima shouted. "It's time to grow up. I made it possible for you to become an officer in the service of the Emperor, and look at what you've done. I'll save your life and your career, but you must do our family honor."

"But I don't know how to approach Li Mae Tang, or her mother. The girl won't even look at me since I killed her cricket four years ago."

"Then do something nice for her, something she doesn't expect. You studied the military tactics of the great sage. What does he say about deception and gaining the confidence of one who opposes you? You must find allies, perhaps Li Mae Tang's mother. Yes, charm her, make her think that your previous behavior was that of a foolish child and you have since become a gentleman and a noble officer in His Excellency's service. Show her that you are worthy of her daughter. Then use her influence. Everything in life is shadow and illusion. Study again Sun Tzu's *Art of War*. His strategies and tactics for conquest are not just through force of arms."

***

Li Mae walked with her mother and Ming Zhaojun through the Shanglin Gardens in the Jianzhang Palace. As she exited a pavilion of master calligraphers, Ming nudged her and pointed. There was Prince Shang Gao, wearing his military finery and looking directly at her.

Li Mae stiffened. Shang gave her a tense smile. Holding a fine cedar box, he bowed to her mother and said, "I want to tender my apologies for my childish and insufferable behavior. Please accept this humble gift as a token of my respect for you, your daughter, and the esteemed general. I only hope that I can wipe away the stain of my earlier years. As an officer of the Emperor's army, my only desire is to serve the Middle Kingdom in all its glory."

Jia Zhou Tang accepted the gift without comment. Prince Shang Gao made a courtly bow, nodded again to Li Mae, and strode away.

"Isn't that the most bizarre thing you ever heard?" said Ming. "He even smiled at you."

Li Mae wrinkled her nose. "That's not like him, not at all."

"Lady Tang, are you going to open the box?" asked Ming.

"I guess I should." She walked to a stone bench. Li Mae and Ming were close behind.

"Be careful, Mother, it may be full of dead crickets," said Li Mae.

"Or their body parts," added Ming.

Lady Tang gave them a baleful look. "You two are becoming as jaded as I am."

The lid of the box featured an elegantly carved dragon with inlaid ivory. She admired it, then slowly lifted the lid. "Oh, look at this!" she exclaimed. From the box she pulled out an exquisite blue silk scarf with embroidered butterflies in silver and gold thread.

"It must have cost him a fortune," said Ming.

"There's something else inside, in that smaller box," said Li Mae.

Handing the scarf to her daughter, Lady Tang opened the smaller container, one made of bronze with etched cranes in flight. She peered in and lifted a three-inch glass vial, something so rare that only the wealthiest could afford it. The container, made of multicolored glass, featured a delicate silver stopper.

"Perfume?" asked Ming.

Lady Tang lifted the stopper and sniffed. "Wonderful," she said, holding the container out for the girls to sniff.

"Where did it come from?" asked Li Mae.

"Somewhere far to the west, I believe," said her mother. "The Sogdiani buy expensive things from a place called Parthia, and I'm told that they trade with an empire even further west. But I don't know where that might be. Perhaps your father knows." She handed Li Mae the vial. "I think the young prince actually wants you to have the perfume."

"I don't want any gift from him. If I wear it he'll think I like him, and I don't."

"Then just put it on the shelf where he could see it if he is ever invited to our home."

"I'll hide it and I hope he never comes," said Li Mae.

"One never knows what the Fates may decide for us," replied her mother.

Ming shook her head. "I still don't know why Shang Gao would give such an expensive gift. After all, he's made himself completely despicable for years."

"I'm sure he has a motive," said Li Mae.

"He does, my dear daughter. The motive is you."

"Me?"

"Of course. Think about it and you'll understand. It's like the game of Go. This is Prince Shang Gao's first move with the black stone. I'm certain that there will be others."

"If I were to play," said Li Mae, "I would destroy him with the white stone, and the game would be over. Forever."

***

"I'm gratified that you agreed to promote Lieutenant Pang Kwan, as well as his commander, for their noble actions. In fact, the lieutenant deserves his own battalion. And I presume that you also transferred him to the east," said the Minister of Censorship and Security.

The impromptu meeting, at Chen Tang's request, took place in his office.

"When did he leave the palace?" asked Sima.

"Five weeks ago. I promoted him as you suggested, but I felt that he was needed at the Wall, so I ordered him back."

"I see," said Sima. "I received your invitation this morning. I was to meet with the scholars, but begged off. I absolutely detest their pomposity."

"They do think highly of themselves." Chen put aside his calligraphy pen. "I received two letters from the captain at the fort along the Wall. The first came three days ago, asking when he should expect Pang Kwan. He should have returned by now."

"I would think so, unless something delayed him. Maybe he has a concubine along the way," Sima Gao said with a rare grin.

"Mmm. I rather doubt it. I sensed that he wanted to return as soon as possible, perhaps to get away from here. And I was puzzled, since the young man seemed so obedient.

Then two days ago I received notice that his body was found by farmers a day's ride from the palace."

"He's dead?" said the Minister of Censorship and Security. "I'm amazed, but maybe I shouldn't be. He was traveling alone and was given money for his return trip. Unfortunately, there are still bandits along the roads, despite our decapitations."

"I had considered bandits, but he hadn't been robbed. His horse was down, as if it had fallen on him. I had my doubts, so I sent an officer to inquire. He believes that the lieutenant was murdered."

"If not by bandits, then by whom? A paramour or a jealous husband?"

"I have no idea. We may never know."

"Most unfortunate."

"Yes, especially since he was the only person, except for Prince Shang Gao, who survived the battle against the Chanyu."

"Surely you're not—"

"No, no," said the general, holding up his hand to halt Minister Gao's indignation. "But the little wound through the kidney was well hidden, and the assailant planned it well—a deserted road at night, no observers, and a quick attack. Not something accomplished by an untrained hand. Perhaps I should investigate it further."

"Perhaps, but it's also a matter of state security, which is under my jurisdiction."

Chen stroked his beard. "Do as you think necessary, but I may still pursue the matter. Be advised that I must reply to the post commander."

"Of course," replied Sima evenly. "Does anybody else know about the presumed murder; that is, anybody besides your trusted officer?"

"No. And he was told to say nothing, except to me."

"Good. Then I will investigate it thoroughly," said Lord Gao.

Sima Gao was at the door when General Chen Tang said, "Oh yes, Minister, my wife wishes to thank your son for the fine gifts. It takes a man of special character to offer an apology, even if so much time has passed."

"He told me that he did it as a matter of personal honor. I know that he upset your daughter years ago, but he's trying to make amends. His youthful errors were especially embarrassing to me. I believe he's growing up."

"It can be a lengthy process. I think we both know that, don't we?" Chen said with a grin.

"Yes, I'm afraid so. I dread thinking back on some of my follies. But I do appreciate my son's efforts at civility."

"So do I. Perhaps with that old blemish behind us, you and your family might honor us with a visit to our house this spring."

Sima Gao smiled. "The honor would be ours." He made a slight bow and left the general's chamber.

There had not yet been any indication that the prince had killed the lieutenant. Perhaps he was overreaching. After all, anybody might have done it. But what if it was Prince Shang Gao? That would lead to a host of problems, not the least being that it could be an impediment to any consideration of marriage to his daughter. The victim had been an officer in his own army. Was the possibility of murder being concealed by Minister Gao?

General Chen Tang considered himself an honorable man, but he was well aware of the machinations and intrigues of the court. The accusation of murder against the son of a trusted official could be dangerous and would certainly end any liaison between his family and that of Sima Gao.

Yet, knowledge was power. What power would he have over Sima Gao if the minister knew that the murder was known to the father of the future bride? An obscure but subtle suggestion regarding his son-in-law's complicity would ensure that he'd never be a threat.

And the safety of his daughter? Well, a gentle but terrifying whisper in the ear of young Prince Shang Gao, and she would never have reason to fear.

Murderers made mistakes, and a youthful assailant, surely excited during his vengeful act, had likely made more than one.

Chapter 11

"They're still following us," said Fortunius.

Aurelius looked back at the plodding camels with their Kyrgyz riders, then up toward rocky crags high above. "There are some up ahead, too."

"Maybe we can find a trail off the main road before night and lose them."

"Those people know every trail, every deer path," countered Quintillus. "We're going to have to deal with them sooner or later."

"We can set up a defense in those rocks," said Fortunius. "Kill some and discourage the others."

"We'll run out of water and they can starve us out. But they're traders, perhaps we can give them something for our passage," said Fortunius.

"I doubt we have anything they would want. They may be traders but they're also slavers and murderers," said Quintillus.

"You have that pendant hanging around your neck, the one you took from Tacitus," said Aurelius. "It might give us some time to haggle. Maybe we can fall in with them and teach them a few things before we get away."

"If they don't attack before dark we can build a fire, make it look like we've settled in, then head back. We might get past their rear guard," said Fortunius.

Quintillus snorted. "And head back to the cohorts?"

Relieved that they had not been pursued by their former comrades, they had hurried along the mountain trail. It wasn't until two days later that they became aware of nomads who had given a wide berth to the cohorts.

"I didn't see them when we passed this way before," said Aurelius.

"Of course not. They wouldn't care to take on 400 legionnaires," replied Fortunius. "Now the odds are on their side."

He should not have come, Aurelius admitted to himself. The whole idea of a few men, alien to the country and not speaking the language, making good an escape over thousands of miles was ludicrous. Yet at the time, the pent-up frustration of an endless march had driven him into Quintillus's camp. The plotting, cunning, and manipulation had had their effect. "We'll pillage when we need to," argued Quintillus. "The Primus Pila and the cohorts will never waste the time to chase us down. In fact, they'll think we'll become discouraged and will beg to be taken back."

It would be 60 miles to the first settlement where they could buy food. But Roman coins were not made of gold, and what value would a few denarii have out here? The few people they had encountered on the march since Carrhae appeared wary and usually slunk away from the massed Roman force. It was doubtful that any meeting with the locals could be advantageous.

Now each time he looked back, Aurelius saw men behind them. Turning, he peered up at a precipice and spied a Kyrgyz with a copper mirror signaling to those below. A moment later dozens of men spilled onto the road and the thud of hoofbeats came from behind.

"Don't draw your gladii yet," said Quintillus. "Let's look congenial and try to parley."

The cameleers did not dismount and remained 20 paces behind, but those who descended from the heights quickly confronted the legionnaires. The Kyrgyz leader, a grizzled old man, placed his hands on his hips and scrutinized the three deserters. He gave a toothy smile, then came very close and touched Quintillus's armor. His eyes strayed to the pendant and he made a face as if appraising its value. He reached for it but Quintillus pushed his hand away. The nomad frowned, then looked back at his fellows, raising his palms as if to say, "He doesn't want to give it to me."

Quintillus pointed to the piece then at the leader and finally the road ahead. The Kyrgyz said "Ahh," and also pointed to the road beyond. He moved his fingers, indicating that Quintillus should give it to him, but the legionnaire shook his head and with a movement of his hands suggested that they all proceed together.

The Kyrgyz gazed dispassionately at Quintillus. He turned and spoke rapidly to a youth, who dashed forward to snatch the amulet. But the flash of the razor-sharp *puglio* was faster and his hand, detached from his wrist, spun into the brush beside the road. Screaming, he clutched the stump of his wrist while his companions, eyes wide, stared at the bloody knife.

Three blades now confronted the Kyrgyz as the youth attempted to staunch the gushing blood. Total silence followed and several of the nomads stepped back until their leader shouted an order. With a rush, a dozen charged forward, knives drawn. Three were quickly impaled, while two more lost arms before the three deserters retreated, their backs against a boulder. Facing them were eight men with bows, the strings pulled taut.

"Leave the shields, they'll only slow us down," Quintillus had said before they'd stolen away from the legionnaires' encampment. Now at very close range the archers could not miss. Aurelius could almost feel the arrow penetrating his skull. Dozens of eyes bored into him as bowstrings were pulled tight. If one archer fired, all would follow suit. Only a fanatical charge could disperse the Kyrgyz, but it would be suicide.

A sudden shout came from the nomad leader. There was a heated exchange with his band. Stepping to the front he pointed at the Romans, then the archers, and indicated that the three must drop their weapons. A moment passed as Aurelius exchanged glances with Fortunius, and Quintillus said, "Do what they ask—drop the gladii. We'll plan something later."

Cautiously their weapons were confiscated, including the *puglio*s. Once more the Kyrgyz leader pointed to the pendant, and this time Quintillus removed it and handed it to the gnarled leader.

Chained together and with wrists bound, the three were led away as darkness descended on the desolate Silk Road.

***

"Quadriga Gracchus, don't you dare splash me again!" cried Tullia, brushing water from her long, white stola. The three-year-old boy laughed and stomped in the impluvium, his blond curls glinting in the morning sun.

"He's grown so," said Ophelia. "If only his father could see him, he'd be proud."

"He would be, if he were alive," said Junia, watching the child as he decided it was wiser to splash water on a pigeon than his mother's dress.

"You know I asked Caladria if Tacitus was dead," Tullia said in a hushed voice, glancing toward the plump woman who sat alone in the arbor. "She would know; she can speak to the spirits. Isn't that right, Aunt Junia?"

"Yes, but she usually speaks in riddles. Gaius and his father consulted her and believed that she could see the future as well. But now when she speaks, and she rarely does, it's mostly to herself. The woman just sits beneath a tree, like she did when she was a slave."

"So what did Caladria say about Tacitus?" asked Ophelia.

"When I asked her," said Tullia, "she just sat there and moaned for a long time. Then, when I was about to leave, she said, 'I can't see Azteca anymore and Aspacia is always busy.' I asked her where Tacitus is and she raised her arm and sort of pointed toward the east."

"And because of that you think he's still alive?!" exclaimed Ophelia.

"Well if Caladria can't see or speak to him it means he's not dead."

"But you sent letters to Tacitus after the battle at Carrhae and he has never answered. It's been almost four years now. Surely he would have written if he were alive," said Junia, speaking softly. She peered into the haze coming off the Tiber, then faced Tullia. "When Cassius got back to Syria he had thousands of survivors, but none of them were from Gaius's legion. And Tacitus had to be with Gaius."

"Some think that many were captured by the Parthians," said Tullia.

"Maybe so, but none have ever come home. It's terribly sad, Tullia, but, captured or dead, it's the same; he'll never come back. You must accept that," said Junia.

"I think she's right," said Ophelia. "Sempronius was also with Tacitus and I never heard from him, either." Ophelia was unusually quiet for a moment. "It's time you look at reality, as hard as it is, Tullia. They're all gone. But you are still young and pretty, and little Quadriga needs a father. You can marry and find a man to take care of both of you."

Tullia watched her child play with a toy trireme in the shallow impluvium. "Rome has hundreds of thousands of pretty women, free and slave, and I have a child. What man would be interested in me?"

"My brother Servius asked me about you. I know he likes you."

"He's in the army."

"Who says you have to marry? Many soldiers are posted to garrisons in nearby towns. He would send for you and Quadriga. You'd be his wife in all but name," said Ophelia. "It would be the same with Tacitus if he were still alive. He couldn't marry you, either. At least not until he was discharged, and that wouldn't be for another 15 years. You can't live in your aunt Junia's house forever."

The thought of having no place to go had long worried Tullia. As if reading her mind, Junia put a hand on her shoulder. "I'm not going to ask you to leave. I need your help around the villa now that Delila is too old to do anything, though I'll never sell her for the few denarii she'd fetch. And besides, I adore your son. But you should have a man to help you raise him, and Servius can do that. At least give it some thought."

Tullia slowly nodded. "I'll think about it, for Quadriga's sake." Then turning to Junia she said, "But what if Tacitus comes back? What will I say to him if I'm living with Servius?"

"What could he possibly expect after being gone for so long without a single letter? I'm sure he'd understand," said Ophelia.

"Let me tell you something, Tullia," Junia said. "I never mentioned this before, but Tacitus would still be in Rome if Gaius had been around to see him grow up. He never would have gotten into trouble as he did. He would never have had to join the army, either. Gaius would have given him discipline, something he sorely needed."

"But he wouldn't have met me. I also joined Tacitus's gang, and would have been killed if I had entered the temple like they did."

"Killed? In a temple? What are you talking about?" asked Ophelia.

"It was a few months before I met you," Tullia said, taking a sip of her morning wine. "There were five boys in our gang and several were jealous that Tacitus was getting all my attention. One of them, the leader, wanted to impress me by having us do something extremely dangerous."

"Like stealing things?" asked Ophelia.

"we'd done that already. Our gang was a very naughty bunch. One of the boys was from a rich family, but others like me were poor and lived in the woods outside the Aurelian Wall.

"I've told you about how Tacitus and his father didn't get along. When Gaius Aquilius came home from the war in Gaul he came to this very house. He and Tacitus got into a horrible argument. Tacitus insulted his father and was beaten for it. He wanted to get back at him. Our leader decided that we should steal money from the tithing plate of a temple. He thought it wouldn't be guarded late at night. Tacitus and I were to stand behind a nearby tree to watch for anybody who might come along during the robbery. Suddenly priests appeared and Tacitus ran in to warn the boys, but they had been caught, and one had already been killed."

"Robbing a temple—what a daring thing!" exclaimed Ophelia.

"Worse than that," said Junia.

"It was Tacitus's mother's temple, Diana of the Woodlands, sacred to her, and of course everything about Aspacia was sacred to his father, Gaius," said Tullia.

"But you said that Gaius didn't believe in the gods," said Ophelia.

"He did until Aspacia's death," said Tullia. "Gaius prayed and even gave money to the temple for the goddess to save Aspacia, but she died anyway. The goddess, Diana, was Aspacia's deity and that's what mattered. Gaius paid off the high priest to release Tacitus. He then forced him into the army. I went with Aunt Junia to Campus Martius and begged Gaius to let him go, but it was too late; he had already taken the oath."

"Did Tacitus know about the baby?"

"No. I didn't even know I was pregnant at that time. I conceived the night Tacitus was given a furlough. It was right after he had finished his training. We secretly met at our favorite spot. I remember the splatter of the rain on our tent and how wonderfully romantic it was. He told me that he had to return early the next day or he would be in trouble. But we had exhausted ourselves and fell asleep. That morning Tacitus woke up late. He kissed me goodbye and ran back to the encampment. He and the legions of Marcus Crassus left Rome a week later and I never saw him again."

She was silent for a long moment, then said, "To be honest, I don't think he'll ever come back."

"You'll cherish his memory forever," Ophelia said gently. "But if you wish, I'll tell Servius that he would be welcome to visit."

Tullia wiped a tear from her cheek and nodded. Instinctively her hand went to her chest, where the gold pendant used to be, the one she'd given to Tacitus on their last night together. She wondered where it might be now. If he was alive, might he still have it? What if it adorned the neck of some woman—would she ever know the love it signified? The thought brought forth another tear and her vision became a blur.

***

"Who are they?" Sempronius asked.

Tacitus, along with the other sentries, watched the procession of travelers as they came slowly but steadily toward the Roman encampment. Ibericus and Diomedes joined them on the outcrop above the road.

"Kyrgyz, most likely," responded Diomedes. "Probably traders in gold, rugs, and slaves. Many are thieves and cutthroats. Some were allowed into Ctesiphon, but we kept a close watch on them."

"Do they speak Greek?" asked Tacitus.

"A few words, perhaps. But I learned some of their language since I often had to deal with them."

The sun glinted off metal as the nomads came closer.

"They do have slaves. See the chains between the men," said Ibericus.

Six men wearing loose baggy trousers and heavy coats rode Bactrian camels. Five other Kyrgyz walked, prodding along three bound men, one of whom had to be held up by another. Their approach brought more legionnaires to the low promontory.

"Then you will translate," said Gaius. They, along with the rest of the legionnaires, started down to the road.

"What do you want me to say?" Diomedes asked.

"Just ask a few questions. Look at their leader on the camel and two of the ones walking beside him."

Diomedes and several of the others gave the centurion a curious glance. "See their shoes?" said Gaius.

"*Caligae,*" said Appian, walking beside Gaius. "Either they bought them from Parthian soldiers or ..."

"Took them from their prisoners, the ones tied up," said Gaius. "Only Roman soldiers wear iron-studded sandals."

"Might the shoes have been sold to them by Parthians?" asked Diomedes.

"I don't think so. I recognize the prisoners."

The grizzled leader brought his camel to a halt and stared at the legionnaires. On his belt hung a Roman gladius. A ten-inch *puglio* peeked out from his coat. After a moment he tilted his head, raised his eyebrows, and indicated the blocked road. Gaius, hand on the hilt of his sword, stepped forward. With a little smile, he looked at the unsheathed gladius in the nomad's belt and tapped it. He glanced at the *puglio* and turned to Diomedes. "Ask him where he got it."

There was a quick exchange and the Parthian said, "The man says he bought it from a trader."

"Tell him I don't believe him," said the Primus Pila.

The Kyrgyz stiffened, his jacket parted, and a glint of metal shimmered in the sun.

"Ask him who the slaves are and where he got them," said Appian.

Again there was a brief discussion. "From far away, he claims," said Diomedes. He says that they were captured while stealing from his village and he wants to sell them, but only at a good price. In gold."

"I want to see them." Gaius purposefully walked toward the prisoners, who had been kept a hundred paces from the Roman contingent.

The Kyrgyz shouted to his men, turned his mount, and hastened toward them, the others following. Without a word, two dozen legionnaires joined Gaius and converged on the chained men and their captors. All three of the prisoners were heavily bearded. With chapped and split lips they stared at the legionnaires through narrow, bloodshot eyes.

"Water," one said in Latin. "May I have some water?"

Tacitus and Ibericus pushed their way to the front and Tacitus peered closely at the man. He put a finger on a scar that stretched from the man's forehead to his lips. "An old comrade," he said to Appian. "This one is Julius Fortunius. Though I don't think fortune favored him on his journey."

Moving to the next he said, "I don't know your name. Where did you come from?"

"I'm Gracchus Lucenius Martinus, Legion IV Galicia, from Carrhae. Are you from there?"

"We are," said the Primus Pila.

"Oh, Great Jupiter, please cut my chains!" the man cried, dropping to his knees and touching the centurion's sandaled feet.

"Unchain him!" barked Gaius to the Kyrgyz who sat on his cud-chewing beast.

The ancient nomad sprang off his camel with surprising alacrity and thrust himself between Gaius and the prisoner, making the mistake of pushing the centurion back a step. If given a moment to reflect, the desert dweller might not have reached for the pilfered knife at his side, but he didn't have that time. He slumped to the ground with Gaius's *puglio* in his chest. The other Kyrgyz tried to urge their lumbering beasts past the legionnaires, but camels are stubborn and their riders were torn off the beasts and quickly impaled.

Tacitus leaned over the body of the Kyrgyz leader and slipped the chained broach from the neck of the corpse. He had feared that he would never see it again. It was all he had of Tullia.

Gaius walked past the dead Kyrgyz to the other two prisoners. They shied away and the centurion stared into the eyes of each. "You are Fortunius, aren't you?"

"Yes, Primus Pila," the deserter said in a barely audible voice.

"This one is Aurelius," said Appian. "I bet you're overjoyed to return to your old chums, aren't you?"

"I wanted to come back and tell you about these cutthroats. I really did."

"Oh, I think you'll get your chance," said the trumpeter.

"It was all Quintillus's idea," said Aurelius, his voice pleading.

"Of course," said Gaius. "But you chose to go along with it. Right now you will tell me where to find Quintillus. I really want to exchange some philosophical concepts with him."

"He's in a cave. I can show you where."

His hands still bound, Aurelius deferentially used the title "Primus Pila" and "*optio*" as if he were still a trusted member of the cohorts. The legionnaires, including the freed soldier from the Legion IV Galicia, ignored him. Undeterred, Aurelius chattered on.

***

The camels were tethered to gnarled stumps outside the cave. A man emerged, removed a pouch from one of the beasts, and reentered the darkened interior.

Looking down from a high ledge, Gaius asked, "How many are in there?"

"I counted thirty-two," said Aurelius. "They're well armed and fight over the spoils. They trade only when they're outnumbered. The rest of the time they raid and plunder."

"Tell me about the cave. Does it have more than one entrance? What about the side chambers, the rooms?"

"There are two chambers, but only one way in, the one you see down there. It's a narrow cave, but long. And there's a smoke hole going through its roof."

"What about the wind?"

"Wind?"

"Does the cave suck in air?"

"Oh, yes, Primus Pila," said Aurelius, "the wind enters from the front and the smoke from the cooking fires goes up the—"

"Get him out of here," said Gaius to Appian. "We'll head down and secure the entrance. Have the men gather up brush and get a torch ready."

Ten minutes later, choking and blinded by billowing smoke, the Kyrgyz stumbled out of the cave and were swiftly annihilated. The fire at the entrance was extinguished when thirty-two bodies were counted. When the last of the smoke cleared the hole in the roof, Gaius led a squad inside.

"He's here," said Appian.

Quintillus, coughing and wheezing, was bound to a stake. As the smoke cleared he peered at Gaius with alarm.

"Are there any others?" asked Gaius.

"Kyrgyz?"

"Legionnaires. Captives from Carrhae."

"No, but there's a lot of loot, and some of it's from there," Quintillus said, rubbing his eyes.

A dozen legionnaires scoured the cave. Tacitus returned from one of the chambers with a bundled kit and handed it to Appian, who in turn gave it to Gaius.

"I believe this belongs to you," said the trumpeter.

Quintillus gave Gaius a quick glance, then looked away. "I'm sorry, I just …"

A small folded papyrus fell out as Gaius rummaged through it. He reached down and put it back in his kit.

"Do you want to execute Quintillus right here, or in front of the cohorts?" asked Appian.

"Not here. Bind his wrists. I'll deal with him later."

***

The cohorts stopped for the night. They had not seen any Parthians or Saka since the battle, so Gaius allowed small fires to be built after sentries were posted. Tacitus found Apollodoros sitting on a log and decided to join him.

"Can't sleep?" asked Apollodoros, his eyes on the star-filled sky.

"No. Besides, I have guard duty in a while."

"You seem troubled. Is it the battle, your father, or just your basic outlook on life?"

"None of those just now. I was thinking about the village we raided and the girl whose lover I killed."

"Would you have killed the girl if I hadn't stopped you?"

"Maybe. I've thought about it since then. If she had had a weapon I would have had to."

"She didn't, and you would have killed her anyway. It would have been a useless thing, a mistake, something you'd regret. There are things we regret, Tacitus. I guess you know that."

"What do you regret, Medicus?"

He shook his head, took a deep breath, and again stared at the constellations.

"You never told me about how you came to Rome, or what you did when you were young."

"So you're asking me now? I find that strange, after all these years." The Greek watched a meteor streak across the sky, and then said, "My father, Macenas, was a merchant and a man of many talents. He spoke many languages, and was well versed in medicine, astronomy, and the subtleties of trade. He had also been a soldier and was familiar with the art of war. And he was a fine teacher, just as I am, of course."

"Of course," Tacitus repeated, earning himself a baleful look.

"Even as a small boy I traveled with him. He taught me how to set broken bones and fractures and stitch up wounds. There were always accidents and violence wherever we went. I even tried to repair entrails with occasional success.

"We traveled this very road, buying and selling, and made our way back to the coast at Tyre, then on to Greece. I was to be married to a Greek girl on a nearby island. But we never got there."

"Why not?"

"We were intercepted by pirates, the Berbers, soon after we set sail from the Peloponnesian peninsula. They took us to the African coast. My days as a free person ended and we were put into a cage with other men waiting to be sold."

"In a cage? For how long?"

"Months. We roasted in the sun. Men got sick, got infections, and died. The Berbers gave us a cup of water and a scrap of bread once a day. Men fought over these like animals. One day the son of a pirate chieftain was knifed by a rival. The place was thrown into chaos. The pirates went from one cage to another asking if anyone had medical knowledge, since their own medic had perished the week before. My father was already dying and told me to say that I could help the wounded youth. They dragged me out, promising a great reward, anything if I could save the young man."

"Did you?"

"Yes. They had henbane seed to ease the pain and I stuffed his entrails back in and sewed him up. I spent weeks attending him and I persuaded them to give my father more food and water. I slept in the boy's tent. For some reason I believed that they would free us, but I should have known better. They were evil men.

"There was great excitement in the camp one morning. A ship came in that had captured a Greek vessel with women on board. There'd been no women in the camp for several weeks. Some of them were immediately distributed to minor chiefs, rapacious men who tore off with them right away. But the father of the boy I saved told me that he had a special reward for me."

The *medicus* closed his eyes and folded his arms across his chest as if to ward off the cold.

"What happened then?" said Tacitus.

"The thing I regret."

Like Sisyphus, the great rock weighed down on him and he said nothing for the rest of the night.

RON SINGERTON

Chapter 12

A trumpet blast ripped through the morning air. Startled legionnaires grabbed weapons and scrambled from their tents.

"Assemble. Stand to arms!" Gaius commanded as the men aligned their ranks. "A week ago you annihilated an enemy force of Saka, the same barbarians who savaged our men at Carrhae. In a small way we exacted revenge. It was a minor victory, and we lost four good men, but it made you soldiers once again. From now on you will march in formation and we will carry the standard at the front. You earned the right to be addressed as legionnaires again, and you will behave as such."

The men squinted in the early light. Gaius slapped the *vitis* stick against his greaves. "No more slouching or falling behind. We are a force that will command respect. Word of our victory will spread. That is good, but it will also require us to be continuously vigilant. Nevertheless, you are once again soldiers of Rome."

After breaking camp an hour later, the men reassembled, straightened their ranks, and awaited the time-honored question.

Gaius looked from his centurions to the cohorts. "Are you ready to march?"

"Yes," came the reply. It was a bit ragged, and, in keeping with tradition, the question was repeated. By the third time, the response was stronger and unified. The trumpeter's horn sounded and nearly 400 hobnailed *caligae* struck the ground as one. The march to the land of the Seres people had truly begun.

The cohorts crossed the Oxus river three days later.

"Will the Parthians pursue us across the river?" Gaius asked Diomedes.

"No, this is the land of the Kushans and the Sogdiani. They trade with Parthia but have no love for them. Their interest is the safety of the caravans. I've heard that they trade with the Han from the east, the people behind the wall who make the silk."

"Then the Seres people can't be very far away," said Appian.

"The Great Wall?" Diomedes said. "I've never seen it, but I know it will take years to get there."

"Well, that's where we're going," said Gaius.

"Why travel so far? There are fine cities before that. Why not settle in a place like Samarkand?"

"Beyond the Great Wall, as you call it, is a river by which we shall sail home. I don't want to be a stranger in a foreign land for the rest of my life," said Gaius.

The cohorts had located a shallow crossing, the Oxus being low at the end of summer. Once forded, the legionnaires marched half a mile inland. Despite Diomedes's assurances, Gaius had the men erect fortifications and assigned sentries before dismissing them for the night. He joined Appian and Apollodoros by one of the banked fires.

"I want to tighten things up," Gaius said, glancing toward a few dozen corralled horses. "I've let the discipline lapse. The fear of another Saka raid was enough to drive the men. But now their only concern is the unknown."

"They won't mind the discipline now that they've experienced a victory," ventured Appian. "I think they're proud of being a military unit again."

"What do you think of our Parthian?" Gaius asked.

"He's an enigma," Apollodoros said. "He's a Parthian, alright, obviously raised by a wealthy family, but born a Greek. He fought for Surena and probably killed Romans before turning into a model prisoner."

Gaius heard laughter behind him.

"I am a model prisoner," Diomedes said, coming into the firelight. "And I'd rather not be considered a Parthian any longer." He sat down beside Apollodoros. The fact that he had not been invited didn't seem to bother him at all.

"But you want to be treated as an officer, and you are, or were, a captain of Orodes's cavalry," observed Appian. "If I'm not mistaken, he's a Parthian."

Diomedes waved his hand dismissively, then touched his forehead as if a thought had just occurred to him. "I am no longer in chains, so I am not a prisoner, nor am I a slave. Therefore, I think you should simply treat me as a noble, educated gentleman—a fellow traveler on this great road to oblivion." He cocked his head, smiled, and twirled his long, black moustache.

Gaius grinned, despite himself. Appian rolled his eyes.

"You are a presumptuous bastard, aren't you?" said Apollodoros.

"Well, I never knew my real father, but what does that matter now? But I often wonder about my mother."

"What happened to her?" asked Gaius.

"I was taken from her when I was quite young. I've only a vague notion of what she looked like. She taught me well during those few years."

"And exactly what did she teach you?" Apollodoros asked.

"All the great stories of Greece. The gods on Mount Olympus, Zeus, Apollo, Hercules, and the hero Diomedes, for whom I'm named. And of course Alexander, who with his Macedonians crossed this very river 300 years ago. Right out there," the man said, pointing into the darkness. "That's where he destroyed the army of Darius III, king of Persia."

"The battle of Gaugamela," said Apollodoros. "But now, young captain, since you started it, we expect you to complete the story."

"Ah, a test by another Greek, a fellow countryman, in fact."

"Not exactly. Now, what happened after the battle?"

A smile spread across Diomedes's face. "Darius was murdered by two of his own men. Apparently they wanted to curry favor with Alexander. But when the Macedonian heard of it he was furious. He said that no man had the right to kill a king except another king. As it was, Darius died in the arms of Alexander and the great man was said to weep."

"And the murderers?"

"Oh, they received a very special punishment," said Diomedes, rubbing his hands together. "Alexander directed his men to bend two yew trees to the ground and secure their tips. Each of the culprits had his feet tied to one and his hands bound to the other. On Alexander's command the ropes holding the trees were severed and the murderers were flung into the air and ripped into pieces. A fitting end, wouldn't you say?"

***

"I have lost all track of time since we left the Parthian lands," said Appian. "I don't even know what day or month it is. I'm not even sure about the year. This road is interminable and the men are bored to death."

"Apollodoros tells me that there is a city about two days' march from here. He said it's called Samarkand," observed Gaius.

"Then we should stop there, give the men a break. It would cheer them up."

"You think we need happy warriors?" Appian gave Gaius a baleful look.

"We have 18 sick men, some with battle wounds," Appian told Gaius just as they reached the outskirts of the city of Samarkand. "Perhaps we should build a camp and allow them to recover. If we don't, I'm afraid we might lose half of them."

Gaius studied the towering Pamir-Alay range of mountains surrounding the city. "I don't like delays."

"Maybe only for a month or so; a respite would be good for morale. Besides, winter is coming. You can see snow on the peaks." Appian grinned. "And, there are women in the city who would welcome legionnaires with their Parthian gold."

Samarkand lay in the fertile valley of Polyimetus, named by Alexander when he had conquered the city.

"Diomedes tells me he knows about the city," Appian Dio said to Gaius.

"Why name it Samarkand?" said the Primus Pila distractedly, looking for a road over the mountains.

"That's a good story," said Diomedes, as he and Apollodoros warmed their hands on the morning fire.

"A very short one, I hope," sighed Gaius.

"Well, sort of. The ruler of the land, once named Maracanda, had a beautiful daughter named Kand who fell in love with a pauper. Her father forbade her to see him, but they met secretly in a garden until they were discovered. The boy was executed and the lovesick girl jumped to her death from a parapet. The boy's name was Samar and the village folk, saddened by the tragedy, renamed the town Samarkand. By the gods, I swear it is true."

Gaius spent the next day supervising the erection of towers, walls, and a moat. The Roman encampment was close enough to the city for lively traffic between legionnaires and the fortified town. Despite Gaius's admonitions, liaisons between soldiers and the local women became a nightly diversion from the monotony of camp duties. The chilling winds of winter eventually ebbed with the advent of spring. Gaius led the men in one training exercise after another, and though many of the sick recovered, some grievous disabilities lingered.

"A few of the men need more time," said Apollodoros when Gaius entered the hospital tent.

"How much more?"

"Until late summer."

"Early summer is the latest I'll allow." Gaius examined the slowly recovering men, then strode out, only to encounter a legionnaire on crutches.

"Primus Pila, the *medicus* tells me that my leg will never heal. I'm afraid that I will be a burden when we attempt to climb the Pamirs."

"If you can't climb or fight, we'll have to leave you here."

"Yes, I understand. I sorely want to return to Rome and march with my friends, but ..."

"Of course. It would please us if you could, but there's really no alternative. You'll receive enough in coin to make a new start here. It's not Rome, but I think they'll welcome you."

The legionnaire nodded and gazed toward the city. "Primus Pila, I would never have guessed that my days in the legions would end here. It's a city I had never before heard of."

***

On a cool spring evening, Tacitus, Sempronius, and Diomedes approached Apollodoros, Gaius, and Appian, as they sat beside a roaring fire.

"May we join you?" Diomedes asked, something that he rarely did.

Gaius indicated an open space and the former Parthian sat. Tacitus and his friend looked on from the shadows until Appian said, "You'll freeze out there. You might as well come in."

Tacitus glanced at his father, who said nothing. The conversation waned.

"Do you know what happened with Alexander here in Samarkand?" Diomedes said.

"I'm sure you'll educate us," Apollodoros said, pouring himself a cup of wine.

"Of course I will, and most gladly," Diomedes replied. There was an audible sigh as the men prepared themselves for another historical onslaught. "Well," he began, looking at each with intense dark eyes, "as great as Alexander was in battle, he was a consummate drunk. Often there were arguments, but cooler heads would prevail before there was carnage. His orgies of intoxication usually ended with morning sickness."

"I haven't had morning sickness, have you Primus Pila?" Appian asked.

Diomedes waited for the laughter to die away. "One night Alexander became mindlessly drunk and a bitter debate broke out between himself and his finest general and closest friend. Who here knows the name of his best friend?" Diomedes asked, as if they were young students at his tutorial.

"Clitus the Black," Tacitus said half under his breath.

"Clitus, indeed! A scholar in our midst!" proclaimed the former captain of Parthian horse. "I, Diomedes the Wolf, challenge you, legionnaire, to finish the story for me."

"The Wolf?" Gaius remarked.

"A nickname. He has a birthmark on his back," said Appian. "I saw it when we captured him."

Diomedes looked expectantly at Tacitus, who glanced about. "Alexander was drunk, as the 'Wolf' said. Clitus had fought alongside Alexander from the day he conquered Athens. Insults flew back and forth and, in a rage, Alexander grabbed a spear and thrust it into Clitus. The man died that night and Alexander was grief-stricken. Clitus was given a hero's funeral. Alexander never recovered."

"He still marched on," the Primus Pila said after a moment of silence. "And that's what we're going to do."

"When?" asked Appian.

"As soon as the weather breaks. Those who can't march will stay here. The rest of us are going to Rome."

***

The cohorts resumed their journey, marching into the Tien Shan mountains. Suddenly, a great quake sent tremors rumbling through the mountains. Enormous boulders careened down the valleys, crushing bridges and tearing away the earthen road.

"This way!" yelled Tacitus as he scrambled up a winding trail. The cohorts had come to a halt as the earth trembled beneath them. Gaius waved the men back from a precipice.

"Up there! Tacitus has found a pathway," added Apollodoros.

Gaius looked back at the crouching legionnaires and saw Appian pointing toward Tacitus. "Yes, follow him!" shouted Gaius over the din of cascading rock. Hurridly the cohorts streamed up the hillside.

A couple of minutes later the quake ceased, but tremors continued throughout the day. An encampment was made on the summit of a barren hill. That night as Appian sat with Gaius, he said, "We could have lost half the men. Lucky that Tacitus spied a way out. You should commend him."

Gaius stared into the campfire and replied, "How many were hurt?"

"Seven, but no broken bones."

"We will push on to the next town in the morning. I want us away from these mountains. Get the men up early. We leave at first light." Nothing more was said about Appian's suggestion.

It was at the Chirchik River near Tashkent, in the principality of Chach, where the legionnaires came to a halt. Tashkent, already an ancient city, was a major trading center for Sogdiani and Turkic nomads. There was a lively exchange of horses, cattle, gold, and precious stones, as well as the importation of silk and jade from the distant Middle Kingdom.

The crisis stemming from the earthquake resulted in an investigative sortie by a contingent of Sogdian cavalry. Upon seeing them, Gaius had the men form a defensive line across the road, but the Sogdian commander drew no weapon. Instead, he dismounted and walked his horse to where Gaius stood. He looked at the assembled cohorts, grunted, and said in Greek, "You can't go much further and neither can we. There was a bridge out there across the chasm, but it's gone now. Everything has stopped."

Clouds of dust rose in the distance as another aftershock rolled like a shaken carpet across the land.

"The gods!" exclaimed Appian, raising his arms to steady himself on the trembling earth. The great forces beneath their feet made all feel insignificant.

"We need you. We've heard of the great roads and aqueducts of Rome, and we know that Roman soldiers know how to build them," said the Sogdian officer. "We require a new bridge. Without it our commerce will die. I am Katyusk, commander of this district. I have at my disposal 22,000 horsemen and 15,000 infantry."

The gorge where the earthquake had centered plunged down to the Syr Darya River. In its turbulent waters lay the remains of the bridge, like the bones of a dead beast. On either side of the gorge, the road slid away into the chasm. Caravans on the opposite side had halted, and figures could be seen peering into the void.

Ignoring the man's comment, Gaius said, "Is there no other route, no way to get to Tashkent?"

"Look around you, Roman. Those peaks join the Atlas Mountains. There's no pass within hundreds of miles, certainly not for all those people," said the officer, pointing to the diminutive figures across the gorge. "So, can you build the bridge? We'll pay you with food and women, if you wish. We'll provide laborers too."

Appian and the other two centurions joined the assemblage. The early apprehension of opposing forces began to dissipate as the leaders surveyed the extent of the damage. That the gods were so angered was troubling, explained Katyusk. Such quakes were a constant threat and any new bridge would have to withstand them.

"Do you have surveyors or engineers?" the Sogdian asked.

"One. Flavius Antonius," said Gaius, searching for the legionnaire in the ranks. "He helped build a great bridge in Rome."

"Then you will begin tomorrow," said the Sogdian.

"I haven't said that we will do it," Gaius replied. "We might just turn around and find another route."

The Sogdian casually pointed to his mounted troop. "And just how far do you think you'll get?"

"That depends on how many men you care to lose."

Gaius could hear his legionnaires aligning their ranks behind him. There was a prolonged silence. Then, to his surprise, Katyusk held up the palms of his hands.

"I wish to see my sons grow up, so let us be reasonable men. I'll pay handsomely. I'm going to see what can be done. I invite you to join me."

Gaius nodded and the legionnaires parted, allowing them to pass. A moment later they were joined by the engineer.

"All the boulders on those hills have to come down first," said Flavius Antonius. "Only then will it be safe to rebuild the road and the bridge. It will be dangerous work and there may be many deaths."

"But it can be done. We will pray to our god, Ahura Mazda, that it will not cost too many lives," replied Katyusk.

"It will take years," Gaius said to his assembled men that night. "In battle I lead you as soldiers of Rome. But this road, this bridge, is not for Rome, so the decision is yours."

"What if we choose not to build it? What if we search for another route?" Appian asked.

"We have no guide through the mountains and the Sogdiani won't provide one. Their threat was real. We would kill many of them, but none of us would live to tell about it."

"What if we go back and take our chances with the Parthians?" a centurion asked.

"That wouldn't be wise," Diomedes said, leaning against a boulder. "They will know about the killing of my men and they'll be waiting. These Sogdiani will pay you in gold; you know how the Parthians will pay."

"Tell them to build a town and stock it with food and wine," a legionnaire said. "We'll build the bridge if they promise to do that."

The men laughed. "Primus Pila," said another, "make them supply women for all of us and we'll do the damn work!"

That brought forth a rare grin from Gaius, who turned to Appian. "Well, I guess we build the damn bridge."

"May it please the gods," said Diomedes.

Gods be damned, thought Gaius, *may it please the Sogdiani or we'll never see the other side of this hill.*

***

Wearing only their tunics, hundreds of Sogdiani and legionnaires clambered up the precarious cliffs overlooking the remains of the road. Great stones near the summit were levered, creating a thunderous rumble as they cascaded into the gorge, bouncing and splintering into deadly shards. Men worked their way down the sloping sides until the last of the overhanging rocks had splattered into the ravine.

"The roadway must be cleared and leveled," the engineer said to Gaius and the Sogdian commander. "Then we must dig a ditch for the heavy stones. Our Roman roads are 13 feet wide so that two wagons can pass at the same time. We use many layers of material, starting with an inch of thick mortar, followed by one-foot-high stones bound together with mortar. On top of that is ten inches of rammed concrete, then the *crusta*, three-foot-long slabs with flint between the stones."

"But we have no volcanic ash to make concrete here," Gaius said.

"No, but we can make a serviceable road the way we did before we had concrete. We'll have drainage ditches and layers of rock, then pressed gravel and sand."

"And what kind of bridge will you build?" asked the Sogdian commander. "The river's not very high now, but we get flash floods from snow melt, and it rises very fast."

"A segmented bridge that spans the river. That way there's nothing to impede the flow, and nothing to knock it down. It'll have an oval arch made with shaped stones, and the roadway above the arch will slope down toward each side of the bridge."

"How long will that take?" asked the Sogdian.

"The whole thing? The roadway and the bridge? Two years, maybe three. Unless there's another quake."

***

A month after construction began Tacitus overheard yet another debate between Diomedes and Apollodoros.

"Are they still going at it?" Sempronius asked Tacitus as they struggled to dislodge an overhanging boulder.

"Of course. They don't do anything else. When was the last time you saw Apollodoros or Diomedes do any real work?"

"I saw the Parthian pick up a rock last week," Ibericus said as he hefted a supporting beam onto his shoulder. "But it was a very small rock, and he put it in the wrong place."

"Of course, he's a nobleman and a great intellectual," Appian added, pushing his nose into the air. "He may call himself a Greek, but he's a Parthian to the core."

"The two of them are useless," stated Sempronius.

"They keep us amused," said Tacitus. "They're inseparable."

"Do you think Apollodoros knows?" asked Sempronius.

Tacitus looked at his friend and grinned. "He doesn't have a clue."

"And neither does the Parthian," Ibericus said.

***

Every night, a fire was lit outside the Roman camp where the legionnaires, Sogdiani, and townspeople often congregated. One night, as the flames crackled and sparks whirled into the night sky, Appian said, "Diomedes, you were a captain of Parthian cavalry, so I was wondering if you were in battles before Carrhae."

"Most certainly, but against bandits and Arab raiders, nothing like Carrhae. At Carrhae I valiantly led a detachment of Surena's cataphracts."

"Valiantly, you say," said Appian. "He must have put a lot of trust in you. How did that possibly happen?"

"By the strangest of coincidences. And, yes, he trusted me implicitly. Why not?"

There was a chuckle around the campfire, but the Parthian seemed oblivious to it.

"As you can see, we are anxiously awaiting another saga," Sempronius said with a wink at Tacitus.

"Well, since you all wish to hear this most amazing story," said Diomedes expansively, "I shan't keep you in suspense. I was only six years old when I discovered my first and earliest talent."

"We know what the other one is," said Sempronius.

Diomedes ignored the laughter. "My earliest talent was as a mime, or more correctly, an impersonator. I was a slave, as was my mother, and my owner required me to stand in the bazaar and impersonate people who walked by. Many laughed at my antics and placed coins in a pot. Then one day a very wealthy man and his entourage came to the market and I began to imitate him. My owner was horrified and tried to stop me. Everybody had stopped laughing. I suddenly realized that I must have done something terrible. I began to cry."

The Parthian sipped his wine and watched as his audience leaned forward. "The rich man, a noble, dismounted and appraised me.

"Without saying a word he began to strut up and down very pompously and winked at a pretty girl who rode beside him. Then, with a flourish, he pointed at me, indicating that I should do the same. I hesitated for a minute, but my owner pushed me forward. I began to strut up and down, gaining confidence all the while. The man began to clap and, seeing this, the crowd did the same. Some laughed so hard they actually fell on the ground. The pretty girl said something to the nobleman and he tossed a bag of coins to my owner. The man thanked the noble and bowed obsequiously. Then the rich man put me on his horse and took me away. I'm sure my mother was horrified. I never saw her again."

There was a moment of silence.

"And that's how I came into the household of the Surena family, the richest in all of Parthia. For a few years I was only an entertainer. But at the age of ten I began training in the art of war."

Diomedes stood. "Now tell me, who is this?" He began to walk around the fire, two fingers at his temple, closely examining his hand, then picking up what might have been an insect and staring at it intently. He assumed a stooped posture and began mumbling in archaic Greek. He gazed at the heavens, momentously pointed upward, and said, "Star!"

Men laughed and pointed to Apollodoros. Then, spreading his legs and placing his fists on his hips, Diomedes took on an angry, scowling look. He stomped around, picked up a stick, and slammed one imaginary legionnaire after another. "Worthless, lazy scum!" he yelled. Another whack with the *vitis* stick and he grabbed his stomach and rolled on the ground. The legionnaires roared and shouted, "The Primus Pila himself!"

In the shadows Gaius merely shook his head and strode back to the encampment. There were rumors of bandits and he wanted vigilance this night.

Chapter 13

With the bridge finally complete, there were great celebrations. Dozens of caravans crossed the span with horses, camels, and wagons festooned in braid and ribbon. Gaius had lined the legionnaires in two rows, their armor and shields spotless, as cheering travelers passed between them. The revelry that evening surpassed all others, the wine flowed, and harlots welcomed all. Gaius estimated that at least 100 children of legionnaire fathers were seeded that very night.

His men and the Sogdian military worked continuously to keep peace amongst a dozen nationalities, all vying for the same women and trade goods now that the road was reopened. That night he was invited into the lavish tent of Ok Katyusk and presented with the final payment owed the legionnaires. He sat beside the Sogdian commander and shared his finest wine.

"You leave tomorrow?" Katyusk asked.

"If any of my men can stand up."

Katyusk laughed, swilled more wine, and leaned toward Gaius. "It would be far better if you remained in Sogdiana. You are welcome here, and your men would continue the pleasantries they enjoy tonight. You will never make it back to Rome, Centurion. The road you take tomorrow certainly leads to the Great Wall, but the Emperor will not allow you to pass beyond it. And you will have marched almost to the end of the earth."

Gaius shrugged, his eyes blurry from the wine. "How many men get to see the end of the earth?" he slurred.

"Let me tell you," the Sogdian said as the sounds of inebriated men and women settled into a predawn stupor. "What you experienced after Carrhae is like a walk in a Persian garden compared to what lies ahead. I know this because my cousin is an ambassador to the Seres people and travels that road. Sogdiana is vital to the silk trade; he and his entourage are honored emissaries to the Middle Kingdom. For that reason he travels in peace, except of course for nomad cutthroats."

"Aside from what you've already told me, what else should I expect on the road?"

"The mountain passes are five days' march from here. It's already too late to start. The weather up there is freezing, the trails become impassable, and the winds are ferocious. It will take a year, maybe two to reach the Wall, and the bandits, well ..." Katyusk shook his head. "The people you see here are traders. Most are honest. Out there every man not riding a laden camel is an enemy. I can't tell you how many caravans are lost each year to Afghans, Tajiks, Kazaks, and the nomadic tribes east of the Taklamakan Desert."

"What is this desert?" Gaius asked.

"The Taklamakan is between the Tian Shan and the Kunlun Shan Mountains, and it extends for 500 miles. Taklamakan means a place you go in and never come out. You can't go through it; you must go around it. And don't even think of skirting it before winter. There is a river in it, but it dries up in summer.

"We Zoroastrians believe in the presence of good and evil. The people east of the desert are called the Chanyu. They're the embodiment of evil. They come from the most inhospitable part of the world and their character is shaped by that. Be on guard and trust no one. Beware of false friendship and feigned hospitality. Sleep as close to your sword as you would to the most beautiful woman in the world."

***

The village of Kochkor was a thousand years old, and its residents claimed that it was a place from which Alexander sent walnuts back to Macedonia. But like much else about Kochkor, this was probably a lie. Though the town harbored thieves and murderers, it was located on a hill called the "Throne of Solomon" because of a story that King Solomon visited the site. Located in rugged mountain country 200 miles before the Torugart Pass, the village played host to the caravans of the Silk Road.

"The men would like to visit the village. They haven't seen women for a long time," Appian said to Gaius.

"And that includes you, my woman-crazed friend," said Gaius. He scratched his balding head and studied the palisade walls of stone and timber. "Take 20 men into the village and look the place over. These people are not Sogdiani; they call themselves Kyrgyz and they live by a different set of rules."

"There's only one gate into the village," Appian said. "That's a bit unusual."

"Anyone going in has to exit the same gate. I don't want any of the men staying in the village overnight."

***

Tacitus was amused by the excited children running around the legionnaires who had entered Kochkor that morning. They stared at the armor while their parents, wearing an assortment of fur caps, rough woolen pants and high boots, hawked their wares. The overall impression was of a happy and festive village. A rollicking wedding party made the rounds, and celebrants offered wine to the Romans, who were invited into cramped passageways between mud brick hovels where girls waited. A toothless man scurried to Sempronius, Lepidus, and Ibericus, leading a tattered woman of uncertain age.

"Not that one," Sempronius said, laughing and waving them off. The villager signaled the legionnaire and his friends to wait. He returned with a much younger girl. Upon seeing her, Sempronius and Ibericus stopped in midsentence. A jeweled headdress and golden braids set off an enchanting face with beguiling eyes. Barely fifteen, she wore a tight bodice, a long silk dress, and slippers that peeked out like faces of tiny mice.

"Oshka," the Kyrgyz said, taking her hand and offering her to Sempronius. The girl stared at the legionnaire and repeated her name.

"Sempronius," the legionnaire said before introducing his companions. The toothless man reached into his pocket and produced three coins, then gestured to the girl. Soon other women appeared, all escorted by men armed with curved knives in ornate copper sheaths. Some Kyrgyz grinned and motioned to the women, while others stood in shadows and spoke amongst themselves. One tapped the steel of Sempronius's *segmentata* and nodded approval.

"I want to come back here tonight," Sempronius said to Lepidus and Ibericus when they departed the village.

"You'll need the centurion's permission," Lepidus said.

"Appian Dio's already arranged it. The last time we bedded women was in Samarkand, six months ago. Hell, the Primus Pila might even come with us."

Lepidus snorted. "*Our* Primus Pila?"

"That girl's the most beautiful thing I've ever seen," said Sempronius. "I think she likes me."

"I don't think she has a choice in the matter. The old man was either her father or her owner and he'd sell her to the first camel driver who comes along," said Ibericus.

"I don't like it. The village seems too content, too inviting," said Tacitus. "I think it's a snake den. I would stay out, Sempronius. A pretty girl is not worth your life."

"I'll stay alert. We will be fine. You worry too much."

***

"Where are they?" Tacitus asked Ibericus as they ran across the boulder-strewn valley toward the fortified village of Kochkor.

"A hundred yards from their wall. I almost passed them; they looked like white rocks. Lepidus is still alive and he'll be okay in a few weeks. They must have taken him for dead, but he may be able to tell us what happened."

Their footfalls slowed when they saw the two fallen legionnaires. Both had been stripped. Sempronius's testicles had been stuffed into his mouth.

Ibericus removed the organ from his friend's mouth. "They shouldn't have died like this," he lamented.

"They shouldn't have died at all. But it's not over." Tacitus bit his lip and struggled to keep his voice steady. "I warned them not to go." He looked toward the village and the men who stared back at them. From their defensive wall he heard laughter and crude taunts. One fired an arrow, which struck a rock and spun away.

"They had better save their arrows," said Ibericus.

"It doesn't matter. They won't have a chance to use them."

***

Gaius and Appian watched the lacerated man who lay in Gaius's tent. Apollodoros and Tacitus sat at his side.

"Can you talk?" Apollodoros asked.

The legionnaire's breathing was shallow, but he nodded.

"They let us in, very friendly-like, and gave us wine," Lepidus wheezed. "A lot of wine. Sempronius wanted to see the girl right away. He even offered the Kyrgyz ten extra denarii. There were women for all of us. We were led to four huts."

"So you were all separated," Gaius said.

"Yes. The women had us remove our armor and weapons. I was pretty drunk by then. The girl I wanted removed her clothes and then ..." Lepidus let out a deep sigh. "And then they broke in."

"The men, the Kyrgyz?" asked Appian.

"Yes. I heard a scream, but it was muffled. I was stabbed and clubbed, and I don't remember anything after that." Lepidus closed his eyes and coughed. "Primus Pila, I'm sorry. We only intended to stay an hour or two. They are a nest of vipers."

Lepidus looked as though he was about to say something else, but drifted off to sleep. Tacitus stood. "Primus Pila, can we talk?"

Gaius walked to the entrance of the tent and motioned for Tacitus and Appian to follow. He would permit his son to speak with him this one time.

"Sempronius was my friend," Tacitus said as they walked up a hill overlooking the village. "I personally want to avenge his death."

"You want my permission to kill the man who murdered Sempronius?"

"No, I want to kill all the men. We'll never learn who stabbed Sempronius and sliced up Lepidus."

"In that case we can simply block their gate and burn the whole place to cinders," Gaius countered.

"And what about the women?" asked Appian. "Why not find the one who was with Sempronius? We can take the others if we don't burn the place down. The men would appreciate that."

"Very well, they can visit the men until we march; if they come, they'll slow us down and cause problems." Gaius turned to Tacitus. "How many men did you see in the village?"

"About 300 and the same number of women and children."

"This will be your operation. You will plan it, and if I approve the tactics I'll consent. The village must be taken by surprise. I will not lose a single man, understood?"

Gaius ran a hand through thinning hair as he watched Tacitus hasten back to the encampment. Had he ever moved with such purpose before?

"So you're giving Tacitus a command?" Appian said. "You surprise me, Gaius."

"He's been a soldier for years. I want to see what he can do."

"You're thinking of promoting him?"

"I'm not saying anything of the sort. As I said, I want to see what tactics he's capable of planning and executing."

"You have to admit it – he's become a valuable and trustworthy legionnaire," said Appian.

Gaius nodded. "Acceptable performance. But it's one thing to be responsible for just yourself. Commanding a force is quite different. That requires constant assessment of the battle, and the ability to adapt as well as anticipate enemy tactics. He's done none of that."

"Then perhaps you should start training him."

Gaius shook his head. "No, he's going to have to think on his own; it's got to be innate. And it's his fight. But I want you to stay close in the attack. Just in case."

"You're not going in?"

"No, I'll be watching. I don't want men looking to me for guidance. Or you, for that matter, unless, of course, things go very badly."

Sempronius was buried with honors the following day, and, as the Kyrgyz watched, the Roman encampment was dismantled. Before darkness the cohorts, with the exception of the scouts, packed their kits and began an eastward march. After ten miles they halted, fashioned scaling ladders, and concealed themselves from any Kyrgyz patrols.

"We'll strike during the hour before dawn," Tacitus said. "Thirty men will remain outside the gate. Archers will eliminate their sentries, then the cohorts will scale the walls. I want to seal off streets, so no one area can reinforce another. Teams will be sent into each house. Once the sentries are killed, every legionnaire goes in."

"No reserves?" Gaius said.

"No. Complete inundation, total surprise. No shields. All women and children will be forced into one corner. We'll herd them out after we kill the men. Then we burn the town."

Gaius considered the concept and glanced at his centurions and Ibericus. They nodded.

"I approve. But there must be total silence before you scale the walls. Once done, the only sounds I want to hear are their screams."

"Great Jupiter will be with us," said Ibericus.

"Perhaps, but I put my faith in the gladius," Gaius replied. Then to Tacitus he said, "it's a worthy plan. I thought well of your friend. Now avenge his death."

***

"Is he still breathing?", said the Centurion.

A legionnaire hastened to where Gaius, Diomedes, and Apollodoros stood. "Yes, but barely. Appian is with him and asks you to hurry."

The village burned fiercely in the light of the new dawn. It took only a few minutes for Gaius to reach the spot where his son lay. He and Apollodoros knelt beside Tacitus. The wound beneath the clavicle was deep, and blood oozed steadily.

Gaius grasped his son's hand. "Stay awake."

Tacitus nodded, closed his eyes, and reopened them.

"I heard that we got them all," he said in a whisper. "They're all dead, aren't they?" His eyes moved to Appian, who nodded decisively.

"Yes, it was brilliant. We killed them all. You did well."

Apollodoros examined the wound. "The knife missed the artery. I'll give him henbane to lessen the pain. I can stitch up the wound and stop the bleeding but ..."

"But what?" said Gaius.

"If the knife was rusty, the wound will fester. That may be fatal. I'm not telling you anything you don't know. He must rest. We'll just have to wait."

Gaius turned to Appian. "We'll build a fortified encampment on the crest of that hill. Tell the men that we will stay here until this man recovers or dies."

Gaius took one more look at Tacitus, then started toward the women and children who were being contained. Over his own footfalls he could hear Appian's voice behind him.

"I didn't think he cared."

"Oh, he cares," replied the *medicus*. "But I didn't think he cared that much."

***

By midday the defensive ditch had been dug, the ramparts erected, and a stout timber palisade was in place. Four guard towers rose over the encampment and the new hut sites. Gaius supervised the construction and turned as Appian said, "We found the woman Sempronius lay with."

"Did you question her? Does she speak any language we can understand?"

"Diomedes understands some. He says that she's not Kyrgyz, but comes from further east, belongs to some nomad culture."

Gaius watched heavy timbers being lashed together to create one of the two gates. "Tacitus was the only casualty, Appian. What happened in there?"

"Until he was stabbed, everything proceeded as planned. Since many of us had been inside the village earlier, we knew exactly where the living quarters were, the houses for the prostitutes, and the hiding places for stolen goods. Once we'd scaled the walls, we divided the town into four sections and placed guards. Each unit knew where to attack. At the sound of the horn we ripped into the houses. It was quick and lethal. The Kyrgyz thought we had gone and their guard was down. Nearly all of them were dead by the time their alarm bell rang."

"Then what?"

"I was with Tacitus when we learned that three or four Kyrgyz had fled to a storage room. It was dark in there and the room was divided up. We hadn't been in there before, but we went in anyway. We were immediately attacked. Tacitus killed two and I sliced up one. We thought it was over when your son was stabbed. The man had been hiding under a carpet and we didn't see him. He tried to deliver one more fatal wound, but he didn't get that far. By that time the women had been taken from the village and the fires had been started. I got Tacitus outside and sent a messenger to you. If it hadn't been for his injury, the entire operation would have been perfect. Absolutely perfect."

***

Tacitus felt cool water on his forehead and heard a voice say, "The fever has broken." The visions had reappeared again. There was Tullia the night he had taken her into the forest, the screams of dying men at Carrhae, and the horrible face that flashed before him with the upraised knife.

"How long before this soldier will be able to march?"

He knew that voice; it was the same one that had been so scathing many years before. It was raspier now and rarely spoke to him. "Soldier," was the word he used. When had his father ever referred to him as a soldier? Tacitus opened his eyes, but the man was gone. He was certain that he had heard it, but during the previous weeks he'd thought that he had heard many things.

"So, you're not dead," Lepidus said, peering down with a sly grin.

"That's what Apollodoros told me. He studied medicine so he must know. What about you?" Tacitus said, seeing the welt on Lepidus's arm.

"This? Your father's *vitis* stick. It's a real morale booster, Tacitus. I couldn't do without it. Now that you're better, he might use it on you instead of me. Somehow I seem to get in its way when he's swinging it around."

"I'm glad that your morale is so high. Now get out of here – I want to sleep."

"Would you like me to send you any of the women? We have quite a few, you know."

The snore may have been faked, but it was quite audible.

***

It was another two months before Tacitus regained his strength. They took down the camp and prepared to send the women and children off to Kochkor. Gaius was checking supplies when Appian and Diomedes approached him with a woman.

"This is Oshka, the one Sempronius bedded," Appian said. "She doesn't want to go with them."

"We can't take her with us; she won't make it over the pass," said Gaius.

"I don't know, Centurion," Diomedes said. "She came here by way of that pass, and not on a camel. She's not a Kyrgyz and wants nothing to do with them since they only used her for sex."

"Kyrgyz, no," Oshka said, shaking her head and waving her hand at the same time.

"She might be useful as a guide, and she does speak a language used on the eastern end of the road," said Appian.

"Do you want her?" Gaius said to Diomedes between curt instructions to a legionnaire.

"Not really. But I know someone who does. In fact, he likes her very much."

"Who, Tacitus? I saw her trying out some Latin on him yesterday."

"No, she doesn't interest him. But Lupus Ibericus would like to have her. He's lost Sempronius, his best friend, and he's been in a funk. The woman might bring him out of it."

"He doesn't blame her for his death?"

"No. She was a slave, and she didn't kill him."

The chief centurion studied the woman, who gazed at him hopefully.

"I don't want any problems. Tell Ibericus that she can't sleep in the same tent with him and his mates; he'll have to sleep separate from them. She'll be his responsibility. If there's a point where she can't go on, he must carry her or leave her behind."

Diomedes translated in broken Kyrgyz and a smattering of Latin. The girl bowed very low, but still sounded concerned when she replied.

"Centurion," Diomedes said, "She's worried that you might try to cross the Torugart Pass. We're still a hundred miles from the pass and it's too late in the season. There's a town before the mountains called Tash Rabat. We can winter there."

Oshka nodded vigorously.

"We'll march that 100 miles, then see where we are," Gaius said. "Appian, assemble the men. I want to get started."

***

The cohorts had erected their encampment outside Tash Rabat. Gaius directed his gaze at the mountain pass two miles distant. He had Diomedes question Oshka again and she repeated the same dire warning, but the days were still mild and only a sprinkling of snow appeared on the distant Pamir peaks.

"We're wasting time here," Gaius said to Appian. "We could be over the mountains in five days of hard marching."

"If the weather holds. You heard what the woman said. Those are the highest mountains we've ever seen. They may even be higher than the Alps."

"Hannibal made it over the Alps in the dead of winter."

"He lost almost all his elephants and many men. And there's something else to consider."

Gaius tapped his golden arrow against his greaves and gave his friend a petulant look.

"The men are grumbling. They're listening to Quintillus again – he heard what Oshka said. He's trouble; you should have run the gladius through him when he deserted."

"That's still a distinct possibility." Gaius stared at the pass again. "I'm not waiting any longer. We're going to do it. Take 15 men, go into the town, and buy warm clothing and boots. We leave here at dawn."

***

Tacitus pulled his cloak tightly about him, but it didn't mitigate the bitter chill that swept through the pass. It was the second day of the ascent and, just as Oshka had predicted, the snow came early as heavy clouds tore across the blue sky. Little white slivers that floated down quickly melted, but it seemed an ominous sign, for the upper reaches of the road were still many miles ahead.

Only a single caravan had passed them all day. It had come down from the 12,000-foot summit and was accompanied by 50 guards, all heavily armed. The legionnaires made room on the narrow road for the procession of Bactrian camels and heavily clothed traders. Gaius had Oshka questioned the caravan's headman, but the man was in a hurry. "Storm coming," he declared, pointing upward. "Go back or die!"

"Are there any more caravans coming down?" Oshka shouted as the traveler passed her in the last light of day.

The trader turned and hollered, "We are the last one. No more until spring. You must go back."

Ignoring the admonition, Gaius had the cohorts erect tents, build fires with dried dung, and settle in for the night. The storm gathered all the next day, as if the army of winter was marshaling its legions for a great assault. The road began as a series of switchbacks, and narrowed as it climbed. Gaius led the march, followed by Appian and the legionnaires in a column of twos. Tacitus trod up the path beside the giant Ibericus. Behind him stomped the petite Oshka, who gallantly tried to keep pace. Taking pity on his woman, Ibericus had her climb onto his back and, exhausted, she nodded off.

"Quintillus was at it again this morning," Ibericus said as they rounded another hairpin turn.

"I wasn't there. What are the men saying?" asked Tacitus.

"Not much. Most still don't want to associate with him, considering that he's such an ass, but they're getting disillusioned and some are listening. I overheard him say that he's meeting with some men tonight."

"Maybe I should be there," Tacitus said.

"He won't say anything if you're around. But I might just sit in."

***

The cabal took place after dark at the rear of the encampment. Ibericus watched as men in clandestine groups looked over their shoulders, then drifted to the banked fire where Quintillus waited. Quintillus had sounded out those of like mind, men he would have little difficulty in convincing. A few had been posted to watch for the Primus Pila or any other centurion. Others hung back, wary but curious. Ibericus wandered toward the dampened fire and met Quintillus's eyes. He hadn't been invited, but Quintillus didn't make an issue of it.

"I know what most of you think of me," Quintillus said when everyone had gathered around the fire. "I did a disgraceful thing and have paid for it ever since. But what I have to say tonight is what many of you are thinking. You're worried about the consequences if the Primus Pila finds out. But I curry no favor with him. I'll say what I wish and leave it to others to convince him of the folly of going up this pass in winter."

The deserter spoke in a quiet, measured voice.

"We have been marching and campaigning for over a dozen years because of a rumor that there may be a river in the land of the Seres people; a river beyond a great wall that will allow us to sail back to Rome. Now, think about it, comrades. We march in the dead of winter over this horrible pass into a land we know nothing about. Then we must cross a terrible desert and enter a foreign kingdom uninvited. And what do we say to the king of that empire? 'Oh, excuse us, but our little armed band just wants to sail down your river, fuck your women, and kill anyone who gets in our way.' Now, let's be honest. In reality what are we?"

He looked about at the ragged, tired men and gave a wan smile as he raised his hands. "Certainly we are no longer an army. Do we still represent Rome way out here? A Rome that doesn't even know we exist? And, if the Republic did know, would it care about fewer than 400 men who fled the disaster at Carrhae all those years ago?"

In a strident voice Quintillus said, "We are a bunch of aging men pretending to be what we once were: an army of vital warriors loyal to a civilization that now thinks us dead. Our effort would be a Greek comedy if it were not so tragic. We all know that continuing means that we will never see our families again.

"Now let us refer to immediate matters," said Quintillus. "We have met people on this road who laughed and shook their heads when we told them we were marching east to get to Rome in the west. And crossing this mountain in winter is suicide. Our war with Parthia is long over and there is no reason for them to deny us passage home, especially if we come in peace. We must go back on the road that brought us here. If we gather together the Primus Pila will not fight us; too many will die. And, given the chance, most will join us. Then we may actually convince him of his folly, and he can still lead us back the way we came."

There was a murmur of agreement. From out of the gloom, Oshka approached the gathering. She spotted Ibericus and pulled on his sleeve. He made a show of brushing her away, but the petite woman was insistent. Finally, throwing up his hands, he allowed her to lead him from the conspiracy.

"Did I do good?" she asked him when they were out of earshot.

"Very good." The big man bent down and gave her a kiss. "Now go to our tent and wait for me. It's too cold out here."

Ibericus made his way to the Primus Pila's tent and poked his head in. A candle flickered uncertainly as Gaius and Appian studied an ancient map of the route beyond the pass. The centurion looked up, saw Ibericus, and listened. Throwing his cloak over full armor the centurion promptly strode toward the gathering, with Ibericus following from a distance. Gaius watched from the shadows, then he moved to the fire with the same determination all had seen before.

"My turn?" he said to the conspirator. A glint of fear appeared in Quintillus's eyes, but he merely raised his palm, inviting the Primus Pila to speak.

"I am going to Rome by way of the pass ahead of us. I will not jeopardize your lives by leading you through Parthian territory because we cannot fight 100,000 men. No one we met ever said anything about peace between Rome and the enemy that slaughtered 20,000 of our legionnaires at Carrhae. I, therefore, assume we remain at war. Roman prisoners may still be at Merv, and Merv stands in our way if we go back. Personally, I don't care to be a slave or corpse of the Parthians. Now, since I will not lead you to your deaths, who will? Are you ready to put your trust in the deserter Quintillus, a man whose complaints are legendary? You are strong, resilient soldiers. How long will you abide by the decisions of this mutineer?"

Ibericus grinned. The Primus Pila could calculate when indecision reigned. He knew when an enemy was on the verge of losing and when the javelin must be hurled for that final, fatal moment.

"You have been trained as soldiers of Rome," he continued. "You know the importance of discipline and cohesiveness on the march and in battle. True, we are few in number, but we have been tested and word of our prowess has spread. We are both honored and feared, which has served us well. If you turn back without discipline you become rabble, a degenerate band of wanderers and outlaws. You will be silenced one by one and will die in ignominy."

The Primus Pila looked around at faces he had led for years. Ibericus could feel the trust returning. With the barest hint of a smile, the centurion said, "Now, legionnaires, what if we find and befriend the Seres people we meet beyond that wall? What if we trade them our knowledge for their silks and become ambassadors for their court in Rome? Certainly they will assist us and perhaps join us on that glorious journey. Would we not be rich and famous for such an exploit? Think of it, comrades, we would be the very first Romans to visit the Seres people and return to tell about it. How many books will be written about us, how many generations will relate our tale to their children? All we have to do is get there. I start tomorrow, and I expect to see you at dawn when the trumpet sounds."

***

"How many are gone?" asked Gaius when Appian stuck his head in the tent.

"None. They're cold and hungry and some are sick, but they're all here."

"And that bastard Quintillus, where's he?"

"Hunched over a little fire at the rear. He's alone. What should we do about him?"

"Nothing. He can come or freeze to death."

"I heard your remarks last night. You were very persuasive. I thought that was quite ingenious about being ambassadors for the Seres people."

"I thought it was pretty good, too, but I don't think I can convince them again; they will have heard it all. We must get over this pass as quickly as possible. Now check on the men. We have to march."

Chapter 14

Excitement coursed through Ling Qui Seng. It was not money or the prospect of advancement within the battalion of castrated men who watched over the emperor's concubines that drove him now. His body shuddered with anticipation, his mind screamed with insatiable need. The possibility that lay before him was something he had fantasized about for most of his life. It was deviously delicious, even greater than gaining confidential knowledge for the loftiest eunuchs.

Rumors and deadly schemes floated like phantoms in the palace corridors. It was imperative to know who would live, who would die, and who would reward him for what he could learn. Indeed, there were many to fear: ministers, the most valued concubines, and even the soothsayers with their incontestable magic.

He was trusted by his superiors and allowed to come and go when not guarding the Emperor's multitude of concubines. But Ling Qui, while showing deference and loyalty, had his own agenda. With utmost discretion he cultivated the dependence of a number of aristocrats.

It would appear unwise for members of the royal family to be seen in the squalid alleys of Chang'an, where potions, poisons, and smuggled exotics were secretly passed from the hands of thieves and alchemists to scheming concubines and dilettantes. But Ling Qui knew the labyrinth of passageways, where the odors of smoke from cooking fires mixed with incense and unwashed bodies. Half-lit corridors burgeoning with pots and spices, silks, and fly-speckled meat created a maze of squalid tunnels in which lurked intrigue, lust, and deceit. The shouts, the wailing of infants, the barking of dogs, the clamor of fishmongers, and the incessant hammering of metalsmiths crated a cacophony of sounds that only subsided just before dawn.

Ling Qui had grown up in this squalor of desperation, in the same blighted alleys, until the age of thirteen when his father could no longer feed him. For a handful of coins he was sold to the court and castrated the next day.

He'd had sex only twice in his life before they cut him. He had relished it and wanted more, so much more. The indescribable pleasure of the girl's response to his thrusts had made him delirious with joy. But that was over, a delight he would never experience again. And he had been so young, so inexperienced. If only there had been time to learn all the tricks older men knew. The thought of what had been ripped from his young life was more painful than the knife.

In time the excruciating pain of castration subsided, but the humiliation and the hatred never did. Recurring nightmares of the slashing knife and the hot chili sauce anesthetic assaulted him. He recalled with dread the plug that was placed in the hole for three days, until it was determined that he could urinate. Boys who couldn't died a most painful death. And, unlike others who shrugged off the contempt of the mandarin bureaucrats, he shuddered when they disdainfully referred to him as a bob-tailed dog, denoting the loss of testicles and penis, the "three preciouses."

The removal of all genitalia had left him with a high voice, a thickened stomach, and an embarrassing lack of bladder control. Far too often he found himself wetting his clothing. Like all other eunuchs, he carried his severed genitals, the bao, in a little sack hung from a sash at his waist. Upon burial he hoped to be reincarnated as a complete and whole man. "It must be buried with me," recited Ling Qui every morning before beginning his tasks for the day.

Many eunuchs rose to high status, could speak casually to the Emperor, and had daily access to him. There were over 40 ranks, and those at the top experienced lives of opulence and power. For some, that influence compensated for the loss of sex, but not for Ling Qui. Someday, somehow, he would do something that would give him pleasure and vengeance.

Days before he'd been sold and castrated there had been a rebellion by court eunuchs, resulting in the extermination of dozens. They had had to be replaced by those, like Ling Qui, who were untainted by the lust for power. The world of Ling Qui Seng became an austere cocoon of house slaves, castrated males, and untouchable concubines. As he matured, he came to understand the value of power, and he ingratiated himself with the lords and ladies who required intelligence within – as well as beyond – palace walls.

It was not money the middle-aged eunuch craved. Rather, it was what had been denied him, the pleasure of women. Standing outside the bedchambers of the royals he could distinctly hear passions and agonized about what had been torn from his body. In his younger years the voyeur in him had had to be satisfied with only the sounds. Of course he knew that he could never have a woman; indeed, the very purpose of the eunuch was to ensure that such a union was impossible. But no one could deny him his fantasies.

He had not seen a nude woman for years. He could only imagine what sumptuous flesh existed beneath the robes of concubines. Though he was responsible for escorting them from one location to another, any physical contact was expressly forbidden. The slightest touch could result in execution. Yet he had to know, had to see, what happened behind those doors. What was it that mature men did to make the women moan and plead with such abandon? And what was it the women did to please their lovers, to be allowed to live in luxury within the palace walls?

He wondered how he could possibly satiate his innermost needs. What devious method would induce an official to let him enter the chamber and observe? He weighed the use of blackmail, discarding the idea as too dangerous. Unsolved murders happened all too often. Indeed, the absence of a eunuch would hardly raise an eyebrow. There had to be another way. It would require great thought. And luck.

Ling Qui made a study of the clandestine trysts of high officials who dared take the Emperor's concubines to their bolted, private chambers. But there were men of lesser status who had not been awarded offices of their own, and these needed a secret cubicle to satisfy their lust. Thus, it was imperative that he know every hidden niche and half-completed parlor in the sprawling Weiyang palace.

Informers and spies were everywhere. As one of them, he knew them all. The delivery of a paramour to a man had to be done with the strictest secrecy.

Any hint of a liaison with the Emperor's concubines would result in immediate execution, and none dared to take a girl beyond the palace gates.

It was nearly a year before he cultivated the trust of an imperious young royal. The eunuch had seen how the boy hungered for one of the concubines, an enticing girl named Xi Shi who had not yet slept with the august Emperor of the Celestial Empire. The concubine had been warned of the dire consequences of her flirtatious eyes, but, upon seeing the young man, her adolescent desire overwhelmed her discretion. She was only one of hundreds of young women made available to the Emperor, and it might be years before he would call for her. Unfulfilled, she lay in her bed each night and listened to the consummated women whisper about their night with the exalted one.

"I must have her," the young royal whispered to Ling Qui. "Can you arrange it? No one will ever know."

"It will be extremely dangerous for you and for me, my lord," said the eunuch.

"But it can be done, can it not? I will pay whatever you want."

"I don't need money. I want something else."

The boy stared at him. "What else could you want?"

"I am entrusted with the girl's safety. I'm required to observe everything, and I cannot allow you to be alone with her," Ling Qui said archly. The part about observing was a lie, but over this youth the eunuch would flaunt his impeccable credentials.

The young royal was silent for a moment. "You could be nearby. Perhaps you might hide behind a curtain. I wouldn't mind that."

"I would have to be close, very close. For her safety I must be able to hear and see everything."

"Yes, exactly," said the excited youth.

"And she must not know that I am there." He scrutinized the boy, sensed his desperation, and wondered how long before he could sit only inches from the writhing girl.

"And you, eunuch, will make no noise and say nothing about it to anyone."

"And you will do the same." Ling Qui put his hands together and bowed low, but not too low.

They would have to plan carefully. A very special room was needed, a small one with a rear entrance. The palace had over a thousand rooms and was a labyrinth of secret passageways. Though he had spent much of his life in its confines, he hadn't realized how extensive the hidden places were until he'd begun silently exploring for just the right location.

After locating a tiny, unlit cubicle, he hung brocaded curtains through which he cut a discreet slit. Next he positioned a chair behind the curtain and surveyed his handiwork. Yes, he thought, as the excitement bolted through him, he would see it all.

Ling Qui could not sleep the night before the assignation. His insatiable and unfulfilled desires caused him to gasp, and he worried that he might emit an impassioned, strangled moan during the coital act itself. But if the Fates played tricks and alerted the girl, she would not dare say a word. To do so would implicate her, and that would mean death.

Xi Shi feigned illness when the other concubines were shunted to an adjoining room of the palace to await their choosing. Later that night, the eunuch led her through a maze of corridors to a narrow and forgotten cubicle once used by construction workers. Over the course of several days he had cleaned the room and readied it for the appointed night. Not daring to light a candle, he had the girl follow closely as they moved through dim passageways. His own excitement and fears were compounded by the girl's. Her anxious breathing was audible. She shivered. With one hand she held up her long gown, lest she trip as they ascended steep stairs to the nondescript room.

The eunuch tapped lightly three times. The door opened and the boy hungrily pulled her inside. Ling Qui waited a moment, then made his way through an adjoining room and back into the draped alcove.

He willed his hands to stop shaking and made sure that the bottom of the heavy curtain had been secured to the floor so that it would not swish if he touched it. Three oil lamps glowed in the lovers' cubicle, throwing shadows onto the wall.

Ling Qui seated himself behind the curtain, his heart pounding with anticipation. For this he had put his life in jeopardy, but it was worth it. It mattered not that he would engage in the act vicariously; it would be the closest he would ever come to the real thing.

The two youths stared at each other for a long moment, as if they weren't sure of how to proceed. Their eyes were wild. The boy tugged at the girl's silk robe.

"Wait," she pleaded breathlessly, "it mustn't be ripped or stained. They'll know."

"Then hurry!" The boy stared at the slim, exotic figure as the fabric plummeted to the floor. A moment later he threw off his own robe. The flickering lamps cast an uneven light on his erection. The girl's hand went to her mouth to stifle a gasp.

"Take it, hold it."

She did as he commanded. Her arm shook and her body shivered. A droplet oozed onto her hand and she released the boy's organ to stare at it.

"Taste it." he said, and again she did as he asked.

In the sallow light Ling Qui could see it all. He involuntarily touched the place on his own body where they had cut him. Feeling the scar, he tasted a tear that ran down his face.

The boy pulled Xi Shi to him, lowered his head, and sucked one pubescent breast. His hands began to explore her body. He clutched her bottom and slid his hands between her thighs until he found her sex. He knelt and toyed with it, then lifted her up and threw her on the bed. Her legs were spread and the eunuch stared at the dark patch. To Ling Qui's amazement, the concubine grasped the royal's erection and nuzzled it into her vagina. A second later the youth thrust forward. The girl issued a stifled moan. As the penetrations began, the young royal looked not once toward the curtain. The eunuch worried that the girl's uncontrolled moans and rapturous pleas might be heard in the silent halls.

Suddenly it was over. The boy let out a startling gasp, his organ still inside the concubine. Her thighs were tight around his waist. They seemed lost in reverie until she gave him a concerned look. The boy took no notice as they quickly dressed. As it had been arranged, Ling Qui slipped out the back door of the cubicle and, after seeing no movement, quickly escorted the girl back to her chambers. Moments later the boy scurried away in the opposite direction.

"You must do it longer and I must be closer, right beside the bed," the eunuch exhorted the young royal when he was approached two weeks later.

"But the girl will see you there, she might be ... distracted."

"I don't care. It's for you to keep her mind occupied."

"But you mustn't touch her, at least not while I'm inside of her."

"Not while you're doing it, but I must see, I must touch if even for a moment. I cannot do what you can, so do not fear."

This time, the eunuch emerged from behind the curtain once the boy's penetrations began. Xi Shi looked up with a start when Ling Qui kneeled beside the bed only inches from her. She began to scream and the boy instantly covered her mouth. He was so close, staring at her undulating body as the young royal penetrated her. The boy was in better control now, willing himself to last longer and enjoying the thrill before the spurt.

Ling Qui moved the oil lamp closer. He could see everything. His heart pounded. Incapable of waiting a moment longer, he squeezed one of the girl's breasts and licked a nipple. The boy tried to push him away but the eunuch wouldn't budge. The girl moaned deeply from the frantic sex that enveloped her. This time the boy pulled out of the girl seconds before he ejaculated.

"Go!" said Ling Qui, "I'll take her back once you're gone."

The boy hesitated for just a moment before arranging his robes and scurrying into the dark corridor. Xi Shi started to rise, but the eunuch pushed her back down and put a finger to his lips. "Soon," he said. He knelt between the concubine's legs. He could feel the quivering of her thighs as he peered at her. He had heard of what men did between those thighs before the penetrations and now, alone with the girl, he had to try it.

Later, after he had snuck her back into the concubine's quarters, he reveled in his success, that just with his tongue, he had given the girl as much pleasure as she'd had with the boy. She had even whispered as much, asking him to do it each time once the boy left.

It went on that way for the next four months. None of them ever saw or heard the woman who slipped in and out of alcoves, listening by the door, melting into the inky blackness with a tight, knowing smile on her ancient lips. But Lady Xie Bingzhong had learned what she needed to know and what secret she would keep for a more propitious time.

***

The concubine was worried about her illness.

"I haven't been feeling well for the last three weeks and especially since we enjoyed our lotus and stalk time," she said to her young lover. "I've been vomiting in the morning. I told my friends that I have a cold, but I know it's not a normal illness. I think I'm with child."

The eunuch and the boy exchanged worried glances. They could not allow an examination by the court doctor. There were already telltale signs of pregnancy. They did everything they could not to alarm the girl during their final liaison. The act did not alter, except that the girl's eyes showed fear rather than lust.

Upon the young royal's departure from the cubicle, the eunuch walked with the concubine toward her chambers. He suddenly stopped and pretended to hear footsteps. Grasping the girl's hand, he spirited her up steep stairs to a precarious landing. They waited in nearly total darkness until he said that it was safe to descend. He was two steps behind her when in one calculated move he shoved as hard as he could.

The girl screamed as she plunged headlong down the marble steps.

"Is she dead?" asked the boy, staring into the lifeless eyes.

"Quite dead," said the eunuch. "Now go and forget about this. Never ask me to do such a thing again."

It was four days later when the Minister of the Household and his aide arrived at the quarters of the concubines with instructions to select three young women for the Emperor's pleasure. Ling Qui stood beside the aide as all 231 were assembled. The minister of household read two names, and the girls came before the aide, heads down. Then in an imperious voice he called, "Xi Shi."

No one moved. The name was called a second time by an impatient assistant.

"Xi Shi," said the Five Pleasures Concubine, an older but greatly favored woman. "Has anybody seen Xi Shi this morning?"

"No, mistress, but perhaps she's sick. She's often sick," said a slender girl.

The aide turned to Ling Qui. "Go to her quarters, find her. I don't care if she's ill. The emperor requires her presence."

After a suitable amount of time the eunuch returned and shook his head. "My lord, she is not to be found. Perhaps she is hiding, or worse. I fear she was greatly distraught and fearful of not being able to please the Emperor. She might have even been suicidal."

"That frightened?" exclaimed the aide.

"Sir, the girl had been here for over a year and despaired that she had not been chosen by the august one. She worried that she was unfit or not pretty enough and had been passed over."

"But you did not report this?"

Ling Qui bowed his head. "I did not think it proper for a mere eunuch to suggest such a thing. I assumed that the Five Pleasures Concubine, being responsible for the health of the women, would be aware of the girl's fears."

"I never heard any such thing from her," retorted the head concubine.

"This will displease His Celestial Being. There will be questions," said the Minister of the Household. Quickly he looked over the assembled concubines, motioned to a fetching replacement, and, accompanied by all three, exited the chamber.

*****

The Minister of Censorship and Security removed the slip of paper from the silk envelope and studied the elegantly penned calligraphy. Sima Gao, like many in the Weiyang Palace, had heard about the missing concubine. Having never shared the emperor's bed, the girl was not yet favored, but she was his property nevertheless.

A lieutenant had found the envelope upon opening the door four days after the girl was reported missing. No name was penned beneath the script that simply said, "Beneath the stairs in the unfinished mall. Ghosts and evil Fates waft in a cocoon of mist. And a royal fears."

Two dozen soldiers were dispatched to the incomplete chambers and the crumpled body of Xi Shi was found. Sima Gao immediately ordered an inquest. In his presence were assembled the Five Pleasures Concubine, the Minister of Heraldry, and the imperial doctor who also acted as coroner. Also present were Ling Qui and the Most Exalted Eunuch, who represented the status and credibility of all palace eunuchs. In the court a threat to a single eunuch was a threat against all, and no accusation dared go unchallenged.

"How could the girl have departed the concubine chambers without being seen?" said Sima Gao, looking at Ling Qui.

Imperiously, the exalted eunuch responded. "She was rumored to have ghostly afflictions. Surely that allowed her to slip through walls without detection. This was reported to me by the late sorcerer Madam Wu. And I suspect that she had great fear of performing the sex act with the Son of Heaven. That, most likely, is why she chose suicide."

"I'm not so sure," said the Minister of Censorship and Security. "Fear, perhaps. I'm sure many girls are decidedly nervous in the presence of the Emperor. But suicide? Here in this forgotten spot? She hadn't even been introduced to the Celestial Being, and who's to say she would have been selected that evening? Other girls were already in his chamber for the night."

"But surely if she had special powers, she might have used them to her advantage, I mean in pleasing the emperor," said the Minister of Heraldry.

"The girl was quite strange," the Five Pleasures Concubine chimed in. "For the safety of His Celestial Being the suicide might have been a good thing. Who knows what mischief she might have made?"

The doctor gave a slight shake of his head. Sima, seeing the motion, ordered all to leave except the physician.

"You examined the girl; what is your conclusion?" he asked.

"Most certainly she died of a broken neck. It might have been suicide."

"Might have been?"

"The girl was with child, my lord. She must have known that she would be executed for her indiscretion."

"Who would have had access to her?" asked Sima.

"Anything can happen in the palace, even though she was being watched wherever she went. And if it was rape and she knew the man, then—"

"He would die," said Sima Gao.

"The rooms at the top of the stairs were unfinished and boarded up. I have no idea why she would have been at the top of the stairs. She may have jumped to her death or ..."

"Or what?"

"Pushed," said the doctor.

"Murdered by someone who didn't want to be accused of bedding a concubine of the Celestial Emperor," concluded Sima.

"And one more thing," said the doctor. "The girl was also drugged."

"Drugged?"

"Well, actually, poisoned. My suspicion is that the perpetrator knew she was pregnant and decided to poison her, but it was taking too long. So he threw her to her death before the Five Pleasures Concubine found out."

"And you're sure it's poison?" quizzed Sima Gao.

"I know the symptoms of *wu tou* when I see them. It induces vomiting, which was found on her clothing. Yes my lord minister, the girl was definitely poisoned."

***

In the early morning Sima and General Chen Tang sat beside a lake in the deserted Shanglin Gardens. The general studied the slip of paper handed him by the Minister of Censorship and Security.

"Who do you think wrote it?" he asked.

"I don't know, but if I were to guess it would be Lady Xie Bing Zhoung. She wanders the Weiyang Palace like a specter and is challenged by no one."

General Tang nodded. "My wife had her rid our house of the hungry ghosts. Jia Zhou thought that her grandfather came back and ate her rice and dumplings. I think some mice got into a storage bin, but she demanded I hire the woman."

"Did her grandfather's ghost go away?"

"No more rice went missing. Of course, I also killed every mouse I saw," said General Tang with a little smirk. "So you think Lady Xie Bing Zhoung saw the person who murdered the emperor's concubine?"

"It's quite likely. Why else would she have slipped the indictment beneath my door? She's quite good at divining the future. They say that she sees everything."

"Have you interrogated her? She would know who bedded the girl."

"I haven't. Lady Xie Bing Zhoung has many enemies at court and I don't want to be one of them. Such an investigation can have unfortunate repercussions—spells and the like. And of course, she's the Emperor's sorcerer. She'd complain directly to the Son of Heaven, and I wouldn't care to be interrogated by him."

"But she's caused a lot of distress, and her enemies would like nothing better than to see her demise," said General Tang.

"She's too cunning, manipulating, and devious to allow that to happen, but she won't live forever. It's said that she's ill."

"Perhaps," said the general. Looking at the slip of paper again he said, "Her note mentions 'royal fears.' Is she suggesting a perpetrator in the palace?"

Sima shrugged. "She was dallying with someone who could afford expensive poison. That wouldn't be a lowly servant."

"So it was a wealthy man. A royal."

"Yes. But the girl was quite young and probably fell in love with someone about her own age. That would narrow the field. I also suspect he had an accomplice."

"But surely she wasn't bedding two men," said Tang.

"No, I'm sure she wasn't, but if there was an accomplice he would want something in return—money or information."

"Even more curious is how any man could approach one of the Emperor's women and spirit her away without alerting the Five Pleasures Concubine."

"The only male allowed in the concubine's presence would have been a eunuch," said Sima. "As for the poison, did she take it rather than face certain execution, or did her lover force her to?"

"But why poison her? She died from a broken neck."

"She ingested the poison first. Poison isn't always fast acting. It's possible that she took it, could not stand the pain, and chose suicide. Then again, he might have killed her because she wanted to be treated by a doctor. The man could not allow that; she would be forced to give his name." Sima pondered it all. "The doctor maintains that she was definitely poisoned. That much is established. I wonder where the murderer got the poison," said Minister Sima.

"It's not an easy thing to procure, but there are people in the poor areas of Chang'an who know how to concoct it. In fact, there's a poison the army uses. It's derived from a plant with blue flowers and we apply it to arrowheads. It's quite lethal, but requires two or three days to kill. It's made only during times of war because its effects dissipate with time. So this royal had to have somebody outside of the military procure it for him. That would require knowledge of the underworld. Poisons like that aren't allowed to be made without official permission," said Chen Tang.

"So it would be someone with a source on the outside, perhaps in those putrid village alleys where one can buy anything if one knows where to go. Who would be able to leave the palace and negotiate that labyrinth?"

"Someone whose coming and goings would not arouse suspicion," said the general.

"We questioned one eunuch, but he was defended by the Most Exalted Eunuch and no one at court is ready to challenge his power. At any rate, I will keep my eyes open. Anyone who has gotten away with the seduction and murder of a concubine may try it again,"considered Sima Gao.

"Do you think the Emperor knows about the girl's pregnancy or the poisoning?"

"I had an audience with him. He was irritated to learn that he had been deprived of a beautiful concubine. I could have mentioned the poison and the pregnancy but the girl was already dead. I didn't care to further disturb the harmony of the Son of Heaven by implying that there was a murderer loose in the Celestial Palace," said Minister Sima. "I wanted to carry on the inquest myself without others involved."

"Have you any suspects?"

"Nothing for sure. But the culprit would have to be a royal so smitten and so determined that he would take a terrible chance."

"And yet so naïve or incompetent to think that he would not impregnate the girl."

"Or, worse yet," said Sima, "not caring about pregnancy if he had already decided to murder her."

***

Ling Qui was lightheaded with relief that the investigation had not singled him out for interrogation. Whereas he occasionally made excuses to avoid an onerous chore, he now made a point of diligently manning his post and fulfilling every request of the Five Pleasures Concubine. Further setting his mind at ease, the young royal had not once acknowledged him, though they had passed in the halls when the eunuch escorted concubines from one place to another.

Nevertheless, Ling Qui listened to everything that had to do with the death of the concubine Xi Shi. He had heard, for instance, that the Minister of Censorship and Security had visited the place of the incident on numerous occasions and had finally banned all from approaching the site.

Yet the eunuch was a curious man who told himself that his existence depended on what he as well as others knew. It was important that he monitor the place of the murder since the investigation was still ongoing. It was not difficult for him to locate a deserted workman's loft above the stairs and slip into it. He believed anything of significance would occur after dark, including perhaps the ghostly appearance of the dead girl.

He half expected to see Lady Xie Bing Zhoung when he heard footsteps. She would carry no lantern, for it was said that, guided by spirits, she could see in the dark. The hesitant footfalls the eunuch heard were accompanied by a flickering candle.

But those were followed by other, more decisive footsteps, perhaps belonging to someone of authority. In the half light of the sallow candle Ling Qui saw the familiar face of the Minister of Censorship and Security. He inched into an alcove behind a pillar and waited. The first set of footfalls approached the stairs from which the concubine tumbled. The candle was lowered as if the seeker was looking for something left behind. The figure stood, listened, and peered again, then hastened down the hallway. He tripped over a pile of stones, and the candle flew to the floor. Unsteadily he rose and was about to retrieve the faltering light when the Minister of Censorship and Security picked it up and held it before his face.

"Never come here again," hissed Sima Gao.

Trembling, the youth backed away, but the Minister thrust the hot candle into his hands and walked off.

"Yes, Father," said Shang Gao as he slumped against a pillar. It was a long moment before the youth, visibly shaken, continued on his way. Ling Qui smiled and knew that he was safe.

Chapter 15

"Stay together! Close up the line!" the Primus Pila shouted as the wind whipped sleet into frozen faces. Men had been sent ahead to clear drifts from the road but their effort proved futile. It had been six days since they'd begun the ascent, and although fur-lined boots and trousers had been purchased in the villages, the possibility of frostbite was on every legionnaire's mind. At night men huddled close to the fires. They erected stone and brush barriers to blunt the wind and cut shelters in the sides of the mountain, but nothing could ward off the cold. Sleep was impossible. If nothing else, that kept the men from slumbering into a frozen death.

"How much further to the summit?" Gaius asked one of the exhausted road crew, his breath visible in the campfire's glow.

"It's not that far. However, the switchbacks are treacherous, the ascent is steep, and the wind can tear you off the road. Centurion, it would be wise to tie rope between the men. It's a long way to the bottom."

"I want to reach the summit and start down to the tree line as soon as possible," Gaius said to Appian. The wind whipped the flames and sparks of the fires. "We'll start again at first light. Push the men hard. We'll lose them if they fall behind."

Appian's smile seemed forced. "The snow is two weeks early, Gaius. I'll tell the men that there's warm food and warmer women in Kashgar on the other side. That should give them an incentive."

"Just don't tell them that our stay will be short. Once over this, there's a desert waiting."

"At least it will be warm. Maybe a bit too warm," said the trumpeter.

***

"Centurion, there is a problem; you must come," said Apollodoros, the words coming as little puffs of mist. A weak sun filtered through damp fog.

Tacitus knelt beside Lepidus and held a cup of tepid wine to his lips, waiting for his father. At last, he saw Apollodoros lead Gaius down the snow-clogged road to where Tacitus and many other men had gathered.

"It's Lepidus. Look at his leg," Apollodoros said quietly.

The legionnaire's boot had been removed and the barbarian-style pant leg rolled up to reveal a blackened foot. Lepidus lay against a rock and shivered uncontrollably despite the cloaks wrapped about him. Six men had complained of blackened toes and fingers the night before, but none were as stricken as Lepidus.

Gaius knelt down, examined the foot, and pricked it with his dagger. "Soldier, can you feel this?"

Lepidus mumbled and shook his head. His words labored through chattering teeth while sweat ran down his face. Gaius peered into the man's eyes, rose, and led Apollodoros aside. A few minutes later, Apollodoros returned and motioned to Tacitus.

"Gaius wants to speak with you."

Standing before his father, Tacitus said, "Can't we take him with us? We can make a stretcher and carry him."

The Primus Pila shook his head. "We still have a 1500-foot climb, and it's got to be done today. The trail is too steep for him to be carried; it will only put others in danger."

Tacitus glanced at Apollodoros. "There's nothing …?"

"The foot would have to come off, Tacitus. I've done amputations before, but it was in a field hospital where we could apply clean bandages. He would likely bleed to death if I tried that here. And carrying him up the mountain is beyond the endurance of the others."

"Your friend is going to die, and there's nothing any of us can do about it," said Gaius. "You may stay with him for a short time, then you must leave him. He has his gods to pray to. Tell him that he has been a good soldier and his memory will be honored."

"But he'll die alone."

"Not if you're there and he decides to end it quickly. It can be done with little pain. It's his choice."

They returned to the stricken man. Lepidus looked at Gaius and Tacitus with glassy eyes. He attempted to sit up.

"No, don't exert yourself; you've stood for me many times before," Gaius said. "You have been a fine soldier of Rome, Lepidus, one of the best. You will be welcomed on the Field of Mars, and sooner or later we will join you there. Now rest; your next journey will soon begin."

Unexpectedly, Lepidus looked clearly at the Primus Pila. He issued a weak grin. "Centurion, this journey hasn't been too bad. I hope to see you on the other side. But you can leave that lovely *vitis* stick here, if you wish."

"I promise not to use it on you until we meet again," Gaius said with a tight grin. Standing, he turned to Tacitus. "Speak with him as we discussed."

A number of men squeezed Lepidus's hands and bid him well. With Tacitus at his side, Lepidus mouthed his thanks as he spoke the names of his comrades. Within a few minutes only three legionnaires remained as the cohorts prepared for the final ascent. A wind began to whip little eddies of snow, and Tacitus wiped flakes from his friend's brow.

"We survived Carrhae," Lepidus reminded Tacitus. "You, me, Sempronius, that big lump Ibericus, and a few others." He coughed. "Funny, I feel warm now." He tried to grip Tacitus's arm, but his strength was gone. "It's like we're in Rome again, at the Forum on a summer's day. Remember Rome, Tacitus? Now it seems so far away and so long ago..."

"But in a way you may be there again. Like the Primus Pila said, we may all be there someday."

"Yes, all together again. That would be grand..." His eyes lost their focus.

"How do you want to end it?" Tacitus said after a moment. "I'll do whatever you wish, but it must be soon."

A coughing spasm wracked Lepidus. When it subsided he whispered, "I don't want to see them all march away without me. I want to be with them, at least in spirit."

Spittle formed on the man's lips. He closed his eyes and nodded to his *puglio*. Tacitus drew the knife and held it to his friend's jugular. His hand trembled and he hesitated.

"Do it," Lepidus blurted.

It was quick; there was a spurt of blood and the labored breathing ceased. Tacitus wiped the knife clean and put it back in Lepidus's scabbard. With the help of two waiting legionnaires, he covered the body with stones to keep the wolves at bay. The last cohort was already 50 yards up the trail, disappearing into the fog. Tacitus mouthed a quiet farewell and hurried to join the column.

***

Great stones had dislodged with the previous storm. The road had become a jumble of ice-covered boulders in the thin air. Breath came in little gasps as each man strove to put his feet into the print of the soldier just ahead. A rope stretched from man to man, looped around the waist, but two of the advance party slipped and fell to their deaths in the abyss below. Appearing like white lumps, the men bent at the waist, struggled against the wind. They could not see the bodies at the bottom of the cliff and were too numb to care. Blinded by icicles frozen to lashes, they stumbled onward.

One man, exhausted, untied himself, sat down beside the mountain wall and told passers-by that he would rejoin them as soon as he could. No one believed him. A few nodded and issued encouraging words. A centurion lifted the man to his feet, attached him to a rope, and nudged him on until he sank to the ground. Cut from the line, he again sat against the rock wall. No one stopped for him a second time.

Heads down, shoulders hunched against icy snow that trickled down their necks, they appeared as ghostly specters. Groping upward, they slipped on boulders, fell, and pulled others down with them. Another man plunged into the chasm, his scream barely audible in the shriek of the wind.

Where the path widened, Gaius stood to the side, encouraging the men. He tried to judge their mental and physical condition, knowing the point at which even the staunchest would fail. They hadn't yet; the legionnaires merely stared back at him.

"I suggest that you give them a break," Apollodoros said.

"It's too soon. If they stop, they'll freeze. They've got to keep going," Gaius rasped.

Another hour would do it, maybe less, he thought, but there was no way to tell. The trail snaked upward between snow-encased boulders and flinty shale. He heard an avalanche somewhere above, and a blast of frigid air swept over the cohorts, slinging darts of ice.

And then it happened. The men simply stopped as if they were one. They became as immobile as the monoliths that towered above them. Gaius, staring at the stolid, hunched forms that appeared like so many gnomes, hastened stiffly to the head of the column.

"Why are you stopping?" he asked a legionnaire. The man looked at him incredulously through filmy eyes. He mouthed the words, "Can't go, Centurion." Another, his face numb with frozen mucus, said the word, "Dying."

"Come on, march!" commanded Gaius. But his words were whipped away like the stones of slingers. Not a man moved. He looked toward Apollodoros, then Appian, who raised his hands in a gesture of helplessness.

Tacitus saw his father's incredulity, as if he couldn't believe men he led would actually refuse his order.

"March!" Gaius again shouted, but not a muscle moved.

When, if ever, Tacitus reflected, had these men, these survivors, ever hesitated to follow the centurion's command? Improbable as it seemed, his father locked eyes upon him, tilted his head slightly, and gave a nearly imperceptible nod. He raised his palm, a gesture that was not exactly a plea, more of a forlorn hope. Perhaps he actually said, "Do something," but Tacitus could not hear the words. Never had the dour disciplinarian ever asked him for anything before. His father's enmity had never faded.

Turning to the line of men, Tacitus had no idea of what to do or say. He had known most of them since training days at the Campus Martius and all of them since their terrible disaster at Carrhae. His mouth felt frozen. He, too, understood the absolute limit of endurance and the termination of will. Indeed, it could be like that battle all over again: an ultimate and ignominious defeat. For the immobile cohorts, death was 20 minutes away.

Willing himself forward, Tacitus began to walk amongst them. "If we don't go on, we will die here. We will all die for nothing. We've come too far for that."

They gazed at him with blank expressions as if he spoke an alien tongue. Another blast of air, grasping like the tentacles of squid, enveloped them. He grabbed Fortunius's arm and shook him. The man nearly fell, his vacuous eyes wandering about.

"Can't go. You see?" Fortunius said, his arm motioning slowly toward the men.

A shadow swept over them. Tacitus raised his eyes. "Look!" he said, shaking Fortunius. "Look at the sky."

A blast of wind rent the clouds and the summit suddenly loomed stark and glowing above them in the effervescent light. An eagle soared across the sky, its shrill screech a clarion call that caused men to raise their heads.

"That's it!" Tacitus shouted with sudden strength. "The eagle! It's a sign, an omen just like the *aquila* carried by the legions. We may die in battle, but we will not die here!"

Again he clutched at Fortunius and dragged him a single step. The piercing call sounded again, and the men stared skyward, pointing to the soaring bird of prey.

"We are soldiers and we will not be beaten by flakes of snow. We will not quit and allow the Parthians to laugh and debase us. We are of the legion!" he shouted with all the strength he possessed. "Come, Fortunius, look at Ibericus who still carries Oshka. It's not time to die."

Like that moment when the tide ceases to flow toward the sea and begins to lap the sand, a single foot stepped forward, then another. Dumbly, but incontrovertibly, the movement began. Each man nudged the one before him forward. Clouds whipped across the summit, and again the cohorts heard the bird's shriek as it circled above them, screaming like the gods themselves.

"Follow the eagle!" Tacitus beseeched, again and again. "He sails the pass, he sees us." Turning to Appian he shouted, "Trumpeter, answer the eagle. A blast on your horn; let him hear the trumpet's call."

As incongruous as it seemed, Appian unslung the instrument from his shoulder, put his lips to the cold metal, and blew a long, quivering note. The sound reverberated through the pass and rose skyward. The eagle plummeted downward, streaking 50 feet above the cohorts, then shot toward the distant peak.

Tears froze on the men's faces. Their eyes followed the great, outstretched wings as the bird angled up toward the mountain's glistening heights. Never had Tacitus seen such high peaks before. They appeared to rise to the heavens themselves, but he knew that the will of the legionnaires had returned.

***

None noticed the subtle change in grade as they crossed the summit that afternoon. It wasn't until they had to lean backwards to compensate for the sloping switchbacks that they understood that they had challenged madness and won. The trek down was nearly as demanding as the climb. Legionnaires who tripped caused an avalanche of men. But the very thought of descending spurred them on, and they reached the tree line an hour before dusk.

Tired as they were, Gaius had them build shelters and start fires. Like the evening before, they huddled together and endured the frigid night. The worst was behind them, as were the bodies of 12 men.

The centurion sat beside Apollodoros, his onetime mentor, and Appian, his boyhood friend. He stared into the flames that flickered in the thin mountain air and thought of the moment when Tacitus spied the eagle.

"Your son is a fine soldier," Appian said, as if he read his thoughts.

"They are all fine solders," Apollodoros said. "Your son is a true leader."

The men follow him, Gaius thought. *What horrible fate would have befallen the command had Tacitus not been there when paralysis gripped the men?* Not even he, the feared Primus Pila, could have inspired those helpless lumps on the glacial road. And what would he have done if not a soul had budged? Would he, the intrepid veteran, decorated by Caesar himself, have simply gone on and left them to die?

It had been over a dozen years since Carrhae. Age had begun its ceaseless onslaught. It wasn't a thought on which Gaius cared to dwell. Not he, the indomitable Primus Pila. The growing stiffness in his back, his legs, old wounds—pains he had once shrugged off had now burrowed deep like the trenches they had dug around Alesia. Rarely had he given the slightest thought to who his successor might be when time dispatched him on his eternal march. Certainly no change would happen on this day. Yet it was something he would have to consider.

Then there was the matter of his judgment. That, too, he preferred not to dwell upon. Dare he acknowledge that he had made a mistake? Certainly the crossing had been too late in the year; he had been warned of that by people who were far more familiar with its challenges than he. But the snow had been early. Without the unexpected snowfall there would have been no faltering, and indeed no crisis of leadership. Perhaps he should have waited and not lost a dozen irreplaceable men and others so badly injured.

But it was the burden of command, and it had been his decision. It was the men's willingness to give their all that would result in success or failure. Men had been known to follow leaders because they feared them more than they loved or even respected them. He thought of Marcus Crassus, who invoked the decimation, killing every tenth man for cowardice in the war against Spartacus. Those who bludgeoned their comrades to death felt shamed and vengeful, and then followed Crassus until victory was achieved. Other men followed leaders because they worshipped them as gods; such was the allegiance given to Julius Caesar.

Gaius's thoughts returned to his son, once a wild and irresponsible youth he had despised. Something besides age and maturity had changed in Tacitus over the years. He had noticed it, but never acknowledged it. Tacitus, he suddenly understood, had the rare ability to lead men who would not otherwise be led. If there was ever greatness in leadership that was the test.

Tired as he was, Gaius remembered a similar act from a long time before. It concerned Caesar and a battle all but lost, a legion stopped cold before a seemingly invincible and overwhelming enemy. The great general tossed his helmet away so all would recognize him, grabbed the sacred eagle, and alone strode forward to the enemy line. Abashed and ashamed of their hesitation, the legion, his own Tenth, charged and slaughtered their foes.

Yes, his son had the same spirit. What Tacitus thought of his father was likely a very different matter. Did he still carry that deep hatred? Gaius knew the youth's expression so well —the clenched teeth, the exaggerated salute, and, above all, the deadly silence. Except for the tactical discussion of revenge for Sempronius, his son never spoke to him. But of course Tacitus was merely a *munifex*, a soldier with no privileges whatsoever. How could a man of such lowly rank speak to a chief centurion who had once commanded 6,000 soldiers? And, certainly, such permission had never been tendered. Now he wondered how this day should change all that.

As the evening wore on he listened to the snores and coughs of exhausted men and marveled that any were still alive.

"Appian," Gaius said when his friend came to the fire, "I want you to carry the standard and be my second-in-command."

"I'm honored, but then you'll need someone to lead the first cohort. Who will that be?"

"I'm still thinking about it."

"May I suggest someone?"

"I know your suggestion. I'm still thinking, Appian. Don't rush me."

"He's different from you, Gaius. But I remember how you were as a boy—wide-eyed, a playful trickster. Toward your father, of course, you had plenty of contempt, though it was well deserved. And, had Aspacia lived, you would not be the man you are. You would have remained a loving husband and a caring father."

"You think I was like Tacitus before I dragged him into the army?"

"You didn't associate with a bunch of petty criminals, though you did spend a good deal of time with me, and I wasn't the most sterling influence. But there was a time, before Aspacia died, when people enjoyed your company. That changed when you joined the legion."

The men felt good about Tacitus even though he appeared less communicative since the death of Sempronius, thought the centurion. No, he was not like his father: dour, stern, uncompromising, and feared.

Gaius's orders had never been openly questioned before this day. Obedience gained through discipline bonded the legion and every soldier within. He, Gaius Septimus Aquilius, understood that and had always brought forth the steel in men. Now he wondered if it was still within him. Would the men unquestionably follow him again or would they look to someone else for approval?

Regardless, he knew who had gained their respect on this day, and it had to be acknowledged.

***

"Form line of battle!" the Primus Pila commanded as the men descended a slope above the mud-brick city of Kashgar.

Still laboring from the exhausting trek, Tacitus limped into formation with the others and looked about for a hostile force. The stern, resounding voice brought him to attention. He squared away his shield and held tight to his javelin.

"Stand straight in rank, look sharp there," Gaius ordered, striding before them, his helmet topped by the red transverse crest. He slapped the *vitis* stick against his greaves to remind them of his office. They had armored up after spying Kashgar an hour before. The tight formation he now required was due less to marauders than to building morale. That was still tenuous and would have to be quickly resurrected. He would also want them to make an impression. Even if they were not descending upon the town as conquerors, they needed to command respect.

The Primus Pila walked up and down the ranks, eying each man. He stopped in front of Tacitus, stared at him, and moved on to the next man. Then he stopped and went back.

"You did well yesterday, soldier," said the Primus Pila in a voice just strong enough for others to hear. "Very well, and I am grateful."

He abruptly turned and continued down the line. Ibericus stood with his woman beside him; Gaius glanced at Oshka, but said nothing about her presence. The giant stole a glance at Tacitus and raised his eyebrows before staring ahead once again.

The Primus Pila came to the head of the formation and removed his helmet. "It is now time to honor our fallen," he said quietly. The men removed their helmets and a somber moment of silence ensued. There was a far-off tolling of a bell in Kashgar. Each clang echoed as a dirge across the valley floor.

How strange, Tacitus thought, that his father had actually praised him. Surely it was the first time he had done so since he had been dragooned into the army. The Primus Pila rarely praised anyone.

Tacitus, nearly immobile, had pleaded with the men the day before. But what would have happened if the eagle had not appeared? Would they now be covered by the unforgiving snow?

Nothing had changed. And Lepidus was dead. Tacitus sighed, looked straight ahead, and wondered what terrible strength would be needed for the next leg of the endless trek.

The centurion had thought about the march through the city. It must be one that would hearten and encourage the men for their next challenge; for, surely, that would come soon. Nor was he blind to the way the men had honored one of their own. There was a nod of respect, the admiration and desire to be acknowledged by the legionnaire, the son of the Primus Pila.

Having concluded his inspection, Gaius replaced his helmet and in a measured voice said, "Rome honors its heroes for valor on the field of battle and for indomitable courage when all hope is gone. It honors leadership and motivation even when the gods fail us or, indeed, when we fail them. Some men are born leaders; others must be beaten into that role like the steel of the gladius in the hands of the armorer. We honor that steel, that sword, for we are all soldiers of Rome no matter how distant we may be." He fell silent, and Tacitus wondered what oratory might follow.

"Legionnaire Tacitus Aquilius, to the front!"

It took a second for Tacitus to recognize that his name had been called. He was in the second rank of the first cohort. A sharp nudge from Ibericus, and Tacitus wheeled and came to attention before the chief centurion.

"As Primus Pila I have the honor of conferring upon you the rank of centurion. For your courage I award you this phalera, the medal I wear on my armor, awarded me by Julius Caesar, general and consul of Rome."

With a steady hand he attached the round bronze medallion, recently polished, to the chest of the stunned Tacitus. "You will lead the first cohort. Centurion Appian Dio is now my *optio*, second-in-command. Cohort, salute your new centurion!"

The first cohort was joined by the second, third, and fourth as iron javelins slammed against the faces of shields. A raw, unrestrained cheer rose from the throats of hundreds. Gladii were drawn and shaken at the sky. Tacitus stared back at them as they shouted, "Centurion Tacitus Aquilius!" again and again.

"Call the question," the Primus Pila ordered. Plucked from the ranks, the idea of being in command felt terribly strange.

Tacitus turned to the cohorts. "Are you ready to march?"

"Yes!" the men shouted, their fatigue a distant thing. The cohorts stood straight in disciplined ranks. Here and there smiles appeared on faces. Tacitus had been given his command.

"Are you ready to march?" he called again, sensing a growing resolve. Then, as tradition required, he called out the question a third time and received an overwhelming response.

"Centurion Primus Pila, the men are prepared to march."

"By fours, quick step, march!" the chief centurion commanded.

Cob nail *caligae* thudded in unison as the cohorts paraded down the road of Kashgar. With the late afternoon sun glistening off their armor, the legionnaires strode to the cadence, while a stunned populace stared in wonder at soldiers from the opposite side of the earth.

Chapter 16

"I saw him!" said Ming as she hurried to greet Li Mae in the Shanglin Gardens of Chang'an.

"Who did you see?"

"Tai Donc Quin. You remember, the son of the Sogdian ambassador. He's all grown up now and he's an official, a junior minister for their state records. He recognized me and was very friendly. He even introduced me to his father. I couldn't wait to tell you."

"I always hoped that he would come back," said Li Mae. "Did he ..."

"Ask about you? Of course he did. I think he really wants to see you again. He's very handsome."

"What else did he say?" Li Mae asked excitedly.

"He didn't have much time to talk, but he asked if you still collected singing crickets. I think he was joking."

"I hope you told him that I'm grown up and more mature than that."

"I started to, but his father told him to talk later. Tai said that there will be a state reception and everybody will come and he hopes to see you there. It's being put on by the Minister of Heralds."

They had only been children then, thought Li Mae, when they'd played together on the palace grounds. The boy, a year older than she, spoke Mandarin as well as the strange language of a people far to the west. He said it was used by Sogdian royalty, and even gave her a coin with the face of a long-nosed conqueror who'd come to Maracanda hundreds of years before. It had been Tai who had taught her how to speak the guttural language of the long-ago invaders who had given their language to his people. It was devoid of the musical rhythm of Mandarin, and her mother had said that learning it was a waste of time. But Li Mae thought differently—the barbarian dialect had become a secret code between her and Tai, spoken by nobody else in the Middle Kingdom.

***

The last time she'd seen him was several years ago in the Weiyang Palace. Since then he had become quite tall, with piercing black eyes and a large hooked nose. She was engaged in animated conversation with Tai and Ming when, to her surprise, Shang Gao made his way through the crowded hall and approached them. Tai stiffened and became silent.

Prince Shang Gao, in an elegant military coat, tilted his head toward the princesses, then gave a slight bow to Tai Donc Quin. In a high but precise voice he said, "I wish to apologize for the barbaric and totally improper conduct of my childhood. I know that I deeply offended you, and I wish to make amends if that is possible. I am certain that you will achieve a prominent position at court, as will I. Perhaps in time we, together, will deal with matters of state. My Emperor requires that such affairs be harmonious and I will do all I can to make them so. So I ask for your forgiveness, and perhaps we might attain true friendship in the future."

Again the prince nodded to the young women, his eyes lingering on Li Mae for a moment. He bowed to Tai Donc Quin, turned, and strode back to the assembled guests.

"Can you believe that?" asked Ming.

"How presumptuous of him to think that he'll have a prominent position here at the court," said Li Mae.

"But it did take courage to apologize," said Ming.

"You're assuming it was his idea. I bet he did it because his father told him to. I still think he's a snake."

They debated the matter until Ming saw her mother motioning to her and left Tai alone with Li Mae. "I have a present for you," he said, lifting a charm necklace from a silk cloth.

"Is it from Maracanda?"

"No, it's from Chang'an. I don't remember seeing you with one, but I'm told that it's mostly worn in May."

"Oh, a 'five poisons' charm." Li Mae admired the highly decorated metal with its gold chain. The medallion was round with a square hole in its center. Around its edge were stylized images of five poisonous pests of the season. "Yes," she said, "it's entering the dangerous time of the year when we see scorpions, centipedes, spiders, and even snakes."

"And the three-legged toad, the fifth evil."

"That one, too." Li Mae laughed and held a silk fan to her face. "Thank you for the charm. The gift is timely—the fifth day of the fifth month, what we call the Double Fifth, is the most dangerous day of the year."

"And the charm protects you from all of that?" said Tai with a flirtatious smile.

"Of course! And to protect the house we hang artemisia, or mugwort, because its leaves resemble the paws of tigers."

"Is that so? I mean, absolutely! It makes perfect sense to me. Maybe I should wear some in my hair."

"Do you always tease girls, Tai?"

"Only you."

"Really? Han men are much more reserved."

"Well, we're a jocular people and we enjoy life." His face became somber as he watched an elderly woman in dour clothing move into the shadows. Li Mae followed his eyes.

"That's Lady Xie Bing Zhoung," whispered Li Mae. "She's a seer. Many people have their fortunes told by her, especially when they're about to marry. She's quite good at face readings, but it's also said that she's a spy, so many avoid her."

"I suspect that she is. I have watched spies at our court and I know one when I see one. But whom does she spy for?"

"No one really knows. It could be the Minister of Censorship and Security, the Grand Chancellor, or even the Emperor."

Tai turned to Li Mae. "This may surprise you, but I've thought of you ever since I left here all those years ago. I'm so glad to see you again. Perhaps you and your parents would visit us during our stay. I know that my father would welcome that."

"That would be nice." She was standing close to him and he touched her hand. As she looked up she saw Shang Gao staring at them, and he was not smiling.

***

Sima Gao looked up from his documents when his son stepped into his opulent chambers. "I want to cement a relationship with the family of General Chen Tang," he said before his son could interrupt his thoughts.

"Yes, Father. You mentioned such an alliance. I think it is a very fine idea."

"You know how that must be accomplished," Sima said, glancing back at his papers.

"I'll marry Li Mae."

"Precisely. But there is a problem. You know what it is."

"Surely nothing of significance."

"Then you are ill informed. Wei Yao Quin, the Sogdian ambassador, entertained General Tang, his wife, and daughter last week. I know this for a fact. I also know that the envoy's charming son made a very favorable impression on the general and his wife, not to mention the girl."

"The general would consider marrying his daughter to a barbarian? It would be out of the question."

"Then you are ignorant of political realities. In fact, Jian Wong, Minister of the Imperial Clan, and the Emperor himself, have been advised of its possibility."

"And they countenance such a union? It's like giving princesses to the Chanyu. It's practically tribute."

"It's hardly tribute, and it is precisely the Chanyu that the Sogdiani are worried about. The Chanyu are the real barbarians. They've endangered Sogdian trade with recent attacks. That lavish event put on by ambassador Wei Yao Quin wasn't done for showmanship. They badly want an alliance with the Middle Kingdom."

"Is the marriage finalized?"

"No, and since a foreigner is involved, it may not require the Six Etiquettes, a dowry, or an official blessing by the court. But the Sogdiani have a problem which may be to our advantage."

Shang's eyes narrowed. "I want that girl, Father. She is exceptionally beautiful and I have wanted her for a very long time. Li has a difficult nature, but I think she will come to care for me and will give you many grandsons. So I hope that you know more than I do."

"Your hope lies in the fact that I have spies and you do not. At least for now. Their problem is the eunuchs who insist on controlling the court and want the ear of the Son of Heaven," said Sima. "The eunuchs believe that an alliance will lead to war with the Chanyu. Money spent on a military campaign means less money for them."

"They are a despicable, scheming lot."

Ignoring the intrusion Sima said, "The eunuchs are allied with the Emperor. The Emperor is willing to buy off the Chanyu—he doesn't care how many princesses we give them —but he doesn't want war. With the eunuchs, it has to do with power and influence around the Emperor. They'll do anything to deter a marriage between the general's daughter and the Sogdiani. Of course, the Grand Chancellor Bi Hangyong and General Tang think very differently. They would crush the Chanyu."

"But the marriage of his daughter to the Sogdian?" asked Shang. "How does he feel about that?"

"He would be inclined toward it, but he's also aware of the importance of a union with our family. The outcome depends upon your ability to gain their trust and respect."

***

Lady Jia Zhou Tang sat on a stone bench in the Shanglin Gardens. She looked pensively toward the Nine Flowers Pavilion, where Li Mae and Ming were admiring a magnificent lily pond. Troubled thoughts of her daughter's future were interrupted as the Minister of Censorship and Security's wife approached her.

Jia Zhou issued a smile and indicated a place on the bench for Liu Wen Gao.

"The gardens are quite lovely today, aren't they?" said Liu Wen as she fanned her face. "My son, Shang, was very impressed by the banquet put on by the Sogdian ambassador. I'm told that his home is also very pleasant."

"It is. Of course it's decorated in the Sogdian style, but he happily accepted the Chinese vases we gave him on our visit a few days ago."

"Yes, it was gracious of him to invite you. I've heard that Tai Donc Quin is very much taken by your daughter. Excuse me for being so candid, but my son also admires Li Mae. I believe he shared a moment with her at the ambassador's banquet. Did she mention it?"

"In fact, she did. The apology was a very noble gesture."

"He has matured greatly, as you can see. I think he'll advance quickly in the army under your husband's tutelage."

"I'm sure he will," said Jia Zhou without enthusiasm.

"Please forgive my lack of etiquette, but I must speak with you about a very important matter: your daughter and my son. I am very fond of Li Mae, and I'm worried."

"I appreciate your candor, but what could possibly worry you?"

"I know that Tai wishes to marry Li Mae, and that your husband and the ambassador favor such a union. But I doubt that the powers of Heaven will be pleased."

"How can you possibly say that?"

"Think of it, Lady Tang. Tai is hardly a barbarian, but he is not Chinese. If he marries your daughter, she'll go with him to Maracanda, a distant city you will rarely, if ever, visit.

And when he's on diplomatic missions, she'll be alone in a foreign city, with none of her own people. And Maracanda? It's hardly Chang'an."

"But she may still visit us."

"It's a terribly dangerous route," said Lady Gao, "one I would not wish on any young woman, especially if a child is involved. And her son would not be Chinese. Oh, she will teach him Mandarin, but his father will raise him as a Sogdian. He'll never be one of us. But my son will always be here with Li Mae. Your family, together with ours, will be a true Chinese family. And, of course, my husband, just like the general, has the confidence of the Emperor, not an insignificant thing."

This strategy had surely been planned by Liu Wen's husband, and it was quite bold, if not rude. Thus Jia Zhou did not feel it indelicate to raise an issue of her own. "This may be a strange question," she said, staring into the lily pond. "I'm curious. Did you ever hear anything more about that incident at the Wall, the one involving Shang and the soldiers?"

"I was never informed about any such thing," said Lady Gao. "Those are men's affairs, and it wouldn't be proper for me to ask questions. Anyway, it's up to our husbands to determine whom our children are to marry."

Jia Zhou nodded but said nothing.

"I know that all of this is weighty and difficult, but we can influence our husbands. In matters such as these they may be swayed by intimate talk. We women are more sensible and have powers of our own. I know that you will help him make the right decision for our children."

***

"I would understand if the Minister of Heraldry or the Grand Chancellor were entertaining the Sogdian ambassador, but what would induce Sima Gao to put on such a banquet?" said Jia Zhou to her husband the following day.

"He told me there may be an impression that his office had not shown proper etiquette to Ambassador Quin. So he's hosting this gala event to erase any notion of discord."

Jia Zhou gave him a skeptical look. "Well, I guess you have to attend, but I really don't wish to."

"And neither do I," said Li Mae as she handed her father a cup of rice wine.

"I will not require it, but Tai Donc Quin will certainly be there," said the general, glancing with raised eyebrows at his daughter. Then to his wife he said, "I would think that your absence would be noted, especially by Liu Wen. Her husband told me how much she enjoyed speaking with you, Jia."

Jia Zhou put on a sour face. "She virtually gave me an ultimatum, going on about how fond Shang is of Li Mae, and how difficult it would be if she married the Sogdian."

"I didn't know that the minister's wife spoke to you about marriage," said Li Mae, eyes wide.

"Well, she just plopped down next to me and after a few inane comments started right in as if we were simple peasants. I was stunned! I wonder how she found out that Tai Donc Quin hopes to marry you. There has been no formal proposal, with or without the Six Etiquettes. She sounded quite worried that her son would lose out, as if we would welcome Shang Gao with open arms." Jia Zhou cast a suspicious look at Chen. "Husband, have you spoken to Minister Gao about marriage between his son and Li Mae?"

Chen sighed. "Not in specific terms. I know that Prince Shang Gao was once quite uncivil. He's made mistakes, even military ones, but he seems to have matured into a courteous officer. His father and I are colleagues, and Sima Gao is in the confidence of Emperor Wudi."

"But I detest that boy! I am your only daughter and though I must obey, you have practically wed me to a monster!" cried Li Mae.

"Very well," said Jia Zhou after an excruciating silence, "we shall attend the banquet, but only because I want to keep an eye on everything, especially Lady Gao and her son. It will be the Double Fifth, an auspicious date."

***

Tian Zhoung Jie was the fifth day of the fifth month of the lunar calendar. It was strange that Sima Gao would choose that very date, mused the general. Yes, he and Minister Sima Gao were "colleagues" as he had told his wife, but his conversations with the minister were of an uncomfortable nature. The minister always seemed to be searching for a devious plot. Dialogue with Sima Gao was nothing less than subtle interrogation.

With the Minister of Censorship and Security nothing was ever as it seemed. It was as if he assiduously studied Sun Tzu's *Art of War* with all its subterfuge and deception. But Sima Gao, with all his spies, did not command armies of obedient troops. He lived in the shadow world, where a mistake could be costly. He needed allies, men of high repute who commanded the Emperor's respect. General Chen Tang had that, and cultivating an alliance had become central to the minister's very existence.

***

It had been five years since the frightful night when Xi Shi, the Emperor's concubine, had been thrown to her death in the Weiyang Palace. Since then Ling Qui Seng had climbed 14 ranks in the pernicious world of the eunuchs. By employing diligence, flattery, and obsequious devotion, he was awarded a multitude of duties that allowed him to move easily between the palace and the village. He supervised lesser, younger eunuchs in their motley tasks and, through bribes, even gained enough money for a change of clothes whenever his bladder suddenly discharged its rancid contents.

Despite the close call of the concubine's murder, he had never forgotten the heart-stopping excitement of watching and even touching the girl during her sexual encounters. Though those moments were long past, he still prayed for another opportunity. The prospect seemed terribly remote until, once again, it suddenly appeared.

"There is something I want you to do," said Prince Shang Gao clasping Li Qui's shoulder in the dimness of the palace wine closet. He gasped and tried to bolt, but the hand remained firm. Slowly, very slowly he turned around.

"You will get me killed."

"There will be no danger, and it will be a chance to actually see what you dream of every night. And it can be for a very long time. I will make sure of it."

A slight tremor ran through Ling Qui. "How can you ensure that? I was nearly executed the last time."

"I am no longer a naïve and frightened boy. I'm an officer and will be promoted into the highest ranks. That equates to power, influence, and protection. I intend to have many concubines in my own house, girls you can observe each night. But there is something you must get me to earn that reward. It will be simple since you have done it before."

"Poison?"

"Just bring it to me and say nothing."

"That is all? I need do nothing more ..."

"Exactly. I can't get the drug myself. I have never been in that part of the village and it is foreign to me."

Ling Qui shuddered and his eyes showed his fear. "Is this person, the one to be murdered ... important?" he said in his high voice.

"It doesn't matter, at least not to you. The Office of Security requires this death, so you'll be doing the Emperor a favor. But I must do it with absolute stealth."

"When do you need it?"

"In three days."

"And my reward?"

"Soon. It will all be arranged. I'll make a special place for you, so you can see everything; you will even be able to touch them," said Shang. "And one thing more: with the power of my father's office, I will liberate you from the palace so that you can supervise my women. You'll answer to no one but me."

"You can do that?" said Ling Qui, sensing that he was losing control of his bladder.

"I can and I will," replied the prince. "Go to the village and get what I require."

The eunuch accepted a small bag of coins and with a slight bow said, "I shall do it tonight."

Then he hurried away. He desperately had to change his clothes.

***

The great pavilion was filled with nobles, scholars, merchants, and eunuchs of varying status, all assigned tasks to make the occasion a stunning success. The center of attention was the Sogdian ambassador and his son, who were in jovial conversation with the Minister of Heraldry, the Chancellor, the Minister of Censorship and Security, and General Chen Tang.

Jia Zhou stood beside her daughter and watched Shang Gao approach the exalted men. He bowed to the ambassador and Tai Donc Quin, then excused himself and hurried off. Wending his way through the crowd, he approached a eunuch whom he led to a corner of the pavilion.

Jia Zhou whispered to Li Mae before she followed the prince. She stopped beside a red lacquered pillar.

Certain that nobody was watching, Ling Qui removed a vial from his robe and offered it to the prince.

"I've changed my mind. You will do it," said Shang, spurning the vial.

"No, that was not the agreement. What I did was already too dangerous. I might have been followed. I'm sure they're watching me."

"No one is watching you. Two drops, that's all. It will only make him a little queasy today. It will take him several days to die, and his death will be blamed on the season and the Double Fifth. Now go to where the tea is being prepared and take the tray of cups. Just be sure the intended man takes the right one."

"Two drops, that's all," Shang Gao repeated before going back to where his father was entertaining the Sogdian ambassador.

Perplexed by the exchange but not hearing the discussion, Jia Zhou rejoined her daughter. "Shang Gao just spoke to a eunuch who seemed very frightened. Perhaps I should mention it to the general."

"Something doesn't seem right," said Li Mae. Her gaze went back to Tai, who glanced her way and smiled.

Jia Zhou was about to hurry to her husband when she saw Ling Qui step toward the tearoom, beside which was a table piled with a cornucopia of fruit and little knives. He spied a tray of cups being carried out by a eunuch and said, "I will take these for you."

"No, it is my job, my responsibility," the other eunuch protested.

Ling Qui pulled on the tray, his shrill voice rising. "You don't understand. I have been ordered to do it. Now give it to me!"

"I will not. I am a twenty-ninth rank. I am We Yang Nu, your superior. Now let go!"

Fearing that he had already attracted attention, Ling Qui tore the tray from the man's grip. The offended eunuch slapped Ling Qui, who picked up a knife and slashed the man's wrist. With a shriek We Yang Nu ran back into the tearoom, blood streaming from the wound. Without another thought, Ling Qui slipped the knife inside his robe and worriedly glanced about.

It was not unusual for arguments to break out between temperamental eunuchs. The guests turned away, shaking their heads, and made disparaging remarks.

Ling Qui had only been in one fight in his life and he was scared, having injured one of higher status. He would hear about it. His face stung from the slap, and his hands shook. Finding a small alcove, he took the vial from his pocket and poured a drop into the designated cup. Again he looked nervously about. His hands shook as more drops spewed into the vessel—how many, he could not count. He stared into the cup. The poison, like eddies of mist, swirled into the tea. He dared not spill it, though the thought came to his mind. Fidgeting, he recapped the vial and saw that it was empty.

"Two drops," he'd been told, but he had poured more, so much more. The eunuch hesitated. How long before the effects would be felt? He saw Shang Gao staring at him from across the room, mouthing the words "Come. Come here now!"

Trembling, Ling Qui made his way to the clique, bowed, but said nothing. He prayed that he was virtually invisible.

"Ah, the finest tea comes from the Middle Kingdom," announced Wei Yao Quin, the ambassador.

"We are pleased that you enjoy it," said Sima Gao taking the cup offered by the eunuch. General Tang, the Chancellor, and Shang Gao took theirs in turn. The last to receive his was Tai Donc Quin. The eunuch turned away and scurried into the crowd.

Quite suddenly the ambassador's son gasped, clutched his stomach, and sank to the floor. His father knelt beside him, shouting his name, and the Grand Chancellor hollered for a doctor. Sima Gao placed towels beneath Tai Donc Quin's head. The ambassador knelt and spoke rapidly as the youth's eyes flicked back and forth. The general saw the blood drain from the youth's face and said, "He must be taken from here."

Li Mae and her mother had been watching and Jia Zhou Tang shouted, "That's him, the eunuch, he did it!" Without thinking, she and Li Mae started toward the ambassador's son. All eyes turned to the general's wife. Ling Qui, caught in the crowd, desperately tried to push past her.

In a state of mindless panic, Ling Qui pulled the knife from his pocket and drove it into her shoulder. She screamed and fell. Lunging forward again, he swiped at Li Mae, who backed away from the blade. Pandemonium erupted as Li Mae tried to staunch the blood from her mother's wound.

Shang Gao bolted forward, wrapped his arm around the eunuch's neck, ripped away the knife, and slashed his throat. Blood gushed from an artery as Ling Qui worked his mouth and tried to make sounds, though no words came. He stared at Shang Gao, but the prince pushed down on his face and covered his mouth. The eunuch was still; the light fled from his eyes.

Seconds later General Tang was at his wife's side. The blood seeped through layers of cloth as a gaggle of doctors hustled to her aid.

"Go to Tai Donc, he's dying," the general said to Li Mae, who hesitated to leave her mother. She knelt near Tai. His breathing came in ragged gulps. Tears ran down her face as she held his hand. He turned his head and vomited onto the floor. A doctor wiped his face. Tai Donc gazed at Li Mae and tried to smile. His smile was replaced with a grimace. "The fifth day of the fifth month, the Double Fifth," he managed to whisper.

"No, it's superstition. But you will live," she said. "We'll be together, I promise." Her chest heaved with the horror of it all.

"Take him to the infirmary," ordered Sima Gao, "and get some wine and cinnabar. It will help him. Hurry!"

But he knew it was already too late.

A troop of guards carried the ambassador's son out of the pavilion, trailed by the Grand Chancellor. Li Mae tried to follow, but Sima Gao turned to her and said, "You will remain here. This is a matter of state and may involve the Emperor himself. You cannot be in his presence unless invited."

"But Tai Donc Quin may die," she said. "I want to be with him. I must be with him."

"You have to do as my father asks," said Shang Gao, who had returned from the eunuch. He put his hand on Li Mae's arm. "I'm sure he'll let you see Tai when he recovers. Our friend will be okay; it's only the heat."

Li Mae recoiled from him, but guards allowed her to go no further. She turned and fled the pavilion. "Don't!" she said to Shang, who had followed behind her. "I just want to go home. My mother is hurt."

The assemblage of aristocrats and dignitaries hurried away, horrified by what they had seen and mystified as to why it had happened. Many wagged their heads, saying that no state event should have taken place on such an inauspicious day. Some felt badly for the Minister of Censorship and Security, for it was obvious that he had tried to make the ambassador welcome. Others were more concerned about the fallout, for surely there would be repercussions.

Lady Xie Bing Zhoung had remained in the shadows until everyone had left. Even the eunuchs vanished, fearful of being seen in a place where one of them had tried to commit murder.

Prince Shang Gao, failing to accompany Li Mae, turned back to the pavilion. It would be unwise, he realized, to have anything lying about that would raise questions. He entered quietly and abruptly stopped.

Kneeling where the killing had taken place, the sorcerer picked up a tiny vial that glinted in the afternoon sun. Xie Bing Zhoung examined it closely, sniffed it, and put it in a pocket of her robe. She looked about and, seeing no one, allowed herself a little smile. A moment later she slipped out

of the pavilion, oblivious of the young man who watched her
go.

Chapter 17

"I found this in front of the door when I unlocked your chamber this morning," an aide said, handing the silk-wrapped box to the Minister of Censorship and Security. Sima Gao looked at it curiously and said, "Did you see who left it?"

"No, my lord. The hall was quite empty. It must have been put there during the night, but the guards saw no one."

Sima was about to open the package when Grand Chancellor Bi Hangyong and the Sogdian ambassador stormed in. Sima Gao stared up at the angry officials and prepared himself for the onslaught.

The entire palace was stunned by the sudden demise of the ambassador's son.

"The Emperor demands a full investigation, but I hold you responsible," said the Grand Chancellor without the slightest preamble.

"I have already begun rounding up eunuchs," said Sima. He wondered if the Chancellor's show of anger was really for the ambassador. "This time they will not get away with murder."

"This time?" said the ambassador.

Hangyong glanced at him. "Four years ago a concubine was murdered, but Eunuch Number One defended him and he wasn't prosecuted. There will be no repeat of that; I want executions this time. One hundred eunuchs will die as a lesson. I will not tolerate their impudence and treachery."

"Yes, they will die," said Sima. "I only wish that my son hadn't been so diligent as to kill the eunuch who attacked the wife of General Chen Tang. I would have interrogated the man. He might have had accomplices."

"Wasn't he the same one involved in the concubine's murder?" asked Hangyong.

"Exactly the same. We should have put him to death then; I regret that I didn't overrule the Most Exalted Eunuch."

"We drank tea just before my son collapsed," said the ambassador. His voice was almost calm, but his fists were clenched. "Was there a potion in that drink?"

Sima gazed down at his silk-wrapped gift. "I checked with the eunuchs in the tearoom; the tea we drank came from the same pot. If it had contained poison we would all be dead. Obviously we know that yesterday was the Double Fifth. That could have—"

"That's a senseless myth!" raged the ambassador.

"Perhaps in Sogdiana," bristled Sima, "but not here. Pestilence, disease, sudden death ... we have known of the day's horrors for a thousand years. It is not mere superstition. The day, indeed the very hour, is a matter of record."

"Not to me. I regard it as murder, and in Sogdiana the chief of security would be held accountable. I will personally speak to your emperor, and I would be delighted to see your head on a stake beside the 100 eunuchs!"

The Sogdian ambassador turned and stormed out of the chamber.

"I wouldn't worry about the threat," said the Grand Chancellor. "He may demand a treaty as compensation for his son's death, though."

"There might be token assistance for Sogdiana against the Chanyu, but the Son of Heaven will see the execution of his eunuchs as payment enough," said Gao.

The Grand Chancellor stroked his long beard. "It doesn't make sense. How could only one person have died when we all drank the same tea?"

"The ambassador doesn't believe in the Double Fifth, but you and I do, my Lord Chancellor, and so does everybody in the Middle Kingdom. The curse of the day mysteriously strikes, particularly against a disbeliever."

"Nevertheless, I wish the doctors had had an opportunity to examine the corpse."

"Wei Yao Quin expressly forbade our doctors from touching his son's body," said Sima. "He believed we would desecrate it. He had it immediately sent home."

"Then we shall never really know, shall we?"

"The eunuchs will be tortured before their beheading. Perhaps one of them will confess. Especially if it's to save his own life. But as far as anybody is concerned, the ambassador's son died because of the dreaded day, not anything else."

The Grand Chancellor departed. Sima sat down and leaned back in his chair. The entire matter would, after official regrets and executions, be swept away like the dreaded humors of summer. The rumors would evaporate, there would be no worrisome accusations, and everything would work to his advantage. All would praise Shang for his bravery in saving the life of Jia Zhou Tang and perhaps that of the general's daughter as well.

Sima looked again at the little package wrapped in silk. A gift. But why had it not been given to him personally? He untied the string and extracted a red lacquered box. With growing curiosity, he opened the lid. A wilting blue flower lay in the box. He examined it closely and set it aside. A second object rested in the box, also wrapped in silk. He lifted the little bag and a tiny vial rolled onto his desk. A slight shiver ran through him. Sima stared at the vial, then sniffed its dried residue.

"Poison," he whispered. Somebody had found the vial and may have witnessed its use. Somebody knew and made sure that he alone received the vial. Perhaps it was to keep the evidence from reaching anybody else. On reflection, however, he realized that it was sent as a curse—a warning of doom. But he had spies. They would discover who set the box beside his door.

The minister sighed. He would ignore it all; no one could prove anything. And he only believed in superstitions when it suited him. This time it did not.

***

The whole thing puzzled General Chen Tang. He wouldn't allow himself to believe that the Double Fifth was the real cause of the death. And the speed with which Shang Gao had thrown himself at the eunuch and dispatched him so quickly —that was interesting. Yes, the eunuch had attacked his wife, but it seemed that Shang had been ready to strike even before the assault. What did the young prince know?

He entered the garden of his house and found his wife sitting beside a pond.

"Prince Shang Gao left here an hour ago," said Jia Zhou. "It's the third time this week he's tried to see Li Mae."

"Is she still in her room?"

"Yes, she just plays that sad song on her zither and writes her poetry. She's mourning as if she had been married to Tai. And of course she refuses to see Shang."

"He is persistent, though. His father wants to speak with me."

"About Li Mae and his son, I presume."

"That and the departure of the Sogdian ambassador," said Chen. "He's already left for Maracanda with his retinue. The death has caused diplomatic problems, despite the fact that the murderer was killed on the spot."

"There was something very strange about that."

"I thought the same. Still, Shang Gao did kill the eunuch. Perhaps he saved your life."

Jia Zhou grimaced. "I doubt that he would have been so vigilant if I was his only concern."

"What do you mean?"

"It's something I should have mentioned to you earlier. I think the eunuch was greatly involved. I saw Shang Gao speak to him before the tea was served. The two were having an angry conversation. Something was going on. Then there was that scuffle between that eunuch and the one carrying the tray." Jia Zhou stared straight ahead. "You were still with the ambassador and his son when Shang killed the eunuch. He tried to say something after his throat had been slashed, and Shang put a hand over his mouth. It was done with great force so, that the eunuch could not utter a word. And then, without any concern for my wound, he rushed back to Tai."

"To see if he was going to live?"

Jia Zhou gave a little snort. "No, husband. To see if he was going to die."

"Was that Shang's intention? I mean, all the eunuchs in the tea chamber would have been incriminated."

"The one incriminated would have been Prince Shang Gao and perhaps his father."

"Do you think Sima Gao was involved?"

"Well, I can't think of any reason why a eunuch would murder the ambassador's son," said Jia Zhou. "If it was planned by Prince Shang Gao, there is another question."

"And that is?"

"Whether Shang Gao would murder Tai Donc Quin without his father's consent, no matter how badly he wants to marry our daughter."

"So you think Sima Gao is complicit?"

His wife merely shrugged.

"The fact is that Tai is dead, the ambassador has left the Middle Kingdom, and, for whatever reason, Shang Gao probably saved your life and that of Li Mae," Chen stated. He was pensive for a moment. "Shang spoke with me after he left here. He said that he hoped your shoulder would mend quickly. He also said that he completely understands our daughter's seclusion since Tai Donc Quin was her very close friend. In fact, Shang claims that he got to like him, too. I won't say that the prince was obsequious, but he was extraordinarily polite. He hopes to see Li Mae soon."

"And you didn't discourage him?" said Jia Zhou.

Rather than answering, Chen said, "He wanted to give her a gift, but since she would not speak with him he gave it to me. I told him I would make sure she received it. I examined it."

He handed her an exquisite silver box with an inlaid gold dragon.

"This is very expensive," said Jia Zhou, turning the box slowly and running a finger over the artwork, thinking of the last one she had received.

"Not nearly as expensive as the other gift inside."

She opened the lid, sucked in her breath, and stared at five perfect jade stones. "These are worthy of the Emperor. How could he possibly afford them? Not even his father has enough for these."

"The prince has suddenly become a wealthy man, and that may require some rethinking on our part. These gems were a gift to Shang from the Sogdian ambassador. He also presented him with a jeweled sword in the presence of the Grand Chancellor before he left for Maracanda. Wei Yao Quin, bitter as he was over the death of his son, wanted to honor Shang for killing the eunuch. He recommended quite strongly that he be promoted. As a conciliatory gesture, the Grand Chancellor did exactly that."

"Promoted?"

"He gave Shang an entire infantry regiment and made him my close assistant. He also presented him with a sumptuous house near the Shanglin Gardens."

Jia Zhou's shoulders slumped. "So, because he's rich, you think that he is entitled to marry Li Mae," she said softly.

"It might be hard to argue against it, since there's no evidence implicating him in any wrongdoing."

"I guess the Fates have played their parts," Jia Zhou said, sighing deeply. "I shall wipe our daughter's tears and pray that Shang is an innocent man."

Chen let the moment pass. "Sima Gao requested that I meet with him tomorrow. You know what he'll suggest." He started for the house, then turned and said, "Oh, I almost forgot. Ming's father came to me today. He was quite upset. Apparently Lady Ti, the concubine who was given to the Chanyu, has died. The barbarians said that she drowned in a flash flood, but the Grand Chancellor suspects suicide.

Anyway, the Chanyu warlord, Zhizhi Chanyu, is here demanding a replacement."

"How does that concern Ming's father?" asked Jia Zhou.

"The Emperor required the Grand Chancellor to make a list of nine princesses that would be suitable for Zhizhi Chanyu. Ming is on the list."

***

Shang did not return to the general's home to visit Li Mae. He would not prostrate himself before the girl. Marrying him was not a matter for her to decide. And now that he had been promoted and honored by the Grand Chancellor, it would be extremely difficult for General Chen Tang to refuse the marriage proposal. Indeed, even the general knew that everyone was praising his swift action in killing the eunuch, and how deferential various lords, officials, and courtesans had been to him since the incident. His status had radically changed. He was no longer a minor officer attached to the command of General Chen Tang. Nor was he an easily dismissed son of the Minister of Censorship and Security. Shang Gao had become a notable figure, and a very eligible bachelor in the Emperor's court.

***

Li Mae stood in a far corner of the Grand Chancellor's chambers and watched as nine princesses were paraded past the Minister, the warlord Zhizhi Chanyu, and his son, Xion Wen Chanyu. Of all the girls, she noted with a heavy heart, Ming was the most attractive.

Their eyes downcast, none of them looked at the Chanyu until ordered to do so by the Chancellor. Many trembled while the warlord's son looked them up and down, a salacious smile on his face. His father motioned Ming closer, studied her face, and untied her robe, ignoring her obvious discomfort. She stood in her undergarments while the elderly man appraised her and stroked his beard. He waved her back into the line. A moment later his son whispered into his ear. The warlord motioned to the Chancellor, and the three men repaired to an antechamber.

Li Mae could hear the warlord's high whine, but his words were muffled. "It is not allowed! It is impossible!" the Grand Chancellor said in response.

"Then you will make it allowed and she will be delivered!" shouted the warlord's son.

Ming sniffled as she and Li Mae walked away from the Grand Chancellor's chamber. "Did you see how the barbarian was looking at me," said Ming through her tears. "I know he'll pick me and I'll never see you again. I'll die in that wasteland."

"I'll go with you if it comes to that," said Li Mae, "but there are eight other girls, and their fathers are far less influential than yours. I'm sure your father can appeal to the Emperor. And I'll have my father speak to him as well."

"Dearest Li Mae, I'm sure it's already decided, and you cannot go with me because ..."

"Because?"

They rounded a corner near the chamber of the Minister of Censorship and Security and nearly ran into Shang. "What happened?" he blurted after seeing the expression on Ming's face.

"Chanyu," was all Li Mae said as she and Ming hurried past.

***

"I just saw Li Mae and her friend. They seemed quite upset," said Shang Gao.

Sima nodded absently and stared at the contents of a little box on his desk. "The Emperor pledged another princess to the barbarian warlord, a token to keep him happy. Princess Ming Zhaojun may be his treat." He looked up and said, "You look quite smug in your new garments. You know we have a little problem of our own, don't you?"

Shang Gao remained silent as his father lifted a small vial from the lacquered box. "Do you, by any chance, recognize this?"

"I returned to the pavilion after the incident and saw Lady Xie Bing Zhoung pick something off the floor. I was hoping to find anything that might have been incriminating."

"But she found it first, and this box with the vial was laid at my door!" shouted the Minister. "She knows that the ambassador's son was poisoned. And who does she assume poisoned him? None other than our hero, my sublime and honored son!"

"Father, I believe she gave the vial to you in exchange for favors. She always curries favors and expensive gifts. If she really wished my downfall, she would have given it to the Grand Chancellor or even the Emperor."

"That sounds neat and tidy. But I can't tell you how many high officials that woman has destroyed out of sheer spite. I have seen their heads on poles. She doesn't want favors; she's toying with us. She delights in staying in the shadows until she strikes, and then she's the talk of Chang'an. I told you before, it's all about power. First she will destroy me, then you. The woman is a witch!"

"Then I shall have to concoct a spell just for her," said Shang.

"Just be sure it does not come in a vial like this," said Sima, crushing it between his fingers.

"Yes, father. This time no one will know."

***

After cordial meetings with the Minister of Censorship and Security and his son, General Chen Tang acquiesced to the marriage of Shang Gao to his daughter. Aware of the prince's ascendency and his pronounced devotion to Li Mae, Chen Tang overrode the concerns of his wife.

"It's done," said Li Mae to Ming as they sat together. Tears streamed down Li Mae's cheeks. Ming held her hand and said, "Is there nothing we can do?"

"My father will not change his mind. I have to do what he says. He doesn't know how terrible it will be."

"Maybe Shang Gao has really changed. He seems to have become a real gentleman, and if he longs for you so badly, then surely he must care," reasoned Ming.

Li Mae shook her head. "If only it were so, but I just don't trust him."

They sat in silence until Li Mae said, "I must be virtuous and obedient. I will marry him. There is one thing I ask of you, dear Ming. Pray for me."

"I shall pray every morning and every night. It will be okay. You shall see," said Ming wiping away a tear of her own.

In short order the gifts and formalities of the Six Etiquettes had been completed, and now only the divination had to be finalized, a delicate examination beyond the powers of all but the most experienced seers.

Liu Wen Gao insisted on being present, since the fate of her son would be tied to the evaluation of his future wife. It was not that she particularly valued the word of Lady Xie Bing Zhoung. In fact, she would have wished for anyone but her. But she acquiesced to the desire of Li Mae's mother, who feared the woman far less than most.

It was late in the afternoon when Liu Wen Gao accompanied Lady Xie Bing Zhoung to General Tang's home. Jia Zhou and her daughter were nervously waiting for the practitioner of face divination.

As a courtesy, Liu Wen busied herself with overseeing the pouring of tea by Jia Zhou Tang's servants. When reentering the garden, she stopped to overhear what she thought was an innocuous conversation between the diviner and the general's wife.

"Have you had an opportunity to speak to Lord Sima Gao about the divination?" asked Jia Zhou Tang.

"In fact I am required to speak with him tomorrow. I received the notification early this morning."

"Required?" said the general's wife. "That sounds a bit ominous."

Lady Xie Bing Zhoung glanced about. "I am not in the slightest worried. There are things I know that will keep me safe. Things that I might use to my advantage, if the need arose."

The seer said it with a satisfied smile and touched a finger to her lips. A frown appeared on the face of the general's wife and she was about to comment when Lady Xie Bing Zhoung spied Liu Wen Gao and said, "So kind it is to bring the tea." She took a sip, motioned Li Mae to come closer, and began her examination of the girl's nose, ears, and cheeks. Closing her eyes, she commenced the five elements of face divination, occasionally sighing with dismay. The seer then consulted her 78 divination sticks. She gazed at a scroll to ascertain the exact meaning of each. Taking Li Mae's hands in hers, she traced the palm lines and with a "tsk, tsk," shook her head.

"Is it bad?" asked Liu Wen Gao, exchanging a worried look with Jia Zhou.

"I'm not entirely sure, and I don't want to be hasty. I will return tomorrow morning with the determination of the Fates." The woman stood. "I wish I could stay longer, but I must be going."

"Of course," said Jia Zhou. "My daughter and I will look forward to tomorrow's visit."

"It will be dark soon," said Sima Gao's wife. "I'll be pleased to escort you home. You shouldn't be out alone at night."

The diviner smiled sweetly. "That would be kind of you. I am old and sometimes a little feeble."

As the two women approached the home of the sorcerer, Liu Wen said, "Are you sure that Li Mae has faults that the Fates disfavor?"

"It's probable, but I didn't want to alarm the general's wife just yet. This is a very serious matter and carries great consequences. Of course the demons can play with us, but I know their tricks. They will not fool me."

Liu Wen had to choose her words carefully. "Lady Xie, what might you recommend if the signs are not encouraging?"

"Under no circumstances should the marriage proceed," said the seer emphatically.

"So, whether my son marries the princess is really up to you and your assessment."

"That is so," the sorcerer said with utmost confidence. "And as I said, there are inauspicious signs which only I am qualified to interpret."

"Ah, yes. That is quite true. Well," Liu Wen said, "we await your determination and pray that it is to our mutual good."

***

"I passed by the house of General Chen Tang," said Shang upon entering his father's chambers. "He told me Li Mae was expecting Lady Xie Bing Zhoung this morning, but she hasn't arrived."

"Are you attempting a macabre sort of humor, or are you vying for my job?"

Shang gave Sima a blank look.

"You're getting good at killing people. I do that quite efficiently too, but my victims are never found."

"What are you talking about?"

"The reason Lady Xie Bing Zhoung isn't at the home of the general is because she is dead. Her body was found in a canal. You could have done better."

Shang Gao stared at his father. "I didn't kill her. I haven't seen her in days."

"Really? So who did?"

"I have no idea. She had many enemies. But perhaps she simply fell in. The stones beside the canal can be slippery, and it rained last night."

"She was found with numerous tiny holes in her neck and throat. She was definitely murdered. I'll have to carry out another investigation; the Grand Chancellor wants answers."

Shang glanced at the door to make certain that it was closed. "Father, regardless of who killed her, the witch is gone. She cannot accuse us in the death of Tai Donc Quin, and she cannot foil my marriage to Li Mae Tang. Her sudden demise is most fortunate."

Lord Sima Gao's fingers tapped his table. "That's certainly true." Then with a tight smile he said, "Perhaps you should be my assistant rather than the general's."

Shang returned the smile. "Perhaps I can do both. You are always in need of a good spy."

***

General Chen Tang sat with his wife, Li Mae and the frightened Ming Zhaojun in the garden of his house. It was past noon and Lady Xie Bing Zhoung had not yet come. That was unusual; the seer was unfailing in honoring her commitments.

"Lady Bing Zhoung seemed quite hesitant during her divinations yesterday when she examined Li Mae's face," Jia Zhou said to her husband.

"Do you think Lord Sima Gao will still want his son to marry me if she finds me unsuitable?" asked Li Mae.

"I don't think he cares about the shape of your facial bones or the creases in your hands," her mother replied. "His goal is power. Yes, he will not flinch, no matter what predictions the lady makes."

Li Mae turned to her father. "If Lord Gao is persuaded to change his mind ..."

"Shang Gao will be a good husband," the general said with finality. "He promised me that. And, as his general, I will deal with him if he fails."

Ming touched Li Mae's hand. "At least you'll be here in Chang'an. I don't know where I'll be after I pass through the Gate of Exiles."

"I'll speak to the Grand Chancellor tomorrow about that," said General Tang.

"You will?" said Ming. "Oh, that would be wonderful!"

***

The quiet afternoon was broken by the drumming of hoofbeats. A cavalry squad reined up beside the gates of the villa, and a lieutenant approached the general.

With a deferential bow the officer said, "I'm sorry to intrude, Your Excellency, but you and your family are to proceed to the palace with all haste. A carriage is here for you."

"Is this about the Chanyu? Am I to call up the regiments?"

"All I know is that the Grand Chancellor requires your presence, as well as that of your wife and your daughter."

"And what of Princess Ming Zhaojun? Should she come too?" asked Li Mae.

"Yes, I intended to mention that. Much is happening, and the Grand Chancellor may call for her. Lord Anshi Zhaojun, her father, is already there."

"Already there?" blurted Ming. "Oh no! That means—"

"Many ministers have been called in," said the lieutenant.

"Yes," said Jia Zhou. "It doesn't really mean anything."

"At least not yet," added the general.

***

"Turmoil, absolute turmoil," said the Minister of Censorship and Security as he passed General Chen Tang outside the chamber of the Grand Chancellor.

"We were waiting for Lady Xie Bing Zhoung when we were ordered here," said the general.

"She's dead. Murdered."

"Is that what all this is about?" asked a horrified Jia Zhou.

"No, my lady. It's about the miserable Chanyu and their demands about the princesses," Sima Gao said and stormed away.

"What princesses? Where is your son?" the general called.

A moment later, Shang appeared, out of breath. He paused, watching his father walk briskly down the hall.

"What's happening?" asked Li Mae.

"I'm not sure, except that everything is very confused."

"What of the wedding? I mean, with Lady Xie Bing Zhoung dead?" asked Jia Zhou.

"I must ask my father. I know nothing." He bowed to the general and scurried down the corridor.

The Grand Chancellor's door swung open. The general was summoned and the door closed behind him.

Ming turned to Li Mae. "Was that my father in there?"

Muffled sounds of astounded voices seeped beyond the door as Li Mae, her mother, and Ming anxiously waited. A seemingly endless time passed before, stone-faced, General Tang, Anshi Zhaojun, and the Grand Chancellor exited the chamber. The general and the Minister of the Histories stood to the side while Bi Hangyong called the women to him. The three bowed while the Grand Chancellor cleared his throat.

"What I have to say to you is based on the decision of the Son of Heaven, the Enlightened Emperor Wudi." He glanced at the girls. "You know that from time to time certain princesses honor the Son of Heaven by going to lands beyond the Middle Kingdom. This is done to further our treaties of friendship and to keep the peace. You must think of it as that, a sacrifice, perhaps, but an extremely noble one."

A terrible sense of foreboding fell over Li Mae as she absorbed each word meted out by the Grand Chancellor.

"Are we ..." Li Mae began timorously.

Bi Hangyong raised the palm of his hand. "Please allow me to finish. As you know, the chief of the Chanyu looked very favorably upon Princess Ming Zhaojun." He gave her a tight smile. "But, perhaps under the influence of his august son, Xion Wen Chanyu, he decided that you, Li Mae Tang, would be awarded to the warlord instead. In a sense you are our ambassadress– an representative of love and devotion, something beyond the politics of men. You are to depart Chang'an in two days under military escort, and will rendezvous with the Chanyu beyond the Great Wall."

Li Mae's hand flew to her mouth. Her words came out in a whisper. "No! It can't be."

"But my daughter was to marry the son of the Minister of Censorship and Security," said an anguished Jia Zhou.

"She will marry. But her husband will be Zhizhi Chanyu," said Bi Hangyong. "We wish you the very best, and we shall offer up our prayers. This is an auspicious moment. The Emperor will provide you with gifts for the Chanyu, and he has commanded that a contingent of our troops will make certain your safe arrival. You are to honor us and yourself by being a good wife. You will always be welcome if the warlord permits you to visit Chang'an."

"I'll go with you," said Ming.

Li Mae opened her mouth to protest, but Ming wrapped her arms about her and squeezed so tightly that she could barely breathe.

"I am your *laotong*. You shall not go alone," said Ming.

"I cannot let you do that. You have a life to live here. I love you, and as much as I can't bear to leave you, I cannot have you come. And, besides, your father won't allow it," said Li Mae.

"He will. I will beg him to let me go or I will take my own life right here this very day. I, too, will be an ambassador for the middle kingdom. The Emperor will understand."

***

"Your mother and I will pray for you. We will miss you and you should know that you are a very special lady, a true princess. I know how difficult it will be beyond the gate, but perhaps you may have influence with the Chanyu warlord as the Lord Chancellor and the Emperor hope."

Li Mae nodded and murmured, "I will do what I can to honor the Celestial Son of Heaven."

"I know you will. And, if you have sons, tell them of our family," said General Tang the day before leaving Chang'an.

Li Mae wiped a tear and said, "I will do what the emperor requires, but the only sons I want would be born here, even if the father was Prince Shang Gao."

The general looked into her eyes and said, "I want to think that he would have been an honorable husband, but I would be less than truthful if I didn't admit that it was for political reasons that I overrode your concerns. For that I do apologize."

"It does not matter now, Father. If it was a choice between the prince and the Chanyu, I would gladly marry Shang Gao and give you many grandsons."

"Yes, that would have made me proud." He deliberated a moment, then reached into his coat and extracted a long thin blade with a jade handle. "Put this into your sleeve so that you can easily use it if necessary. I hope that the warlord protects you, but there may be a time when you must protect yourself. It is the only gift I can give you, daughter."

"No, Father, you have given me love."

"That is a sweet thought, but just in case," he said. "There may be bandits." Yet it wasn't bandits she was thinking about. She would marry a barbarian and would attempt to bear the unbearable. But if that proved impossible ...

Then she looked at Ming and realized that suicide was out of the question. What would happen to her one and only friend in that wasteland? The answer was too painful to consider.

***

It was decided that General Chen Tang, along with Shang Gao and 100 cavalry, would escort the princesses, but the general would only go as far as the Great Wall. Once beyond the Gate of Exiles the prince would continue, with 80 soldiers.

The procession trotted through the streets of the capital, followed by a baggage train of tribute. Many watched in silence. The mood was sullen and prayers were said since no one ever expected to see them again.

Shang Gao saw his parents as he and the general rode past the palace. Conscious of his military bearing, he kept his eyes straight ahead, regretting that he'd had no chance to speak with Li Mae before she and Ming had entered their high-wheeled carriage. Upon reflection, he didn't know what he would have said. Though he had pursued Li Mae relentlessly, he had never engaged her in a meaningful conversation.

She was supposed to be his. Another week, a month at most, and the wedding would have taken place. The princess would have been beyond the reach of the Grand Chancellor, for it was he, Shang knew, who had so influenced the fate of Li Mae Tang. Now bereft of an alliance between the two families, he pondered just how far his military career could possibly go. There were already rumors about his father falling into disfavor over the death of Tai Donc Quin. What would be his own fate if the wrath of the Emperor or the Grand Chancellor fell upon his father? And what calamity might befall him if the true story of the Sogdian's murder were revealed by the ghost of Lady Xie Bing Zhoung?

As the princesses' carriage rumbled over the cobblestone streets, Shang wondered if Li Mae would have embraced him as his wife if she had had a choice between him and the aging warlord. He sighed and cursed the Fates.

***

Liu Wen Gao, her face and hands heavily powdered, repositioned her new hairpin and watched in bitter silence as her son passed by. Nothing had turned out as it should have, she thought. A shudder passed through her as she reflected upon the horrific event two nights earlier. It had become apparent that the diviner would render a poor judgment of Li Mae. And that, Lady Gao had determined, had to be avoided at all costs. There had been no way to influence the old woman. The Fates, she would say, were predetermined; no mortal could change that. All one could do was interpret the signs, and only a diviner could do that. Not even a subtle threat from the wife of the Minister of Censorship and Security could alter the expected pronouncement.

Despite the glow of a multitude of lanterns, the night had been quite dark as the two women had walked along the canal near the seer's home. A drenching rain had begun to fall, which pleased Liu Wen Gao.

Lady Xie Bing Zhoung appeared frail, but that belied reality. She was thin but sinewy, and the wife of the minister suspected that the next few moments would not be easy.

Hurrying through the rain, the sorcerer had seemed distracted. Lady Gao made a calculated misstep and the seer tumbled forward. Instantly, Liu Wen thrust her silver-tipped hair pin through the sorcerer's neck. She plunged it in again and again as the old woman screeched and her fingers tore at Lui Wen with two-inch-long nails. The murder had to be quick or the woman's piercing screams would wake the neighborhood. A jab of the jade pin through the diviner's eye ended a disbelieving shriek.

A dog barked in the distance and a few residents emerged, but the rain made shapes indistinct. Lady Xie Bing Zhoung fell face down. In frantic haste, Liu Wen tried to withdraw her hairpin, but it lodged in the skull and broke in two.

The canal water, usually a sluggish stream, now roiled through the village with the downpour. Soaked, her hands torn by the seer's nails, Liu Wen dragged the woman's limp body to the water's edge and rolled her in. The corpse tossed and bobbed in the turbulent gush. In a lantern's muted glow, the woman, her one eye still open, stared at her assailant. Then, with her robes ballooning, she flipped over and was swept from sight.

Still clutching the splintered hairpin, the wife of Sima Gao tore through the gloom. Only after she returned home and made a cup of steaming tea did she wonder how a seer of such high repute could not foretell her own demise. The sorcerer, Liu Wen finally concluded, had been a fraud. Ridding the capitol of such an imposter could not be a bad thing. Whatever trace of guilt she might have felt quickly washed away.

***

The Minister of Censorship and Security rolled the dark green fragment between his fingers. It was only three inches long, but Sima instantly knew its owner. It had been extracted from the eye socket of the body that had washed up the following day. The bloated corpse of Lady Xie Bing Zhoung had been identified, and once again questions were being asked. The doctor who had dug the silver-tipped pin from the woman's head was sworn to secrecy. With the spate of recent murders, he assured the minister that no incriminating words would ever pass his lips. But, despite that pledge, the physician feared that a terrible judgment about him had already been made.

Sima Gao tossed the remnant of his wife's hairpin into a smoldering brazier and watched the silver tip discolor and melt away. She had not confided in him. Had the pin not been found, he would never have suspected that she could be capable of murder. Any suspicion he harbored would have fallen on his son.

Lord Sima Gao had not had a happy marriage. He knew that he was loathed by his wife, and the fact that she was capable of such a heinous murder disturbed him. Certainly he would never tell her what he knew, and the forthcoming investigation would take a very long time. And, of course, no suspect would ever be found. But he would never sleep well again.

Chapter 18

Gaius allowed the exhausted cohorts to rest a few miles from Kashgar, until the first week of spring. With snow still falling in the Torugart pass, he was surprised to see a procession of four stately Bactrian camels plodding toward them. The animals halted 50 yards from the legionnaire's camp, and their driver, a small man wearing a great sheepskin hat, leaned forward on his saddle and regarded the Romans with a mixture of curiosity and mirth. His woman, wearing a colorful wrap of woolens, was perched on the second beast and looked on indifferently.

The man flicked a switch and his mount kneeled with a loud and indignant bleat. Meeting Gaius's eyes, he left the Bactrian and walked stiffly toward him. With a nod and a lopsided smile, he seated himself. Appian and Apollodoros joined them. There was a ribbon of laughter as a crowd of legionnaires gawked at the man's insouciance. Gaius simply stared at him, then shook his head and sat across from the gnarled traveler.

"Ulugbek," the man said, pointing to himself.

"Gaius Septimus Aquilius, Chief Centurion."

The trader nodded and uttered a sentence in a language Gaius had never heard before. He glanced at Apollodoros, who shook his head and shrugged. The centurion raised his hand to interrupt the traveler. Standing, he looked about, saw Diomedes, and ordered him to bring Oshka. When she and Diomedes joined him they all sat in the lee of the tent.

"What's he saying?" Gaius asked.

Diomedes repeated the question to Oshka. She spoke a few words, and the man repeated what he had said. In a mixture of Greek and Latin she said, "Everybody knows about you and where you are from. They know that you are trying to go to Rome. And he says that you have a very difficult name."

The old man smiled and Gaius did the same. The Tajik pointed back to the Torugart Pass and spoke. "I am a Tajik and you are Roman, yes? Rome is that way. You're going in the wrong direction and you are a long way from home," Oshka translated.

"Where we go is our choice and my decision," replied the Primus Pila, offering the man a wineskin. "What do you know of Rome?"

Ulugbek looked curiously at Gaius, raised an eyebrow, and spoke rapidly to Oshka.

She nodded. "He traveled to Merv two years ago. That's as far west as he goes, but he spoke to a Parthian trader whose news comes from the Roman province of Syria. He says he knows things about Rome that you don't, since you've been traveling so long."

"Tell him we have heard nothing except a few rumors. Is that what he has, rumors?"

Ulugbek sniffed, and his words sounded more clipped than before. "I've heard more than rumors," Oshka translated. "But what I know and what you want to know comes with a price. In my world everything does. I hear it's also the same in yours."

Gaius looked closely at Ulugbek and tossed him a gold Parthian coin. The Tajik peered at it, grunted, and put it inside his tattered coat.

"Perhaps you could share some food with me and my wife. It will take time to tell you everything," Oshka said after listening to Ulugbek's reply.

After they ate, the Tajik seated himself in the middle of men who were anxious to hear of Rome, Oshka at his side. "Julius Caesar is dead and so is your Republic," Ulugbek began.

There was instant commotion, which Gaius silenced. The Tajik sipped his wine and looked into alarmed faces. "Ah, so much to tell. You cannot imagine what has happened since the slaughter at Carrhae. Yes, I know about Carrhae, if that surprises you. A general named Cassius escaped with many men and got back to Syria. But I will speak of that later.

"Now about Caesar. After the death of Marcus Crassus there were only two consuls left, Caesar and his rival, Gnaeus Pompey. Their union only existed for political purposes. Their rivalry grew despite the fact that Pompey was married to Caesar's daughter. See, I even know about Pompey, Dives, the rich man, yes?" The Tajik sat straighter, clearly impressed with his own knowledge.

"Caesar was a hero for having conquered a place called Gaul, a land I hear that is much like Sogdiana, though of course I can't be sure," continued the nomad.

Gaius spun a finger in the air to indicate that he had little patience with the man's speculations. Ulugbek ignored the reproach. "So I'll tell you the true story. Julius Caesar wanted control of Rome and was appointed dictator."

There were astonished looks on the legionnaires' faces as the Tajik said, "Oh yes, it is so. He even attempted to crown himself, but changed his mind when the crowd was displeased. They say he did it in jest, but many doubted it. Anyway, now Pompey hated Caesar. He took an army and the Senate to Greece, to escape. But he was followed by Caesar."

"Did they fight?" asked Gaius.

"Yes, of course they fought. It was a great battle, named Pharsalus, mostly at sea. I have never seen what a sea really is, but never mind. Anyway, Caesar destroyed Pompey's forces. Pompey fled to Egypt, hoping that he would find sanctuary. But what do you think happened when he got there?"

"I have no idea," said the astounded Gaius, seeing the Tajik's enjoyment as he played out his story.

"Well, we must envision the scene, the one the Parthian told me. Caesar arrives on the dock at Alexandria with dozens of soldiers and is met by the Egyptian court. There they are—priests and functionaries all hoping to please the mighty general with a gift in a bejeweled box. Curious, Caesar appraises it; perhaps it's filled with precious gems. The high priest rips off the cover and there is the head of Pompey!"

"Murdered?" said Gaius, stunned by one revelation after another.

"The Egyptians thought they were doing Caesar a great service. And what did they give him? The bald and gory skull of a consul of Rome and a one-time friend of Caesar. The great conqueror is horrified, cuts down the Egyptians, and marches into Alexandria. But it doesn't stop there, Centurion. You will marvel at this part, and again I shall describe the scene." The Tajik looked into Gaius's eyes with obvious delight as Oshka continued to translate.

"A huge Egyptian eunuch comes to the palace that Caesar has taken, and with great drama unrolls a carpet before him. And what tumbles out? To the general's astonishment it's none other than Cleopatra herself, the queen of Egypt."

The legionnaires looked at one another, as if the moon had fallen from the sky. With only the briefest pause the Tajik continued. "Now you Romans must remember that the pharaoh queen is a Ptolemy, whose ancestor was a general with Alexander of Macedonia, the man who gave Greece an empire. The wily queen is about to lose her crown and she is in desperate need of help. She is clever and cunning, and though not beautiful, she seduces the great Caesar. He marries her and saves her throne, and she accompanies him as he enjoys a triumph through the streets of Rome!"

Gaius could hardly believe what he was hearing. "This is true?" he asked Diomedes.

The captain of horse consulted Oshka, who quizzed the Tajik. The man nodded vigorously.

"Go on," Gaius commanded.

"Cleopatra, an Egyptian, was terribly unpopular with the Romans. Meanwhile Cassius, the general who had escaped Carrhae, and Caesar's former wife, Julia, plotted against him. They believed that the Republic should be reinstated and worried that Caesar would proclaim himself dictator for life. So he was murdered by Cassius and many others on the fifteenth day, the Ides of March. This was about eight years after you and your men fled Carrhae."

"You said that the Republic is dead and so is Caesar. So who rules Rome?" asked Gaius.

The Tajik leaned back and chewed on a piece of dried meat. "Rome was divided up between Octavian and another general, Marc Antony, who also fell in love with Cleopatra. She would seduce anyone who would help her keep her crown. Octavian, afraid that Antony wanted to rule Rome along with the Egyptian woman, went to war against him. He defeated Antony in a battle called Actium, in Greece. Marc Antony and Cleopatra fled to Egypt, where she supposedly committed suicide."

"Supposedly?" said Appian.

"It's said that she was killed by the venom of an asp, but many suspect that Octavian had her murdered. The woman was a survivor; it's doubtful that she would have taken her own life. She had a son and he ran into the desert. He was found and also murdered. Anyway, Octavian became the supreme ruler of Rome and renamed himself Augustus. He rules over the Senate as an emperor, not a consul. I've heard he's even elevated himself to a god, but on that I can't be sure. Rome has become an empire, and a frightening one at that."

"One last question," Gaius said as Ulugbek began to rise.

"What of the Roman prisoners at Merv? Have they been released? Have they gone back to Rome?"

The Tajik ruefully looked at the Roman centurion, then turned to Oshka. "They will remain there for the rest of their lives. There are 6,000 of them. They have women and children now, and the children will become Parthians. For those legionnaires, Rome is a fading memory."

"Should we presume that there is no peace between Rome and Parthia," asked Appian Dio.

"The Parthians still keep the eagle standards you lost at Carrhae and refuse to return them. What do you think?"

Ulugbek ignored the dismay of the legionnaires, rose, and called to his woman. They mounted their camels. He prodded his mount into a plodding gait and soon became a distant speck on the great Silk Road.

***

Like a miasmic pall, a sense of purposelessness settled over the cohorts. Having been on the march for a dozen years, the men had heard little of Rome. They could never have imagined the cataclysm that had befallen the Republic. Men sat in sullen groups around their fires, shaking their heads as a cold wind buffeted their encampment.

"This isn't solving anything," said Gaius to Tacitus and Appian after three days of immobility. "We can't stay here. We're exposed and too vulnerable. We will march. I'm told there is a town beyond the desert. The men can rest there."

Tacitus, pleased to have been taken into his father's confidence, said, "I will speak to the men in my cohort. I'm sure they will see the importance of starting soon."

"They will do what you ask," said Gaius putting a hand on his son's shoulder. The Primus Pila watched Tacitus call his men together and was pleased.

As Gaius turned, he felt the stomach pain once again. It had begun months ago. At first he'd ignored it, assuming that it was an old battle wound—there were many—and that the throbbing and twinges would eventually subside. He became increasingly concerned when he felt a lump where there had been no wound. The pain seemed to be increasing, and Apollodoros hadn't been able offer any advice.

"I might be able to cut it out," said Apollodoros, catching Gaius wince.

"I won't have that, *medicus*." Then, to Appian, he said, "Get the men in order. Sound the trumpet. We march."

With the advent of spring the caravans had begun to travel the high Silk Road. The weather had warmed, and though the trek was arduous, it paled in comparison with the Taklamakan Desert, which lay east of the mountain pass. There were no landmarks in the five hundred-mile-long desert. Eddies of sand were blown by ceaseless winds and the drifts entombed every structure ever made by man.

After leaving Kashgar the cohorts journeyed to the city of Yarkand, where Oshka prevailed upon Gaius to take the southern route around the great desert. It was the one she was familiar with, having been carried that way by bandits many years before. Two hundred and fifty miles beyond Yarkand lay the tiny village of Khotan. It was there that the cohorts rested beside an ice-melt river.

The men had marched more than 3,000 miles since leaving the Roman province of Syria. From the frigid heights of the mountain passes they had descended to the great desert in the Tarim Basin. To Tacitus it seemed a land of nightmares and death, where the bleached bones of despairing travelers and their animals appeared and disappeared with each sandstorm. The nighttime temperature dropped to 20 degrees Fahrenheit and rose to over 80 during the day. It would continue upward to 125 as midsummer came on.

"It's red, as if it were on fire," Ibericus said. The giant had become Tacitus's *optio*, second-in-command of the cohort. Together they inspected the placement of guards, and Ibericus, proud of his promotion, made a show of concentration and diligence. The men knew Ibericus well. They grinned at his newfound importance but gave him his due; he was good in a fight and he was loyal.

Two days later, Tacitus stuck his head into Gaius's tent. Appian Dio sat with him, and the talk was raucous and slurred.

"Night guards are posted," he said. Gaius belched in response, and Tacitus slowly backed out.

"Where do you think you're going?" said Appian as he let loose a monumental fart. "Get your ass in here!"

Startled, Tacitus wrinkled his nose. "I don't think so. Your tent has a peculiar odor."

"None of your insolence! Get in here. We're draining our wine and you're required to drink. That's an order, isn't it, Primus Pila?"

"An order, yes, trumpeter," Gaius slurred.

Tacitus stared at the two men. He had never seen his father drunk. How long had they been at it?

"Sit here, soldier," Appian commanded, pointing to a spot of sand beside the dung chip fire. He tossed Tacitus a cup and filled it, the sour wine gushing over the top.

Gaius looked up with a silly, unfocused expression and motioned for his cup to be topped off. He leaned back against his kit, laughed, and ran a hand over his balding pate.

"And you remember the girls, the ones in the cemetery," Gaius said, turning back to Appian.

"The whores?" Appian asked, grinning.

Tacitus gave his father a quizzical look. "What whores? When was this?"

Appian waved his had dismissively, then slurped his wine. "Before you were born. Gaius, what were you, fourteen, fifteen, then? Still a virgin, gawking at every girl? Didn't know anything about sex."

Turning to Tacitus he said, "So I lead this wide-eyed boy to a graveyard in Rome where we find two *lupae*, they howl like wolves. I take one and the other grabs our future hero. He thinks she's as beautiful as a vestal virgin because in the dark he couldn't see a thing. And that was damn fortunate! The bitch was four leagues beyond ugly."

"But she was very considerate. She made all the lustful sounds so Appian would think that I was really something," said Gaius, his head bobbing up and down.

"Of course she did. I paid her extra to screech and squeal. 'Oh Gaius, you're such a stud! Oh, you fill me with such womanly joy!'" The trumpeter mimicked in a falsetto voice. "You creamed all over her faster than you recited your oath to Rome, and that was really short. It was hilarious."

"You set it all up?" howled Gaius.

"Of course I did, Great Jupiter be pleased! I was worried that you would do something really stupid, maybe with a Roman virgin, and that would have finished you."

"You dog! You tell me this after all these years?" Gaius shook his head in amazement and mock horror. The wine dribbled down his chin as Appian laughed and clutched his sides.

"You wouldn't have recognized your father back then ... What? Thirty years ago?" Appian said, wiping his eyes. "He was a naïve child, held in contempt by his father, and detested by his society-climbing mother. I had to arrange everything, and now look at the thanks I get."

Gaius beamed. "It was the least you could do, since you were in bed with my mother."

"She was doing half of Rome. But I really had no choice; she was feeding me and I was dirt poor. But Tacitus, your father, this sweet kid, was made of hammered steel, something I didn't know till later. And then he nearly killed me."

"Because of you and his mother?"

"No, no. When I was training him for the army. After Aspacia." Appian stopped and glanced at Gaius, who had a faraway stare.

So that was his father. A young man he'd never known and couldn't imagine. But here he was in this rollicking stupor. Certainly none of his men had ever seen their Primus Pila drunk, like a simpleminded recruit.

"Anyway," Appian said, his grin returning, "then along comes his father's slave girl, and this boy's innocent world ends as fast as a bolt from a scorpion. Consumed! Head in the clouds, reduced to a babbling idiot. Thank the gods that I was already in the legion. The slobbering child is stricken with love and there is no cure. Apollodoros can do nothing to help him. Gaius commits a monumental defiance of Roman law by stealing the girl from his father. He then manumits and marries her. What did you call her, a 'lady of Rome?'"

"A lady of Rome," Gaius said. He smiled and his eyes narrowed, as if he was peering into a world so long ago and so far away.

"What was she like, my mother?" Tacitus asked gently.

"Your mother? A bewitching goddess, an enchanting thing men can only dream of." Gaius looked directly at him. "She was as the sun, full of light and joy and everything radiant."

"And you loved her."

"More than you could imagine."

"And you see her. In your mind, I mean."

"Every day and every night."

Yes, Tacitus thought. He saw Tullia the same way.

"I wish I had known my mother."

"She is in you, her kindness. You even look like her. She would have liked you."

There was a long moment of silence.

"I never told you how sorry I am for what happened," said Tacitus.

Gaius looked at him as if trying to remember.

"You know, at the Temple of Diana. I didn't know the gang was going there to steal from it. I would never have gone had I known."

"It wasn't your fault. I guess I always knew that. You weren't to blame. I was afraid of what might happen to you, though, even after I paid the priest to let you go."

"So the army was to be my salvation."

"As it was mine. Enrolling you in the legion was the only thing I could do. I had no choice. But since you offer an apology, I accept, as your mother would wish me to. You are our son."

"And now I have also become a centurion. What would she say about that?"

"Aspacia would say that we are the playthings of the gods. We become what destiny requires of us. She adapted, flowed, and made the best of it, as you have. She would have wanted us to be friends."

"Were you ever friends with your father?"

"Not for a very long time. I hated him, until Aspacia changed that," Gaius said somberly. "But we became friends before she died."

"You and I might have been friends if things had been different. If she had lived," ventured Tacitus.

"She would have insisted on it. But for a while we have not been enemies."

"For a while, Father. Yes, I think we have been friends."

***

The chill air of dawn was invigorating. The wind whistled through Gaius's armor, and he savored it as much as the wine he had drunk the previous night. He was pleased that he had spoken to Tacitus. It was something he had wanted to do for a very long time. He felt that a great weight had been taken from him and the path ahead was clear.

He had climbed high above the desert through rock-strewn defiles to a small, flat stretch from which he could view the encampment below. The strap slung over his shoulder held a cloth satchel, its contents light. Within was a carefully wrapped object that had been tucked into his kit since he had departed Rome so many years before. Now he would untie its bindings and secrete it in a little niche facing his homeland. It would have to be a spot protected from the elements—a place of eternal rest.

The stillness of the desert descended and its heat sucked life's moisture dry. But it was so peaceful. He had long cursed and repudiated the gods, the mythical deities who had failed to save his wife. But if the gods did exist, they would reside here. This arid place, so desolate, seemed a sanctuary of all that was holy.

Peace had eluded him since her death three decades before. From that time on he had never known it, never wanted it. He dreaded it. Peace offered moments of contemplation, a time to examine the spirit and the soul. He had told himself he was devoid of a soul. He was a soldier, a killer of men and, to his regret, sometimes their women. He was the very antithesis of peace. But he would not reflect upon that now. This was as close to tranquility as he would ever come.

Gaius glanced up to a towering cliff. Yes, up there, a little escarpment jutting out. He could put it there and pile rocks beside it so that neither wind nor animals could dislodge it. And it faced west, the right direction. She would be pleased.

Grasping the satchel, he climbed upward. From behind he heard a stone dislodge and rattle downhill.

Gaius wheeled and drew his blade as the first bandit came within striking distance. A quick thrust to the neck and the attacker fell forward, hands clutching an impaled throat. A second, then a third assailant expired before him as a dozen more took their place. The gladius parried and thrust, slicing off one arm and then another. He whirled and engaged a man behind him, and he felt his knees buckle. Something had struck him. He became weak, too weak, and he fell. They were on top of him, their knives slicing mercilessly. He twisted and grappled as they tore away his armor, not unlike hyenas fighting over portions of writhing prey. Attackers fought one another to claim the precious *segmentata*, the greaves, and above all, the vaunted helmet.

His gladius was gone as was the *puglio*, ripped from its sheath by a nomad who scurried away with the prize. The wounds were deep and his blood flowed. A torpid feeling came over him. Why hadn't they finished him off?

The Kyrgyz who had stolen Gaius's knife bent beside him, reached into the satchel that was still slung over his shoulder, and began to pick through the contents. Through excrutiating pain, Gaius pulled himself to his knees. With one last gasp of strength, Gaius raised his fist and slammed the man's face into the ground. The thief didn't move again.

Weakness was gaining on him. The special niche he had seen a few moments ago now seemed so far away. He unslung the satchel and pulled himself forward. He would not have enough strength to put as many rocks around it as he would have wished.

He removed the small, sacred object from its stiffened wrappings. It was still undamaged. His eyes blurred and he fought for each breath. With trembling fingers he placed the statuette in the crevice. Then he nudged a stone beside it, so that the goddess Diana would gaze toward the shrine for all the days to come.

He envisioned Aspacia now, the sprightly girl with the jouncing black curls, the twinkling eyes, and the soft lips that had caressed him in the night. She would know his final act, and she would be pleased.

He lay back against the warm rock. Images, some crisp, some faded like autumn flowers, flited through his mind. "Never venture out by yourself," he had berated the men. And, yet, here he was, alone and dying, having done what he had so often told them not to. But this was an act of devotion that had to be done alone. It was his obligation. And something told him that it was time.

He would die beside the little statue, a goddess that had adorned a shelf in his father's house, and the only object he had taken from that villa upon the death of his parents. Aspacia worshipped the goddess and he worshipped her.

Gaius could envision the valley between its great rock sentinels, a road that stretched interminably toward the west, and the urn that held her remains. Now the centurion and the little statue would gaze in the same direction. Now he would be at peace.

***

It was still early when Tacitus led the first of two cohorts up the steep hill. Sweat ran down his face, and his steel helmet felt like a caldron, but neither he nor the other men slowed their advance. Telltale footprints could be seen in the shallow sand. One set was made by *caligae*, most certainly worn by the centurion. Tacitus found other prints, sandals of numerous men. It had been hours since Gaius had started up the ravine. Only the guards had been awake; they told Tacitus that Gaius had said he required no escort and would soon return.

Tacitus ascended the promontory, and looking down could see the rest of his cohort close behind. The shriek of a hawk faded as it plummeted into a canyon. Vultures had already smelled the scent of death.

"There!" Appian exclaimed. He pointed to a half-dozen bodies that lay in contorted positions. There were still dark splotches where the blood had pooled. He looked into the faces of the dead. "He's not here."

Lupus Ibericus scanned the crags above them. "Something's up there," he said, pointing with his gladius. A moment later he clambered up the ledge. "Centurion!" he called to Tacitus. "The Primus Pila is here."

The body was carried down and placed on a cloak. Tacitus peered into the face of his father and saw a serenity that, in life, it had never had. He knelt by his father, and it seemed as though the world stood still.

Chapter 19

The body of the Primus Pila was carried down the hill and placed in his tent. Tacitus and Apollodoros entered and were followed by Appian, who handed Tacitus the satchel that his father had carried. He gazed down at the fallen centurion, then, curious, opened the leather bag and sorted through it, laying its items beside his father's body. Tied with a cord was a small bundle of papyrus letters. He was about to release the string when Appian shook his head. "It would be better if you read them after the funeral."

With a questioning glance at the *optio*, Tacitus placed them beside the other contents.

"Yes," said Apollodoros, "after we do honor to your father."

By dusk all was prepared. Torches illuminated the ground in the Primus Pila's last encampment. His body lay on a bier atop a pile of brush and gnarled branches. Tacitus asked Appian to give the eulogy, since he had served with the centurion from their days in Gaul.

Nearly 400 men clad in full armor stood silently behind their shields.

"He was like a father to many of us," the trumpeter extolled. "Unflinching, honored and honorable, dedicated to Rome and to us, his legionnaires. Others have attempted to achieve his heights but few ever have, for he stood boldly at the summit. Gaius Septimus Aquilius was the epitome of Rome, all it was and shall ever be. We honor his memory, we will carry forward his spirit, and we dedicate ourselves to his glory and his quest. We now place our trust in Great Jupiter, the sacred bull of Mithra, and all the deities of Rome."

Tacitus opened and closed his father's eyes as was the custom. A coin was placed under Gaius's tongue to pay Charon for passage across the River Styx. Beside him lay the gladius and *puglio* he had carried for 30 years. In unison the legionnaires shouted the man's name three times, followed by three blasts of the trumpet. Tacitus touched a brand to the wood and watched the flames reach upward in the soft evening breeze.

***

The ash still smoldered in the light of early dawn. Grey wisps floated in the still air as Tacitus placed a handful of white powder into a lidded metal box he had purchased in Samarkand. At the time he had had no idea what he would do with it, but the incised carvings of tigers and dragons had captured his imagination. They were fitting for the remains of a warrior.

He snapped the lid. In his hand he held the essence of his father. How strange that seemed, a man whose presence had been so constant, so intimidating, was now reduced to a few ounces of ash.

For a moment he thought of carrying the urn to Rome. It was logical, considering that Rome had been his father's final destination. But then he'd died here, on the great march.

This was the end of his journey. All was peaceful below the silent promontory, and what sufficed for an urn need go no further. Tacitus searched for an appropriate place.

"Up there," Apollodoros suggested. The Greek pointed to the rocky ledge above them where Gaius's body had been found.

"Yes," Tacitus said, studying the sheltered crag. He climbed up and gazed toward the camp below. It was eerily quiet. The men stood in small speculative groups. There was no banter, none of the usual camp bustle. A solemnity, a residue of the night's mournful requiem, hung over the encampment.

Reaching the ledge, Tacitus spied a suitable cranny, a small flat place beneath a little overhang. He pushed aside a rock and suddenly withdrew his hand. The little marble goddess of Diana stared at him. His mouth went dry and a presence coursed through him. He would not touch it. The goddess was there, he understood, because that's where his father wanted it. Tacitus sat back, motionless, and said nothing when Apollodoros called to him.

Why did his father put it there of all places? Indeed, why did he even have it? The Primus Pila had never mentioned the statuette, and Tacitus had never seen it. Surely his father had considered it sacred, not because he was a believer, but because it embodied the spirit of his wife. To disturb it would violate his father's final act.

Gently, reverently, Tacitus placed the box of ashes beside the goddess. Both the urn and the figurine became a columbarium, a final resting place. The sun rose higher and a radiant light illuminated the little bronze box and the white marble figure. An omen, a presence.

He placed protective stones beside the objects and descended to where Apollodoros and Appian waited. "It's done," he said. "His remains will be safe there." Someday, he thought, he would ask Apollodoros about his mother and her goddess.

Legionnaires offered words of condolence as Tacitus walked to his father's tent. Once inside, he arranged armor that had been recovered from the bandits who had been tracked down and killed. His eyes flited over the helmet, the war-battered lorica *segmentata* with its torques and phalerae. After so many years, he could not imagine his father's solid frame without armor strapped to it.

Tacitus sat in the stillness of the tent. He closed his eyes and imagined his father staring at him. It was unnerving; he felt like an intruder. He blinked and studied the objects he had arranged. There was the furca, a four-foot pole with a crossbeam that every soldier carried on his back. Beside it lay his armor, the greaves, and the rectangular shield with its gold-painted lightning bolts. There was the *vitis* stick and the little golden arrow given to Gaius by Julius Caesar. And beside that was the bronze patera, the cup that his father had drunk from each day. This was all that remained of the man's life and possessions.

Apollodoros peeked inside the tent. Tacitus motioned for him to enter.

"When I went up to the ledge I found a statuette of a goddess, Diana of the Woodlands. It was my mother's goddess. Did you know that Gaius was going out to find a place for it?"

"He didn't tell me, but I suspected it. The act was a very private thing. That's why he went out alone."

"But surely he knew that tribesmen were near. Without guards, he was putting himself in danger," said Tacitus, perplexed.

"It did not concern him. He had something to do and that's what mattered. He knew that he would probably die."

"Die? Die here, now? That doesn't make sense."

"He didn't tell you. He didn't tell anybody, but he was dying. He has had a growth that has been causing him great pain since we left Samarkand. He consulted me. I confirmed it and told him that I could operate, but he thought it too risky. It might have worked if there was no internal bleeding. It was just a matter of time. He always wanted to honor Aspacia and die in battle. And he did exactly that."

And he made peace with me on that strange evening, thought Tacitus. That inebriated, drunken banter had been so out of character. Only now did Tacitus recognize that it had been his father's farewell.

"He made me a centurion, a leader of a cohort, and awarded me the medal given to him by Caesar. Was that part of his plan?"

"The men had to continue on and they needed a leader. He had to grant you stature by promoting you. He wanted you to take the men home," said Apollodoros.

"But why not Appian? He's senior, and the men respect him."

"Both Appian and your father wanted you to lead the men as you did in the Torugart Pass. No one else could have done that."

Tacitus nodded silently. The Greek rose and left him alone. Tacitus extracted a packet of letters from the torn satchel and considered them, wondering if they were too private for him to read. But they belonged to him now, and curiosity again took hold. Strange, he thought. Both Appian and Apollodoros had counselled him to wait until the funeral was over. What did they know that he did not?

Tacitus gazed at the tightly rolled papyruses. They were old, very old, and he wondered why his father would have carried them as he had for so long. Surely they must have been keepsakes, perhaps letters written to him by someone very close. Aspacia came to mind, but she had died before his father joined the army. More likely they were from Toronius, Gaius's father. If so, they would make interesting reading—a window into a past, one of which he knew precious little.

A knife prick cut the bindings and the letters tumbled out. Though sealed well, the papyrus was brittle. Carefully Tacitus unrolled them and saw a slip of hair fall to the ground. He picked up the strands, studied them, and placed them on his father's cloak. His eyes went back to letters written in a cramped hand. The first began, "Solicitations, nephew. I hope these tidings find you well and of good heart. I know that it has been long since I have written and I've learned that you're in our province of Syria. I send you my prayers. Were your dear parents alive, they would surely have made homage to the gods. I cherish the thought of them.

"I think of Aspacia often and with the greatest affection. I honor her memory, as well as that of my sister Livia and your father, Toronius. Be safe, be well, your loving aunt."

Tacitus laid the papyrus aside and began to read the second one, a short letter with a wax seal that had been broken decades earlier.

"I, Julius Caesar, general and consul of Rome, hereby bestow the honored rank of Primus Pila upon Centurion Gaius Septimus Aquilius, for extreme bravery in defense of the Republic. By recovering the sacred eagle standard he infused my Tenth Legion with the determination that has led to victory on this extraordinary day. I also award him the

Golden Arrow with my personal gratitude and that of the People and Senate of Rome."

Who, Tacitus wondered, had seen this extraordinary letter? How many on this march might have known of these exploits? Surely not he. The Primus Pila would not have shared them with him in earlier years. There had simply been too much hatred then.

Tacitus rolled up the letter and picked up a third. Intrigued, he saw that it was again from Gaius's mother's sister, the woman who had tried so desperately to raise him before his father had dragooned him into the legion. The writing had to have been done by a scribe, since she was illiterate.

"Dear Gaius," it read, "I heard of the terrible voyage to Syria by the legions of Marcus Crassus. The husband of one of my best friends drowned when his trireme foundered in the storm off Sicily. How pleased I am to have received your letter signaling your safe arrival. I have also heard of the ancient Greek city of Carrhae, and I do hope that your winter there is warmer than ours. I have acquired a slave woman to help me tend the house and do the cooking. I bought a new brazier, but charcoal is becoming more expensive. I pray that Great Jupiter and Mithra will protect you in the coming war with Parthia. I trust that with Crassus's seven legions victory will be quick and you will return soon.

"Oh yes, I almost forgot. Tullia, the girl so infatuated with Tacitus, had a baby boy. She named him Quadriga, a strange name. I'm told that it signifies a general's chariot pulled by four horses. I will be seeing her baby next week and will write you more after that. May the gods protect you, Junia."

Tacitus read it twice more. "Tullia, the girl infatuated with Tacitus, had a baby boy."

"My son," he said aloud. He stared at the letter and bolted from the tent. Apollodoros was walking toward a group of men when Tacitus grabbed his arm and swung him around. Thrusting the papyrus at the Greek he shouted, "Did you know about this?"

Tacitus's face was hot with fury. His body shook, and spittle appeared on his lips. He ignored the small group of legionnaires who turned and stared.

Apollodoros wrenched away his arm and snatched the note. He scanned it quickly, as Tacitus's eyes bored into him.

"Take it," the *medicus* said, shoving the letter back.

"Did you know about my son?" Tacitus repeated angrily.

"I knew of a child."

"You and my father refused to tell me for all these years! Did Appian know?"

"He knew. Now come with me," Apollodoros said brusquely. They walked away from the men, who stood about uneasily.

"The letter came while we were in Syria. Your father showed it to us. He was afraid that if you learned of it, you'd try to get back to Rome. He knew that you would be caught and executed as a deserter. And after the battle of Carrhae, what was the point of showing it to you? You couldn't go back, none of us could, and he would have always had to watch to see if you slipped away with Quintillus, to certain death."

"But it was my child," Tacitus protested. "Years have gone by and I've changed. My father even said so. You could have told me. You and I always talked. You told me everything."

"Not everything. Not about me or even about your mother's sister, the seer who could foretell the future. Besides, it's questionable if the child was even yours."

"Not mine? Of course it was."

"Did you read the other letter, the one that followed?"

"No, what does it say?" asked Tacitus warily.

"Well I suggest you read it and speak to me more civilly next time. I am a free man, if you recall, and I'm here of my own volition."

***

"Dear Gaius, or do you prefer Primus Pila? We are so proud of you. I have little time just now with the coming of the Equinox holiday, but promise to write tomorrow. I pray that you and Tacitus are safe. I know that Tacitus has a new life and I hope that he eventually adjusts to the army. He is young and in time will likely put the thoughts of Tullia to rest. May Great Jupiter protect you, Junia."

Tacitus flung the letter aside and searched through the next two, but there was no more mention of Tullia. The letters ceased just before the battle of Carrhae.

"May I come in?" asked Apollodoros.

"If you want."

The Greek sat on the ground across from Tacitus and offered him wine. "You see, another reason we didn't tell you," Apollodoros said, pointing to the script tossed onto the ground. "What if she did marry? It would have been quite sudden. What does that tell you?"

"She probably needed somebody to provide for her and the baby and someone to make her respectable," said Tacitus.

"She was pregnant with someone's child. The girl was unmarried and had sex with you. Why not with others? What if she was more than just friendly with all those boys," Apollodoros insisted.

Dismayed, Tacitus shook his head. "Still, I believe the baby was mine. We talked of being together at some future posting. You should have told me."

Apollodoros sipped his wine and looked at Tacitus. He put a hand on the centurion's shoulder and said, "I would not have been the one to do so. And how could your father speak of it after so many years? The child, if it even lived, never knew you. And Tullia? If she's still alive she would only remember you as a boy. That is, if she even remembers you. I wonder if she can recall your face at all."

"I can remember hers," Tacitus said quietly.

"But it's all in the distant past. You have other things to consider, and they matter right now."

"That's the damn truth," said Appian, barging into the tent. "You have to deal with that slime Quintillus. He's been grumbling all the way, and he is at it again. He couldn't even wait a decent amount of time."

"What do you mean?" said Tacitus, still reeling.

"With your father gone, he thinks he can talk the men into going back over the pass—back the way we came."

"Who would want to do that? It would be winter before we got there," said Apollodoros.

"I know that, but he's spreading dissention," said Appian.

"You could just banish him, cut him loose. He won't be able to do us any harm that way. No Parthians will come after us out here," said Apollodoros.

"Quintillus can't be trusted. He might join some Tajik band and do something stupid. If it were me I'd just put a gladius through him," said Appian.

"Then do it, but first you must take command," said Tacitus flatly.

"I'm not taking command, you are."

"The choice should be put before the men."

"It already has been, and they want you. I'll remain your *optio*."

Tacitus turned to Apollodoros. "What do you think?"

"A Roman centurion asks a former slave what he should do?" said Apollodoros, displaying a toothy grin. "It doesn't really matter what I think. I'm here for the wondrous delight of this jaunt. It's been a total thrill and I'm joyfully delirious."

"By the gods, you're no help."

"Look," said Appian, "I know that leading this mob is a bit of a task, but your father took charge of 60 cohorts when he was your age. And I'll remind you of what the Primus Pila used to say: 'There are two, and only two, types of people in the world. The first sees a challenge, ponders all the pitfalls, and does nothing. The second sees the same challenge and dreams of possibilities.' If he were here now he would say, 'Tacitus, son of Gaius Septimus Aquilius, which one are you?' You better make up your mind. The men are waiting."

Tacitus strapped on his gladius and moved into the sunlight. "Then it would be wrong to keep them waiting, wouldn't it, old man?"

"Old man? Insolent child," mumbled Appian.

"Assemble the men, *optio*. We're going to march, insolence or not."

***

The ancient town of Niya was the halfway point on the route around the great Taklamakan desert. Nights, even in May, were terribly cold, but Niya was an oasis where poplar trees and cultivated fields broke the monotony of the desert. The legionnaire's encampment, pitched a mile from the town, sat at the base of the Kunlun Shan Mountains, the vast chain of great snow-covered peaks overlooking the desert.

Tacitus had gotten used to large caravans on the Silk Road, so he was surprised to see a lone traveler plod toward their camp with a string of heavily packed mules. The man dismounted and stepped up to a guard. "I would be honored to speak to the chief centurion of the camp," he said in accented Latin.

Tacitus walked over. The muleteer was a large, elderly man with a bushy grey beard, a heavy Chinese coat, and a woolen cap. When Tacitus led him inside his tent, he arranged a blue and white striped shawl on his shoulders and squinted in the dim light.

"I'm Elizar ben Josephus," he proclaimed in a heavy accent. "I have traveled this road for 20 years." He said it as if he were stating his credentials. Wrinkling his nose, he glanced at the weapons arranged in the tent. "I still have a few precious items from the west—Rome, Greece, and Parthia. You'll need valuables when you meet the Chanyu up the road. The nomads expect gifts." He placed a small box on his knees and stroked it with loving fingers as if it were a cat.

"They expect gifts?" Appian said.

"Oh yes. Even the Son of Heaven, the exalted Emperor of the Celestial Kingdom, gives them gifts: princesses, silks, gems and such, to keep them from pillaging Han villages." The man nodded gravely and again looked around the tent. "But you don't have gifts for them, do you?"

"For gifts we would want something in exchange," said Tacitus.

The old man smiled knowingly. "Certainly, certainly. The 'gift' may be letting you live and cross their lands, Roman. You don't want a repeat of Carrhae, do you? Same weapons, same tactics; get you in the open, then ..." He raised his palms and looked upward.

Tacitus watched him but said nothing. The old man waved dismissively and said, "Soldier, I've known those barbarians for years. Nasty bunch on their little horses, and they do love war."

"Do you speak their language?" asked Appian.

"I'm fluent in six languages and can make myself understood in many more. Hebrew was my first language. I also have a very keen memory for faces and names. It's a tool of the trade, you know, like a gift or a weapon, depending on the circumstances," He raised his bushy eyebrows, then looked up with an amused smile. His eyes fixed on a shaft of light that illuminated Tacitus's armor.

"You have a hole in your tent," he said, pointing with his forefinger. "You should have that fixed before winter."

"And you happen to know somebody who can repair it," said Tacitus.

The man sighed and raised his palms again as if in prayer. "I'm not a tailor, but I know of two. One is Euripides and the other is Eumenides, but they are very busy and won't travel this far to mend your tent." He waited a moment; Tacitus didn't laugh, and neither did Appian. He sighed and almost to himself mumbled, "Romans, so dour."

The trader cleared his throat. "I deal in precious goods. Only the finest. My business takes me from Alexandria to Dunhuang near the Great Wall. No other man travels as far. Just me and my wife. It takes me many years, but I'm known to everyone. I give good prices, so they say, "When is that old Jew coming again? Maybe he'll bring something special. And I always do."

He looked about. One eye focused on a wineskin bag. Tacitus took it from a tent pole peg and offered it."

"I shouldn't, my wife would say only on the Sabbath, but ..." He folded his hands over his ample stomach, settled himself on a camp stool, and closed his eyes. Then as if suddenly wakened, he leaned forward. "Roman soldiers in Egypt and Romans in Jerusalem. Yes, yes, I understand the use of power, but you Romans had better be very careful in the city of the Holy One. We will not burn incense to your emperor or kneel like slathering supplicants." With that, he settled back and sipped his wine.

"Aren't you going to invite me in?" said Apollodoros, standing beside the tent's open flap. Without waiting for an invitation, he entered and nodded to the guest.

Elizar ben Josephus stared at him, stood, and extended his fingertip to within an inch of the Greek's nose. "I know you," he said, straining his one good eye. "You were much younger then. It was, let me see, Tyre? No, not Tyre. Alexandria. Yes, in my father's shop. We spoke Aramaic. You were with a boy and his father. Of course, now I remember it clearly, you negotiated for the Roman and bought scarabs and other antiquities."

Apollodoros looked closely at the old trader. "By Zeus and all the gods on Mount Olympus, yes, I remember you!" In a most unusual display, Apollodoros threw his arms around the man. "I, Gaius, and Toronius bought ancient Egyptian pieces from this man to take back to Rome. He was the only honest trader in all of Alexandria." Turning to Tacitus, he said, "You remember I told you that I helped your grandfather buy valuable artifacts, and he sold them to wealthy patricians."

The rotund trader turned his attention to Tacitus. "The boy was your father? What a wonder! A fine young man, even for a Roman."

"You actually met them?!" exclaimed Tacitus.

"Yes, of course. I heard there was some trouble afterward and they had to leave Egypt rather quickly, but ..." he waved his hand again. "So long ago, it doesn't matter. Is your grandfather still ..."

"Alive?" Tacitus said. "No, and neither is my father."

The traveler looked down at his hands. "Such is the way of things. The Lord does what the Lord does."

"Why don't you show us what you have to sell; I should carry on my grandfather's tradition."

"Yes, that is what binds," said Elizar, bobbing his head. He extracted several objects from a threadbare sack. "I have saved these for someone special; this occasion is exactly that." He opened a rosewood box and displayed two vials of multicolored glass and three jade rings. One ring was deep green, another was yellow, and a third, gray.

"Years ago it was said that only the Son of Heaven could wear the gray jade; that's how precious it is, Centurion." He held up the glass vial. "Roman glass, very precious to the Chanyu and the Chinese."

Tacitus had seen hundreds of such bottles in Rome, but here they would be extremely rare. "How much for the vial?"

"Five sestertii for one, nine for two," the man wheezed.

"I only want one. I'll give you four sestertii," Tacitus countered, holding out the coins.

Elizar ben Josephus rolled his eyes, laughed, and put out his hand. "In memory of your father and grandfather," he said with a labored sigh. "So you will be meeting the Chanyu, yes?"

"I assume we will. We haven't heard anything good about them, so I'd like to know more," Tacitus said, carefully wrapping the vial.

"Indeed, good intelligence is priceless, be it in war or business." The man ran his fingers through his beard. "The Chanyu are China's thorn and have been since the barbarians rode out of Mongolia hundreds of years ago. Some of them, and there are thousands, have made peace with the Han people. But there are rebellious clans led by hotheads, young men who insist on making their mark. They're fierce warriors like the Saka you encountered at Carrhae, but they sometimes augment their ranks with foreigners who have special skills."

"Can any of them be trusted?" said Appian.

"When it suits them. Their life is simple. They worship the horse since it takes them everywhere, and they like fine gifts. In return they give peace when it is to their advantage."

"How do the Chinese deal with them?" said Tacitus.

"Sometimes they go to war, but the current emperor prefers to placate them in the Taoist tradition: 'Drink rice wine and flow with the nature of things.' There are others in the Middle Kingdom who would prefer to ride them down with a hundred thousand men."

It was dark when Elizar ben Josephus departed the Roman camp. Tacitus and Apollodoros walked him to his mules. "How far is it to the Great Wall?"

"About 700 miles. The Wall is hardly complete. It's made up of many separate sections, mostly made of rammed mud. That's why the Han are so vulnerable. But I won't be going there anymore. I'm going west."

"To Alexandria?"

The old man shook his head. "No, my wife and I have enough time left for one final journey, and it will not be to Egypt. It will be to Jerusalem, the city of David." With a wink he said, "Before you Romans desecrate it, as you probably will."

Tacitus almost protested, but anything might happen with Augustus leading the empire. Putting the thought aside, he said, "So you haven't been there, after all these years?"

"No, but my wife and I talk of it. We Jews often say, 'O Jerusalem, if I ever forget thee may my right hand lose its cunning.' Sarah tells me that such a calamity would be an unholy thing, even at my age." Elizar ben Josephus winked with his one good eye. "I rarely wish Romans good fortune, but I do wish you well, Centurion. If you make it to the Great Wall and beyond you should write about it. The story would make great reading in Rome if you ever get back there."

The moon was nearly full when he mounted his mule and resumed his journey.

"Do you think he's going to make it?" Appian asked Tacitus.

"He came this far, and he's bound for the city of his god. I'll wager he'll eventually get there."

How strange to encounter a man out here who had actually known his grandfather. A chance encounter, to be sure. It was too bad he'd never see him again.

***

Appian burst into Tacitus's tent.

"There's a problem with the villagers, and it's damn serious."

"What did they do?" Tacitus asked, alarmed. They'd marched 300 miles from Niya to a tiny hamlet, and up until now they'd had cordial relations with the local inhabitants, the Kyrgyz.

"Not them, one of us. You better hurry."

"Who is it?"

"Quintillus, who else?"

"He wasn't to enter the village. I gave strict orders. Was he drunk again?"

"If it were only that simple."

They strode toward the village. The sun had just risen and it shone bleakly through scudding clouds.

Surrounded by angry men, his tunic ripped, Quintillus screamed defiantly at the menacing crowd. The village headman spied Tacitus and beckoned furiously. A couple brought forward a girl not yet 13. Sobbing, she covered her swollen face.

The headman pushed villagers aside and had the girl open her bloody mouth, revealing three missing teeth. His hand snatched the ripped clothes and pointed to the trickle of blood that stained the dress and ran down to her bare feet.

"Raped!" the girl's mother shouted in Turkic. Although the language was barely understood by the legionnaires, the meaning was clear. The distraught woman spat at Quintillus, her face twisted with hate, then grabbed a rock and hurled it at him. The stone grazed Quintillus's cheek. He cursed her as the villagers, armed with an assortment of swords, knives, and farming implements, moved toward him. They halted as a dozen legionnaires hastened forward.

Striding to Quintillus, hand on his gladius, Tacitus said, "Did you rape her?"

"No, not rape. She wanted me to do it. It wasn't rape. I swear by the gods, Tacitus!"

"Don't you dare call me Tacitus!"

The centurion approached the girl, now struggling to stand.

The girl's father looked into her eyes and spoke rapidly. Staring at the ground, the pubescent child nodded.

Taking her daughter's arm, the mother motioned Tacitus toward their hut. Away from the eyes of Romans and massed villagers she raised the girl's dress and pointed to the still bleeding vagina. Tacitus nodded and mouthed the word "sorry." He stormed out of the tent and to the legionnaires said, "Take him!" Turning to the headman and pointing to Quintillus, he said, "Thirty lashes and banishment."

"No! You kill him!" the headman shouted. "You kill him now!"

"Thirty lashes," Tacitus repeated. "It will be done right here. Appian, get the rope."

Blurry-eyed and tipsy, but a veteran of a dozen campaigns, Quintillus broke the grasp of a legionnaire and grabbed a villager's sword. He backed a few feet away, and as the crowd surged forward he struck, severing a man's jugular. There was an outraged cry as Quintillus spun from the mob, slicing the arm of one more Kyrgyz. Then he looked down at the gladius deep in his chest.

Quintillus stopped and stared in disbelief, his hand grasping the offending weapon. His knees buckled. He only had time to say "Centurion" as Tacitus withdrew his sword.

The crowd that had swelled to hundreds stared at the lifeless Roman. Moments later they filtered away, leaving the corpse in the muddied street. The headman nodded to Tacitus while the girl's mother watched, her daughter held tightly by her side.

Turning to Appian, Tacitus said, "Strike the camp. We've outstayed our welcome. We march at the third hour."

***

They had trod past Endere, Cherchen, and Miran. Tacitus had the cohorts halt briefly in Charkhlik at the eastern end of the Taklamakan Desert. Only a few dried mud huts remained of the oasis where poplar trees once cast shadows over orchards and green fields. Now sand covered the streets and only a few souls ventured into the eye-stinging wind.

Trundling behind the legionnaires was a multitude of caravans whose traders led their protesting camels. Sogdiani, coming from the west, led beasts laden with alfalfa to feed the "heavenly horses" they sold to the armies of the Son of Heaven. Other merchants brought spices, musk, and flax as well as silver bowls and carpets from distant Persia. As the cohorts neared the fabled city of Dunhuang, an oasis beside a crescent lake, they met travelers from across the Indus River who transported precious stones, lace, and filigreed scarves.

Donkeys laden with fruit were led by Turkic men who rubbed shoulders with Kazakhs and Chinese. Kyrgyz riding bullocks and wearing peaked hats, heavy coats, and boots with high heels added to the diversity of peoples on the great Silk Road. Bizarre as the mixture of cultures appeared to the legionnaires, it was apparent that they themselves seemed even stranger to the people of Asia. Never had they seen Roman cohorts, armored and marching in solid ranks to a cadence uttered in such a foreign tongue.

Caravans moved to the sides of the road to let the soldiers pass, the people craning their necks to get a better view of the swaggering, helmeted men. Marching beside the first cohort, Appian signaled Tacitus.

"There was a man with a chained and hooded falcon on his wrist, riding a shaggy horse," Appian said. "He was staring at us. I think we've met our first Chanyu."

Tacitus shielded his eyes from the sun with his hand and looked around, but Appian shook his head. "He's gone. He rode off quickly."

Tacitus sighed. The cohorts had passed many armed men, usually guards for caravans, but they never presented a threat. The Chanyu would be a different matter.

Two days following the appearance of the falconer, the cohorts were quickly encircled by Chanyu, bringing back images of Carrhae. Tacitus immediately had the men form the square. The dozen scorpions they had laboriously constructed were rapidly pieced together and armed, their bolts within easy reach of the horsemen.

While Tacitus watched, two riders broke from the assemblage and galloped toward the square. They halted, dismounted, and ambled toward the Romans. Tacitus asked Diomedes and Appian Dio to join him. He told the nearest legionnaire to get Oshka, since she understood the Mongolian dialect.

"Fierce Slaves, the Han call them," Oshka said to Tacitus with disgust, "but they're hardly slaves. They eat raw meat and drink horse blood. They also like fancy clothes given them by the Son of Heaven."

"Can they keep their word if we strike a deal?" asked Tacitus as the two Chanyu drew near.

"Only if they're paid enough. I would not trust them, Centurion."

"Do you know the old man, the leader?"

"This man I know. He's the warlord of a big clan, maybe 4,000 horsemen."

"Are they at war now?" asked Appian.

"I'm not sure, but they raid the Han villages when they want more tribute."

"Time to talk," Tacitus said. He and his small party walked purposefully toward the Chanyu. They were small, lean men with sunbaked faces and long braids tied with colorful ribbons. The older one was slightly stooped and appeared nonchalant. The younger one, a little taller and wearing a peaked bronze helmet, followed a few steps behind. Except for their knives, neither was armed.

Standing before Tacitus, the nomad studied him, tilted his head, and offered a hint of a smile. It seemed condescending, an expression a father might give an immature and naïve son. Tacitus nodded but said nothing.

"Zhizhi Chanyu," the warlord said, pointing to himself. He spoke rapidly to Oshka.

"He says that you are trespassing on Chanyu land, and if he wanted to he could annihilate you right here and now." said Oshka.

"Tell him that depends on how many of his thugs he wants to bury today."

She uttered the reply and the man gave Tacitus a piercing look. And then he laughed. Almost as an afterthought he pointed to the younger man. "My son, Xion Wen Chanyu."

The son gave a perfunctory nod, but his eyes were on Tacitus's armor.

Redirecting his attention to Oshka, Zhizhi Chanyu continued to speak in terse, rapid sentences. She stiffened and replied in a sharp tone.

"He doesn't like speaking through a woman. He says that he speaks a little of another language, one from far away that you might understand."

"What might that be," Tacitus asked.

"The language of Diomedes and him," she said, pointing to Apollodoros.

"Greek?" the *medicus* said incredulously. "How would he have learned any Greek? Alexander never got this far."

Zhizhi Chanyu looked at Apollodoros. "You Greek?"

"Yes, Greek."

"You speak that language too?" the warlord asked, studying Appian and Tacitus.

They nodded, and the old man said a few words to his son before turning to Tacitus. "Exactly where do you think you are going?"

"Rome, by way of a river past a great wall."

"Beyond a river and a great wall," the warlord repeated. He smiled and said, "And you imagine that the Son of Heaven, the exalted emperor of the Middle Kingdom, will simply let hundreds of foreign soldiers march across his land?" He cackled and shook his head. "Sad that you have come so far for such folly."

"We will march to Rome through this 'Middle Kingdom,'" Tacitus said.

"Of course you will," replied the Chanyu disdainfully. "But you will need friends to negotiate for you. That is, people who know the ways of the Han, people the Chinese honor and respect. Not a band of adventurers who know nothing of the Empire beyond the Wall." Zhizhi Chanyu emphasized his statement with his fingers as if skipping across an imaginary landscape.

"And the Han honor you?" Tacitus said, an eyebrow raised.

"Oh, yes. They give us many gifts and insist on remaining friends. With gifts from you we may intercede with the Han, but that will take time. Negotiations with Emperor Wudi and Chancellor Bi Hangyong must be delicate; it's all about statesmanship, you see. In the meantime we may allow you to stay on our land, but we will require your services. A gift to us, you understand."

"And what 'services' might that be?"

"We will call it 'protective services' for my villages when I am away, perhaps when doing your bidding. I'm rather interested in foreign tactics—those unfamiliar to our enemies. The negotiations with the Han may take a year. We must send a delegation, but I have many appointments before that." The warlord nodded as if agreeing with himself. "If all goes well, you may pass through the Wall. Then you can march to the river and down to the sea, if there really is one."

Xion Wen Chanyu spoke to Oshka.

"He says it would be unwise to continue on without agreeing to his father's offer. The road is long and many bad things can happen between Dunhuang and Jiayuguan, the fort at the start of the Wall."

"Then you should be careful if you go there," Tacitus replied. After a moment of hard silence he said, "We will consider your offer. I'll give you my decision tomorrow."

The warlord nodded and mounted his horse. "To cross my lands, you will need my approval. Without it," he gestured toward his warriors, "you will have to face many more Chanyu than this. Consider it well. I shall return in the morning."

Chapter 20

"She ignores me," Shang said to General Tang as he entered his superior's tent.

"And that leaves you angry? Depressed? Both?" asked the general. He put down his cup. "Lord Gao, what do you expect? Should she throw her arms about you and beg to be saved from the barbarians? There is nothing that any of us can do. I will lose a daughter, you a wife. The Son of Heaven has spoken and there is no discussion, no wallowing in misery. It's not the way of a soldier."

"What happens if the Chanyu precipitate war, General? Would it be possible to rescue her, invade the barbarian lands as they have ours?"

The general sighed. "My daughter was given as tribute to prevent war. It would be quite foolish for the Chanyu to attack the Middle Kingdom in force. Don't spend time on false hopes. Li Mae and Ming belong to the Chanyu. The only prospect we ever have of seeing them again is by invitation, through a fraternal visit to their lands, with additional treasure. And you know as well as I do that we have never been invited. They're an insular people."

Shang nodded and turned to go.

"This is the last night I will see my daughter," General Tang said. "Tomorrow you'll escort her through the Gate of Exiles. It's six days' travel before you meet the Chanyu. She must arrive there in the same physical condition as she is now. Anything less, and the ramifications could be quite harsh."

The general locked eyes with him. Was the comment a cautionary note or a veiled threat? Aside from an accident on the road, "in the same physical condition" could only mean one thing.

Again Shang nodded. "One thing surprised me, my Lord General. Ming Zhaojun's father has not accompanied his daughter to the Gate of Exiles. Might you know why?"

"The Minister of the Histories was seen speaking to men outside the court. It appears, according to your father, that Anshi Zhaojun wanted these men to appear as bandits and kidnap his daughter before reaching the Wall. She was to be hidden away, incognito, in a remote village far from Chang'an. He and his wife were to slip away and join her later. Had he succeeded the agreement with the Chanyu would have been jeopardized."

"What happened when my father found out?"

"Anshi Zhaojun was forbidden to escort his daughter. He's under guard in the capital and may lose his position."

***

Tents were erected for the princesses each night. For the first two evenings Shang Gao stayed close to his troops. On the third evening, he walked toward the princesses' tent.

Li Mae saw him approach and hesitated. She could have hastily disappeared inside, but she willed herself to remain where she could be seen. Ming excused herself and slipped into the shelter.

Their meeting was something that Li Mae had expected ever since they had passed beyond the Wall. She knew that he watched her every movement. On several occasions she had considered speaking with him, if for no other reason than scuttling the thought of any future relationship.

Shang Gao had never intimated that he loved her or even had feelings for her. Certainly she harbored none for him, but his attention on the journey was touching and she thought that it should be acknowledged.

There had been those persistent rumors from his pubescent years, and hushed talk of a concubine's murder. There had been no direct implication; afterall, his father was the Minister of Censorship and Security. Li Mae had never known Xi Shi, the girl who had fallen to her death in the palace. A whispered conversation between her parents late one night was all she really had to go on, and yet, there was something that made her tremble. And there was the death, or more likely the murder, of her friend Tai Donc Quin, whose quick end had never been fully examined. How complicit the young prince had been would always remain a mystery.

He was three paces away when he made a courtly bow and asked if there was anything she required.

"I and Princess Zhaojun have been provided all we need. I thank you for your attention," Li Mae said, showing as little trepidation as possible. There was an extended silence. Unwilling to initiate conversation she simply waited.

"Despite what you might think of me, Princess, I was hoping that our union would become pleasant and fruitful. I'm sure that you would have honored me with a fine son."

"But the Fates have decided otherwise. I truly hope that they'll show kindness and allow you to find a lady worthy of your position."

"The Fates are fickle. Situations, even the most dire ones, can change. The Chanyu make mistakes, Lady Tang, and for that there are consequences. Consequences that might change everything."

The sky had darkened. Li Mae could see Shang only by the glow of the campfires and an oil lamp inside the tent. He looked about, then took a step toward her. She moved back, held up one hand, and knitted her brows.

"Please," said Li Mae, "it wouldn't be right, and it would displease the Son of Heaven. There is nothing to be gained by it."

The prince hesitated, his expression contemplative, perhaps even fearful. An unsettling moment passed, and then he bowed stiffly and strode away.

***

"How much further?" asked Li Mae

"Maybe three miles," said Shang's aide as he rode beside the high, two-wheeled cart. "We sent scouts ahead, and should be meeting the Chanyu very soon."

There had been no more contact between Li Mae and Prince Shang Gao. There was little reason for haste, yet the small party rarely stopped. Ming held Li Mae's hand and wept, wondering aloud why her father had not chosen to accompany them to the Gate of Exiles as had General Chen Tang.

The mindless drudgery of the journey lulled Li Mae into a fitful sleep. She didn't know how much time had passed when she was suddenly wakened by hoofbeats.

"What's happening?" asked Ming.

"I'm not sure." Li Mae parted the curtains to hear the exchange between Shang, his aide, and the scouts. A driving wind pelted fistfuls of sand against the side of the cart, making it hard to understand anything. She gazed blankly at the dun-colored hills that rose from the parched earth. Gnarled brush rustled in the wind, its sparse leaves barely clinging to tinder-dry branches. A darkening sky lay on the horizon, and the soldier's mounts were skittish.

"They're coming, Excellency," said the aide, pointing to a dust cloud rising in the distance.

Li Mae had seen the Chanyu at court and had come to accept the disaster that had befallen her. Yet, until now, her exile and future existence as a tribute wife had been a nightmare that would fade with the dawn. With the sudden appearance of countless horsemen, her fate was no longer a calamity in the abstract. It was very real, and she shuddered.

***

"I did not expect that they would send so many," said the aide, watching the horde charge over a low rise.

"An intentional show of force," said Shang. Perhaps it was meant to show respect to the warlord's future bride, but the numbers were ominous. "Very well," he said tersely, "we'll let them come to us. Have our men form behind me. Wagons and attendants will station themselves to the rear."

He glanced at his pitiful force and saw how vulnerable they were. The princesses' wagon had halted, and its occupants watched the approach of the Chanyu with ashen faces. The once elegant interior with its silk upholstery was coated with layers of grit. Sunlight illuminated tiny motes that swirled with the wind. The cavalry horses, pelted by sand, nervously pawed the ground, making it difficult for

Shang to present the appearance of a disciplined force. Nevertheless, he ordered the long banners removed from their sheaths and watched as they rippled with each gust. One as important as he, a prince of the court, should have been given a force of hundreds to impress the barbarians. He felt pitifully inadequate.

The Chanyu stormed over the rise as an undisciplined mob. Though they were a militaristic society, they assumed no fixed formations.

"Barbarians," said the aide. "How many princesses do we have to give them? What happened to the last one?"

"She died," said Shang, his eyes fixed on the Chanyu.

"Then what chance have these two? Princesses or not, I wager they'll be dead within a year."

The leader of the Chanyu reined in his shaggy mount and trotted up to Shang. Neither dismounted or exchanged courtly words, as would have been expected in Chang'an.

The nomad leader wore coarse pants and leather boots. His braided hair was festooned with long streamers that pirouetted in the wind. He studied Shang, then glanced at the women in the wagon. Li Mae parted the curtains and stared at him. The curtains were quickly closed. Shang saw a faint smile appear on the Chanyu's face.

Turning back to Shang the nomad said in halting Mandarin, "My name is Xion Wen Chanyu. I'm charged with delivering the women to my father, His Majesty, Son of Heavenly Wisdom."

It was a mocking honorific. Shang made little effort to hide his contempt.

"We have been instructed to accompany you," said Shang.

Xion Wen Chanyu shook his head and pointed to the approaching storm. "We must travel very quickly to reach the camp before we're caught in this. Anything else will be very dangerous for them." His eyes flicked to the princesses. "You and your soldiers must return to Chang'an."

Shang Gao shook his head and sat taller in the saddle. "I've been ordered by the Son of Heaven to observe the wedding of the princess to your father. I am also to witness that the gifts of silk and gold are properly delivered to the warlord. That is my duty."

Again the nomad shook his head. The Chanyu horsemen moved to the flanks and rear of the Chinese escort. Shang Gao willed himself to remain stoic.

Xion Wen Chanyu sighed with a show of exasperation. Then, in a more diplomatic tone, he said, "Circumstances change. Being a reasonable man, I will allow ten of your soldiers to accompany us. You are wasting precious time by arguing. My men will transfer everything to our packhorses and you shall inform your emperor that all is well."

Shang's aide tensed, and his hand went to his sword. The prince frowned and the man removed his hand from the hilt.

"The Son of Heaven will be greatly displeased. This contravenes the agreement he had with your father. I have every right to return the princesses to Chang'an."

"That wouldn't be prudent," Xion Wen Chanyu said, toying with his stringy moustache. He swept an arm back toward the extent of his force. Then he motioned his men toward the wagons.

"Ten soldiers," he repeated.

The valuables were quickly transferred to the pack animals. The princesses were pulled from their wagon and shoved onto waiting horses. Their long dresses were pulled up to accommodate the rough saddle. Li Mae looked embarrassed and Shang's aide grabbed a saddle blanket and sprang from his mount to cover her bare legs.

Two Chanyu grabbed the reins of the princesses' horses as the nomads regrouped.

"Report back to me after the marriage," Shang Gao said to his aide who would lead the Han escort to the village.

With a terse command from Xion Wen Chanyu, a thousand horsemen whipped their mounts into a dead run. A terrible wail erupted from Ming Zhaojun. Li Mae Tang glanced up and caught a glimpse of hundreds of strange men on a distant knoll. They wore glinting breastplates and metal helmets and appeared nothing like the barbarians who surrounded them. Arranged in mounted ranks with an officer and a standard bearer at their front, they suddenly turned, formed two columns, and descended the hill to join the captors.

Dark clouds billowed over the returning Han squadron and a raw wind lifted sand and pelted Shang. He reflected on what he would say to General Chen Tang, and what the general might say to the Grand Chancellor. Deep in bitter melancholy, he began the long march to the Great Wall and whatever might await him in the court of Emperor Wudi, the most excellent Son of Heaven.

***

Exhausted and in excruciating pain, Li Mae slid off her horse when they finally arrived at the Chanyu village. The entire procession had slowed twice when she and Ming had tumbled from their mounts onto the rocky terrain. Unable to stand, they were separated, carried to yurts, and deposited on piles of disheveled blankets.

"Where are my Han attendants, my escort?" asked Li Mae apprehensively.

"They were lost in the storm," answered Xion Wen Chanyu. "We sent a search party to find them, but I'm afraid they may never be found. Few foreigners venture here, and most disappear."

"That's very enlightening. And just how many of your men were lost?" she asked, her anger rising.

"None. My people know the terrain and the signs. Apparently your escort did not and became disoriented."

"Oh," she replied with disbelief. He gave her a salicious grin. "Then there will be no representative from my emperor when I marry your father?"

"We will send an emissary with all the details. But you needn't concern yourself with that. Once you and I marry, you will be a Chanyu woman."

Li Mae's eyes grew wide. For a moment she could not utter a word.

"We?" she finally blurted. "I was promised to your father, not you."

"My father is infirm and can no longer lead this clan. I have taken his place. You will be my wife, my ... princess." Again, the grin.

"This will not please the Son of Heaven," she said. A feeling of horror spread through her body as she imagined sharing the man's bed.

"You are a gift to the Chanyu. You are barter, tribute, because the 'Son of Heaven' is afraid of us. In my world you are less important than my horses. You will do exactly what I require. I don't worry about your emperor. Our wedding will take place tomorrow."

"And what of Ming? What will become of her?"

"She will be my concubine, and when I tire of her she will go to someone else," he said as he stormed out of the tent.

Moments later a guard opened the flap of the yurt and Ming was thrust inside. She rushed to Li Mae and threw her arms about her.

"Have you seen him?" cried Ming. "He's horrible."

"Xion Wen Chanyu?"

"No, his father, Zhizhi, the one you are to marry. He's had a stroke. He's a cripple, paralyzed. His hands look like claws and he can't even stand up. He has to be carried everywhere."

"He's not the one I'll be marrying. I must wed his son."

"Who told you that?"

"Xion Wen." Li Mae glanced at her friend, then looked away.

"What will they do with me? Who will they have me marry?"

"He didn't say anything about a marriage for you. You will have to be his …"

Ming sank to the floor, her face streaked with tears. "Do you think he's as cruel as he looks?"

"I suspect so. These are mean and arrogant people."

"They have no respect for the Son of Heaven?"

"None. And I'm afraid that they have less for us, dear Ming."

Hours later, a small, bowlegged man pushed open the tent flap and eyed the two princesses. Li Mae and Ming inched to the rear of the yurt when the nomad put a hand on a long curved knife strapped to his waist. Then, with abrupt motions, he pointed beyond the flap.

Confused, the princesses stared at each other. Suddenly, the man grabbed Li Mae's hand and dragged her outside. Ming quickly followed, blinking in the harsh sunlight.

With a repeated flick of his hand, the Chanyu motioned that they should walk. Taking cautious steps the princesses proceeded down a rutted path between dozens of felt tents yellowed by sun and dust. The yurts stretched over a large hill surrounded by a wooden palisade. Beyond the flimsy perimeter lay a sluggish stream and a copse of wind-whipped trees. Nearby were corrals for thousands of horses, sheep and goats.

"Why are we allowed to go out?" whispered Ming.

"I don't know. Maybe they want us to go somewhere special," said Li Mae, noting that only a few people took notice of them.

"Everything looks alike. I don't see any place special. I think they just want us to see how impossible it would be to run away."

"There's no place to go even if we could," replied Li Mae.

In the distance was another hill, with an encampment surrounded by a moat, a staunch wooden wall, and four guard towers.

Ming pointed to the palisade. "Is that a Chanyu fort?"

"I don't know. I guess we'll find out eventually."

Small gardens amongst the yurts grew a variety of vegetables. Children milked and herded goats and yaks. Li Mae and Ming walked past metal workers forging iron swords; the clanking of hammers resounded throughout the village.

A group of women sat upon quilts and sewed felt panels, chatting while they worked. Many were festooned in Han jackets as well as Chanyu traditional dress. One woman with graying blonde hair looked up from her task and saw Li Mae and Ming. She studied them for a long moment. "Good morning," she said in halting Mandarin. The woman had neither Han nor Chanyu features.

"Good morning," Li Mae replied. She and Ming, urged by their guard, returned to the yurt.

"I've never seen a woman who looks like her," said Ming after the flap was closed behind them. "Did you see her eyes and the color of her hair?"

"My father said the officials we sent to Parthia have seen many people like that," said Li Mae. "In fact none of them look like us. Some even have red hair and green eyes."

"But she speaks Mandarin as well as Chanyu."

"I don't know where she's from. But our guard didn't want us to speak to her."

"I wonder why not," said Ming.

"Because we're not 'honored guests.' We're prisoners."

***

The shaman was the first to file into the over-sized yurt. He was followed by two men who carried the crippled warlord. They set him upon a pile of blankets, but not in a place of honor. Behind him came Xion Wen Chanyu, who glanced at Li Mae with a blank expression. Ming was required to sit alone. Soon ten men filed in, but Li Mae and Ming were the only women allowed.

At the rear of the tent was an altar, upon which rested a gold-covered horse skull. The priest was cloaked in bright woolen garments, his face stained crimson. He made what Li Mae assumed was a prayer to the sun, the moon, and the heavens. He raised the skull and held it aloft, his bare arms thrust through his cassock. Then, raising a goblet, he took a sip of koumiss and passed the fermented milk from one man to the next.

The priest launched into a long, rambling oration, often interrupted by shouts and murmurs of approval by the assemblage. He then directed Xion Wen Chanyu to rise. The shaman turned his gaze upon Li Mae and pointed to the space beside the warlord's son. A chalice of koumiss was offered to the groom, who gulped it down to the applause of his compatriots. Another cup was given to Li Mae, who hesitantly took a sip and, seeing reproachful looks, drank the remainder of the brew.

The holy man stepped forward, held the ornate skull over their heads, and uttered an incantation. This was followed by the binding together of the couple's hands with a horse-hair rope, which quite suddenly completed the marriage ceremony. Li Mae and Ming were taken outside. Still crammed into the corner of the yurt, sat the old warlord. He stared into the distance and lolled his head from one side to the other.

The newlyweds stood in the middle of the throng. Xion Wen acknowledged their applause but glanced not once at his bride. Moments later she was escorted back to the tent, where she and Ming were ordered to wait. With darkness, the sounds of the clanging metal smiths and shouting children abated.

Ming sat hunched over, tremors coursing through her. "It might not happen tonight," Li Mae uttered in a hushed voice. "He may not take you for weeks or even months. I imagine that he has many mistresses."

"What about you?" Ming sniffled and wiped her nose with her sleeve. Surely he'll have you on this, his wedding night."

Li Mae sighed. "I have to do what the Son of Heaven commands. It's my fate. My personal wishes hardly matter."

Xion Wen Chanyu was quite drunk when he finally threw open the flimsy door and stood swaying before the princesses. Li Mae cringed. The man's body stunk of koumiss, sweat, and horse.

Through bloodshot eyes he stared at Li Mae, then Ming. Li Mae instinctively backed away when he shuffled toward her. With surprising swiftness his arm shot out and grabbed her. He pulled her body tightly against him and kissed her with fetid breath. Ripping her dress, he tossed her onto a pile of horse blankets and straddled her, his hands tearing open the front of her jacket.

Li Mae was stunned by the sudden assault. She attempted to push him away, but he was bigger and stronger. She dug her long nails into his arms; he seemed not to notice. Ming rushed forward, but Xion Wen's fist shot out, connecting with Ming's chin. She spun backwards, screamed, and fell hard against a stove.

Li Mae's move was instinctive. She reached for the knife hidden in her sleeve. The razor-sharp blade tore across Xion Wen's face and then jabbed deep into his arm. The man shrieked as blood gushed from the wounds. Li Mae rose, the knife clutched in her hand, her breathing coming in ragged spurts. A guard rushed in. The warlord pointed to Ming and spit out a torrent of words. The man rushed forward, grabbed the princess by her hair, and dragged the wailing girl from the yurt.

Xion Wen stared at Li Mae and again stepped forward. She raised the knife as her father had taught her and tauntingly beckoned him closer. If it was time to die, she decided she would not die alone. Xion Wen stared at his wife, mouthed another stream of epithets, and backed out of the tent.

The rage she saw on the man's bloody face was more malovelent than anything she had ever seen. He hated her. Perhaps, she thought, his loathing was greater than his lust. Yet his fury might still result in rape, so she sat immobile for hours.

He could have come back after tending to his wound. Xion Wen could have disarmed and easily killed her. Li Mae expected him to do that. She kept the blade in her lap and expected death all night.

Li Mae cried throughout the long night as Ming's shrieks tore through the hours of darkness.

Chapter 21

The city of Dunhuang was an oasis of fruit orchards that abounded in pears, peaches, nectarines. There were abundant stands of walnut trees and fields of poppies that in spring and summer painted the landscape in pink and burgundy. Wagtail birds flitted from one flower to the next.

It was the most splendid city since Samarkand. The cohorts swore that if the city had not bordered the Taklamakan Desert, they might have thought themselves in southern Italy or Spain. But a place of such fertility was not for the Chanyu. They led the cohorts past the city and around the edge of the desert to an isolated and barren land near the desolate town of Hami.

There was a small stream ten miles beyond Hami where the nomads had established their yurt city. It was a barren place, with nothing but sand, rock, and stunted trees.

Tacitus chose a low hill beside the stream to erect the legionnaires' encampment. It was within easy walking distance of the village, out of range of Chanyu bows, but not out of range of the legionnaires' scorpions. The locals, having never seen those weapons fired, could only guess how far the bolts could travel. That was just fine with the centurion.

As in every Roman encampment there was a moat, a palisade, gates, a corral, and guard towers. The Chanyu watched the construction—and the legionnaires—with interest. There was little that Tacitus could do about it, though he told the warlord that, once completed, only legionnaires could enter the camp without his express permission. Xion Wen Chanyu said that the same would apply to his village, but since his people produced trade goods, the foreigners might be allowed in from time to time. Thus began a guarded and wary peace between the two peoples.

Once the encampment was complete, Tacitus ordered a reconnaissance of the surrounding hills with their many caves and occasional watercourses.

"We've been invited to visit their village," Tacitus told Appian. "I guess the elders want to know more about us. But only six of us will be allowed in. I think that should be you, me, Oshka, Apollodoros, Diomedes, and Ibericus."

"Why Ibericus?"

"Because that lout is bigger than any two of them put together and he'll make a nice diversion," said Tacitus, observing a group of Chanyu exercising their horses. "I want you, Apollodoros, and Diomedes to sniff around while I talk to the warlord."

"I hate this place," said Appian. "I can't wait to get out of here."

"I feel the same. Hopefully we won't be here any longer than necessary, but we must retain a semblance of friendship with them. Still, I want the men to keep their distance; no fraternization with the Chanyu women. We can send groups to Dunhuang for women."

"Speaking of women, did you hear the screaming last night?"

"It's every night," said Tacitus.

"Who do you think that is?"

"A captive, I would guess. It's not our affair."

Appian stood beside Tacitus on the parapet of their wall. "I'm curious, did you ever see any of the Seres escort once we came back here?"

"No, they were mixed in with the Chanyu. Maybe they strayed and got lost in the storm. It was impossible to see anything."

"I did see two groups of Chanyu split off on either side of the Seres people, but nothing after that."

"We'll probably never learn what really happened," Tacitus said. "Have the men up early tomorrow. I want them to drill hard. Things won't stay the same, not with these barbarians. There will be no complacency."

"If I didn't know better, I'd swear I was talking to your father. Thankfully, you carry no *vitis* stick."

***

"The old warlord, Zhizhi Chanyu, is dying," Appian said once he and the others returned from their visit to the Chanyu village. "I saw him, paralyzed and hidden away in a yurt. He was babbling, but no one listened to him. It's as if he's already dead."

"That's why I couldn't meet with him," said Tacitus.

"I thought it strange; I'd heard that elders and ancestors were given great respect."

"It sounds like a power struggle. His son didn't want to speak about his father. He wanted us out of there once we started asking questions."

"Xion Wen is going to be very difficult to work with. I'm sure he has no interest in speaking to the Seres on our

352

behalf, Tacitus. He's young and ambitious. He wants power and he'll get it, even if he has to murder his father."

"It happens in Rome; it can certainly happen here."

"And then what happens to us and their commitment?"

Tacitus seated himself on a log next to a fire. Appian watched the course of a meteorite, then sat beside him.

"The man's all about war. He needs victories to boost his image, and he has to make a name for himself amongst all the clans. I'll wager that he'll eventually attack the Seres. And it won't be for tribute; he wants heads to put on poles."

"So our agreement with them is nothing more than smoke," said Appian. He nodded in greeting to Diomedes and Apollodoros, who had walked over to join them. "Surely we won't help them in a fight with the Han."

"I saw something very strange in the village," said Apollodoros. "There's a woman who speaks Chanyu, but she's not Asian. Nor was she Chinese or Kyrgyz, and certainly not Sogdian. I could be wrong, but she looks Roman or even Greek. She has a straight nose, big eyes, and there is blonde still in her hair."

"Did you speak to her?" asked Appian.

"No, but she gave us a real long stare," said Diomedes.

Appian turned to Tacitus. "Did you get anything from that monster Ibericus?"

"The monster is here," Ibericus said, plopping down and scooting everyone over.

"Great Zeus," Apollodoros moaned as the weathered log tilted dangerously.

Ibericus munched on a piece of bread and gave the Greek a contented look. "Does my magnificent bulk not leave you stupefied and in awe, *medicus*?"

"Stupefied, yes," Apollodoros said as the fire shot embers high above.

"Do you hear anything?" Diomedes asked.

Tacitus cocked his head. "Hear what?"

"That's just it. She's not screaming tonight. It's the first time in weeks."

"The woman might have been the new warlord's bride," said Ibericus. "But why would she scream every night?"

"Women see you and scream," ventured Appian.

"Only at first. Then they enjoy it."

"Well, I don't think that woman enjoyed it. I think she's dead," said Tacitus.

"Oh, by the way, Centurion," said Ibericus, repositioning his mass on the teetering log. "I was snooping about like you told me to, and I saw two other women who were not Chanyu. They were young and dressed in silk clothes as if they were rich or important."

"Rich or important won't do them any good here," said Appian.

"Remember the day we were with the Chanyu, when they met that Seres detachment?" said Diomedes. "Xion Wen didn't want us to get close, but we could see some women thrown onto horses. I wonder if they were the ones Ibericus saw?"

"Apollodoros," said Tacitus, "why don't you do some probing tomorrow. Find that strange woman you told us about, the one who looks Greek. She might be able to tell us things about Xion Wen that we should know. I think it's important."

***

The woman was shooing away a half-dozen goats from a tiny vegetable patch, energetically waving a stick at the intruders, when Apollodoros found her. He guessed that they were about the same age. She glanced at him, then looked over her shoulder.

Apollodoros came closer and said in Greek, "They eat everything. My father had some when we lived near Athens. I never got to like them."

Tilting her head, the woman smiled. "But tending them gives me an excuse to go outside the village."

"Do you need an excuse?"

"I'm afraid so," she said. "You have an Athenian accent, but you're with the Romans. I find that strange. I presume you're not a slave."

"I'm a *libertus*. I was born in an Athenian village, but I work as a *medicus*." Apollodoros pointed toward a detail of legionnaires tending their horses. "I've been with them for many years. Your Greek is flawless. May I ask you how you came to be here?" asked Apollodoros.

"You may ask, but it's not something I enjoy talking about."

"But you're so far from home. It must be a fascinating story," he said. "And surely you don't have the likes of Herodotus or Thucydides rushing up here for interviews."

She laughed and shook her head. "You are a funny man. And, yes, you're the first Greek I've met since I left Parthia over 20 years ago."

"Well, this Greek is pleased to make your acquaintance. My name is Apollodoros," he said, "What were you doing in Parthia?"

She put a finger to her lips and tapped slowly, as if deciding how much to reveal. "I and my son were slaves. We were sold to a Parthian trader, then to a Sogdian, and I was sold again to the Chanyu.”

She related it without emotion, as if it were a natural occurrence, one that was simply expected in life.

“I was also a slave, captured by pirates along with my father, then sold to a Roman. In fact, I was the teacher of the son of the man who owned me, and that young man is now the leader of the legionnaires on that hill.” Apollodoros nodded toward the encampment.

“I see. So you attend to Roman soldiers.” Her comment hung in the air for a lengthy moment.

“The young man, the centurion you might have seen in the village, is named Tacitus,” said Apollodoros, not wishing to meet her rebuff. “His father was a Primus Pila, a—”

“I know what that is, Apollodoros. I have seen Romans. They were the people who enslaved us, as I recall. But, that aside, I imagine you’re wondering how I became a slave, aren’t you?”

“It’s a delicate question. I assumed that you would tell me if you cared to.”

“It’s not a pleasant topic, as I said, but I’ll tell you anyway, since we’re being so chatty.” There was a flicker of a smile and Apollodoros thought that he would have enjoyed knowing her years before.

“I was to be married to a Greek boy on the Island of Samos, a place my father used to visit. Our ship was also taken by pirates. My father was killed. My mother and I were taken as slaves to a bestial place on the Berber coast. My mother died there and some terrible things were done to me, things that most men take lightly.”

“You were assaulted, you mean?”

“As no woman should be.”

"I think I understand. Our centurion killed a legionnaire for committing that act."

"Really?" she said, studying him closely.

"Did you ever learn who did it, I mean who offended you?" Apollodoros asked, looking into the woman's dark eyes.

"No, he was just a young boy, a Greek like me, captured and put in a cage. I don't think he wanted to. At least that's what he said while he did it. The pirates threatened to cut him if he refused. It was a long time ago and it hardly matters now."

With apprehension, Apollodoros said, "May I ask your name?"

"Hera."

"It does matter, Hera," Apollodoros said, eyes wide, stepping back from her. "It matters very much."

She was staring at him now, trying to imagine a youth, one whose face had been burned into her mind. So much time had passed, and now this aging, frightened man stood before her.

Shaking, his mouth fell open and he hid his face in his hands. "Oh, Hera," he said, his voice quaking. He stumbled backwards and repeated her name again. The words "Forgive me, please forgive me," came out as a muffled sob. He turned and staggered off. He looked back once at the stunned woman, then ran as fast as his skinny legs could carry him.

***

In the following days the princesses were allowed to drift about the Chanyu village without their guard, since escape seemed impossible. The pathway they took led past the group of women they had seen earlier. The Chanyu women

357

were curious about the Han girls and asked Hera to speak with them on their morning walks. It wasn't long before Li Mae invited the Greek woman to visit, since she could not communicate with any of the Chanyu.

The day after the encounter with Apollodoros, Hera knocked lightly on the door of Li Mae's yurt. Li Mae quickly ushered her in.

"He's come here with those people." Hera sat on a goatskin mat. How frail she looked, with her long, greying hair spilling down her face. Li Mae exchanged a worried glance with Ming while Hera slowly rocked back and forth and wiped away tears.

"A nightmare, the most terrible thing, and I tried so hard to forget it. Now it's come back to haunt me in flesh and bone. How could he have come here? Did he try to find me, to seek me out and punish me? What have I done to deserve such a fate? Oh, the gods," she cried as the tears rolled down her weathered cheeks. She sighed and stared into the hearth, but shivered all the same.

***

Hera made her way slowly to Apollodoros, who sat on a rock beside the stream and gazed into the swirling eddies. He did not see her until she sat beside him. He glanced at her, then quickly looked away. He seemed to shrivel into himself. She wondered if by going to him she had made a mistake. He always sat in the same place, head bowed. Then he would rise and walk about, always coming back to the same rock.

Two weeks had passed since he had run from her, two weeks during which she sobbed each night. She had lain in her yurt, rarely venturing out. Often she thought about the knife she had hidden and whether the pain she had endured should be inflicted upon him. Then a strange resolve compelled her to walk to the rock beside the stream.

"I wanted to kill myself. I wanted to die after I saw you here," Apollodoros said quietly. "But I didn't want you to think that you were responsible for my death. Maybe I am simply too afraid of dying."

They did not speak for a time.

"Every day and every night I thought about how to murder you. In my mind I played it over so many times that I thought of you as already dead."

"You should have, Hera. What I did to you was the worst thing I have ever done." He took a deep breath. "Oh, I've tried to repent by becoming a *medicus*, saving wounded men. But the gods have punished me by sending me here to confront my past. I am in moral exile. I'll never see peace again."

"Then we share the same fate." Hera said, watching a hawk fly east.

He followed her eyes skyward, then looked at her again. "Why did you decide to speak to me?"

She shrugged and shook her head. The breeze lifted a strand of grey hair, and she tucked it into her wool cap.

"The decision wasn't an easy one, Apollodoros."

He closed his eyes and nodded.

"We're both prisoners of our past. I've heard it said that life is a circle and we race around it as fast as we can to escape our destiny. But our fate is always there, always waiting. So you travel around the circle of life and eventually you run into your fate. You can't escape yours and I can't escape mine."

"And what is yours, Hera?"

"To have seen you again and, if the gods favor it, make peace with myself. And with you." Then, almost inaudibly, "And maybe the gods will let me see my son again. I haven't laid eyes upon him in a very long time."

"A mother should be able to do that," he said in a comforting way. "I was afraid to see you again, but I sat here hoping that you might appear. I didn't want our meeting to end as it did, with never another word."

"If you hadn't done what those horrible men demanded, they would have killed you," Hera said. She fished around in a cloth sack, extracted a chunk of goat cheese, and offered it to him.

"I have heard that the Romans hope to march to a river in the Middle Kingdom and go down to the sea. Is that true?"

Apollodoros gave her a wan smile. "They hope to."

"Is that why the Romans stopped here?" Hera asked. "Are they allies of the Chanyu?"

He shook his head. "It wasn't a matter of choice. The cohorts have to cross their land and need Chanyu permission. They don't have enough men to fight their way to the Wall. So they agreed to a deal. The legionnaires watch over the village when the young men go to the clan rendezvous. The Chanyu are supposed to parley with the Han. It's an unhappy arrangement, but the only one the Romans could make."

"The old warlord, Zhizhi Chanyu, may have honored such a commitment, but his son will not. It would be very naïve to think otherwise. Xion Wen will allow the legionnaires to remain here until he has no further use for them. Then there will be war."

Apollodoros finished the cheese. "For many nights we heard a woman scream. It was quite unnerving. Then the screaming stopped. Do you know anything about that?"

"A rape, what else? A Chinese princess, a tribute, was raped by many men."

"Is she still alive?"

"In body, but it has affected her mind. She screams in silence now. The bastards enjoyed hearing her. Sometimes she whimpers, but they like that, too."

"We saw two Seres women. Who is the other one?"

"Another Han princess. She was married to the new warlord, but he shuns her. She cut him on their wedding night. They hate each other."

"But Xion Wen hasn't murdered her."

"No, not yet. A previous princess met a bad fate, but Zhizhi Chanyu, the old warlord, had enough influence to demand a replacement. His son does not, and the death of the one he married will bode ill if the Chinese learn of it. So for now the barbarian allows her to live. She is even worse off than I am."

"A prisoner."

Hera nodded.

"The centurion also saw the Seres woman, the one married to Xion Wen," said Apollodoros.

"And he's curious?"

"What man wouldn't be? She's beautiful."

Hera smiled. "It would be very dangerous for her if he showed any attention. Xion Wen Chanyu detests her, but he's a dangerous and jealous man. Tell your centurion to be very careful. The Son of Heaven gave Li Mae to the Chanyu. Nothing can alter that except the Emperor, and he's not coming here."

***

It was the second time Li Mae had glimpsed the Roman officer with the red transverse crest on his helmet. She and Ming had been allowed to take their morning walk when they saw the man ride from the legionnaire's encampment. He trotted his horse toward the village, then dismounted to adjust a stirrup.

"He's tall, said Ming. Taller than Chinese or Chanyu. I wonder why he's here."

"I don't know but I've never seen any man like him," said Li Mae.

Tacitus remounted and trotted his horse to the village perimeter. He halted his mount when he saw the women.

It was a sweltering day. A gust of wind whipped past and the morning light illuminated a shock of curly hair.

The princesses suddenly stopped. "Look, it shimmers like golden thread," exclaimed Ming, clutching Li Mae's hand. They stood transfixed, staring at the centurion in his polished breastplate with the gladius belted to his waist.

"He's looking at you," Ming whispered. "Don't you want to say something to him?"

"I woldn't know what to say. I have no idea what language he speaks."

"He looks so impressive. Look at his eyes. They're blue like the pools in the Shanglin Gardens."

"Yes, I guess they are."

The soldier issued a little smile, a nod, and, after replacing his helmet, spun his horse about and trotted back to the palisade.

That night Li Mae lay awake thinking of the young warrior with the golden hair and the way he had gazed at her.

She wondered what he was really like and what thoughts had come to him that morning. A myriad of questions assaulted her, but, having no answers, she pulled the blanket closer. The last thought before slumber possessed her was what the fates might hold for her and the soldier with the golden hair.

***

"What are those barbarians like, Hera? I mean the ones on the hill."

"They're the same as any men who think they should rule the world. In China the Emperor speaks of the 'Middle Kingdom' as if it's the sun and everything revolves around it. Those Romans are no different; neither are the Parthians, Sogdiani, or Chanyu. They all want power. They think they have a right to it and will fight to get it. It has always been that way and always will be."

Li Mae sighed, frustrated with her confinement. She wanted so badly to fly away, to go someplace else.

"I'm no longer interested in politics, Hera. I grew up in a court. But I'm still curious about people."

"Like the Romans on that hill?"

"Well, yes. The barbarian officer, for instance. What did you call him, a centurion?"

Hera leaned forward and peered at the princess.

Li Mae turned from the woman's stare, feeling her pale skin flush.

"Oh, you are playing a dangerous game, aren't you?"

"Not at all! I'm just interested; they look so different. Their features are like ..."

"Mine?"

Li Mae glanced at Hera. "Yes, in a way. I mean their eyes, noses. They look, well, impressive, noble."

"They might look impressive in all that armor, but I'm not so sure about noble," said Hera, chuckling. "I know nothing about the centurion. I do know about Xion Wen, the warlord you had to marry. Do not provoke him, princess."

"He hasn't murdered me yet, and I've certainly given him cause. Besides, whatever happens has been decided by the fates. I can't escape that."

"And what have the Fates decided for the centurion if you show any interest?"

"I don't know. But nothing is accidental. He's here for a reason, and that's his fate as well as mine."

The Greek woman shook her head. "I wish I could be hopeful. But the Fates, my dear, are rarely kind."

***

Hera was washing village clothing beside the stream when she saw Apollodoros walking up to her. Over the weeks their meetings had become more frequent.

"Just what did you tell the centurion about the princess?" she asked him, beating the cloth against a rock.

"Only what you told me about her. That she was tribute to Zhizhi Chanyu but was forced to marry his son after the old man's stroke. Don't worry. He understands that it would be dangerous to approach her. Besides, he doesn't even know how to say hello in her language."

"Really, now? And you believe that will stymie his interest?"

"He hasn't actually met her, and there are more critical things for him to deal with. In any case, it's been many years since he's shown any serious interest in a woman. The last one was in Rome."

"Oh," said Hera, "Such a long time ago."

"We've been on the march continuously. There has been very little time to develop relationships."

Hera bent to her work again, but was distracted by a horseman with a regal bearing. She raised her chin toward the foreign-looking officer who was drilling the Roman cavalry. "Who's that?"

"Our resident Parthian. He was captured by the Romans years ago."

Hera shielded her eyes from the morning sun and watched the officer command with casual self-assurance.

"He was a captain of horse for the Parthians, but was born as a Greek. He's a terribly vain fellow, but we like him. He keeps us entertained."

"So he's kind of like you," Hera said, trying her best to staunch a grin.

"Me? I am hardly vain, just amazingly well versed. True intellect doesn't require vanity, my lady."

She laughed again. They chatted a while longer as Hera placed the damp clothes into a sack. Apollodoros promised to meet her again the next day.

***

"No members of the princesses' escort have returned," said General Chen Tang to the Minister of Censorship and Security. "They should have been back here months ago."

"I've had no communication from the Chanyu about them. I can't imagine the escort would still be at their village." Sima Gao set a document down on his desk and turned to his son, who stood at Chen's side. "They were to rejoin your force after the wedding to Zhizhi Chanyu."

"Father, I suspect that they have been murdered or killed in battle. The lieutenant who accompanied the escort had precise orders."

"You said that there was a great storm approaching when they were riding to the Chanyu village," said Chen. "Perhaps they became lost?"

"It's possible, but how is it that none returned? Now I believe the princesses are in grave danger. I volunteer to lead a thousand cavalry to their camp and determine their fate."

"A noble but provocative thought, one that will lead to war. The Son of Heaven and the Grand Chancellor won't condone it. But I have dispatched a man to investigate," said the Minister.

Turning back to Chen, Sima said, "Do you remember Yao Peng, the hostage given us to ensure the safety of a princess?"

Chen thought back. The barbarian boy had been the younger brother of Zhizhi Chanyu. "Of course, but that was 20 years ago. I thought you had him strangled when the princess was reported dead."

"We kept that fiction as a warning. No, Yao Peng was allowed to live a quiet life. In fact, he has a Han wife and two children. He is quite indebted to our clemency."

"So you used him as a spy," said Chen.

"I did. Apparently he blended in quite nicely. No one recognized him all these years later, and he has just returned."

"But he is still a Chanyu; he might give you false information," said Shang.

"He wouldn't want his wife and children's heads on pikes," replied the Minister. "At any rate, he's here, and his report is quite interesting. Xion Wen Chanyu has murdered his father but shuns your daughter, General. Unfortunately, Princess Ming Zhaojun has not adjusted to her new place and suffers greatly."

Chen Tang thought for a moment. "So with Zhizhi Chanyu dead, the validity of my daughter's marriage to his son is questionable, if not unlawful."

"Perhaps, but that must be determined by the Son of Heaven. He may sanction it just to keep the peace," said Sima. "What we do know is that there is no sign of her escort at the Chanyu village, and the son of the old warlord has been unifying Chanyu clans.

"So I should be concerned about our villages and the unfinished Wall. Does the Emperor know of the Chanyu violation?" asked Chen.

"The Grand Chancellor has informed him. The Son of Heaven is quite concerned."

"But my daughter is safe."

"For now."

Chen gave the Minister a short bow, as did the prince, before they turned to leave. They had almost reached the door when Sima said, "Oh yes, Yao Peng did mention one thing more. A force of barbarians, some three or four hundred, have joined the Chanyu and erected a fort outside their village."

"Sogdiani?" asked Chen.

"No, people from the west, perhaps the *li-jin*, the enemy of the Parthians we heard about. But we're not sure why they've come this far. Our spy only observed; he was not to arouse suspicion by asking questions."

"Are these barbarians a threat to my daughter?"

"Not directly. In fact, Yao Peng says that their leader and your daughter may have an interest in one another. He even saw an exchange of presents. Something is happening right under the noses of the Chanyu."

"The princess and a barbarian exchanging gifts? That is intolerable," said Shang.

"I wouldn't give it much weight," said Chen. "The western barbarians are still in Chanyu territory and I doubt they're going anywhere." He sighed. "And neither is my daughter."

"She won't be there long. There will be war." With that, Prince Shang Gao stormed out of his father's chambers.

Chapter 22

To Li Mae's surprise, no one paid much attention when she first accompanied Hera to the goat pens. Perhaps, she thought, since there was no place to escape to, there was no reason for the Chanyu to care if she strolled beyond the village stockade. As time passed she ventured out alone, finding a place of solace away from the village clamor.

A haphazardly latched gate was easy to slip through, and a pathway meandered beyond the sight of the village and down to the stream. Beyond the stream was a place of rolling hills where the Roman cohorts drilled. It was also out of sight of the inquisitive Chanyu.

Over the weeks she noticed that the leader of the legionnaires, the one Hera called a centurion, appeared more often. Sometimes he would detach himself from the cavalry troop and ride to the stream opposite the bank and watch for her. Occasionally he waved, and she waved back. Then she would gather up her belongings and walk back to the village.

Except for her talks with Hera and Ming, the silent encounters were all Li Mae had to look forward to. The man who rode down the hill to see her was so foreign that she could only guess his real nature. Indeed, she did not even know his name. What might become of these clandestine but wistful meetings was impossible to contemplate, but she did remember her dreams.

***

Tacitus, sitting astride his horse, watched the young Han woman as she walked back to the village.

"Was she waiting for you again?"

Tacitus looked to see Appian grinning up at him. "I don't know if she was waiting for me. Maybe she just found a place where nobody bothers her."

"You can certainly be more inventive than that. Of course she's hoping to see you. I just wonder where this peekaboo is heading."

Tacitus shrugged. "Nowhere, but she's nice to look at."

"I think you're infatuated. And considering her circumstances, that could be a problem."

Their meetings became a daily ritual, and they began to leave little gifts for one another. Neither opened the packages until the other departed. Sometimes Tacitus left nuts or fruit that he had purchased from traders out of Dunhuang. One day he carefully wrapped the little glass vial he had purchased from the Jewish trader Elizar ben Josephus and laid it on a rock where she would find it. It was the only thing of value that he possessed. He wondered what her expression would be when she found it.

The next day Tacitus discovered a pair of mittens wrapped in a silk kerchief.

"They're really quite pretty, and functional too. It's a sign of true love," said Appian when he saw Tacitus wearing them.

"Don't be jealous. It was just a nice thing for her to do."

"Oh yes, a very nice thing," said Appian, unable to smother a grin. "And all the men think so too, Centurion."

***

At four months pregnant, Ming had become morose. Li Mae encouraged her to leave the dimness of her yurt and accompany her and Hera through the village. The stark surroundings were terribly depressing. Ming abruptly stopped, and in a tone of utter desperation yelled, *"Trepema, foberos! To miso afto!"*

Hera, wide-eyed, stared at the princess. "What did you say?"

"I hate this terrible place."

"Where in the world did you learn that?"

"It's Sogdian," said Li Mae, feeling a wave of sorrow pass through her as she remembered their lessons with Tai Donc.

"Nonsense! That's not Sogdian, it's Greek. Where did you learn Greek?"

"From the Sogdiani, who else?" said Ming. "They were at court in Chang'an. A Sogdian boy, the son of their ambassador, taught us to speak that strange language. It was our secret, a kind of code."

"The Sogdiani came to talk trade and spread their Zoroastrian religion. Sometimes we even rode horses with the ambassador's sons," said Li Mae.

"You two actually speak Greek," said Hera. *"Thamasios, thamasios!"*

"Wonderful, wonderful," Li Mae translated.

"But why is the Sogdian language the same as Greek?" Ming asked.

"It's not. Only higher-class Sogdiani speak Greek. A famous general from a place called Macedonia marched through Samarkand and brought the language to those people."

Li Mae pointed to the Roman encampment. "Do they speak Greek?"

"They speak a language called Latin, but many know Greek."

"Does the centurion?"

"I imagine he does."

"Interesting," replied Li Mae. "You and that old man speak the same language, don't you?"

"Apollodoros? Yes."

"He visits you a lot," said Ming. "You two must be great friends by now. Are you fond of each other, I mean romantically?"

"Romantically?" Hera looked startled. "Remember when I told you about my captivity by the pirates? That something terrible happened to me? It's the same thing that happened here to you."

"You were raped?" Li Mae said with alarm.

"Yes, by a Greek boy. I never thought I would see that person again but—"

"And you actually speak to him?" Ming said, an expression of horror on her face. "If I ... I could never ..."

Hera took Ming's hand. "The circumstances were different. It's a long story, but he was forced into the act as much as I was. I've since found him to be very caring, and he comes from my part of the world. And what happened was a very long time ago. So we have come to terms."

"And now you two are as the jade stalk and the lotus, the stallion and the filly?" Ming asked.

"More like the gelding and the old mare. We are far too old for anything romantic, and, as you know, I was used for much of my life. It's a stain that never really washes away. Men have only brought me pain. But a little friendship is not a bad thing."

"Oh," said Li Mae, disappointed.

"It's alright. For Apollodoros the past is so bitter, it's doubtful that his 'jade stalk' would sprout anyway. So we've become like brother and sister, and that will only last until the Romans are gone."

"But he might stay. I mean, stay with you," said Ming.

Hera smiled wanly. "Why would a man stay with an old woman? Even old men have dreams, princess. You must remember that."

"It's important if one lives to be old, Hera. I don't think that's my fate."

They walked in silence for a while until Hera proclaimed, "He's staring at you again."

Li Mae looked in the direction of Hera's gaze and saw the centurion with another Roman. A stiff breeze caught the centurion's red cloak and it lifted in the wind. He slowly raised his hand. After checking to make certain that nobody but Hera and Ming could see her, Li Mae also waved.

One soldier turned back to the encampment, and the centurion touched his heels to his mount and quickly followed.

"*Li-jin,*" Li Mae said.

"*Li-jin?*" said Hera.

"The people you call Romans, we call '*li-jin*'. I guess it's the name of a military unit. We Han made trade agreements with the Parthians, and they must have fought the *li-jin*. But the *li-jin* people have never come to Chang'an."

***

The haunting strains of music floated from Li Mae's yurt in the late afternoon. Hera listened for a while before tapping softly on the door and peeking in. Li Mae's fingers rested on her *qin*, one of the few possessions she'd been able to rescue from the wagon when she was taken by the Chanyu.

"Please don't stop," Hera said upon entering. A crude bench lay between her and Li Mae; draped over the bench was a length of silk. Beside it was a fan, an inkpot, and a calligraphy brush. Hera gazed at the delicate brush strokes that played upon the fabric and shook her head with amazement. The strumming of the zither faded again, and Li Mae laid the instrument on a yak-skin rug.

"I learned to speak some Mandarin from other Han women imprisoned here, but I could never read it," Hera said, gently lifting the brush. "What have you written, Princess? Is it a poem?"

"A rather sad poem, I confess," said Li Mae with a doleful smile. "Most Han songs and poems are sad, particularly ones about love at court. Court is very competitive; there's a constant struggle to gain prominence. Life there is fragile and very often brief."

Hera wondered how she would have fared in such a swirling and discordant microcosm. Could it be any more venomous than this wasteland village? Though still a slave, she had become a member of the women's gatherings. Moreover, she could go anywhere she wished in the village. Having no importance, she had no fear of jealousy. Nor at her age would she likely be the object of rape, though she disappeared into her yurt on nights when men became mindlessly intoxicated. Yes, she had a certain amount of latitude in her world; she could feed the goats and horses and sew with the women at her discretion. No one ordered her about any more. And life for her would end quietly, like an icicle's last drops in a spring thaw. That would be better than the terror of a knife or hatchet in the cold corridors of a Chinese palace.

Hera drew the soft bristles of the calligraphy brush across her palm. "I've never heard Han poetry. I don't even know what Han poetry would be like. Would you mind reading it to me?"

"This is just a fragment of a much longer poem, but I'll read it if you wish." Li Mae held the silk so the characters caught the fading light. "I should tell you that we believe heaven has four parts. One quarter is in the south where the sacred red bird flies in summer. It's a wondrous place of beauty where Taiyi—the supreme deity—reigns, and where one can find eternal happiness. The land is so sacred that even the Son of Heaven makes sacrifices to Taiyi on a place called Taishan Mountain. That's where I'll find happiness when I die."

Hera gazed at the enchanting young woman with the heart-shaped face and sad eyes and thought what a waste her life had become. Then Li Mae spoke as softly as a summer breeze.

"I pray that my soul shall fly with the red bird and take me to Taishan Mountain to repose with celestial joy.

How wondrous it would be to lie in the willow grass and contemplate the harmony of emerald hills and silver ponds.

I will fly from this wretched place of sand and wind where evil fills my heart with dread and foreboding.

Red bird so high and swift winging above me on this horrid day,

May my spirit be carried on your wings to Taishan Mountain where I shall find harmony for all time to come."

The princess placed the silk on the table and sipped tea in silence.

"Were you ever in love?" Hera finally asked, gazing at the coals in the mud hearth.

Li Mae shrugged. "I was greatly enamored of a Sogdian boy, a man, really. I had known him for years. He was an assistant to his father, the ambassador from Samarkand. The one who taught me your language."

"And you had to leave him behind."

"He died. Murdered, I believe. Perhaps by the man that had been chosen for me, an army officer who still serves my father." The princess's face was devoid of expression.

"That's astounding. Obviously you have no affection for the officer," said Hera.

"None, but it no longer matters. I will never see him again. Besides, love is not terribly important in Confucian thought. Filial piety and the birth of a son are treasured above everything else. Parents in the Middle Kingdom arrange marriages for their children to improve their social status, not for the happiness of their offspring."

"It's much the same where I come from. I didn't know the boy I was to marry. Sometimes I wonder what he would have been like and how our lives might have been different."

Hera looked at the fan on the table. "The last princess here, a Lady Ti, had a fan like that. She used it to hide her face when she laughed. But she did not laugh often."

"My friend Ming and I saw her leave Chang'an with the Chanyu. We never learned what happened except that she died"

"It was very sad," said Hera. "Zhizhi Chanyu had four pleasures: his animals, drink, gambling, and women. One night he got drunk in a game of chance and lost nine horses to another clan elder. Hoping to get them back, he bet the only valuable thing he had left, Lady Ti. He lost the bet and the princess was given to the other warlord and his friends. She had a very bad night and the next day I found her body in the stream."

***

In late spring, hundreds of Chanyu horsemen rode out of the village in an armed mass for a gathering of clans on the distant steppes. For many days there would be a brisk trade in slaves, horses, and tribute goods given them by the Chinese. The festivities, fueled by fermented goat milk, resulted in mock battles and real feuds with many casualties. The great gathering left the village virtually empty of military men, and a more relaxed environment gave Li Mae, Hera, and Ming time to gather in Li Mae's yurt.

Ming's morning sickness had passed, but the fear, guilt, and depression had not. She sank into a fathomless melancholy and talked in whispered tones of escape. She sobbed about giving birth to the child of a barbarian.

"But it will be your baby, too," Hera said. "Women here raise the child until he's of military age. You can teach him to speak Mandarin. He'll think of the Middle Kingdom as his real home."

"And he will honor you, his mother," said Li Mae.

"There will be tranquility along with the pain," added Hera. "As Li Mae has said, having a male child is a very important thing."

"We are not in Chang'an," the girl wept. "And it may not be a male child. I'm going to have a baby because I was raped. There was no wedding, no matchmaker, no ceremony, and no groom!" She buried her face in her hands and, through the tears, said, "Oh sisters, I just want to die!"

***

Silky black hair brushed Tacitus's face as the girl's tender lips touched his and he kissed her deeply. Penetrating warmth flowed through him and he heard the princess sigh. She had undone the top buttons of her gown and he glimpsed a breast, delicately white and supple. He tried to pull her closer, but the elusive beauty, like a specter, began to dissolve before his eyes. He saw sadness come over her, perhaps a longing for something or someone she could not have. She withdrew, an arm still reaching out to him. "No, don't go. Please stay with me," he pleaded. She only whispered utterances he could not understand. Emptiness enveloped him and he let out an audible moan.

"They're gone, you better get up," Apollodoros said, shaking him.

"Gone? Who's gone?" Tacitus said, his mind still in the dream.

"The princesses. Hera found me near the village and said that Li Mae went after her friend who rode out earlier."

Tacitus sat up and reached for his armor. "Where would they possibly go?"

"I have no idea and neither does Hera."

Setting out alone, Tacitus circled the village until he found the tracks of two horses. One set of prints was more windblown than the other. Both led into the wasteland and the craggy hills that bordered it. He looked toward the darkening horizon and spurred his horse. Sand whipped through the air and stung his face. He found Li Mae four miles from the village, beside a narrow trench. She held the body of her friend and, sobbing, rocked the dead princess in her arms.

Tacitus brought his mount to a halt. The princess looked up with alarm, then relaxed when her eyes met his. She pointed at her friend's horse and spoke in Mandarin.

The animal had a broken leg. Tacitus nodded his understanding. He surmised that at a dead run and in a moment of misjudgment the horse had plunged into a hole and tumbled forward, throwing the girl onto the rock-studded ground. Li Mae stroked her friend's face, wailed, and shook her head. The wind tousled the dead girl's hair, rippling through her dirty, ripped gown.

"She came to this wretched land because of me and look what I've done. I killed her!" Li Mae said in the language taught her by Tai Quin.

Tacitus stared, reeling. "You speak Greek?"

"Sog— yes, Greek. Hera calls it Greek."

Without thinking, he wrapped his arms around her. "Oh, Great Jupiter, by all the gods!"

"Jupiter?"

Under any other circumstances he would have laughed with unabated joy. He hugged her again, and she winced when his *segmentata* pushed hard against her chest. He pulled back and glanced at the steel plates. "Oh, I forgot." Then he gazed at the still form at their feet and said, "I'm so sorry for your friend, princess. I am so sorry."

Kneeling beside the limp, almost childlike figure with the bulging stomach, Li Mae looked beseechingly at Tacitus. "I can't just leave her here. Wild dogs, vultures ..."

The centurion wrapped his cloak around the body of the princess and strapped her to the saddle of Li Mae's horse. He then mounted his horse and helped Li Mae sit behind him.

"What of her horse?" she asked as she wrapped her arms about his waist.

"He's crippled and will die. Do you want me to destroy it now, finish it quickly?"

She shook her head. "No, I don't want to see anything else die."

***

We must leave this desolate place as quickly as possible, thought Tacitus. He considered returning to the safety of the Roman encampment, but ominous clouds hovered above and the shearing gusts already whipped sand about them. The ride back, he realized, would be far too perilous.

He held her tightly to himself as he had in the dream, but in that she had appeared as a mirage, a fleeting image tantalizingly close, yet so elusive. His somnambulant words came back to him: "Stay with me," but they'd been to no avail. She had vanished like morning mist. He knew so little about her, not even her name, but he did know that she was too precious to lose again.

She was shaking. *Is it fear?* he wondered. *Is it due to the death of her friend, or something else?* After all, they came from different worlds, and they had never spoken to one another until moments before.

He had told Appian that his interest in the princess was all quite innocent, a mere diversion from the tedium of everyday camp life. What could possibly transpire between the two of them? They didn't even speak the same language. Yet, in an instant, that barrier had fallen away, and now what?

He had lied to Appian. He dreamt about the mysterious girl night and day and mused over romantic possibilities, and, on rare occasions, the consequences. Now he would flee to shelter with her. *What is in her mind?* he wondered. *What are her dreams?*

It was time to go.

***

The storm chased them across the parched landscape. Li Mae tried not to look back at her friend's body strapped to the horse behind them. She should have had Ming stay with her during the night. Hadn't Ming intimated to Hera that she would not live long? That the princess, six months pregnant, had ridden the horse in near darkness was an unimaginable act of desperation. Was she was simply running away without a word to her lifelong friend? And where was she going except to a calculated and fatal end?

Surely Ming would never have thought that anyone would follow her. Her death and disappearance would have been a mystery, and a missing horse amongst thousands would have gone unnoticed. *Suicide*, thought Li Mae. *It could have been nothing else.* Now she was gone. Somehow it seemed inevitable, as if they were both dead the moment they passed through the Gate of Exiles.

Never before had Li Mae held so tightly to a man. But for her father, she had rarely touched one. Now she clung to the centurion as tightly as she possibly could. Tears streamed from her eyes as the horse pressed on. Like skeletal fingers, the wind ripped at the sand and the skies opened up for a rare deluge.

They neared the dun-colored hills with their jagged outcroppings, and the centurion turned the horse toward a cave he had spied before. Its entrance was dark and forbidding and blasted by shearing gusts. Sheets of water ripped across the rock face. Its interior had been chiseled out, likely by those seeking sanctuary from nature or from men who hunted other men.

They dismounted. The centurion led the spent animals inside the cave. He lifted the body of the dead princess and carried her to a ledge cut into the rock. Wisps of straw and cloth lay upon the ledge, evidence of long-ago slumber. Li

Mae arranged her soul mate's gown and wiped rain from her face.

"She should be clothed in white, that is our color for death," she said. "There would be priests and mourners and incense, but here," she said, indicating the cold sepulcher, "there is nothing."

"But you are here, and that's what matters," said the centurion. "Everything else is smoke and noise. The lamentations of strangers are rarely sincere. It is the same where I come from—the dead don't care about the grandeur of the funeral. Perhaps your friend knows that you are with her now. That would please her. In fact, it might have been her final wish."

The dead princess appeared serene. Li Mae touched her face, then the man's, wondering if Prince Shang Gao or even her father would say such kind words.

"My name is Li Mae Tang," she said in a hushed voice. "We, my soul sister and I, owe you our gratitude. I think she will be at peace here. Someday I would like to come back to visit her again."

The centurion nodded. "You are shivering." He led her into an adjoining alcove where the storm's fury was muted. She followed him, her feet touching the dusty floor with the daintiness of a kitten.

"Will the Chanyu find us here?" she asked.

"No, the storm will have blown away our tracks."

"I'm afraid of what might happen to me when they find me, when I go back."

"You're not going back to Xion Wen. You will stay with us."

"But they'll come for me," she said, her voice rising.

"They won't like the reception."

The centurion led her to another small room in the cave. He spread his cloak on the ground, and they sat against the wall. The cold and fear that had gripped her dissipated as she leaned against him. He removed his *segmentata* and helmet and held her close.

Only the dimmest light filtered in. The muffled wind sounded like a spirit beating ineffectually against a distant window. They huddled together in the shadows. He buried his nose in her long, damp hair and wrapped his arms tightly about her.

This foreign soldier who gave her shelter had to be nearly twice her age, thought Li Mae. Certainly he was older than Shang. She only came up to his shoulder and felt child-like beside him. How strange it was to be protected by one regarded as a barbarian, this resolute centurion from so far away. It was this man she had asked Hera about, had made gifts for and had dreamed of since he had first appeared by the village wall. She had tried not to stare as he sat on his horse across the stream, but she had memorized every feature of his face. But touching that face had been as improbable as touching the moon and the stars. His visage was the image that came to her each night.

What could he possibly be like, she had wondered? What sort of man would travel so far? What quest was he on? Surely, he had no intention of remaining in this barren land. Though he and his men appeared to be a stalwart force, was he a captive of the same people who imprisoned her? Or was he allied with the Chanyu? But surely, this man who held her so close would not countenance the evils of the Chanyu. None of that mattered now, she thought. He had saved her and that was all she needed to know. Certainly the fates had set it all in motion, just as they had everything else.

For the first time she remembered her dress, which she'd torn while chasing after Ming on horseback. The tight gown parted still further, and she tried to cover herself. He grinned and said, "I will buy you a new one in Chang'an, or a stola in Rome."

"I might need one before that," she replied in the simple Greek she had learned as a child. She looked into his eyes. His lips brushed hers. A shiver coursed through her body. No man had ever kissed her before. She put her fingers to her lips, and then to his. The next kiss came with an intensity that left her breathless.

"Centurion... Centurion," she murmured when their lips finally parted.

"Tacitus, Princess, my name is Tacitus."

She wrapped her arms about him and succumbed to passions that she had not even dreamed of.

Their breath intermingled. Her thighs wrapped around him with hardly a moment's hesitation. She felt his strength deep within her, a glowing, seamless sensation that transported her to a world far away. She closed her eyes and willed the coming of each movement, their pent up desire bonding them together like the lightning and thunder in the heavens above. Every carnal need cried out, their bodies reached a crescendo, tensed and held for a brief moment before falling into weightless bliss.

***

Tacitus awoke to wailing sobs. Though the princess in his arms uttered her lamentations in Mandarin, he needed no translation. Finally, drained, she lay in his arms as if she were a very young child.

Tacitus couldn't remember when they had shed the last of their clothes. The fire he'd made the night before had faded to flickering embers. He gazed into her eyes, searching for the mystery within her soul. The princess's cheeks were still damp. Then she smiled. It was a shy, self-conscious smile, but it was the most joyous thing he had ever beheld. Tacitus traced a line around her nipples until they were taut again, then ran his fingers lightly down her belly, between her legs, and was pleased to hear a soft moan. Their first coupling had been searing lust, every carnal need crying out, their bodies reaching a crescendo before satiated exhaustion. This time their desire was tender and lingering. Entwined, they lay in consummate rapture deep into the night.

She seemed so small, so fragile. And she was so young, no older than he when his father took him from Rome and Tullia. The image of that girl flitted across his mind. So much time had passed. For years he had repressed the need for the warmth of a woman other than Tullia. There had been moments of need with harlots along the way, but nothing worth remembering. Never like this. Tacitus willed away all thoughts of the future. Breathing deeply, he simply wanted the world to stand still.

With the addition of a few sticks, the fire glowed again. Li Mae snuggled beside Tacitus and said, "When you are alone, who do you pray to? Who are your gods?"

Sleepily, he considered the strange question. "I rarely think about the gods, but we Romans have many. Some are our own, others are imported. There are deities from foreign lands that have been approved by the high priests. Most of our soldiers worship a god from a land called Syria, on the other end of the Silk Road. That god is Mithra. He's celebrated on Sunday with the sacrifice of a white bull."

"Do you believe in it?" she asked, and kissed him again.

"Not really. I don't put much faith in the gods. I think they're myths and inventions made by men who crave power. The priests want to be rich. They want people to tremble before them and they want to be honored. No, I have little faith in the deities. The most important thing in the Roman world is *virtus*. It's even more important than the gods themselves."

"What is *virtus*?" Li Mae asked, the fingers of one hand tracing a line around the centurion's lips.

"It means courage, strength, and excellence in everything."

"And that's what you believe in?"

He nuzzled her ear. "All I believe is that I care more for you than anything else. And if you were a goddess, Princess Li Mae, I would believe in you."

"What will become of us?" she asked in the hour before dawn.

Us, she'd said. The thought of them as a union, a single element, brought Tacitus a sense of wonder. No girl since Tullia had spoken to him in such a way. But now this enchanting creature wanted to be with him. She had become more than his responsibility or passion; she had become his world.

"We will persevere," he said.

"Will the Fates allow it?"

"By the gods," he said, "they damn well better!"

He was pleased that she laughed; but, he knew that gods, manmade or not, were capricious, and he held her very tight.

In the morning, Tacitus woke again to find Li Mae staring up at the ceiling of the cave. "Will my friend be safe here?" she asked.

"She is safe here with the memory of you."

An uncertain light broken by scudding clouds had filtered in, revealing chambers that he hadn't seen during the night. It was time for them to leave, but the labyrinth of rooms and passageways seemed to have secrets, and Tacitus had suspicions of what one might contain.

Holding a taper aloft and with Li Mae clutching his other hand, Tacitus cautiously peered into one cubicle after another. In some the ceiling had collapsed, littering the floor with shattered stone, while others showed signs of human habitation. A musty smell pervaded all as they went deeper into the cave. They approached the end and Tacitus stopped.

"Wait here," he said, releasing her hand. The odor had changed. It was one he had smelled many times before. The taper flickered as he entered an aperture with a low ceiling. He sensed what he might see. The light played across the decaying remains of men still clothed in bloodstained, quilted uniforms. Arrow shafts protruded from a few. The murdered soldiers of the princesses' escort had been tossed into a pile. Some skulls had detached and lay amongst the ashes of long-ago fires.

"What is in there?" Li Mae asked when Tacitus emerged.

"Your soldiers, the escort from Chang'an. They were murdered and their bodies were dumped here. Nobody was to find them."

"So it was a conspiracy from the start," said Li Mae.

"True, but most likely on the orders of Xion Wen, not his father," Tacitus said. "Xion Wen wanted your escort, and his father, dead. No one in Chang'an would know anything, there would be no report to your emperor. Xion Wen would be the new warlord and gather all the clans."

"And what then?" she asked.

"War. It's what he wanted from the start."

Li Mae nodded slowly. Together they walked toward the cave's entrance.

"Say goodbye to your friend, Princess," said Tacitus as he saddled the horses. "It's time to leave. There's another storm coming, but it's not wind or rain."

Chapter 23

Grand Chancellor Bi Hangyong laid a map of the incomplete Great Wall on his desk and studied it. Chanyu patrols had been seen near the Wall. It was still an incomplete barrier of wattle, stone, and earth that could be easily penetrated. Bi put a finger on the map and traced the area where the barbarians had made a minor raid, most likely to judge the response of local Han forces. The response had been ineffective, as the Han solders weren't allowed to pursue the nomads into the wasteland beyond.

Although he had tacitly supported the pacifistic views of the emperor, Bi was a Legalist, one of many who saw the Chanyu as eternal enemies of the Middle Kingdom. Now, with Xion Wen Chanyu's power grab and increasing hostilities, he counseled the Son of Heaven that the rootless barbarians only behaved themselves at the point of a sword. Thus, he was in little mood for compromise when his aide, Quing Liang, approached him.

"The honorable scholars have arrived, Excellency."

The Grand Chancellor looked up from his map. "Have them enter," he said wearily. "I already know what they want."

"They're such idealists."

"We must flex like the willow in the autumn wind and follow the dictates of the Son of Heaven."

Quing Liang left the antechamber and welcomed the scholars with a deep bow.

Hangyong watched as the five academics returned the courtesy with a curt nod and filed into a hall decorated with tranquil garden paintings of beautiful pavilions and exotic animals. The men kowtowed three times; their black caps with two long, horizontal feet on each side grazed the polished floor.

Looking up, the senior scholar rested his eyes on the mural. "Hill beyond hill, pavilion behind pavilion at the West Lake of Hangzhou, will the singing and dancing never cease?" he quoted.

Bi nodded approvingly. "Honored scholar, I'm told that you and your colleagues have just returned from the border in the northwest corridor."

"That is so," the Confucian academic replied. "The Minister of Culture wanted to know the condition of our peasants."

"And?" Bi Hangyong said, taking his seat on a raised dais, a subtle affront to the five who stood before him.

The senior scholar smiled wanly. "I think his Excellency has been apprised of the hardships they face. The entire weight of taxes has fallen on those who could least afford it. That may not distress the military, but we believe the peasants must be spared. As you must realize, their labor feeds the army. The situation is most unfortunate and certainly displeases the exalted Son of Heaven."

When Bi remained mute the scholar continued, his voice a degree more forceful. "As his Excellency knows, the wars against the Chanyu have cost us great treasure, quite to the detriment of the masses. Every year thousands of peasants are required to defend the frontier and toil at hard labor. Their crops yield nothing and starvation is rampant."

"Our earlier policies of retribution against the barbarians have always cost us more than we have gained," stated another scholar. "We, therefore, beseech your office to reconsider any hostile action. There are less costly and more responsible ways to achieve our goals." He folded his hands; the long, polished fingernails glistened.

Enlightened words until our villages are burned to the ground, thought Bi as he nodded sagaciously. How they loved to recite the words of Confucius and cite benefits of a balanced yin and yang. Did they really think that the barbarians would sip gingered tea and pontificate on the joys of peace? What fools, that they would shackle the war wagons and assume that the harmony of mankind would be influenced by goodness and virtue. Real virtue lay in the swords and pikes of 50,000 men and 500 chariots.

"So, honored Chancellor," the chief scholar concluded, "we believe it is the wish of the Son of Heaven to ameliorate the hardships of our people while binding the barbarians to us through our superior culture. As the eyes of the cobra will paralyze a mouse, so the wealth of the Middle Kingdom will transfix our enemies. In time they will kneel in awe and supplication."

What was it that the great general Sun Tzu had said? Oh, yes. "Parry the inevitable stroke and await the moment when weakness shows." Let these spineless dreamers prattle on until the Chanyu slice the heads from the bodies of our peasants. Then we'll see what noises they make, thought the Chancellor

"I recall the first time Zhizhi Chanyu sidled into Chang'an pretending to be our heartfelt friend," said Bi. "He was feted and honored as if he had been praying on Taishan Mountain. I can recite from memory the tribute we bestowed upon him: 50 horses, 20 *jin* of pure gold, 70 rolls of silk, and 34 *hu* of grain. But their raids continued and our people still died."

The chief scholar shrugged. "The court of the Son of Heaven will invite the Chanyu. We're certain they'll renew their allegiance. We recommend a special inducement: another princess to add to those we have given in the past. We expect their delegation to arrive during the Catching Cool Breezes festival."

A bitter taste welled up in Bi's mouth. The barbarians would festoon themselves in garish silks like children playing dress-up.

"You realize it will all be in vain. A stopgap measure at best before we unleash our fury upon them."

The scholar opened his mouth to reply. Bi held up his palm and said, "Yes, I know. It's the will of the Son of Heaven and all has been approved. We must patiently await the barbarians and offer whatever princesses happen to wander by."

The scholars kowtowed again, the elongated attachments of their caps flexing with the motion, and backed out, no doubt pleased with the thought that they alone would bring peace and harmony to the land.

The Grand Chancellor rolled his maps and willed his anger to subside. To Quing Liang he said, "The wind changes with the seasons. When it grows cold and blows from the north, we'll be ready. Apprise General Chen Tang of what has transpired and instruct him to prepare the army."

Bi wondered how the scholars would react if they knew the real plans of Xion Wen Chanyu. He could have told them, but they would only equivocate. No, let the full disaster fall upon them. He would not be played again.

***

Shang considered the game board and placed a white stone on the fourth line, a strategic move that expanded his territory. He looked at General Chen Tang to observe his reaction.

Chen rewarded the prince with a telltale smile. "A bold move," he said, "but a dangerous one."

He and Shang had inspected the troops earlier that morning, having received orders from the Grand Chancellor. However, the timing of any military move had not been determined. The Emperor, influenced by the scholars, had made no commitment. Playing *weiqi*, an ancient game of strategy, allowed the general time to contemplate and reread the sage advice of Sun Tzu while again weighing the military mind of the prince.

Chen considered the board. How might he isolate Shang's stones, cut them off from reinforcements, and annihilate them? He lifted a black stone and placed it next to a line of black stones that supported one another. He then opened his volume of Sun Tzu and thumbed through it until he found the passage he was looking for.

"'Caution is effective,'" he read. "'Do not advance boldly without due consideration. Be able to concentrate strength decisively, anticipate the enemy, and annihilate the adversary.'"

"Yes, I believe that to be wise counsel. We must concentrate our strength and launch an attack on the Chanyu. Destroy their villages and annihilate them," said Shang as he placed a white stone on the board in an attempt to isolate the general's stones. "And we must bring back your daughter before she becomes entangled with the *li-jin* barbarian," he added.

"The strange foreigners are the people who interest me. I'd like to know their strengths and weaknesses. I presume that they were part of a great fighting force. Perhaps we can utilize their tactics."

"But if they are allied with the Chanyu, we must destroy them," said the prince.

"Better to capture and use them to our advantage. Sun Tzu also said that. But I think your real concern is the *li-jin's* involvement with my daughter."

"Isn't there reason to be concerned?"

"Perhaps," Chen said. "Li Mae is a beautiful girl."

Then he positioned another stone next to Shang's.

"But she was to be my bride before the Chancellor gave her to the Chanyu," Shang protested.

Chen nodded. "We don't know what the endgame is for the *li-jin*. Perhaps they consider my daughter a prisoner of the Chanyu and wish to rescue her."

"That's for me to do, not them."

"You may have that chance. No former agreement with the Chanyu will be honored if we go to war. My daughter, if she's still alive, can be freed. So I must ask you, do you still wish to marry her, considering that the lotus will have been sullied by the stalk of the barbarian?"

"I'll honor the agreement you and my father made. Nothing has changed in that regard."

Chen continued to study the board. "A worthy thought. By the way, your man has entered an area that I control. You have to be judicious about your moves into hostile territory." He picked up his book and quickly flipped to another page. "Enlightened lords and distinguished commanders can overcome an adversary when action is taken and achieved with unparalleled foresight. That cannot be gained from ghosts or gods. It must be gained from what is learned by men.'" With those words, General Chen Tang, commander of the western frontier, pushed his stone into place and swept those of the prince from the board.

***

The storm had passed, but a stiff wind blew as Tacitus and Li Mae rode toward the legionnaire's encampment. An arrow flew past Tacitus and splintered upon a rock. Turning in the saddle, he saw a tightly packed band of 30 nomad horsemen close behind. The Roman fort was still a mile beyond the hill that he and the princess began to ascend.

The pair spurred their mounts, but the tired animals couldn't outrun the Chanyu ponies. Tacitus cursed. He'd known they should have started much earlier. Now he had put their lives in grave danger.

Li Mae's mount was failing as they pounded up the hill. Another arrow sped past, but a third struck Tacitus's horse and the animal fell to its knees. The Chanyu were 15 yards behind.

"Go!" shouted Tacitus as he slapped the rump of Li Mae's horse. The exhausted animal made a last attempt to reach the top when there was a sudden shout from the crest. A mounted cohort led by Appian charged past her and flung their pila into the startled Chanyu. Twenty were impaled as the legionnaires charged down the rise, hacking to death the stunned riders.

It ended quickly. The wounded Chanyu were dispatched, and the cohort reformed and prepared for a fast ride back to the encampment.

"We assumed you would be coming from the west," said Appian, "but I thought it would be much earlier. I organized the force when I saw the Chanyu leave the village."

"I'm sorry to have put you and the men in danger. My venture out here was an impetuous thing, but…"

"It was, but I would have expected nothing less," said Appian.

Tacitus nodded and said, "They'll all be coming at us now. Prepare the camp for an attack. Has Xion Wen returned from his meeting with the clans?"

"A few hours ago, but he was doing more than just meeting the clans. They had to be raiding. There are a lot of prisoners, mostly Seres women," replied Appian.

Ibericus caught up to the group and walked beside Tacitus.

"Then the Han must be at war with them," said Ibericus.

"And so are we," Tacitus said grimly. "Are all of our people in the fort?"

"All but Apollodoros and Diomedes. They knew there would be trouble, so they went to get Hera," said Ibericus.

"They went into the village alone?" Tacitus asked with alarm.

"Few were awake," Appian replied. "They hoped to get in and out before they were noticed."

A jostling of bodies accompanied by shouts turned Tacitus's attention to the village gate.

"There they are!" said Ibericus. Hera, Apollodoros, and Diomedes ran past the gate, struggling to free themselves from grasping hands.

"Cohort, rapid pace!" shouted Tacitus. Legionnaires tore downhill to the village. Swords and knives flashed in the morning sun as blood spurted at the village entrance. Seeing the oncoming force, the Chanyu released the Greeks, fled inside, and slammed the gate behind them. Their arrows flew from inside the wall.

Tacitus, leading the cohort, lifted Hera. Several legionnaires carried Diomedes, who had been slashed. Once they were all inside the Roman encampment, Tacitus ordered the cohort to join the other two in defensive positions.

"Medicus, take the Wolf to your tent. Hera, go with them," Tacitus shouted as he headed for the ramparts.

"Wolf?" said Hera as she hurried behind Apollodoros.

"Quick now, remove his tunic and clean the wound. I will suture him," commanded the *medicus*.

"Why is he called that?" Hera persisted. The patient was largely hidden by Apollodoros and those assisting him.

"It's just because of a mark he has," Appian said. He handed Apollodoros a strip of linen. "A birthmark, that's all."

"Where?" Hera asked, her voice trembling. "Where's the birthmark?"

"It's not—" Appian turned to see the anguish on her face and pointed to the scarlet mark. "There, right there. Do you see it now?"

Hera stood on tiptoe, but she still wasn't able to see past Apollodoros and pushed her way to the prostrate man. She screamed, her hands suddenly on her face.

"What are you doing? I'm trying to save this man. Get her out of here," said Apollodoros as he pulled the stitches closed.

"No! It's him! It's really him!"

"Who?"

"It's Diomedes. He's my son!"

Everything stopped. Diomedes sat up. His eyes met Hera's. "What did you say?"

"The mark. The birthmark. My son was born with a mark in the shape of a wolf's head, just like the one you have. It was the same color and in exactly the same place. Who was the man you were sold to when you were six? Tell me, please tell me."

Despite Diomedes's wound, the legionnaires made room for the incredulous woman.

"General Surena, the Parthian. The richest man in the kingdom."

"And you performed for him in a village square," she said, vigorously nodding.

"Yes, he played along with my pantomime of him and the crowd clapped. He threw a bag of coins to my owner and took me away." A slow smile came to Diomedes's face. "Mother?" Instantly he was off the table, wrapping his arms about the woman and kissing her.

Embarrassed by the display of emotion, Apollodoros said, "I assume you wish to be alone, so please excuse me."

"You mustn't leave," said Hera, her voice suddenly quiet.

With a questioning look, Apollodoros said, "The wound will heal. It's not as serious as I thought. Nothing vital was cut, and I treated it with honey. There will be no infection, Hera."

"That's not what I'm talking about. Why don't you sit down and think for a moment."

"We don't have time. We're preparing for battle."

"I think it will be worth your time," she said, her eyes meeting his.

"I have to check our preparations," said Appian, as he moved toward the tent flap.

Hera pointed to Diomedes. "Apollodoros, this man is my son. Now remember yourself as a boy of fifteen, and count the years. You were the first and only man I had been with at that time. I bore my son nine months later."

Apollodoros sat on the table and put two fingers to his temple. Diomedes saw the gesture, grinned, and looked at his mother with amazement.

"Great Zeus and all the gods," whispered Apollodoros. His eyes sought out Tacitus, who raised his eyebrows in acknowledgement.

"You knew?" Diomedes demanded.

"We all suspected it a week after we captured you. It was quite humorous, really. Your personalities are almost identical," said Appian, putting two fingers to his brow. "We were waiting for you to figure it out."

Apollodoros stared at Diomedes as if a fog had descended upon him, the realization beyond his grasp.

"Knew that I ..." he began.

"That you are my father, you pompous Greek!" Diomedes bolted forward and wrapped his arms around the *medicus,* and yet another stitch ripped from the wound.

"Great Zeus," Apollodoros said again. "Oh, by all the gods of the pantheon, I have a son!"

"Yes, Father," said Diomedes. "And in a way you also have a wife."

***

Shang hurried past functionaries, scholars and eunuchs who bustled about the palace. "I hope we've not kept him waiting."

"The note just said to be here with all haste," General Chen Tang replied.

They approached the ornate hall flanked by stone dragons and imperial guards. A moment later the officers stood before the stern-faced Grand Chancellor. They bowed, and the advisor to the Emperor returned the courtesy.

"The village of Yongchang in the Gansu Corridor has been pillaged. Men have been murdered; women were raped, then taken away."

"By the Chanyu?" Shang asked.

"Of course by the Chanyu," the Chancellor replied testily. "Several survivors fled and told us about it. We investigated. The barbarians carried out a major raid inside the Wall."

"I've assigned more workers, but the barrier is still incomplete," said General Tang. "I apologize for the weakness."

"The Wall will be completed in due course, but at least 3,000 Chanyu got past it. They were led by Xion Wen Chanyu."

"Does the Emperor know of this?" asked the general.

"Yes, and he has become tired of conciliation and diplomacy. This band of Chanyu will be exterminated. His Excellency regrets that his generous gifts, including Princess Li Mae Tang, have been wasted and abused. I know that you have prepared the army. There will be an immediate attack."

***

"Centurion!" a legionnaire shouted from the parapet. "Chanyu, about 15 of them. And they're armed."

"Optio, I want 30 men," Tacitus said as he sprinted toward the commotion. "And bring Hera."

"The woman! The princess!" Xion Wen spat. He dismounted and strode toward Tacitus. The centurion ordered him to halt and turned to see Hera approach with Li Mae.

"Go back into camp."

Li Mae shook her head. "If Hera is here, then I'm here." Both women stood beside the centurion and stared into the flushed face of Xion Wen.

"That woman was a gift to us by the Han emperor. She belongs to me," the man said, his face twisted with rage.

When Hera finished translating Tacitus said, "Tell him the princess was granted to his father, whom he murdered. We also know he ordered the extermination of the princesses' escort. We found their bodies in a cave. She will not be returned to the Chanyu, and all agreements we had with them are terminated. He should go back to his village before there is more trouble."

Upon hearing the translation, one of the villagers made a dash for Li Mae. Before Tacitus could react, a knife flashed from her sleeve and a gush of blood streamed from the assailant's face. A second villager advanced, only to have his arm severed by Ibericus's gladius. A thick wash of blood spurted across the ground.

The Chanyu leader glared at Tacitus. Thirty legionnaires pointed their weapons at the nomads, who warily backed away.

That evening Tacitus doubled the guard. "They'll attack at first light," he said to Appian. I want them to have a little surprise."

Listening in the predawn hours, one would have detected the sound of shovels outside the Roman encampment. But that sound would have been overshadowed by the screams of captured Han women within the Chanyu village.

Chapter 24

"Form triple line," Tacitus ordered.

The three cohorts assembled 100 feet beyond their gate. The front rank held their shields before them; those behind raised them over their heads like overlapping tiles. Several dozen archers were positioned behind ramparts, waiting for the Chanyu. Behind them were a row of cocked scorpions, their bolts aimed at horsemen assembled on the field.

The placement of the cohorts near the fort made it too dangerous for the Chanyu to attempt encirclement; they would be in range of the bowmen if they did. Trusting in shock and overwhelming numbers, they shouted a war cry and charged the Roman line, giving scant attention to the terrain as their arrows flew toward the line of shields.

Chanyu horses, bunched together, screamed as their hoofs plunged into deep, narrow pits covered by twigs and brush. Their legs snapped, and their riders were thrown into sharpened stakes that rose from the ground in serrated rows. Within seconds, hundreds of mounts pitched forward, bringing the charge to a stunned halt.

"Fire scorpions!" Tacitus ordered, and the metal bolts ripped into packed riders in the rear ranks. Tacitus had his men reposition behind a second line of pits as the Chanyu regrouped. Easily within range, the scorpion darts continued to topple men from their mounts.

Tacitus positioned himself at the exposed end of the line. "Prepare for a second wave," he commanded. Looking over his shoulder, he saw that Li Mae, who had stood beside him, was unshielded and exposed. Blood oozed from her leg.

"You should not be here! It is far too dangerous! Go back!" he shouted amid the din of battle.

"I will not! My place is with you!"

"Quick, get behind me," he shouted, but she pointed to a thick, rising cloud of dust.

"The barbarians are not coming again. They're looking out there, see?" She stared in the same direction as the legionnaires.

Sweat ran down Tacitus's face, but he could still see the dust and the swarms of figures emerging from it.

"Horses, cavalry, thousands of them!" shouted Appian.

Hundreds of silk battle flags flashed in the morning sun as the din of horns and drums rolled over the combatants and the air resounded with strident blasts. The ground shook with the thudding of cavalry and chariots. High-wheeled machines with their archers and pike-wielders were supported by ranks of thousands of infantry.

As they neared the village, the terrified Chanyu fell back toward the Roman position and the withering fire of the scorpions. Like angry hornets, the tribesmen milled about, screaming as bolts tore them from their mounts.

Not since Carrhae had Tacitus seen so many troops committed to battle. Relentlessly the great wave came on. The front rank of infantry discharged their crossbows into the tangled mass of fleeing Chanyu. Behind the bowmen came troops wielding iron flame throwers, terrorizing men and horses alike. In minutes the village was aflame with women and children rushing from its gates.

The princess stared at the oncoming horde and gripped Tacitus's shoulder.

"They're Han," she shouted, pointing to their flags, "it's a Chinese army!"

"They'll think we're still allies of the Chanyu." yelled Appian. "They'll attack us as well."

The stunned Chanyu, their numbers thinned, attempted a defense as the great mass descended upon them. Horse-drawn wagons with archers broke through their ranks, and scythes protruding from wheel hubs amputated the legs of horses and fallen riders.

The force and speed of the Chinese rush was inexorable. Though many fell to Chanyu arrows, the attack continued unabated. The desert warriors turned, their exposed flanks crumbling under the onslaught.

"They're coming at us!" Appian shouted.

The Han cavalry swept toward the second row of pits. Like the Chanyu moments earlier, hundreds of horses plunged into the deep holes, flinging riders to their deaths. As the second wave struggled past the stricken cavalry, Tacitus turned to the scorpions and waved his arm. Bolts shot forward, flinging dozens of men from their saddles. A quick second volley felled chariot horses, causing wagons to topple, their occupants tossed into the path of onrushing vehicles.

Prince Shang Gao, riding beside General Chen Tang, pointed to the Roman cohorts. "Only *li-jin* remain General. My infantry companies will attack and annihilate them!"

"No, I want a three-sided envelopment to push them toward the burning fort. They will surrender when they see the hopelessness of their situation," the General said, but the Prince had already committed his troops to a frontal assault. The Han infantry charged; drums and gongs accompanied troops carrying a vicious curved blade attached to a long staff. Others fired crossbows, bringing down a dozen legionnaires. As men fell in the front rank, they were quickly replaced by those behind. The line held.

"Fire the scorpions," Tacitus ordered again. The bolts, far more forceful than handheld crossbows, tore through the light armor of the Han archers, impaling two or three at a time. When the Han infantry closed to 20 yards, Tacitus shouted, "Pila!" and 300 javelins flew into the front ranks. The advance faltered as survivors struggled to step over the dead and dying.

It was the desperate moment Tacitus had awaited, the critical instant when a small, determined force could inflict great damage on a more numerous foe. "Charge gladii!" he shouted. The cohorts, shields slamming into the disorganized Han, moved like a great plow. Their double-edged sword sliced off limbs and impaled torsos among the startled infantry.

Two of the three companies committed by the Han had been decimated, but the soldiers regrouped and prepared to send a shower of arrows at the cohorts.

"Form testudo!" shouted Tacitus.

***

More legionnaires fell as Shang Gao ordered another charge. He rode forward, accompanied by General Chen Tang, who was furious that his order had been disobeyed.

The General was close enough to see the taut and resolute faces of the enemy who must have known that death was imminent. The lines of the legionnaires began to form a wedge and a space briefly opened between them. To his surprise he noticed a young woman, knife in hand, standing resolutely beside the barbarian leader. Clad in royal clothing she held tightly to his arm, an arrow having grazed her leg. General Chen Tang studied her to see if indeed she was allied with the *li-jin* or a captive. In a moment it became apparent that she would fight alongside him to their deaths.

It appeared to the general that the young woman was seeking out faces of any Han officers. Many on horseback darted in and out of infantry ranks directing the attack. Suddenly the girl began to shout, dropped her knife and waved frantically. Again, the general looked in her direction, spurred his horse through the massed troops, and pushed to the front. He whipped around and shouted until his troops lowered their weapons.

The assault on the Roman line halted as combatants, only inches apart, glared at one another.

***

"My father, my father!" Li Mae cried in Greek, waving her arms. Tacitus, stunned, looked at the man on a caparisoned charger. The gongs, drums, and horns had ceased, as had the shouts of the armies, though wounded men still moaned as they lay crumpled on the ground. The general leaned forward on his mount and, with an outstretched arm, motioned for his daughter to approach.

"I can't walk very well, Tacitus," she said. "Please take me to him."

Tacitus sheathed his sword and lifted her into his arms. The legionnaires parted, and Tacitus moved between them as the Han soldiers stared at the unbelievable pair. Tears streamed down Li Mae's cheeks; she said the word "father" again and again.

Delivering Li Mae to her father was something Tacitus had hardly anticipated. He'd thought that both of them had only moments to live. Her long black hair trailed across his face, and he breathed in her scent.

Li Mae Tang smiled through her tears. Sitting erect on his warhorse, surrounded by an army of 40,000, the general stared down at the strange foreigner who wore the steel helmet with the red transverse crest. The general studied the way she thanked the *li-jin* and clung to him.

Chen Tang dismounted and took Li Mae in his arms. Tacitus saluted, his clenched fist striking the metal of his *segmentata*.

"Please ask your father if I may attend to my dead and wounded," he said quietly.

Li Mae translated his words and received a curt nod. With a flick of his fingers he motioned to allow Tacitus to pass.

"Sheath your weapons. Stack shields and assist with the wounded," Tacitus ordered his men.

Li Mae's father pointed at the dead and wounded Romans, and then to the Han wagons. Tacitus nodded, and the legionnaires, with the help of the Han commander's soldiers, placed them into the war wagons.

Shang Gao hastily dismounted and stood beside Li Mae's father, who cradled his daughter as if she were a small child.

Li Mae's father spoke with her for a moment, then the general again appraised Tacitus. He finally turned and put Li Mae in the arms of the prince with a few curt words.

Shang Gao looked relieved. Li Mae gave Tacitus a final glance. The look did not escape the man carrying her. Quite suddenly he turned and stared at Tacitus with an expression of fury on his face. Tacitus returned the stare and bowed ever so slightly. Then he turned his back and walked toward waiting medics.

The centurion turned his attention to the Han forces. They still surrounded the legionnaires. He watched them with curiosity and a measure of respect.

"We have not been disarmed, but we are not free to leave," Appian said.

"Until I'm told otherwise, we're free men," Tacitus replied.

Without asking for permission he strode to the front of the cohorts and in a commanding voice ordered, "Form fours!"

The troops quickly moved into position.

"You have fought honorably and we have not been beaten. We now do what the general commands, but you are still legionnaires. We will show the Seres the strength and honor of our people."

Tacitus could feel the general's presence behind him. *Let him observe and note the caliber of the men they engaged,* he thought. *We saved his daughter and successfully held off his men. Now I will lead mine, perhaps for the last time.*

Two hundred and eighty legionnaires stared straight ahead. They were fine soldiers. His father would have approved.

Tacitus drew his gladius and raised it high above his head. "Are you ready to march?" he called out. The cohorts replied with a thunderous "Yes!" He repeated the question twice more and was rewarded with the same resolve.

"Draw gladii!"

The Han soldiers stiffened. Tacitus slammed the weapon against his shield, and his soldiers did the same. The sound echoed through the ranks. Appian issued three blasts on his horn. Swiveling with the precision he had learned nearly two decades earlier, Tacitus bowed to the commander, pointed his weapon forward, and said, "We are prepared to march."

No translation was required. The general nodded, and the rapping of swords on shields was soon accompanied by the beating of drums and the hammering of gongs. The Han army had won a great victory over the Chanyu and their determination invigorated his men. Looking across the field at his magnificent force, General Chen Tang allowed himself a smile and gave the order to march.

****

In the late afternoon the army bivouacked beside a stream many miles from the Great Wall. Shang paced outside the *li-jin* encampment, glancing frequently at their leader who inspected his men. The *li-jin*, bereft of tents, camped in the open, surrounded by troops who watched the foreigners with great curiosity.

Shang hadn't seen Li Mae since he'd handed her to the doctors. The thought of her attraction to the foreign officer was becoming unbearable.

With rising anger, he strode to the general's tent, made a cursory bow, and said, "You have not disarmed them, my lord, and they're still a dangerous force. I recommend that they be bound and their weapons confiscated. After all, they allied themselves with our enemies. Indeed I would go further; they should be eliminated lest they cause trouble."

"Eliminate them?" General Tang said in a measured voice. "That is what you think? A foreign force that fights with unique tactics and such skill? I would consider that a waste. They're surrounded by our forces and have displayed no hostility. In fact, they have shown themselves to be quite professional, wouldn't you agree?"

"At this point they have little choice. But it may be a ruse —make us lower our guard while they plan escape, or worse."

"And in what direction would they escape? Back into the Chanyu wasteland or through my army?"

"But surely you will not permit them to proceed beyond the Great Wall?"

For a long, piercing moment, Chen Tang said nothing. He reflected on the disobedient actions of Shang Gao and the loss of hundreds of soldiers. He had not invited the Prince to sit and enjoy tea with him as usual.

"I spoke with my daughter an hour ago," said the general, finally breaking the cold silence. "She tells me that many of the Chanyu dead were killed by the *li-jin*. They had gone to war against our enemies after Xion Wen attacked the Han village. So in a sense the western barbarians have become our allies. Do you remember that we discussed the logic of Master Sun Tzu? I refer to sparing the life of a skillful leader."

"I do," said Shang, attempting to mask his anger. How badly had his actions on the field jeopardized his relations with the general and Li Mae? Until recently he had been a very junior officer, and one of questioned ability.

It would be judicious, he thought, to show a degree of humility. The general was like a spring; the more one pushed against him, the more he resisted, and then a bolt would suddenly fly. He could not allow that to happen.

"The great sage said many things, General, which I shall study more closely."

"A wise consideration. The master taught that one should learn from an ally as well as an enemy. Judging by the way the barbarians fought, there is much to learn. That is all I'll say for now."

"Good evening, my lord," Shang said with brittle deference, and started to back out of the tent.

"Prince," the general's voice called out. "I counsel you not to let motives and desires regarding my daughter influence your military judgment. You must compartmentalize your emotions, lest you jeopardize men's lives."

Shang considered the rebuke, bowed again, and stormed into the night. The insult stung. He believed his actions had been audacious, the sign of a decisive officer. When only the *li-jin* had remained on the field, he'd committed his troops to a frontal assault. Crossbows had brought down a dozen of the barbarians. To Shang's dismay, the fallen men in the front rank had been quickly been replaced by those behind, and the enemy line had held. Still, was his determination any less impetuous than that of the barbarian leader who was now at the mercy of thousands of Han soldiers? The loss of two companies of peasant soldiers was a small price to pay for such a victory.

With the destruction of the Chanyu, nothing should have stood between him and the princess. Had he not participated in her rescue alongside his troops? What right had the *li-jin* officer to interfere with the wishes of a Chinese prince and the son of the Minister of Censorship and Security? He had seen a look of devotion pass between Li Mae and the barbarian. How dare they defy what had been granted him. Bile rose in his throat.

But then he considered the situation. The leader of the *li-jin* was a virtual prisoner and would never again be allowed access to the princess. That thought calmed him. The girl was safe and he had nothing to fear. In time, the general would become amicable again, as was his nature. Putting everything into perspective, he surmised, the Fates were not terribly unkind.

***

"Should we leave you alone?" asked Hera.

"No," said Tacitus ruefully, throwing a twig into the fire. "I brood better with good company."

"Such contemplation is one of your finest attributes," Diomedes said. His eyes took on a mystified and bemused look when Apollodoros and Appian chuckled.

"Son," Hera said reproachfully.

"Mother?"

"It's the Parthian influence," Apollodoros said. "An incurable affliction."

Tacitus shook his head and stared into the flames.

"It's all over," Appian said. "At least the men think so. We're prisoners no matter how it's packaged. The Seres general has showed courtesy—you handed him his daughter —but, like our generals, he takes orders from a senior man."

Tacitus moved a stick across the sand. "A lot of the Chanyu got away. I'm sure I saw Xion Wen ride off with several hundred, and I don't think he'll run too far."

"Do you think he's still a threat?" asked Appian.

"He's been stung, but he's power hungry, and there are many young men in the clans. He can say he fought the Han and lived. He'll brag, raise another force, and bide his time. I know his type. He'll strike when he thinks no one is watching."

"That man, the one the general handed the princess to, who is he?" asked Diomedes.

"A very angry and jealous man," Tacitus replied.

"I'm sure he's Prince Shang Gao," said Hera. "Li Mae was to have married him before she was given to the Chanyu. Now he has her back."

"But you're in the way, at least as far as her affections are concerned," said Apollodoros.

"I don't see how. As you said, we're prisoners. Unless we can get the ear of the emperor, we're of no consequence. This Shang Gao would probably attack us tomorrow if his general would allow it." Again, Tacitus shook his head. "I feel bad for the men. I told them that I would take them home, and now …"

"They're realists, Centurion," said Apian. "An unknown river, a mystical sea, and a voyage back to Rome? I doubt that one in ten ever believed it."

"But they marched!" Tacitus replied vehemently.

"Yes, because of you. They marched because you led them, just as you did over the Torugart Pass," countered the trumpeter.

"And now I've let them down."

"No! We fought like furies against a great army," rounded Appian. "No matter what comes of this, the men will remember what they did for the rest of their lives. All else is fate. The Fates have decided that today we live. And tomorrow, Centurion, we will march again."

Chapter 25

It wasn't what Tacitus had expected. Familiar as he was with the Aurelian Wall surrounding Rome, the earth and mud brick barrier with its incomplete crenellations was disappointing. He had heard of great stone walls manned by thousands of soldiers, and enormous guard towers with pagoda roofs over vaulted tunnels. But as they approached the "Great Wall" he saw that it was a jumble of impediments with gaps in between. Its terminus was here at Jiayuguan. Even the gate was in disrepair.

The cohorts were marched to a section of the wall nearly a mile from the closest village. Scrawled into the bricks were farewell poems and the names of those about to be exiled without hope of return. Tacitus had been told that inside the barrier resided a civilization greater than Rome, but to him it looked the same as the parched land they'd come from. Melancholy descended once again. Having marched proudly amongst the Han soldiers, the legionnaires' future seemed uncertain and their purpose unknown.

Around them toiled several hundred workers, peasants brought in from the hinterland. They gawked at the foreign soldiers camped beside the earthen wall. Overseers shouted when they slowed their work, so their glances were furtive.

***

"I have been ordered back to Chang'an," Chen advised Shang Gao as he finished a letter.

"Am I to accompany you?" asked Shang who waited impatiently.

"No, you shall stay here and supervise the construction of the Wall. I will allow 700 soldiers to remain, and that includes the foreigners. They must not leave the area."

"General, we are few and they are still armed. Wouldn't it be better to disarm the barbarians and put them to work? I'm told they know how to build walls. After all, they're our prisoners and have nothing else to do. And they did kill many of my men."

"They were at war, what did you expect them to do? The *li-jin* are still soldiers; they'll fill a gap in the Wall. I'll ask the Grand Chancellor what he ultimately wants done with them. Who knows, the Son of Heaven might even wish to see these strange people. Do not think of them as expendable."

"Will the princess be returning with you to Chang'an?"

"She is not feeling well and will remain here until I return."

Shang cleared his throat. "My lord, despite my shortcomings I still wish to wed your daughter. As I said before, I will honor you with many sons. I and my esteemed father believe the Fates will bless such a union."

"Let's hope so. I gave my approval to the marriage some time ago. We will conclude the Six Etiquettes as agreed."

"For that I am truly grateful, and in time I hope to regain your confidence. But regarding the *li-jin*, how do I communicate with them? Surely not through the princess."

"There's a foreign woman named Hera who speaks some Mandarin. Use her to translate." Chen added a notation to his letter and then said, "I expect you to observe proper etiquette with my daughter and avoid unnecessary contact until the wedding." He put down his writing brushes. "I also received news that my wife is on her way—apparently she didn't know I was being called back. She'll be here in two days. Be sure that she is shown every courtesy."

Shang bowed. "Regarding the barbarians, may I use force if they show defiance?"

"I doubt that force will be necessary. Treat them fairly. They may be needed if there is war, and we want their loyalty."

"Simply feeding them should ensure that," said the prince sourly. "The Chanyu have been decisively beaten. I see no military usefulness for them."

Chen regarded the prince. "A good commander must expect the unexpected."

Shang bowed again, this time more deeply. "In your absence, I will do my duty."

"I expect nothing less. I'll ask the Grand Chancellor for more workers. This Wall must be finished."

***

Li Mae had been escorted by Han soldiers to a house prepared for her parents. Now it was night and she waited. Hera wouldn't have a hard time finding her. Though constructed of mud brick and stone, their house was the finest in the village, with blue tiles and stone dragons brought by wagon from Chang'an.

Finally Hera appeared. "The centurion will be at the workers' huts beside the old gate," she said without preamble.

"Tell him that I'll be there two hours before sunrise."

"You know how dangerous that is. If the prince sees you or your father learns of it ..."

"They won't. My father has left for the capital."

"And the prince?"

"I've heard nothing about him since we came here. Considering my involvement with the centurion and the Chanyu, maybe he doesn't want me anymore."

"Believe me, he wants you. What you are doing is very exciting and romantic, but it will put the centurion in grave danger."

Li Mae shook her head. "No one will be awake at that hour, and nothing is going to happen anyway. I just want to see him. It may be the last time."

***

The towering silhouette emerged from the shadows, a sickle-shaped moon revealing its form. At first Tacitus could not identify it, but then a horse's snort broke the quietude of the night. There was a burst of rapid, angry Mandarin, and then he heard Hera.

"He asks if you are inspecting the earthworks at this hour or if ... if you—" A loud slap interrupted her shaky voice.

"If you have you an assignation, that will result in your death," she said, completing the translation.

Tacitus could see them now. Prince Shang Gao, riding a great, snorting charger, held the Greek woman tightly and jerked her hard. A dozen Han soldiers rode behind them, moonlight glinting off their pikes. The prince walked his horse closer to Tacitus and spoke in just above a whisper.

"He says you are to go back. The princess belongs to him. On pain of death you must never speak to her again," said Hera.

Tacitus backed away. Like a scolded child, he felt hatred mixed with helplessness and revulsion, something he had not experienced since his father's scorn at Carrhae. There was nothing he could say. He listened to the horse's iron shoes as the prince rode into the shadows. Shang Gao gave a shout, and the animal broke into a gallop. That was followed by a cry and the sound of a body hitting the ground.

Tacitus rushed forward and found Hera crumpled in the dirt. She moaned as he lifted her.

"He knew. He caught me while—"

Tacitus hushed her and led her back along the Wall. "It's my fault," he said, supporting her when she stumbled. "It was a foolish thing and I should never have agreed to it. I put you and the princess in danger."

"That man hates you, but he also fears you, Centurion. You must be careful; he really wants you dead."

"Where is the princess now?" Tacitus asked.

In the moonlight he could see the Greek woman hesitate.

"She was at the house with her mother when I last saw her, but now I don't know."

"I have to find her."

"No. She will go back if you are not at the meeting place. Only at her house will she be safe. But do not go there. Shang Gao has many men waiting, and they are to kill you if you come anywhere near her. There's nothing you can do."

***

He should have been here by now, Li Mae thought. There had been no sound, no movement for an hour. Silent shadows moved about her, and, though she'd been listening intently, the sudden footsteps took her by surprise. She burst out of her hiding place and blurted, "Tacitus, Tacitus!"

Prince Shang Gao grabbed her.

"No, it's not your barbarian, my lady. It's the man you will marry. The *li-jin* is stinking drunk and will never see you again."

He gave an order and a wagon was brought up. Li Mae was shoved inside. The driver flicked a whip and the mud Wall faded into darkness.

***

Tacitus's mouth tasted of ash. He had been caught, chastised, and he had no one to blame but himself. Appian sat beside him in the Roman encampment.

"What if you, a mere centurion, challenged a jealous tribune for the attention of a highborn Roman lady? How far do you think you would get? Even if he allowed you to live, you would spend the rest of your enlistment on the banks of the Rhine."

He was right, of course. Having lost sight of the true objective, the one his father had entrusted to him, he had fallen for a woman claimed by another. Upon reflection, he realized that he knew nothing of her land or customs. In the cave that night they'd talked about how different their worlds were. How could their lives possibly entwine?

He had been living a fantasy, dreaming the impossible. Worse, by opposing the prince, he had jeopardized the lives of his men and put in doubt any chance of journeying to Rome. Who might he now appeal to, and who could influence the emperor on their behalf? His legionnaires had said nothing, but their countenance spoke volumes. They were virtual prisoners with a leader whose abilities they could no longer trust.

The men congregated in small groups and Tacitus had heard their words of despair.

"I have betrayed them all," he admitted. "And it will not happen again."

But Tacitus had been seared by fire deep inside, and flames, even when doused, tend to smolder.

***

Hera came to Tacitus when he was alone. "She is watched all the time, but I know that I can meet with her," she said. "I can at least convey a message."

"The only message is that it's over. I must attend to the men, not a girl I can't have," said Tacitus.

"The princess told me that her father will return very soon."

Tacitus brightened somewhat. "That's good. He might know how long we'll be kept here and if the emperor will allow us to continue."

"I've made friends with some village women. Their husbands are officials and officers. They may have heard something, too."

"You and Li Mae must take no more chances. My men and I are soldiers and will live or die based on our own follies. I don't want to involve any one else. "

Hera took a few paces and turned. "She loves you. You do know that, don't you?"

***

"He says that they're stationed in the wrong place," Hera translated to Shang.

Tacitus regarded the prince, who sat imperiously on his charger. He wouldn't be cowed by the previous week's calamity. "We're too far from the worst gap in the Wall. That's where the Chanyu will come when they attack again."

"The Chanyu?" Shang said with a smirk. "Tell this barbarian that I defeated the Chanyu, and he's been put here because I don't want him anywhere else. In addition, he is not at liberty to speak to me. He will do exactly what I require or face punishment."

"Fine," Tacitus replied, ignoring the censure, "Hera, tell the young fool I'll watch him bury dozens of his men. We'll see if that pleases General Chen Tang."

Upon hearing the translation, Shang tightened the horse's reins; his hand grasped the hilt of his sword. Tacitus clutched a drawn gladius. He could plunge his weapon into the prince's horse and slit the man's throat before he'd even drawn his sword. But the consequences for his men would be disastrous. Instead he merely pointed the tip at Shang's eyes.

The prince's grip tightened. Tacitus stared at him in silence. The urge to kill, to hear Shang scream before all went black, was nearly uncontrollable. But the moment passed. Shang removed his hand from the sword hilt and pointed toward the Wall, where Tacitus was ordered to stay. Tacitus, gladius in hand, glared at the prince until he backed his mount and rode toward the village.

***

Li Mae lay in her bed and stared at the ceiling. There were knots and furrows in the wood and she traced them with her eyes. One timber had many vertical marks and it reminded her of the crest on Tacitus's helmet. A great weariness came over her and she closed her eyes. She wondered what he might be feeling knowing that he would never see her again. Certainly Hera must have told him about the upcoming wedding and that she would return to Chang'an with Shang Gao. Was he in despair or, realizing the absurdity of their courtship, did he consign her to a fond but distant memory?

She had not seen nor heard from him since that terrible night. Even Hera, who was allowed to visit her village, conveyed no message. Surely, thought the princess, the fates could not be so duplicitous as to have bonded them together only to tear them apart. It was beyond her understanding and she tried to put it out of her mind. A tear ran down her cheek. She wiped it away, but the memories remained.

Her wedding would take place in three weeks. Under the circumstances, she supposed, she ought to be happy. She would be home soon, and Shang Gao couldn't be worse than Xion Wen.

She heard a knock downstairs, then Shang's voice. She was fairly certain that nobody had invited him. Li Mae rolled onto her side and wondered if his presence was a violation of prenuptial courtesy.

She heard footsteps coming from the room where they entertained guests. Her mother would be offering tea. There was conversation, but Li Mae couldn't make out what they were saying until she heard the word "indisposed." She'd told her mother that she had a head cold and didn't want to be disturbed. Hopefully Shang wouldn't press the issue.

"I don't know *who* gave it to her."

That was her mother again, speaking just a little too loudly for polite conversation. Li Mae got out of bed, crept across the room, and put her ear to the door.

"Are you saying that she did not tell you or would not tell you?" said Shang suspiciously.

"On that I'll make no judgment. I presume she met many people beyond the Wall of Exiles while she was gone. Perhaps she made friends with somebody." Lady Tang said, with a tinge of annoyance.

"Maybe the leader of the foreign barbarians at the wall?" Shang said.

"I don't know."

Li Mae heard heavy footfalls on the steps and jumped back just before Shang burst into her room and slammed the door hard against the wall.

"You have no right to be up here," said Li Mae.

Shang grabbed her arm with one hand and held up Tacitus's little glass vial with the other. "He gave this to you?"

"It's not what you think. I was so depressed, and—"

"And he gave you a nice little present. Exactly what did you give him?" said Shang, his face flushed.

"Mittens. I made him *mittens*." Li Mae wrenched her arm away.

Jia Zhou appeared at the door, out of breath. "My daughter is right," she hissed. "You shouldn't be here."

Shang turned around to face her. "A girl promised to me accepts gifts from a barbarian devil? Is this what I'm to expect from your daughter?"

"You have violated the sanctity of this house and the Six Etiquettes," said Jia Zhou. "I will tell my husband about this. You must leave this instant!"

Ignoring her threat, Shang held the little vial in a clenched fist and glared at Li Mae. Never had she seen him so enraged or so terrifying. A tremor went through her as she feared what terrors her marriage might hold.

"The centurion saved my life," Li Mae said. "The glass was just a sign of ... affection."

"Affection?" Shang spat and hurled the vial against the wall. "I expect an obedient and loyal wife," he said, pointing a finger at her. "And I will have one!"

He turned and marched down the stairs. Li Mae's mother followed him. The prince suddenly spun about and said, "Please tell the general that despite the poor judgment of my beloved, the auspicious day has been set. My parents have received the expected dowry. My father writes that he appreciates the gifts, and they are preparing for the wedding."

Jia Zhou nodded mutely. "All will be done to your father's satisfaction."

After Shang had slammed the door behind him, Li Mae descended the stairs and looked at her mother.

"Did he really say 'beloved'?"

"Yes, that's what he said," answered Jia Zhou.

"I hate him!" wailed Li Mae. "The *li-jin* rescued me in the desert and carried Ming Zhaojun's body to a safe place. I adored the centurion, having no idea that I would be rescued from the Chanyu. I believed that I would perish there." She clenched her fists. "Shang Gao is a tyrant. You can see that."

"But you will marry him, and you will honor him," said Jia Zhou. "You have no more choice than I did. We women do as we are told. That is our fate. Love is not a requirement for happiness. Your joy will be in your husband's accomplishments and the son you present to him. Sometimes people can change. Perhaps the prince will mellow with age."

Li Mae slumped to her knees and gazed up at her mother. "I'm scared. I'm so scared."

"I was frightened, too, before I was married. I knew nothing about men and what they want from women." Jia Zhou stroked Li Mae's cheek. "But we learn and adapt. Things will become … acceptable."

Li Mae shook her head and put her hands over her face. "No, no, it won't be acceptable. It never will."

Jia Zhou dried the tears that welled up in Li Mae's eyes and gave a reassuring smile. "The banquet will take place here. Hundreds of guests will come from Chang'an. There will be old friends and high officers of the court and perhaps even a representative of the Son of Heaven. They'll all have wonderful gifts. Surely it will be the most memorable time of your life, and it will be so much better than your marriage to the Chanyu barbarian."

Li Mae sighed. "Yes, I'm sure it will be a fine banquet."

But the most memorable time of her life? That had already occurred, and it would remain a secret for the brief time she had to live.

***

Hera watched the wedding procession from a discreet distance. The revelers were accompanied by a dancing paper lion and a Chinese unicorn. Princess Li Mae Tang was adorned in red silk and her hair was illuminated by a glistening tiara. She was borne aloft in a sumptuous sedan chair, from which hung a bronze mirror to protect her from evil spirits. Next to it was a pair of shoes which, combined with the mirror, were a symbol of luck.

Beside her, Prince Shang Gao rode his charger and wore a cap decorated with cypress leaves. The couple was trailed by General Chen Tang and his wife, Shang Gao's parents, and dozens of friends, relatives, and dignitaries. A squadron of cavalry rode escort, followed by musicians and clowns.

The guests arrived at the general's home, with its newly planted gardens, and awaited the festivities. Carrying a tray of sweets, with a hat covering her face, Hera slipped into the garden to witness the marriage ceremony, already in progress. The prince, his face triumphant, accepted a pair of chopsticks, signifying the early arrival of children, and received the congratulations of palace luminaries.

Both Li Mae and the prince were assured by the priests that Old Man of the Moon's invisible thread would happily bind them in matrimony for life.

Additional tables were placed outside the walls of the villa to accommodate the overflow crowd. A pike platoon of guards stood at attention but took no notice of Hera when she left the nuptials and made her way back to the Roman encampment.

"So it's concluded," Tacitus said when he got Hera's report. His expression was stoic. They might have been discussing the weather.

"Yes, it has been done. I have never seen such extravagance."

"And Li Mae?"

"Beautiful, but she seemed in a trance. The girl never smiled once. She only nodded to well-wishers and said not a word to her groom."

Chapter 26

It was nearly dark when Ibericus and Appian's reconnaissance patrol slipped through the gaps in the Wall and met Tacitus and Diomedes.

"We found their tracks," said Ibericus.

"How many?" Tacitus asked.

"Only a few, probably scouts, but they're all out there. We saw a lot of dust in the air and there was no wind today."

"So a few hundred," Tacitus said.

"At least that," said Appian. "I'd bet a triumph through the streets of Rome that they've had spies in the Han village. Xion Wen knows more about tonight's banquet than we do."

"What did Hera say about the Han guard?" Ibericus asked Tacitus.

"That they're honorary, not battle ready. And there wouldn't be enough of them even if they could fight."

"Because Shang Gao is over confident. He convinced General Tang that the Chanyu are no longer a threat." ventured Appian. The trumpeter ran a hand through his thinning hair. "Tacitus, the prince ordered us to stay here. He's already married the general's daughter. Whatever happens tonight falls on his head; it's no longer our fight. So why have you formed up the cohorts?"

"It's the princess, isn't it?" Diomedes said quietly.

"No." Tacitus watched the men put on their armor. "It's about our honor as soldiers. It's about our freedom. Engaging the Chanyu is the only way we can leave."

"Honor and glory doesn't mean much out here," said Appian. "So we fight, but what if this Shang Gao and his father ignore our efforts? What then?"

"I'm not sure. But I'm at war with the Chanyu and I've wanted to deal with Xion Wen since the day I met him. There won't be another chance. You can stay here or fight. It's up to you," said Tacitus.

***

The village was only a mile away, but the surrounding hills were like an amphitheater, making the horns, drums, and cymbals signaling the festivities clearly audible. Tacitus and the others could hear the laughter of assembled guests. As the hour grew late their voices became more strident and inebriated.

"Keep the fires going," Tacitus said to Appian. "I want the Chanyu to think we're in the encampment."

Unlike other nights, there was no grumbling about poor food or boredom. To the legionnaires, the fate that had befallen them had less to do with the Seres people than the Chanyu.

The night turned cold. While they waited for the command, the troops pulled their cloaks around them and stared at a shower of meteorites that streaked overhead.

"Omens," whispered the legionnaires.

The merriment in the village became louder. Tacitus walked amongst the legionnaires offering encouraging words, a ribald remark, or a cautionary note. Soon the cohorts assumed marching order.

"No noise, no talking on the approach. We take no prisoners, none whatsoever. Kill them all," said Tacitus.

The moon hung like a Chinese lantern, and a scattering of clouds scudded beneath its frigid light. It was the only illumination they had. Tacitus motioned his cohorts forward. Shields held before them, they hurried along the Wall until they came to the main breach. The town was closer and so was the cacophony of voices.

A legionary picket peered down from an abandoned guard tower. "Horses!"

"What direction?" asked Tacitus.

"Straight at us."

"I want archers here, and bring the ropes," Tacitus commanded.

"I know what to do," said Appian. "I'll stay and follow when it's done."

Tacitus placed a hand on his *optio*'s shoulder. "This is where they'll come through. Stay in the shadows and keep safe, old man."

The road from the Wall led directly to the village, and Tacitus had no desire to be discovered by Prince Shang or any patrol. The wedding celebration was raucous. Torches illuminated faces as well-wishers passed in and out of the light.

Somewhere in that revelry was Princess Li Mae Tang. Tacitus wondered what she was thinking on this, her wedding night. Shang Gao would be taking her to his bed. He tried to banish the thought from his mind. Yes, he realized, this was really about her. How damned would he be if his men died this night for a woman that he would never see again?

He looked for the Han guard. They were no longer at their posts. Most were drunk and mingling with the guests.

Down, Tacitus signaled, and 280 men lay prone. He could hear hoofbeats. No one in the village seemed to notice.

The ropes lay upon the ground in the gap of the unfinished Wall. One end was tied to a sturdy post; the other was ready to be secured around a rock piling. There was a sudden shout, and nearly 400 Chanyu horsemen tore through the opening.

Appian ordered the ropes pulled tight. A foot above the ground, the legs of the lead mounts snagged the lines and panicked horses toppled onto the road. Riders who survived the fall were struck by arrows, but the momentum of the charge caused horses to leap past the fallen, and the attack sallied on.

Xion Wen escaped the entanglement and led the charge into a now terrified assembly. His mounted archers brought down the few Han guards who tried to block their way. Horses tore headlong into the throng as screams and shouts rent the night air. Tables laden with food and drink were hurled skyward. Horrified revelers ran in all directions.

As the onslaught continued, a few dozen men, led by General Chen Tang and Prince Shang Gao began to rally. They struggled to surround the women and hacked at riders and horses in an attempt to halt the surge.

"Where are your reserves?" the general shouted to the prince.

"Rise, launch pila!" Tacitus ordered. Legionnaires aimed at the horsemen whose advance had been stymied by the struggling mass of wedding guests. Startled by flung javelins, dozens of Chanyu toppled from their mounts. In the sallow light of lanterns and torches, horses threw riders and the attack disintegrated into chaos. Many Chanyu turned, in a desperate attempt to flee.

A moment later a wall of shields slammed into them and those on foot were quickly cut down. Tacitus reached out and tore a rider from his saddle. Coming from the gap in the Wall, Appian and his men joined him.

"Tacitus!" Ibericus called.

Tacitus turned and saw Xion Wen leading a dozen of his men toward Li Mae, her father, and the groom. He raced toward the assault with Ibericus, Appian, and 20 other legionnaires. Cutting through the unarmed crowd, the warlord was making his way toward Li Mae and the prince. Tacitus's men joined the melee, thrusting their gladii into the nearest of the Chanyu. In the tumult, Tacitus found himself beside the embattled prince.

Xion Wen pushed to the fore and sliced at Shang Gao's head. He parried, but not before the warlord's blade had sliced off his wrist. He screamed and a there was a sudden gush of blood. Li Mae, a look of horror on her face, stumbled back as the groom toppled over her.

Seconds later General Chen Tang, his wife, and Shang Gao were pinned against the outer wall of the house, having been impaled by Chanyu arrows. Li Mae rose to her feet and tried to reach her father, only to be thrust away by the wailing crowd. Tacitus clambered over bodies to reach Xion Wen. Slipping in blood that spewed from Shang Gao's wound, the nomad struggled to his feet. He slashed wildly at Tacitus but his sword struck the centurion's shield.

The warlord screamed in fury and raised his weapon once again. A barred throat, a sword lifted too high—it was an invitation. Tacitus thrust his gladius into the man's chest, then sliced through his neck. Xion Wen's head pitched to the ground. Other Chanyu, seeing the bloody corpse, began to back away.

Prince Shang Gao slumped against Tacitus, blood spewing from his amputated wrist. Tacitus, surrounded by bodies, laid the dying man beside the general. He had lost too much blood; it would be impossible to staunch the flow. Tacitus glanced at the blanched face of Shang Gao, who that afternoon had been at the pinnacle of his success.

There was no time to gloat over his enemy's defeat. The remaining Chanyu were trying to cut their way out of the encircling legionnaires.

"No prisoners! None escape!" Tacitus shouted. The legionnaires echoed his cries as they pushed the horsemen into an ever tightening circle. Several Chanyu attempted to jump their mounts over the wounded, but the horses shied, fearful of the writhing bodies beneath their hoofs. One by one the Chanyu fell until the last crumpled atop a lifeless comrade.

A few remaining lanterns swung in the evening breeze, throwing a muted glow on the entangled bodies. Moaning and bleeding, survivors pulled themselves from beneath corpses. The quiet was broken by the sound of hoofbeats. Han reinforcements came at the run, their horns blaring over the screams of the wounded.

A Chinese officer halted and peered at the carnage. With an astonished look on his face, he gave an order. His battalion sheathed their weapons and began assisting Tacitus's men with the wounded.

Tacitus searched the crowd, his bloody sword at his side. Li Mae knelt beside the body of her mother and her mortally wounded father. Her disheveled hair was streaked with blood and her wedding robes were torn. With anguish and a hand to her mouth, she stared at Tacitus and bowed her head. The representative of the Son of Heaven hovered beside Chen Tang as a labored sound came from the general. He crooked his finger at his daughter and she put an ear to his lips. Then she looked up at Tacitus. "My father says that you're free. All your men are free."

"Tell him that I, we …"

She turned back to the general, and he touched her face. His hand dropped, and he said nothing more. Tacitus watched in silence as she prayed over his body.

Finally Li Mae stood and approached Tacitus. "The prince, my husband," she said. "Is he alive?"

"I'm not sure. He's over there with my men."

Wending his way through the dazed crowd, Tacitus followed Li Mae to a wagon where the legionnaires had placed the prince. Silently they made a path for her when she approached. Tacitus stood back, unsure of what to say.

He had loathed Shang Gao. Now he felt nothing. The body of the prince was simply one of many whose world had come to a desperate end.

A legionnaire stepped beside Li Mae and tendered the pike her husband had carried. She accepted it and placed it in Shang's one remaining hand. Then she stepped back, bowed three times, turned, and walked away.

Tacitus tried to say words of condolence, but she simply shook her head. "Later, we'll talk later," she replied. She didn't protest when he put his arms about her. No one saw him do it; no one cared. Then, alone, she walked through the courtyard and into her parents' house.

***

"How long will you mourn?" Tacitus asked two days after the funerals.

"Three years, perhaps even longer, considering that both my parents perished. We Han show respect for the recent dead as well as our ancestors."

"May I be with you? I also mourn the death of your parents."

"Your sentiments are very kind, but I cannot be seen with any man. It would not be proper."

"Then there is nothing I can do?"

She looked up at him and shook her head. "You have done all you can. You saved my life for a second time, and my appreciation is beyond words. But for us there's nothing more. At least not for a very long time."

"And when those years are past, Princess? Will the Son of Heaven still determine the course of your life, our lives?"

"Fate determines everything, even for the Son of Heaven. What mortal answer can I possibly give you?"

No sounds came from the village for the next three nights. The legionnaires' joy quickly changed to despair when a representative of the Emperor made it clear that, despite what General Tang might have said, the cohorts would not march through the Middle Kingdom.

Tacitus sat at a fire with Apollodoros and Appian, looking at the Wall a few feet away and thinking of home.

"What will you do?" Apollodoros asked.

"What should I do?" he asked his old mentor.

"Wait, however long the mourning takes. Stay here with the men; they have nowhere else to go. Personally, I never want to cross a mountain or see a desert again, and neither do any others."

"But surely some will want to go back."

"Back?" Apollodoros shook his head. "The way we came? Oh, no. There are women in the village who will marry the men, peasant women who have lost their husbands. Many have been admiring the legionnaires, their bravery and resolve, you know."

"Even though we're 'barbarians'?"

"They need men to care for them, and the Seres men won't marry widows. What choice do they have? Maybe the women think barbarians can be civilized. We Greeks thought the same about Rome, and in a few rare cases it worked," he said with a wry smile.

"For us it's the end of the great Silk Road," said Appian. "Our venture is over. You're going to have to accept that, Tacitus. Besides, I think in your heart you want to be with the princess, and in time she may want to be with you."

"She gave me very little hope beyond telling me that everything is up to the Fates. She's a vassal of the Emperor; for all I know, she'll return to Chang'an. With her parents gone, what's here for her? Three years from now she will have forgotten me and will be married off to some other prince. There is nothing I can do, no one to appeal to. What Han general will listen to me? I won't remain here to sulk and pine away like a self-pitying adolescent."

"So what are you going to do?" asked Apollodoros.

"I'm going back."

"You're not seriously thinking of walking back to Rome and leaving the cohorts?" said Appian.

"Why not? The men don't need me anymore, and you're the obvious leader. And who knows, some idiot might come with me."

"I'll go, at least as far as Parthia," Diomedes said, coming into the firelight.

"You'll leave me and your mother?" asked the *medicus*.

"I cherish both of you, but I have a wife and child in Ctesiphon and I haven't seen them in many years. I just want to hold them again," he said wistfully. "And then I'll return to you. I'll bring them all."

Apollodoros shook his head and turned to Tacitus. "So what's really waiting for you in Rome?"

"A woman I almost died for. If the princess won't have me, perhaps Tullia will. I've been thinking about her since the battle. I loved her very much, you know."

"A woman who may be dead by now," the Greek countered. "It's been 17 years since you left. If she's alive, she's probably married and has children. Even if you get there, you'll be nothing but a problem for her. What will you say to her husband? 'Hello, I've come back for your wife. I just had to take a little walk to the Great Wall of the Seres people'?"

"To set out on that road is madness, and you know that!" Appian said vehemently.

Tacitus shrugged. "I have no intention of marrying one of those peasant women, and I refuse to just sit here. I'll miss all of you, but tomorrow I shall say my goodbyes."

***

Six weeks after the battle, Li Mae came to the legionnaire's village. In appreciation of their valor, the cohorts had been allowed to settle just inside the Great Wall. They were given a few li in a small valley beside a meandering stream. There they could grow crops and tend animals on the condition that they would defend the Wall. Working under Appian's guidance, they built mud-brick dwellings and, with their women, settled into village life.

Li Mae found Hera and Apollodoros seeding in their garden, and she walked slowly up the small rise to greet them. Hera put her arms around her.

"I missed seeing you. I was afraid that you had gone back to Chang'an."

"No, many things have changed for me." Li Mae let go of Hera and pulled on the folds of her white mourning robe; its fabric glinted in the sun. "I'm sorry for not coming earlier. Socializing, even with old friends, is discouraged."

"Mourning is a lonely thing, no matter where you are," said Hera.

Li Mae looked down the street and said, "The houses look quite different from ours."

"Yes, I imagine they're like houses in Rome, but here they're mud brick. And now many of the men have women folk—widows, survivors of the battle."

"That's good," said Li Mae. There was a silence and then she said, "I want to thank the centurion once more for what he did—how he saved me and tried to defend my parents. Where is he, Hera?"

The Greek woman took a deep breath and looked at Apollodoros.

"I'm afraid he's gone," said the *medicus*. "The centurion left with our son almost a month ago. We don't expect him to return, Princess."

"Gone? Where did he go?"

"He's on his way to Rome. He's going home," Hera replied softly.

Li Mae stared at her with disbelief. She looked past the Great Wall where workers were filling in the gaps.

"But I have something to tell him," she said numbly. "Something he'd want to know."

Hera shook her head and hugged the girl once more. Li Mae returned the embrace and attempted a smile. "It was good to see you again. I shouldn't stay ..."

"May I visit? Is it permitted?" Hera asked.

"I don't think anybody will really mind. I certainly don't," Li Mae said. "I don't live in my father's house any longer. The villagers will show you where I am now."

"Then we shall visit, Princess," said Apollodoros.

"I think I once mentioned that nothing remains the same in Chang'an. Much is up to the Grand Chancellor, the Emperor, and the fates. Many people died the night of my wedding, and some blamed my father as well as Prince Shang Gao. So in retribution, I guess ..." Li Mae brushed a stray hair off of her robe. "I'm no longer a princess. I'm now a commoner, a peasant, like all the other Han who live here. I will never go to Chang'an again."

Chapter 27

The camels of the great caravan trod past the Taklamakan desert with its ceaseless wind, sweltering days, and freezing nights. Tacitus's mind drifted as the beasts ascended the Torugart Pass. Nearly a year had passed since he and Diomedes had joined the procession, signing on as guards and scouts. Hundreds of men who accompanied the caravan discouraged marauders and, except for accidents, the traders progressed without incident.

Tacitus had vowed not to dwell on what he had left behind. He had led more than 300 legionnaires to a dilapidated mud wall that they could not pass and a future they could not escape. And he had left them there. The men had not questioned his decision; there were no derisive comments when he abandoned them, though he suspected that more than one thought him delusional.

On most nights he and Diomedes sat beside a fire apart from the other travelers. Neither had any wish to form friendships that would dissolve when they reached one town or another. It was on those nights when Tacitus felt guilt creep in as well as the loss of the comradeship he had known for all his adult life. He wasn't surprised that none of the legionnaires had wished to return with him. The youngest was thirty-five, and a 6,000-mile journey to Rome through hostile lands would be daunting. Even Tacitus anticipated a weary trek, especially if he had no one to return to.

No, he couldn't criticize their decision to remain at the Wall. Most by now would have women—young, compliant wives who revered them. The legionnaires were still considered "barbarians" like anybody else born outside the Middle Kingdom, but they had been honored by the Grand Chancellor, and that afforded a certain status. The women, especially those from poor families conscripted to toil on the Wall, considered the valiant foreigners a good catch.

Though he did his best not to think about it, a gnawing worry assailed Tacitus. What if the gods played their tricks and he never reached Rome? How would Tullia ever know that he wanted to see her again? Just yesterday there had been a slide, and three camels and their riders had been swept into a chasm. Instant death on the Silk Road could happen any time. So on the day after the accident, he purchased Chinese paper and began to write.

"If anything happens to me, see that this reaches Tullia," he said to Diomedes.

"I will do my best, Centurion, but I can't promise that I'll ever get there. At any rate, I have no doubt that you will see the lady again, if she is still alive."

Tacitus had asked Diomedes to not call him "Centurion." Diomedes ignored the request. He hadn't felt like a centurion, much less a soldier, since he'd left his men. Now the title seemed absurd, if not distasteful. Surely the legionnaires at the Wall would not consider him a centurion now.

"What will you do if your wife has remarried?" Tacitus asked as he and Diomedes watched clouds darken an afternoon sky.

"I'm not going to dwell on it," said Diomedes. "What is, is, and worrying won't change anything. I may remain there if the king is amenable to that. I have traveled to the Great Wall—that may gain me fame. And after all, I was a captain of Parthian horse. I might be so again."

"Even after you said that you were no longer a Parthian?" Tacitus chided him.

"If I live in Parthia, Centurion, I am a Parthian, am I not? But if there's nothing left for me in Ctesiphon, I will go further."

"Where?"

"Greece, where my parents came from. I'd like to see Mount Olympus, and I might even go to Rome, or back to the Wall." He paused, looked at the sky again, and pointed toward the oncoming storm. "If we survive that."

The gale came on more quickly than anybody had thought it would. A freezing rain drenched the caravan, thunder rolled across the sky, and lightning shredded trees. The usually imperturbable camels snorted in terror and mindlessly charged down the trail in a stampeding mass. More than 20 of the shaggy beasts plummeted off ledges, their riders taken with them. The snow that had been threatening all day suddenly fell in a heavy blanket, making visibility nearly impossible.

Tacitus's camel, caught in the rush, tumbled over a fallen mount. He heard Diomedes shout in horror. Tacitus held tight to the Bactrian as it skidded over a ledge and tumbled toward the bottom of the ravine. Thrown from the beast, Tacitus pitched heavily onto an outcrop and grabbed at branches as he spiraled downward. After what seemed an eternity, he came to rest a hundred feet below.

Tacitus attempted to stand, but his legs wouldn't hold him. The camel, laden with equipment, continued its descent while baggage ripped away and spewed into the chasm. He watched the beast fall, then slowly lay on his back. It hurt to breathe.

After a few minutes, Tacitus heard something above him. Diomedes was tying rope to a boulder. He motioned for Diomedes to go back, wincing in pain at the effort, as his friend inched his way down the slope.

"Go," Tacitus implored. "There's nothing you can do for me. My legs are broken."

Diomedes gave no sign of hearing him. When he got to the bottom, he ran to the spot where Tacitus lay, then tied the rope under his arms and climbed back up to the road. He then secured the rope to the saddle of his camel. Tacitus winced with the pain as Diomedes slowly inched him up and over the precipice's edge. Snow lay thick on the road. The corpses of two boys and their camels were half buried in the accumulating drifts. There was no one else to be seen. Diomedes lay Tacitus in a snowbank and wrapped him in a saddle blanket.

"Ribs," Tacitus said. Speaking was almost as painful as breathing. "I broke at least one, maybe two. And my legs."

"I'll build a sled and pull you to Kashgar as soon as the storm peters out," Diomedes said.

"It would be useless and a waste of time; I'm going to die here. Now go, you've been a good friend and you've done all you can."

"Leaving you to die is not the sign of a good friend, Centurion."

Tacitus felt himself losing the ability to focus on anything. The intense pain should have kept him awake, but his mind was clouded and heavy. He wanted to convince Diomedes to save himself. Then there was blackness and the world slipped away.

Tacitus imagined he had woken many times but everything was a fog. Fleeting images emerged and faded. Faces, impossible events, people in places they shouldn't have been, appeared like actors flitting about a stage. Sometimes the scenes were sharp and materialized right before his face. He tensed and cried out, reaching for a nonexistent gladius or calling to Appian Dio to fill in the line.

He often saw his father's face, devoid of decades of bitterness. Tears came as he witnessed the ghostly image of Tullia before him. Her face morphed into that of an old woman in a dark forest, the same where they'd had their tryst so many years before, and he moaned and writhed in agony. The horrible image faded, replaced by a much younger woman who beckoned. She spoke in an indecipherable language but one that, strangely, he understood.

His mind, churning with feverish delirium, sped on, night after night. He envisioned horses and chariots; he was racing for the "Green" team in the coliseum. Once again he was a wild youth of sixteen shouting, "Faster! Faster! Now take the turn!"

Then the congestion in his lungs built and he lay comatose, his breathing hardly discernable. He whispered the word "Princess" over and over.

***

"Grandma," said the four-year-old boy, "There's a visitor at the door. He asked for you and he speaks real strange."

"Did he say who he is?"

"I think he's a traveler. He said something about being the son of a man you once knew."

"Once knew?" the woman said. "Show him into the atrium and have the new slave bring him some wine. Tell him I'll be along."

She shuffled in a few minutes later. The guest, a tall man in a Greek-style toga, sat on a stone bench and sipped the wine, smiling at the inquisitive boy who stared at him. Sunlight streamed down from the roof into the impluvium and illuminated a pool of lily pads. The man stood, adjusted his garment, and bowed when he saw her.

"Thank you for the refreshment, lady. Might your name be Tullia?"

She nodded.

"I am Diomedes, son of Apollodoros, a former slave of Livia and Toronius. Livia's sister, Junia, once befriended you. Do you remember her?"

"Of course. I was very fond of her, but she died many years ago."

"I have been instructed to deliver a letter to you from a friend of mine. You meant a great deal to him when you were both quite young."

"A letter?" she said, looking closely at the stranger. The woman, slightly stooped, appeared much older than her thirty-seven years.

"It has come a very long way. The one who wrote it gave it to me two years ago, the last time I saw him. But he would be pleased to know that you are here to read it."

Tullia opened the wax-sealed envelope. Diomedes smiled and said, "I will leave it with you and you may read it at your leisure."

"No, wait. My eyesight is too poor to read any longer. Can you?"

"Yes. If it pleases you."

Tullia nodded vigorously. "I haven't received a letter in years, not since my husband died. Who is it from?"

Diomedes took the envelope and extracted several sheets of paper. Tullia looked at them with curiosity. They were unlike the papyrus or vellum common in Rome.

"Paper, it's called paper. It's made by the Seres people in a place they call the Middle Kingdom," Diomedes said.

"Dearest Tullia, I, Tacitus bring you greetings."

Tullia's eyes widened and she sucked in her breath. "Tacitus, is it really from Tacitus? Where is he?"

"My dear lady, I will answer all your questions, but allow me to finish reading the letter." He peered at the shaky scribble and continued. "I fervently hope that you are well. I survived the horrible battle of Carrhae and have wanted to return to Rome for all these years, but I fear that I will never get there. Truly, I hoped to see you again and tell you all that has happened since I last saw you. You should know that I have seen your beautiful face in my dreams and only wish that we could have been together. Regretfully, the gods have decided otherwise. But you have always been in my heart and always will."

Diomedes read on for several more minutes, then handed Tullia the pages.

"But I must ask again, where is he now?" she said, her anxious voice trembling.

"My lady, he wrote that letter just before an accident that left him near death. We were together on the Silk Road, a place even beyond the empire of Parthia where I once lived. He was badly injured from a fall and I fear he might not have survived. I am terribly sorry; he was a good friend and a good man. I will leave you to your memories now if it pleases you."

"No, stay, please stay. I pray that you tell me everything. Do so for an old lady who once loved him dearly." Then, not wishing to be impolite she said, "You wear a Greek toga but say you lived in Parthia. Do you have family there?"

"My parents were both Greek, but through circumstances not of our making, my mother and I were transported and enslaved in Parthia. I was taken from my mother and raised by royalty. I had a wife and child, but they died in a plague. With nothing left for me there, I came to Rome to deliver the letter."

"I am sad for your loss, but I'm pleased that you have come here. I have wondered about Tacitus for years."

Tullia's slave appeared at the door. Tullia asked her to bring more wine for her guest, and some fruit and cheese.

"I prayed for him and of course hoped that somehow things could be different," Tullia said. "I, we, were very young when his father forced him into the army, and we knew little of the world. I wrote letters but never received a reply. Then we heard of what happened across the Euphrates, a terrible battle, and I assumed he had died. I mourned his loss for a very long time. I would have liked to see him again. I loved him and he loved me. And I had his son. He's a soldier now."

It was already late in the day when Diomedes left the aging woman to her memories. She still held the letter as he closed the door. He would stay in Rome that night but continue his journey in the morning. He had fulfilled the request of his friend Tacitus and wondered what had become of him. Now he would travel to Mount Olympus and then to Athens, the land of his parents. And after that, perhaps he would venture east again on the Silk Road to live the rest of his days beside the Great Wall. Indeed, the Son of Heaven might even allow him to visit Chang'an. He was, after all, an officer of Parthian Horse. Surely he would be welcome in the Celestial Kingdom in the center of the world.

Chapter 28

Tacitus opened his eyes and scanned the small room. There was a lived-in scent and a shaft of light came through a small window.

"Where is Diomedes?"

"So you decided to wake up," said an old man's heavily accented voice. "My wife was about to drown you with soup."

"I dreamt of soup," Tacitus said, a faint smile playing about his lips. He touched his face and was surprised to feel a thick beard.

"It's good; a man should have a beard. It's a natural thing." The old man stepped closer, and Tacitus saw him for the first time.

"You—I know you!"

Elizar ben Josephus chuckled. "I'd say we're old friends by now."

"But how did I get here?"

"I met Diomedes on the road not too long after that storm blew itself out. He was very surprised to see me. Fortunately, my hut isn't far from where I found the two of you."

"Where is Diomedes?" Tacitus asked again.

"Gone. He stayed for a month, and would have remained longer, but there's a sickness in Parthia. Thousands have died. He wanted to find his wife and child, to see if they are safe. He said that he hopes to see you again, but ..."

"So you and your wife have cared for me all this time?"

"It was winter and I had nothing else to do. I thought that I should heal the grandson of a friend." The man smiled. "I hear you made it all the way to the Middle Kingdom."

"The other legionnaires are still there. But, for me, things changed."

"Ah yes, the princess. You spoke of her in your sleep. Maybe you shouldn't have left her. Oh well, things always change and they will likely change again. Change is the only constant we know."

"You told me that you were going to Jerusalem. Did you get to your holy city?"

"I am still on my way. I just hope there aren't too many Romans there. At least not in the Temple."

"And now you've been taking care of another one. How long have I been here?"

"Four months. We thought you had broken ribs, but they were only bruised. Your friend, the Greek—or was he a Parthian? Anyway, he helped bind your ribs and put splints on your legs. Then a sickness came into your chest and you nearly died."

"There were times when I thought I had." Tacitus tried to raise his head and stopped, suddenly dizzy. "Where are we?"

"Kashgar. Now you must rest. You can thank us later," the old man said with a twinkle in his eye.

***

Five weeks passed. The old man kept Tacitus occupied with recollections of Gaius and Toronius. When at last

Tacitus could walk, he expressed deep gratitude to Elizar ben Josephus and his wife. He offered them his coins, but they didn't want his money. They said their goodbyes, and the itinerant trader and his wife set off for Samarkand.

Tacitus sat in the walled garden of their mud-brick hovel with a dozen chickens and a tethered goat that the couple had left behind. It had been more than two years since he'd left his men at the Great Wall and he was only a third of the way on his trek to Rome. The old Jew had found him suitable clothes for travel. There was nothing to identify him as a Roman, though he kept his gladius and *puglio* hidden beneath a coat and could draw them easily if need be.

"Nevertheless, be careful going through Parthia," Josephus had cautioned. "They are not at war with Rome, but there is no truce either. They still keep the eagle standards captured at Carrhae. There will be no peace until they are returned—and that won't be soon."

Tacitus attempted to recall places he had known in Rome and, based on what others told him, tried to envision how it might have changed. What would the city be like under the leadership of an emperor? Were they at war? No one in Kashgar seemed to know.

And then there was Tullia. What might he say to her at first sight? Indeed, would he even recognize her? He fantasized about how delighted she'd be at his homecoming, how she would greet him with wonder and open arms.

In more somber moments, a darker thought occurred. What if their meeting was a terrible disappointment? After all, the image he had carried for so many years was of a lively, mischievous fifteen-year-old girl with an impish smile and sensuous lips. He hoped that she would simply be a mature version of that. But what if she didn't look anything like he remembered? Of course she would not be a girl anymore and could not possibly look the same. It would not matter, he told himself.

"She's much older now, if still alive. She would likely be married," Appian had said. The words, "still alive" echoed through his head. She would be over thirty now.

He also wanted to see his aunt. She had been a patient woman and he had treated her badly when he was a youth. But she'd been in poor health when he'd left and was probably gone. There would be nobody else. Within a month, he reasoned, he might tire of Rome, a city now as foreign to him as Samarkand. Then what would he do?

Of course, there was the army. He might join a legion. After all, he had been promoted to centurion by the Primus Pila, a soldier honored by Caesar. But who could vouch for him? Indeed, who in Rome had heard of the Torugart Pass or the Taklamakan Desert? Every centurion or legionnaire he'd known was either dead or existing beside the Great Wall. In Rome his adventures, like Homer's Odyssey, would seem a fable. Moreover, after all these years, the authorities might consider him a deserter who had come back to clear his conscience. And deserters, he reminded himself, were executed.

It was at night when the other image came to him, a beguiling face, a petite girl with almond-shaped eyes and jet-black hair. He couldn't rid himself of it. His breathing became labored as the vision of her smoldered in his mind. He would wake suddenly and force himself to clear his head. Then he would prepare himself for another day's march.

With his legs nearly mended, his walk became purposeful, a legionnaire's pace. Indeed, he often imagined he was leading his cohorts, listening to the tramp of hobnail *caligae*, and he amused himself by calling cadence. He glanced behind, half expecting to see over 300 red shields and a column of men, four abreast. Then he would laugh and chide himself for such silliness, and the weight of having left them settled upon him once again.

Endless nights followed endless days. Tacitus's steps had slowed and he often paused and sat by the side of the road. And now the pathway to Rome seemed so very long.

***

The great Silk Road crested a rise, and Tacitus stopped and gazed westward. In the distance a caravan trooped toward Parthia at a sleepwalker's pace. The sun was high overhead and it seemed that the world had ground to a stop. The Egyptians, Assyrians, and even some Romans considered the sun a deity. Perhaps the rays of the great disc would offer him guidance and magically open a curtain to some ultimate truth. He lay against rocks and gazed at clouds high above. The sun's warmth baked upon his face, and he felt himself drift like a boat in a languid current. Nothing made sense anymore. He wondered what was real.

Tacitus finally rose, closed his eyes, and turned twice in a circle. And then he began to walk.

***

Once each month Appian had the men practice their fighting skills and that would take place two days hence. As their centurion, he was proud that he could hurl the pilum further than men half his age. He could still run, and his eyesight was sharp and unclouded. He tilled his garden on the knoll overlooking the village and planned the next exercise for the dwindling cohorts. There were but 229 legionnaires remaining. All were clustered in the little settlement just behind the Great Wall. The men had learned rudimentary Mandarin, their wives some Latin, and their children babbled in a mixture of both.

The legionnaires had not been at war since fighting the Chanyu four years earlier. They still considered themselves soldiers rather than farmers, but putting on the lorica *segmentata* and hurling the javelin was now a festive sport, something to impress the women, more than a military exercise. That most of the men had married was something they never would have contemplated earlier, at least not until retirement. But they were not in Rome, and many rules no longer applied.

On occasion, the Wall was visited by dignitaries and high military officials from Chang'an. The cohorts, as an honor guard, were marched out smartly in full armor, Appian shouting orders as if they were a full legion parading before Julius Caesar himself. Coached by his wife, Appian made a welcoming speech in Mandarin and the notables smiled indulgently. It was during such times that the men from the capitol were reminded of the foreigners' battle against the hated Chanyu. Often the legionnaires felt more like actors than warriors, but they were aging, and few really wished to fight again.

A hawk circled low over the knoll, rose in the light air, and turned toward the west. Appian followed its flight to the horizon. Another movement caught his eye, and for a long moment he observed its progress. It was still quite far, but Appian smiled, turned, and ran to the village.

"Armor up! Shield, gladius, and *puglio*. Make quick of it!" he shouted when he reached the huts of the company street. There was no need for a moat, palisade, or guard towers, but the whitewashed houses were arranged in the style of a Roman town. Hearing the order, men dropped tools and bolted into their houses. "Helmet, lorica *segmentata*," Appian commanded.

His wife grabbed the armor from wall hooks. She quickly secured the straps and ties, a fearful expression on her face.

"It's okay," he said, squeezing her shoulders affectionately. The fear left her eyes, though she still looked mystified. He took the horn she handed him, the same one found by Sempronius the day after Carrhae, and stepped into the street. With a single blast the legionnaires fell into line, their armor and weapons gleaming in the morning sun. Appian inspected the ranks, making sure that weapons and shields were perfectly aligned. The men exchanged glances, looking confused.

Appian Dio said nothing. He quickly strode up and down the double line of troops, keeping a sharp eye out for any slacking in their deportment. But he couldn't quite suppress a smile.

***

"A drill?" asked Hera, looking up from her weeding. "We weren't expecting anybody important."

Apollodoros listened to Appian's trumpet and took his wife's hand. "Let's find out."

When he reached the street, Hera close behind, he was surprised to see the assembled cohorts. Apollodoros looked quizzically at Appian, who pointed to the far end of the road.

Apollodoros walked to the knoll, put two fingers to his forehead, and stared at the slowly approaching man. With the help of his own walking stick, he made his way down the hill to meet him.

"May an ancient *libertus* walk with a wayward centurion?" Apollodoros said, putting his arm around the man's shoulder.

Tacitus smiled wanly. "Centurion, huh? I had hoped to come back in a more heroic fashion, but I must look like a bedraggled old beggar. And now I walk with a limp. Not much of a soldier, am I?"

"All of us are older now." Apollodoros pointed to the village. "They're all drawn up in ranks, but Appian didn't tell them why."

"Ranks? Why would he do that? I'll be surprised if they even want to see me."

"I think they do. In fact, many bets were placed."

Tacitus became pensive. Under the circumstances, he reflected, it would not be inconceivable for the men to simply ignore him or even ask him to go someplace else. Turning to the old Greek, he had a question but was almost too afraid to ask. They walked toward the village in silence.

"Is she still here? I mean, has she gone to Chang'an?"

"She's in another village not far from here. A rather humble place, really. She hasn't the same position that she once had. They gave her a plot of land and a house, but she'll never again grace the palace in Chang'an."

"Did she ever speak of me?"

"So many questions, centurion. Life has many surprises, as you will learn."

"What about Hera? Does she visit Li Mae?"

"On occasion, but Hera is quite frail now. In her sleep she speaks of Athens and our son. Where is he, Tacitus?"

"He went to Parthia to see if his wife and child survived a plague. I didn't get that far—an accident, you see." Tacitus patted his right leg. "But you should know that Diomedes saved my life."

"Do you think he will ever return to us?"

"I don't know. He mentioned visiting Rome and Athens, perhaps even Mount Olympus to see where the gods reside. He said he'd like to return."

"Hera and I hoped that he would come back to us, but if he doesn't, the home of Zeus isn't a bad choice. On the other hand, I always expected that you would return someday."

"Why's that?"

"I think you know."

There were two blasts on the horn and Tacitus looked up. "Draw weapons? Maybe they'll use them on me. At least the ones who lost the bet."

"We'll just have to see," replied Apollodoros. "If I might say, your Excellency, you look like you just came through a whirlwind. You'd best brush yourself off. The men would expect that."

***

Unlike the Han villages, which had been built with narrow, crooked streets to slow down invading cavalry, the legionnaires' roads and houses were arranged in neat rows. As Tacitus neared the buildings, he could see ranks of men and heard Appian's "Cohorts, prepare for inspection!"

Tacitus took a deep breath, stood straighter, and began his descent into the village. At the entrance he halted and eyed the rows of assembled men. Appian gave a slight nod, and the two of them marched between double ranks of legionnaires. Tacitus walked slowly, eyes straight ahead. The men in their polished armor stood motionless, their swords held firmly across their shields. He could feel their eyes upon him and wondered if they were truly honoring his return or merely complying with an order. Appian took his own gladius and handed it to him. Then Tacitus passed through the ranks; he turned and saluted the legionnaires.

"Return salute!" commanded Appian.

Two hundred and twenty nine swords rose and slammed against shields. From the corner of his eye, Tacitus could see women and children who'd been watching from doorways jump at the sudden crack of steel. There followed a long moment of silence.

"I have returned after having deserted all of you. I thought ..." Tacitus stopped, and again there was an awkward silence. "I do not deserve this honor. I can no longer claim to be your leader, much less a centurion."

"You were our centurion," Appian said with calm resolve. "And you still are. You saved us once. We give thanks for your return."

"Then I am honored," Tacitus said softly. "But I hope the remainder of our days will be ones of peace."

His vision shifted to the quiet village and the women and children who gawked at him. "Trumpeter, there is someone I wish to see. I think Apollodoros can show me the way. I will return here soon, and in your eyes, I hope to redeem myself."

"The place you wish to visit is only two miles from here. We have waited a long time and you have walked alone many leagues. But you will not walk these miles by yourself." Appian turned to the legionnaires. "Form column of fours. Marching order, standard bearer forward." He grinned. "Are you ready to march?"

"Yes!" the men shouted. They sounded joyous. Tacitus scanned the crowd again. Standing taller than any was Lupus Ibericus, who met Tacitus's gaze and gave a tiny nod. A great weight lifted from Tacitus as he saw the obvious respect reflected in the men's actions.

Some legionnaires had joined the cohorts in Rome, others in Syria or Gaul, but on this day their loyalty and enthusiasm would have carried them to the gates of Ctesiphon itself.

"Cohorts prepare to march! March!" The standard was raised and the sound of spiked *caligae* resounded as the column took to the winding road.

With Apollodoros by his side, Tacitus stopped on a knoll overlooking the village. "That house down there, the one with the poplar trees and the garden," the Greek said, pointing to a modest dwelling beside a well. A dozen chickens pecked at the earth, oblivious to the men who stared down at them.

"I'll be going now, Centurion. Hera needs me."

Tacitus nodded. "Tell Appian that I appreciate the escort, but they should also return." He was about to ask Apollodoros if he thought she was in the house when a petite, dark-haired woman opened the door and walked into the garden.

"Your hands are shaking, Centurion," Apollodoros said with a grin. "I haven't seen that since Carrhae."

"I haven't been so nervous since Carrhae."

"I suspect this encounter will be more pleasant. Who knows, she might even be waiting for you."

Tacitus stood and watched the lithe figure for a long time. His journey back had begun slowly, hesitantly, but the desire to see her once again had become an overwhelming urge. He had spurned the slow tread of a camel caravan. Despite his limp, he had often jogged the Silk Road on cool mornings. Whereas Tullia's face had faded, the princess's urged him on with enchanting clarity.

It had been nearly four years since he had left, and she had heard nothing of him. The time they'd spent together had been so short. Honestly, how presumptuous it was to suddenly reappear and claim her as if she had been breathlessly awaiting his return. He shivered, though the air was quite warm. Then, breathing deeply, he started down the hill.

***

As a child growing up in the court, Li Mae Tang had never dreamed of the catastrophe that had awaited her. She'd been married twice against her will to men she feared. Her soul sister had suffered a senseless death. Then had come the murder of her parents, followed by the sudden departure of the only man she had ever loved.

That horror was compounded by expulsion from the court. For months she had simply drifted from day to day. Even though her marriage to Shang had never been consummated, she was seen as a widow—a peasant widow at that. No Han of any stature would consider marrying her. She was shunned by all but the poorest villagers. The only women who spoke to her were the wives of the legionnaires and Hera, so old and infirm that she rarely left her house.

Li Mae often lay awake at night and wondered what terrors she might have faced if Prince Shang Gao had lived. Then she dreamed of what life might have been like if the centurion hadn't gone away. If she had been braver, she might have followed him, but rushing after him during her mourning period would have been considered disgraceful, perhaps unconscionable. And then, of course, everything had become far more complicated, and no one besides Hera and Apollodoros knew the reason why.

Now Li Mae knelt in her garden, a weeding spade in her hand. A reflection of light from the knoll caught her attention. She looked up and saw hundreds men in armor and helmets. They were the foreign soldiers, the *li-jin*. Since coming to the Han village they had occasionally paraded around for the dignitaries, but that was always beside the Great Wall. Never did they venture to her insignificant village. Truly puzzled, she stared at the motionless figures. It didn't make sense.

She saw a man standing in front of the others. His clothing was frayed and splotched. What had been white was now faded and stained. The onetime princess felt rooted to the stony ground.

"Tacitus?" she said in a whisper.

Li Mae rose, tiptoed to the edge of the garden, and stared at what had to be an apparition, something the Fates would conjure up. The man slowly raised his arm. She did the same.

Tacitus began to run toward her. She was already beyond the garden and halfway up the knoll when he lifted her into the air, then held her tightly.

"Tacitus!" she exclaimed over and over. "You've come back!"

He didn't put her down until they reached the house. "You are not married—you are alone?" Tacitus asked, his hands clutching hers, his voice unsteady.

"Not married, but not alone."

He looked puzzled, then looked past her to an open doorway. A little boy with almond-shaped eyes and a thick crop of curly hair rushed out and hid behind Li Mae's dress. She looked down at him and whispered. Shyly, he gazed up at Tacitus. The centurion knelt down, held the child's hands, and stared.

"Centurion?" the boy said in Greek.

"My son?" Tacitus said, looking up at her.

"Our son, Centurion."

"What is his name?"

"I know my name," the child said. "It's Li-jin."

"Li-jin?" Tacitus exclaimed.

"Like them," the boy said, pointing to the legionnaires on the hill. Appian raised his arm, his gladius flashing in the morning sun. He gave a sharp command, and the cohorts wheeled from a line to a column of fours. At the sound of a trumpet, they began the march back to the village, a place they would never leave.

Tacitus lifted the child and, as if in Rome, said, "I claim you, Li-jin, as my son. He's beautiful, Princess."

"Not 'princess' anymore," she said. "I am a commoner now, like everyone else in this village."

"To me, you will always be a princess."

Li Mae smiled. Her heart felt like it was going to burst in her chest. There were so many things she wanted to say to him that she didn't know where to begin. But that was alright. They had time now.

"I have tea, the type you like, Centurion. Shall we go in?"

The soldier put the child down and took Li Mae's hand. Together they made their way to the little house. Once inside, Li Mae turned back toward her son and beckoned for him to follow. The little boy took a last look at the departing legionnaires, hurried to join his parents, and silently closed the door behind him

THE END

Author's Note

I am thankful that the great writer Plutarch in his book *Lives* so intimately discussed the histories of Marcus Licinius Crassus, Gnaeus Pompey, and Julius Caesar. He also gave a detailed account of the battle of Carrhae and the escape of Cassius after the destruction of Crassus's legions at the hands of the Parthians.

Unfortunately, neither Plutarch nor the rest of the world knew anything about other survivors of that encounter in 53 BCE. Ancient Chinese documents mention the capture of Roman legionnaires near the Great Wall in the year 36 BCE. Thus began my inspiriation for this timeless adventure of desperate men, epic in their determination to succeed at all costs.

In addition to the literature, Roman helmets have been unearthed, inscribed with the word "prisoner" in Mandarin. There is also an ancient village in the Gansu Corridor in northwest China named Liqian (part of Zhelaizhi village today) where the local people still bake bread in the shape of an ox head, as was done in ancient Rome. The inhabitants of the village have European features, and DNA tests indicate that the inhabitants may be the progeny of those long-ago Romans. The startling discovery of this in the 1950s is attributed to Homer Dubs, a professor of Chinese history at

Oxford University. There is some debate regarding these findings.

Roman prisoners captured by the Parthians at the battle of Carrhae were marched to Merv (now Chorasmia) to defend the eastern region of that kingdom.

It has been suggested by historians that the Chanyu of Central Asia may have been known as Huns when four hundred years later they invaded Eastern Europe.

During the first Han Dynasty, the Chinese offered princesses to the Chanyu as tribute, and there actually was a Han general named Chen Tang who fought the nomads during the time of that dynasty.

The term "Silk Road" was not employed until many years after our story, but the fabled road did cross the Torugart Pass and skirted the Taklamakan Desert. Unfortunately for historians, most of the ancient cities on that road were destroyed by the Mongols in the thirteenth century.

A final note: I used the term "cohort" for clarity, even though the name of the unit had changed to "century" during the events of the novel. A century, like a cohort, was composed of 80 men. Sixty such units, plus non-Roman auxiliaries, comprised a legion.

ABOUT THE AUTHOR

RON SINGERTON

After graduating from California State University at Long Beach in 1965, Ron Singerton joined the U.S. Army Security Agency and spent his overseas time in Asia.

The following twenty-five years were devoted to teaching history and art in Southern California High schools where he developed a particular love for writing and historical research.

During the early 1980s, he authored a series, "Moments in History", of some thirty mini books on famous legendary people and events ranging from Columbus to the moon landing. The books were adopted as supplementary teaching material for the State of California and approved by the Los Angeles School board as a teaching aid. Published by Santillana Publishing Company, the original ones are considered collectors' items.

An avid horseman and saber fencer with a special interest in the American Civil War, he "heard the bugle and the sound of the drums" and became a re-enactor riding with the Union cavalry in dozens of engagements from California to Gettysburg, Pennsylvania.

Always interested in an exciting but obscure story, his historical research meandered from the nineteenth and twentieth Century back to the ancient world. Singerton once said, "Technology of the past often appears elementary to us, the emotions do not." For the writer, the thoughts of peoples long past, as well as civilizations now little more than sand pitted ruins, still evolve into a pageant of love, intrigue and dire conflict. "It is nothing less than a shadowed mirror of our own world."

Through the writings of Plutarch, Pliny and Julius Caesar he uncovered an epic event that would take him from Rome in the last days of Republic to the Great Wall of China. After years of research the tale became the gist of a two volume novel: *The Villa of Deceit* and *The Silk and the Sword*.

Ron is also a professional artist who, with his wife Darla, owns and creates works for their art gallery, Singerton Fine Arts, in Idyllwild, California, where he works in glass, stone, paint and bronze.

If You Enjoyed This Book

Please write a review.

This is important to the author and helps to get the word out to others

Visit

PENMORE PRESS

www.penmorepress.com

All Penmore Press books are available directly through our website, amazon.com, Barnes and Noble and Nook, Sony Reader, Apple iTunes, Kobo books and via leading bookshops across the United States, Canada, the UK, Australia and Europe.

Talon returns to Acre, the Crusader port, a rich man after more than a year in Byzantium. But riches bring enemies, and Talon's past is about to catch up with him: accusations of witchcraft have followed him from Languedoc. Everything is changed, however, when Talon travels to a small fort with Sir Guy de Veres, his Templar mentor, and learns stunning news about Rav'an.

Before he can act, the kingdom of Baldwin IV is threatened by none other than the Sultan of Egypt, Salah Ed Din, who is bringing a vast army through Sinai to retake Jerusalem from the Christians. Talon must take part in the ferocious battle at Montgisard before he can set out to rejoin Rav'an and honor his promise made six years ago.

The 'Assassins of Rashid Ed Din, the Old Man of the Mountain, have targeted Talon for death for obstructing their plans once too often. To avoid them, Talon must take a circuitous route through the loneliest reaches of the southern deserts on his way to Persia, but even so he risks betrayal, imprisonment, and execution.

His sole objective is to find Rav'an, but she is not where he had expected her to be.

PENMORE PRESS
www.penmorepress.com

ROCAMORA

DONALD MICHAEL PLATT

No man is closer to a woman than her confessor, not her father, not her brother, not her husband.

-Spanish saying

Vicente de Rocamora, the epitome of a young renaissance man in 17th century Spain, questions the goals of the Inquisition and the brutal means used by King Philip IV and the Roman Church to achieve them. Spain vows to eliminate the heretical influences attributed to Jews, Moors, and others who would taint the limpieza de sangre, purity of Spanish blood. At the insistence of his family, the handsome and charismatic Vicente enters the Dominican Order and is soon thrust into the scheming political hierarchy that rules Spain. As confessor to the king's sister, the Infanta Doña María, and assistant to Philip's chief minister, Olivares, Vicente ascends through the ranks and before long finds himself poised to attain not only the ambitious dreams of the Rocamora family but also—named Spain's Inquisitor General

PENMORE PRESS
www.penmorepress.com

Fortune's Whelp
by
Benerson Little

Privateer, Swordsman, and Rake:

Set in the 17th century during the heyday of privateering and the decline of buccaneering, *Fortune's Whelp* is a brash, swords-out sea-going adventure. Scotsman Edward MacNaughton, a former privateer captain, twice accused and acquitted of piracy and currently seeking a commission, is ensnared in the intrigue associated with the attempt to assassinate King William III in 1696. Who plots to kill the king, who will rise in rebellion—and which of three women in his life, the dangerous smuggler, the wealthy widow with a dark past, or the former lover seeking independence—might kill to further political ends? Variously wooing and defying Fortune, Captain MacNaughton approaches life in the same way he wields a sword or commands a fighting ship: with the heart of a lion and the craft of a fox.

PENMORE PRESS
www.penmorepress.com